1 9 9 2

Other Books by Tim Winton

Cloudstreet

1992
Happy Birthday aref to
many many more!
Ew & Jody

Tim Winton

GRAYWOLF PRESS

Copyright © 1991, 1992 by Tim Winton
First published in Australia 1991 by McPhee Gribble,
a division of Penguin Books Australia.
First published in Great Britain 1991 by Pan Books Ltd.
Publication of this volume is made possible in part by a grant provided
by the Minnesota State Arts Board, through an appropriation by the
Minnesota State Legislature, and by a grant from the National
Endowment for the Arts. Additional support has been provided by the
Jerome Foundation, the Northwest Area Foundation, and other generous
contributions from foundations, corporations, and individuals.
Graywolf Press is a member agency of United Arts, Saint Paul.
Published by GRAYWOLF PRESS
2402 University Avenue, Suite 203,
Saint Paul, Minnesota 55114.

9 8 7 6 5 4 3 2
First U.S. Printing, 1992

Library of Congress Cataloging-in-Publication Data
Winton, Tim.
Cloudstreet / Tim Winton.
p. cm.
ISBN 1-55597-158-X: $20.00
I. Title.
PR9619.3.W585C58 1992
828—dc20

for
Sam Mifflin
Sadie Mifflin
Olive Winton
and
Les Winton

with love and gratitude.

Acknowledgements

I am indebted to several people who kindly made working space available to me during the writing of this book: to Joe Sullivan and the late Peter Bartlett for Spencer's Cottage; to Leonard Bernstein for the room at Vlihos; and to the Australia Council for the studio in Paris.

Thanks to Erica and Howard Willis for invaluable help, and to Denise Winton for years of hard work.

Some of this story was written with the aid of a fellowship from the Literary Arts Board of the Australia Council and a travelling scholarship from the Marten Bequest in 1987 and 1988.

Shall we gather at the river
Where bright angel-feet have trod . . .

WILL you look at us by the river! The whole restless mob of us on spread blankets in the dreamy briny sunshine skylarking and chiacking about for one day, one clear, clean, sweet day in a good world in the midst of our living. Yachts run before an unfelt gust with bagnecked pelicans riding above them, the city their twitching backdrop, all blocks and points of mirror light down to the water's edge.

Twenty years, they all say, sprawling and drinking. There's ginger beer, staggerjuice and hot flasks of tea. There's pasties, a ham, chickenlegs and a basket of oranges, potato salad and dried figs. There are things spilling from jars and bags.

The speech is silenced by a melodious belch which gets big applause. Someone blurts on a baby's belly and a song strikes up. Unless you knew, you'd think they were a whole group, an earthly vision. Because, look, even the missing are there, the gone and taken are with them in the shade pools of the peppermints by the beautiful, the beautiful the river. And even now, one of the here is leaving.

He hears nothing but the water, and the sound of it has been in his ears all his life. Shirt buttons askew, his new black shoes filling with sand, he strides along the beach near the river's edge nearly hyperventilating with excitement. His tongue can't lie still; it rounds his mouth, kicks inside like a mullet. He tramps through the footprints of the city's early morning rambles and nightly assignations toward the jetty he's been watching the past halfhour. He breaks into a run. His shirt-tail works its way out.

It's low tide so he reaches the steps to the jetty without even wetting his shoes, though he would have waded there if need be, waded without a qualm, because he's hungry for the water, he wants it more than ever.

Three cheers go up back there in the trees on the bank. But he's running; seeing slats of river between the planks, with his big overripe man's body quivering with happiness. Near the end of the jetty he slows so he can negotiate the steel ladder down to the fishing platform. He's so close to the water. A great, gobbling laugh pours out of him. No hand in his trouser belt. The water to himself. The silver-skinned river.

He sits. He leans out over it and sees his face with hair dangling, his filthy great smile, teeth, teeth, teeth, and then he leans out harder, peering to see all the wonders inside. It's all there, all the great and glorious, the sweet and simple. All.

Within a minute he'll have it, and it'll have him, and for a few seconds he'll truly be a man. A flicker, then a burst of consciousness on his shooting way, and he'll savour that healing all the rest of his journey, having felt it, having known the story for just a moment.

From the broad vaults and spaces you can see it all again because it never ceases to be. You can see that figure teetering out over the water, looking into your face, and you can see the crowd up on the treethick bank behind him finishing this momentous day off and getting ready to wonder where he is. And you can't help but worry for them, love them, want for them – those who go on down the close, foetid galleries of time and space without you.

The Shifty Shadow is Lurking

ROSE Pickles knew something bad was going to happen. Something really bad, this time. She itched in her awful woollen bathing suit and watched her brothers and a whole mob of other kids chucking bombies off the end of the jetty in the bronze evening light. Fishing boats were coming in along the breakwater for the night, their diesels throbbing like blood. Back under the Norfolk pines gulls bickered on the grass and fought for the scraps of uneaten lunches that schoolkids had thrown there. The sun was in the sea. She stood up and called.

Ted! Chub! Carn, it's late!

Ted, who was a year older than her, pretended not to hear, and he came up the ladder dripping, pigeontoed, and dived off again, holding one knee, hitting the water so that he made an artillery report – ker-thump – and a great gout of water rose up at her feet.

She got up and left them there. They can do what they like, she thought. Rose was a slender, brown girl, with dark straight hair, cut hard across her forehead. She was a pretty kid, but not as pretty as her mother. Well, that's what everyone told her. She wasn't vain, but it stuck in her guts, having someone telling you that every day of your life. Probably in a minute or two, when she got home, someone'd tell her again, someone in the public bar or the Ladies' Lounge. They'd be all swilling for closing time and there'd be a great roar of talk, and she'd try to slip upstairs without getting caught up. She wasn't in the mood for it this evening. Yeah, something terrible was up. Not the war, not school, but something to do with her. She didn't know if she could bear any more bad luck. In one year they'd lost the house, the old man had been through two jobs and all the savings, and now they were living in Uncle Joel's pub.

Rose had never felt a shadow like this before, but she'd heard the old boy go on about it often enough. Well, she wondered, I bet he's squirmin out there now, out on the islands, feelin this dark luck comin on. She stopped under the trees and looked back out over Champion Bay. The boys were silhouettes now. She still heard their laughter. The sea was turning black. Yeah, he'd be squirmin. And if he wasn't, he should be.

Sam Pickles was a fool to get out of bed that day, and he knew it ever after. In the sagging, hammocky cot he caught the scent of his father, the invalid port and tobacco, the closeness in the sheets of him, and he woke with a grunt. He jerked upright and looked about the dormitory hut. Other men were sleeping in the half-light before dawn with their salt-white boots paired beneath them, their photos and empty bottles awry on bedside benches, and another hard stupid day of labour hanging ahead of them in the twilight. Sam knew, as anybody will know, that when you wake up on a summer morning fifty miles out to sea on an island made entirely of birdshit and fag-ends, where only yesterday the rubbershod foot of a Japanese soldier was washed up, and you turn in your bed and smell your dead father right beside you, then you know the shifty shadow of God is lurking. And Sam knew damnwell that when the shifty shadow is about, you roll yourself a smoke and stay under the sheet and don't move till you see what happens. When the foreman comes in to kick your arse, you pull the sheet up over your head and tell him you're sick enough to die, to give up women, gambling, life itself. And if you're smart you'll let him blow and bellow, but you'll hang onto that bed till you hear whose missus is dead, or who's won the football raffle, or what poor bastard's the proud father of twins, or whose mob it is that's won the war. You stay right there till the shadow's fallen across whoever's lucky or unlucky enough, and then when it's all over, you go out and get on with your business. Unless you're just plain bloody stupid and think you can tell which way the shadow's fallen. Then you'll think: nah, this one hasn't got me number on it. Today's not me day. It's someone elses. And you may or may not be right.

Sam Pickles, who thought today wasn't his day to be worried, and who happened to be dead wrong, just waited for the odour of his old man to leave him, and then cocked his head, whistled through his teeth at the shiftiness of it all, and slid off the cot. Tiny crabs scuttered across the boards away from him. He went and stood on the stoop and saw the ocean, flat as sheetmetal. He headed for the thunderbox with gulls, terns, shags and cockroaches watching him come. The toilet was built on a catwalk hanging off the edge of the island. The seat was only eight feet above the water on a low tide, and on a high tide you were liable to experience what some welltravelled soul called nature's bidet. Or a shark might go for your heart the long way.

Out there, with his bum hanging over the still lagoon, Sam Pickles told himself today was just a day – more work, more sweat, and salt, diesel, guano. Some talk of the war, maybe, and a game of cards in the evening. He looked at his hands which were white with work. Every time he looked at them he knew he was a small man, small enough to be the jockey his father once wanted him to be. What a thing, hoping for smallness in a son. Well, he was small, in more ways than he cared to think about, but Sam never was a jockey.

He rolled a smoke and looked out beyond the Nissen huts and the water tower to where the dozers and trucks and oilsmeared engine blocks were waiting. A couple of scurvy-looking dogs sniffed about at the perimeter of the compound, finding leftover crayfish and abalone from last night's meal. Well, he'd just have to square the day away. It was a dream, that's all.

At the long trough outside his hut, Sam washed in the cool tank water, and as though to arm himself against such a shifty start to the day, he shaved as well. No one else was up yet. There was nothing to distract him. He got thinking about the old man again. When he looked at himself in the shard of mirror hanging from the water tank, that's who he saw.

Sam's father Merv had been a water diviner. He went round all his life with a forked stick and a piece of fence wire, and when he was sober he found water and fed the family on the proceeds. He was a soft, sentimental sort of man, and he never beat Sam. The boy went with him sometimes to watch that stick quiver and tremble like a terrier's snout and see the old man tugging at his beard as he sang 'Click Go The Shears' and tracked back and forth across the sandy coastal plain. Sam followed him, loved him, listened to him talk. He believed deeply in luck, the old man, though he was careful never to say the word. He called it the shifty shadow of God. All his life he paid close attention to the movements of that shadow. He taught Sam to see it passing, feel it hovering, because he said it was those shifts that governed a man's life and it always paid to be ahead of the play. If the chill of its shade felt good, you went out to meet it like a droughted farmer goes out, arms wide, to greet the raincloud, but if you got that sick, queer feeling in your belly, you had to stay put and do nothing but breathe and there was a good chance it would pass you by. It was as though luck made choices, that it could think. If you greeted it, it came to you; if you shunned it, it backed away.

Queer, now he thought of it, but Sam had spent his boyhood sharing a bed with the old man. And he *was* an old man, fifty, when Sam was born. At six every evening, his father retired with the *Geraldton Gazette* and a bottle, and Sam climbed in beside him to doze against that wheezy chest, hear the rustle of a turning page, smell the pipesmoke and the port. As a general tonic, the old man drank a bottle of Penfolds Invalid each evening; he said it gave him sweet sleep.

Sam's mother slept in the narrow child's bed in the next room. She was a simple, clean, gloomy woman, much younger than her husband. Even as a boy, he barely thought about her. She was good to him, but she suffered for her lifelong inability to be a man.

One morning Sam woke to a creeping chill and found the old man dead beside him. His mouth was open and his gums exposed. His mother came in to find him stuffing the old boy's dentures in. He stopped rigid, they exchanged looks, and it appeared, with the upper plate left the way it was, that the old man had died eating a small piano. The townspeople wrote fond obituaries about Merv Pickles, water diviner. In the end they named the racetrack after him in tribute to his finding water there, and probably for having made it his second home. Without doubt, his faithful and lifelong loss to the bookies had probably underwritten the place for a good twenty years.

People had loved him. He was poor and foolish and people will always have a place in their hearts for the harmless. He loved to gamble, for it was another way of finding water, a divination that set his whole body sparking. Sam Pickles grew up on that racetrack, hanging around the stables or by the final turn where the Patterson's Curse grew knee high and the ground vibrated with all that passing flesh. Old Merv had Sam down as a rider. He was small and there was something about it in his blood, but when Merv died the dream went with him. A gambler's wife has ideas of her own. Fools breed a hardness in others they can't know. Sam Pickles tried to knuckle down to his mother's way. He came to love labour the way his father never did, but there was always that nose for chance he'd inherited, an excitement in random shifts, the sudden leaping out of the unforeseen. He did badly at school and was apprenticed to a butcher. Then one day, with the shifty shadow upon him, he shot through, leaving his mother without a son, the butcher without an arse to kick, and a footy team without a snappy rover for whom the ball always fell the right way. A lot of things had happened since that day. His luck had waxed and waned. Like a gambler he thought the equation was about even, though any plant, animal or mineral could have told him he was on a lifelong losing streak. Plenty of queer things had occurred, but he'd never before woken up smelling the old man. It could only mean something big. Even as a boy he'd known that his father's soul had touched him on the way up. He knew that meant something big and quiet and scary as hell.

Men were stirring and cursing now, and the cook was spitting out behind the mess hall. They were hard men here – crims, fighters, scabs, gamblers – but the government didn't seem to give a damn who they were as long as they filled quotas. They were here to mine guano for phosphate, and there was no shortage of that. Some places, a man could get thighdeep in the stuff if he wanted to. Dozers scooped it, trucked it and dumped it on barges. In Sam's hut some wag had painted the motto on the door: *Give em shit*. And that's what they did. Sam didn't mind the work. It was better for his asthma than the wheat dust on the mainland wharf, where he'd been foreman. And the money was good. Right now he needed the dough, what with a wife and three kids to feed. In a single bad year he'd gambled away everything he'd ever owned and he figured he'd see the war out hauling birdcrap to make up. A man could always recover his losses.

These islands were the sort of place to put the wind up a man, though. He knew about all those murders and mutinies. The *Batavia* business. There'd been madness out on these sea rocks since whitefellas had first run into them. Under the night sky they glowed white and when you heard some blokes had found a man's foot in a rubber boot, you wondered whether you weren't living on some outpost of Hell itself. His cousin Joel had worked here as a crayfisherman before he made his pile on the horses. Joel said sometimes you heard the sound of men strangling women at night, but in the morning you always told yourself it was the birds nesting.

Give em shit, boys! the cook yelled as they left the mess hut.

Sam got down to the boat with a full belly and waited for his partner Nobby. Keep the day ahead of you, that's what the old man used to say. Nobby rolled up to the wheelhouse and belched. He was a fat brand of man, balding, with bleached earhair and a great capacity for hatred. He had an ongoing grievance with everybody, all forms of life. As he came in, he made a sturdy beginning to the morning.

That fucken Wilson, I tellya –

Sam pushed past him and went astern to cast off the line.

A man'd be hardly blamed for murderin that barsted in is sleep –

He started the winch to draw an empty barge alongside.

It was Nobby who made the work hard. The sound of his voice was like something grinding away without oil or maintenance, and Sam had learnt to think across the top of it, to look into the water and think of coral trout, jewfish, baldchin, plan another night's fishing, conjure up the sight of himself with a beer by the fire and a drumful of boiling crays. That's what he was thinking of when the cable caught his glove and his hand was taken from him. His fingers were between the cogs before he could draw breath, and he felt his knuckles break in a second. Madness rose behind his eyes as Nobby fumbled with the gears, cursing him, cursing the winch, till he got him free and Sam tore the glove off, squealing, as four fingers fell to the deck and danced like half a pound of live prawns.

Sam was aloft. His body vibrated. Two men in flying suits played cards on his chest. His hand was in a block of ice. The airmen were playing gin rummy.

Orright, mate? We'll land in a few minutes, doan worry.

I'm not worried, he shouted back over the sound of the engines. So this was what a Catalina looked like on the inside.

He thought he'd tell them a cautionary thing or two on the subject of luck, but one of them slapped down a card so hard that Sam felt the reverberations right down his arm and he fainted fair away.

From up here, with hindsight, you can see into every room in the town of Geraldton, through roof and fence and curtain, down alley and beach, along bars and breakwaters, and if you look hard enough you'll see a schoolgirl hurrying home early to the back of the old pub to fetch her mother to the hospital. She clangs up the fire escape, pigeontoed but athletic. The rear of the pub looks like the back of a movie set but from the front, the place looks the real business.

Rose Pickles hammers along the corridor past numbered rooms till she reaches 36. It's locked. She calls out to her mother but there is no reply, though she detects an intake of breath from behind the door.

Now that it's all in the past, anyone can see the woman astride the bed with her dress up. The sweat on her skin. The Catalina pilot with his belt undone and his hat on the table. You can smell the beer on their breaths, you get so close. So close, you hear the blood in their fattened hearts. And out in the corridor you witness the terrible boiling dark in the schoolgirl's head, the confusion, the feeling, the colour she can't put a name to.

Her two brothers will be here soon. She goes out and waits on the fire escape. Afternoon sun cuts it way down from the reservoir of blue. Rose's plaits tug the back of her head. She feels tough all of a sudden, and grown up. The boys can find their own way, she thinks, they can all find their own way. She batters down the fire escape. The metal tolls after she's gone.

Dolly Pickles was a damn goodlooking woman. Anyone in town would tell you so. In some pubs they would know you so, and send a wave of winks down the bar that would always wash up at the far reaches of the Ladies' Lounge. As she headed down to the hospital, she turned a few heads in the street and took in the salt breeze. When this town didn't smell of salt it smelt of phosphate and wheat and rotting crayfish. She liked the stink of salt. Right now, with the rime of sex on her, she smelt of salt herself. Oh, those Yanks are somethin, she thought; Jesus Christ, they're somethin.

Kids were bombing off the jetty as she passed under the Norfolk pines. The water was a flat bed of sunlight and the brownslick bodies of children bashed through into its blue underbelly. Leaning against a fence, a man shelled prawns and eyed her off. He wiped vinegar from his chin and smiled. She gave him a piss-off-useless flick of her hips and went on to the hospital.

Rose and the boys were there. The boys left off whispering by the window and stood straight. They were rangy, sundark kids. Rose was by the bed. She didn't look up. Sam was asleep with his white fist bound up in a salute or a warning – she didn't know which. A private room in the new wing. Government money, she thought. We couldn't afford this.

Four fingers and the top of his thumb, Rose said.

Christ.

Dolly saw it was his right hand. His bloody working hand. A man could hardly pick his nose with a thumb and half a pointer. They were done for; stuffed, cactus. Thank you, Lady Luck, you rotten slut. It was probably time now to pack a bag and buy a ticket, but hell, there was the kids and everything. The whole town knowing. How would she live?

He bin awake?

Nup.

The boys, Ted and Chub, scratched themselves and pulled at their shorts.

We go down the jetty? He's not gunna wake up.

S'posed to be in school, youse.

We'll be back dreckly. Dad might be awake, eh.

Oh, ya mays well.

Don't drown from cryin, Rose said, from the bedside.

Dolly stood in the room with her daughter. You had to watch this kid. She was getting to be a clever little miss. And she was Sam's through and through. She was hot in the face like she was holding something back. Dolly wandered what she knew. She's a kid. I'm a woman. The only thing we've got in common these days is a useless man. Dolly'd always gone for useless ones. But this was the living end.

The room smelt of new paint and phenyle. Dolly tried to spot a mirror but there was none.

The woman and the daughter do not speak. The crippled man does not stir. The breeze comes in the window and stops the scene from turning into a painting.

After her mother left, Rose sat by the bedside and watched him sleep. She hated him sometimes, he was so hopeless. At times she wanted to hit him, to pick up a lump of four-be-two and snot him with it. He was a grown man and yet he didn't have a pinch of sense in him. But he wasn't mean, like the old girl was turning mean. She had to put up with all these catastrophes, so maybe she had a right, but the old man still made you love him. They'd had good times together, all of them, but something sour was coming into everything, and it'd been happening all year. Everything was falling to bits. When the old man was home they fought and swore. The old girl hammered him night and day and he went out and lost money. Even now she didn't know whether to put a cool hand on his brow or shake him by the throat. He looked so pale and busted. Oh, he'd made her laugh so many times, making a dill of himself to make her happy. He remembered what she liked, he told her adult things sometimes, and stories from his stockriding days. Rose saw through him; she knew he was always going to be useless, but she loved him. Hell, he was her father.

Sam began to snore. Rose pressed her lips together and waited.

No one in the pub had a conversation that night that didn't somehow wander into the territory of the Pickles family and their doomed run of luck. They had to do it when the publican wasn't about because he was a loyal relation. They wondered aloud about Sam's future, and the evening was kept alive with conjecture. Luck was something close to any drinker's heart here at the Eurythmic. The place was built and bought on it, named after the great horse that brought it. A photo hung above the bar of the dark gleaming horse with its white diamond brow staring out at them, as if reminding them of his beneficence. The brash, hearty talk rose into the residential rooms at the top of the broad banistered staircase. Rose and the boys listened to it until the closing swill got under way, and when the place was quiet they slipped downstairs to the big dining room and its smells of steak and cabbage.

Alone on her bed in 36, Dolly dreams.

A faint breeze lifts her dress as she approaches the man by the fence with the prawns. He gives her a gaptoothed smile and she stops him. Children drop like jellybabies into the mouth of the sea. She takes a prawn, holds it in front of the man's red nose, rubs it against his lips and takes it away. She puts her tongue out and rests the prawn on her tongue, draws it slowly into her mouth, and bites down. She cries out, and spits it into the man's lap. It's a human finger. There's blood. She spits again and her front tooth lands on the man's shirt and he scrambles up and knocks her to the grass and forces his tongue into her mouth. She feels their tongues meeting through the gaps in their teeth, vinegar between her legs.

For a week Sam Pickles lay in bed and listened to the fans stir the soupy summer air. School was starting up again and the beach was quiet, but in the afternoons when the southerly blew, he could hear kinds bombing off the jetty and shrilling like gulls, setting the loose boards rattling as they ran. He knew his kids'd be there with the rest of them, and maybe they'd be down there at night with heavy lines under the lights, waiting for samsonfish like the others. The days were long and he heard them out. He heard the jangle and crash of the wharf, the wind in the Norfolk pines, the clack of heels in the street, rattles and moans down the ward. He listened instead of looking because everything hurt to look at: the juicy fat bum of the nurse who changed his dressing, the sideways, preoccupied look on Dolly's face when she visited, the angry bloodcrust on the stumps where his fingers had been. There was no use looking anymore. It all said the same thing.

At night the lighthouse divided up the dark, and he let himself watch it because it was just time slipping away.

One day a parcel came from the Abrolhos Islands, and the nurse with the juicy bum opened it for him and gasped. It was a preserve jar. In it, swimming in alcohol, were four fingers and the nub of a thumb. Someone had pasted a label on the glass which read: SAM'S PICKLES. He stared at it, then at the nurse, and laughed like a wounded dog. The nurse just looked at him lying there all gauzed and pale and handsome, laughing at his own fingers in a jar, and she wondered if he wasn't the most stupid bugger she'd ever met in her life.

When Sam came home from the hospital, Dolly had to say goodbye to the Catalina pilot and the smell of his cologne. The two rooms at the pub seemed crowded again, and the kids hardly came home except to eat and sleep. Dolly spent the days tidying up, sometimes even helping the cleaning girls to make beds in the other rooms. She couldn't stand the sight of Sam sitting in the chair by the window with his stump on the sill. That was enough to make her busy.

Afternoons, she pulled a few beers for Joel to show she was still grateful for the roof over their heads, and in the evening she drank more than a few to show anyone who cared to notice that she was still a woman and not a beggar. On Saturdays she went out to the racetrack and watched Joel's horses win, and she looked into the faces of people who stared at her as though they couldn't believe her husband was so unlucky. Men looked at her the way they look at horses. They were bolder now they knew her old man was a crip. She was fed up with this town. She knew it was time to make her own luck and piss off, but she just couldn't get started. It'd be better when the summer was over, when the war was over. There'd be a better time, she knew.

No money came in. No compo. Sam didn't go on the dole. At night she lay beside him in bed, sensed his wiry weight spilling her towards him, and she tilted guiltily his way every time to scramble astride him and pull him into her, watch the harbour lights rise and fall through the window as she remembered the girlhood colour of moonlight on a paddock of stubble and the grind of dirt beneath her buttocks.

At the sound of the air raid siren, Rose and the boys sprinted up the beach toward the trenches in the lee of the showers. Rose followed her brothers across the buffalo grass and over the sandbags as they leapt in. The Japs were coming this time. She heard the sound of an aero engine as she landed in the dark end, ankledeep in turds and newspaper. She crouched in the stinking mire as a plane went overhead, too high to see. They laughed in disgust until the all clear sounded and they ran back to the water and swam the poop off themselves.

That afternoon, Rose bombed off the end of the jetty and got a jellyfish up her bathers that stung her navel until it looked like she'd been hit with grapeshot. Gutshot, the boys said.

Later the same day Rose and her brothers found the foot of a Jap soldier washed up in a twotoed rubber boot on the back beach. It was so horrible they laughed and ran home. When they told their father, he looked more gutshot than Rose.

In the evening Rose went down to the library with the old man. It was the first time he'd been out since the hospital. He walked slowly beside her as she carried her books and, under the Norfolk pines in the moonlight, she saw him stop and look out over the water. She took his wrist and held it gently.

Doesn't matter, Dad. You're okay.

He looked at her and she saw his teeth in the light of the moon. When he stood beside her at the library looking vague in the presence of all those books, she felt so sorry for him, so ashamed, so maternal.

On the way home a man came out of a pub as they passed and gave Rose four big crayfish.

Bastard, Sam said as they walked on.

He gave us a present, Dad.

I used to work for him. He's hoping I'll stay away and take the jinx with me.

Rose smelt the freshcooked crays damp in her arms and felt tired and sunburnt. The welts from the stinger on her belly felt like a fresh tattoo. She thought she'd fall asleep walking.

Some people are lucky, she heard him say. Joel, he's lucky. Got a good business. His hayburners win. See, I got me ole man's blood. Dead unlucky.

Rose yawned. Until your luck changes.

Luck don't change, love. It moves.

In the cool of winter, Sam Pickles began to give up the idea of being a crip, even though he'd grown accustomed, even attached to his new status. Joel set up a serious campaign in July to persuade him, to badger, niggle and nag him to get up out of room 36 and get on with his life.

There's no flamin use droppin yer bundle, he said, you'll just have to cope with six-and-a-half fingers. You need a job and I need a payin guest. Catch my meanin?

Dolly softened a little toward Sam, as though under direction, though she still drifted away at odd times to leave him smoking by the back window and staring out at the Catholics moving on the high ground. She came back vague and cheerful but he couldn't work up any anger. For the kids, the novelty of having an old man who was wounded in the battle for birdshit had seriously faded. Even Rose looked at him these days as though she thought it was time he *did something*.

The furious puckered pink scars on Sam's hand subsided round the finger stumps – the colour of a monkey's bum, some wag in the bar suggested. He'd learnt to button himself and roll a fag. Now he could look at the club on the end of his arm without having bile rise in him. He got restless. In the end, Joel ferreted him out. Fishing was the place to start.

One July evening, as the sun dozed in the sea, he found himself standing on a lonely beach casting and winding, clumsy as a child, with the great dunes behind him turning brown. Haze began to shoulder in and render every form fluid. When he baited up, the gang of hooks always slipped sideways in the mulie and ended up buried in his palm. It was frustrating and silly, but he said nothing to Joel, and Joel said nothing back. As dark came, Sam got the hang of it, and found ways to use his bung hand. He got a half decent cast out now and then and was satisfied by the sound of bait hitting the water. They lit the lamp and shared a smoke. Sam began to feel a crawly, exhilarating sensation in his fingers – all his fingers. He burned and tingled and swore he could feel ten fingers gripping that rod. It was a lie, he knew, but he let the feeling take him in the dark. There was something momentous in it, he thought, like it meant something truly big. The shifty shadow, alright. But he was relaxed. He was with Joel whose luck ran like a fountain. He was a lightning rod for luck, that boy.

He wasn't at all surprised to hear Joel grunt and then shout. It was a big strike. Sam brought the lamp alongside and saw Joel's cane rod arching halfway to the water. Line sang out and ran from the reel. They laughed like kids. Joel feinted and pulled, crabbing along the beach, to worry the

21

fish, wear him down. Sam held the gaff and the light close by; he guffawed and stomped and felt like getting sickdrunk and dancing all night. He whooped and hooted as the great silverflanked mulloway came twisting in through the shore-break. Nah, it was no surprise at all. Not with Joel. He put down the light, swung the gaff into the fish's gills and dragged it in. He turned to Joel and *there* was the surprise. Joel was on his knees clutching his heart. Sam Pickles stood and watched man and fish flap on the sand until neither moved. He stood there a long time after everything was still, letting it soak in. Joel, his only living relative beyond Dolly and the kids. His lucky, wealthy, generous, last relative. In whose pub his family was living. Sam's feet turned stiff with cold. The facts racked themselves up like snooker balls. He was bereaved. He was unemployed. Minus a working hand. Homeless. Broke.

A sea breeze blew.

Sam tried to decide which he would drag back first, man or fish. It wasn't going to be easy. The lamp burned low. He tried to weigh it up. He sat down to nut it out.

Fish Lamb Comes Back

JUST near the crest of a hill where the sun is ducking down, the old flatbed Chev gives up the fight and stalls quiet. Out on the tray the kids groan like an opera. All around, the bush has gone the colour of a cold roast. Birds scuffle out of sight. There's no wind, though the Chev gives out a steamy fart.

You'll have to back her up, Lest, the woman says to her husband. Go on, turn her around.

Carn, Dad! someone calls from behind the cab.

The man spits out the window, lets the brake off, and they roll back. He lets the clutch go, and with a jerk that sends the kids lurching all over the back, the motor grinds up again and the grey-blue bush is full of clatter.

This time the truck goes up the hill in reverse and the kids elbow each other and feel a right bunch of dags heading up like that, but they're the first to see the rivermouth, the oilstill river and roiling sea; it looks so like a picture they're suddenly quiet.

The engine idles, best it can.

Whacko, one of them says.

They shift around on the prawn nets and watch the sun hit the sea without a sound.

Lester and Oriel Lamb are Godfearing people. If you didn't know them you could see it in the way they set up a light in the darkness. You've never seen people relish the lighting of a lamp like this, the way they crouch together and cradle the glass piece in their hands, wide eyes caught in the flare of a match, the gentle murmurs and the pumping, the sighs as the light grows and turns footprints on the river beach into longshadowed moon craters. Let your light so shine.

Around them their six children chiack in the sand.

Get some wood, you bigguns, Oriel Lamb says. Hattie you look after Lon.

The beach widens in the light of lamp and fire. The children see sparks rising like stars.

These are farm people, though Lester Lamb has taken to being a policeman because the farm is on its last legs. Lester Lamb polices like he farms, always a little behind the moment. He'd quit the force if only his wife'd let him. Around town he's known as 'Lest We Forget' and if he knew, it'd break his Anzac heart.

He unravels the prawn net and shucks off his pants. His scrawny white legs bring a smile to him.

I'll take the boys.

They're not tall enough, Oriel Lamb says.

Ah, the girls grizzle too much. Drives me mad.

Put on yer shoes, or yull be stung. Don't want any cobbler stings. Can't stand *your* grizzlin.

He laughs and remembers the last time he was stung, when they had to load him onto the flatbed and Hattie had to drive because no one else could, and they delivered him to the doctor in the main street naked and screaming like a breech birth.

Orright, he says, lacing up the old brogues his father left him, no stings tonight. Give us a kiss then.

With the two older boys, Mason and Samson, Lester Lamb wades out. He holds the lamp over the water while the boys drag the net; it makes a long triangle out behind them, narrowing down to a little sock in the end. Mason is eleven. They call him Quick because he is as unquick as his father. Samson is two years younger and the others call him Samsonfish, or just plain Fish, for his wit and alertness. Everyone loves Fish. Just by dunking a girl's braids in an inkwell he can make her love him. He endears teachers to him by giving them lip. And in town, he'll wait till dark and crap in a paper bag and set fire to it on someone's doorstep so they come out screaming and stamping and get poofooted, only to melt into jolliness when they see it's just Fish Lamb and his fun. Even his three sisters Hattie and Elaine and Red love him, and they hate boys to Hell and back.

Quick knows that his brother Fish is smarter and better looking than him, and that people love him more, though Fish doesn't catch fish as well as his name would suggest, because he's always wisedicking around, talking too loud, being lovable.

Don't smile, Fish, Lester Lamb says. You'll frighten the prawns away.

Oi, Quick, look at Dad. He looks like a statue in a fountain with that light. Wants to be careful someone dunt come over an toss in a penny to make a wish.

What would they wish for, ya reckon? Quick asks.

Yeah, what? Lester Lamb asks.

Prolly wish they could get their money back, I reckon.

Cheeky blighter, Lester Lamb thinks as he wades with the light and lets the talk go away from him.

27

On the beach, Oriel Lamb sees them dragging round the bend and back towards the beach. The fire coughs and she goes back to darning. She doesn't hate being poor the way Lester does. She'll cut garments down and cadge and patch to give things a second life, she'll keep the farm swaying on its back trotters, but not be unhappy. She's prouder than the British Empire. She'll send the kids into town on old Mabel with a shilling between them and know they'll spend it on sherbert and icecream and watch the outdoor flicks for free from a vacant bush. They'll see Randolph Scott back to front through the old white sheet, and they'll see the projector flicker and send out its bolt of light, and they'll watch the townie kids eating popcorn out of paper cups, but they won't for a moment think they're poor. They'll know they're Lambs; they'll know how to treat others with a mixture of pity and respect. *And*, what's more, they'll always come back with change.

She looks up and sees Lester and the boys hauling the net up onto the beach. The water is flat behind them. She can almost see the trees etched out on the other bank, the paperbarks where the dunes begin. There is the sound of surf away across the sandbar. Little Lon is asleep at her feet. She wraps him in her cardigan and he seems no bigger than a kelpie curled up like that.

The boys empty the lummocky mess of stuff into the light, and they fall to their knees to separate jellyfish, gobble-guts, smelt, weed and muck from prawns. In the light, the prawns' eyes are cheap jewels in transparent bodies that warp and flick against the sides of the steel bucket.

Fish skylarks up the beach. Quick whistles as Hat uncovers a fat cobbler, its glossy catfish body bending to show the sting behind its head.

I'll take em out again, Lester Lamb says.

His wife shrugs and lets them go. Her blunt little hands are full of prawns.

Oriel Lamb wipes her hands on her apron, looks up and sees her husband out on the water, his head illuminated and seemingly free of his body. Her men look like they are walking on water. Somewhere a fish breaks the surface.

She leaps to her feet. Lord Jesus, something just falls through the bottom of her heart. She startles the others.

Lest?

Oh, the water has never been so quiet. Quick and Fish and their father move through it like it's a cloud, an idea, just a rumour of water, and when Fish goes down there isn't a sound. Quick feels the net go slack. Lester Lamb smells woodsmoke from the beach; he hears his heart paddling slowly along, but nothing else.

Fish will remember. All his life and all his next life he'll remember this dark, cool plunge where sound and light and shape are gone, where something rushes him from afar, where, openmouthed, openfisted, he drinks in river, whales it in with complete surprise.

And Lester Lamb, turning in alarm at the shout from shore, came round too hard and swung the lamp into the water and left them in hissing darkness. Quick was yelling; he heard the boy beating the water.

Quick staggered and fell over the net and squealed at himself trying to get off, to get it off. A pole glanced off his chin. He felt the net butt under him. Fish! He was on him; he was trying to come up under the net.

Lester Lamb hoisted Quick out of the water and off the net. The sky was the colour of darkness, starless, mute. Everywhere, everything was net.

He's under it, get if off get if off! Quick was yelling.

Lester Lamb could not see. He could only feel water and net and panic.

Oh, I remember. Mesh against the face, the cage of down and up and the faint idea of light as the cold comes quicker now out of the tunnel, that strange cold feeling that's no longer a stranger. Fish feels death coming unstuck from him with a pain like his guts are being torn from him. Fish is having his gizzard, his soul torn away and he feels his fingers in the mesh, reaching up for anything, his . . . someone's . . . and then he's away.

Away.

The net went still in Lester Lamb's hands. A sound escaped him.

Just pull! Quick yelled.

What?

Into the shallow. If he's caught in the net, just pull him in!

When they got into the shallows they saw the shadow trailing and they dragged it up the bank to the woman's feet and the smell of cooking prawns. Lester Lamb saw his son's fingers in the mesh of the net, still holding.

He was dead and they knew it, but the woman beat the water out of him anyway. To little Lon, awake now with all the screaming, she looked like she was giving Fish a good hiding for his cheek.

Quick heard her shouting at the Lord Jesus.

Blessed blessed Saviour, bring him back. Show us all thy tender mercy and bring this boy back. Ah, Gawd Jesus Almighty, raise him up! Now, you raise him up!

And Fish lay there in the mostly dark, eyes and mouth open, lurching like butcher meat as his mother set her fists to him:

Lord Jesus

Whump!

Saviour Jesus . . .

Whump!

And she made sounds on him you only got from cold pastry.

The old man on his knees weeping: Yairs, Lord, yairs!

And the girls strangely quiet there on the sand with waterlap and prawnkick and the smell of mud and rottenness.

Fish's pain stops, and suddenly it's all just haste and the darkness melts into something warm. Hurrying toward a big friendly wound in the gloom . . . but then slowing, slowing. He comes to a stop. Worse, he's slipping back and that gash in the grey recedes and darkness returns and pain and the most awful sickfeeling is in him like his flesh has turned to pus and his heart to shit.

Shame.

Horror.

Fish begins to scream.

The great gout of river hit Oriel Lamb in the face and Lon laughed. Got back on his wet little bum and laughed. Fish started to geyser away and Lon laughed again and they were all shouting enough to hide the awful, the sad, the hurt moan that Fish let out when the air got to his lungs. Never, never, was there a sadder, more disappointed noise.

They brought him into town like that. From the pub verandah men saw the Lambs barrelling down the hill like mad bastards, and they heard them singing and shouting like they were ready for rape and revenge, and the sight of them rioting on the open tray of that Chev suddenly put people in the street.

Lester Lamb swung into the darkened dirt yard of the Church of Christ and got ready to beat down the door. He had to get inside and turn on the lights, throw the windows open, find the minister, tell the people. Oriel Lamb, infant astride her hip, was singing and wildeyed. The horn was blowing and the headlamps tore the darkness.

Out on the tray, as the graveldust caught them up and blotted out the world, the girls laughed like they were famous.

Quick cradled Fish's head in his lap. He felt the blood moving in his brother's body. Fish's eyes were open, unblinking.

We got him back! Quick heard his father bellow to the drinkers across the road. Back from the dead. Fish Lamb is back! Praise the Lord!

But Quick held his brother's head in his hands and knew it wasn't quite right. Because not all of Fish Lamb had come back.

Back in Time

BACK in time there was a big empty house. It was owned by a very respectable woman who had cheated several people in order to get it. The local Anglican priest was the only visitor she ever had, for she was lonely and a widow, though very rich. The priest secretly thought she was a nasty piece of work, but he also believed that there was good in every heart and it only needed to be nurtured. She had such an enormous house – six bedrooms and a library, with grounds full of fruit trees and fragrant shrubs – and in an inspired moment he put a proposition to her. She was lonely and bored, he said, why didn't she open her house? To native women, perhaps. She could be the Daisy Bates of the city.

Somehow it took her fancy, the Daisy Bates bit, though she'd never met one of these natives. Missionary purpose came upon her like the flu. Girls were procured and the house filled. She aimed to make ladies of them so they could set a standard for the rest of their sorry race. She showed them how to make their beds and wash, how to dress and how to walk. She read aloud from the novels of Sir Walter Scott and she locked the house up at night. The mission girls climbed into bed with one another at night and cried. They had been taken from their families and were not happy. They crawled from windows but were tracked down and returned to the house. The widow showed them how to serve at table and wear hats in church. One evening she went into the library to find a girl dead on the floor from drinking ant poison. Before she evicted the rest of them, she made each of them come into the library and take a close look at the twisted death snarl of the poisoned girl. When she got the last one out the door and into the night, she gathered up all the linen and burnt it under the fruit trees in the backyard. Then she sent a neighbour to fetch a constable.

She was at the piano one evening a few weeks after, mulling over the possibilities for diversion, when her heart stopped. She cried out in surprise, in outrage and her nose hit middle C hard enough to darken the room with sound. Her nose was a strong and bony one, and there was middle C in that library until rigor mortis set in. The room soaked her up and the summer heat worked on her body until its surface was as hard and dry as the crust of a pavlova.

That's how the vicar found her when he came visiting to tick her off about the girls. The smell knocked him over like a shot from a .303 and he ran out with a nosebleed that lasted seven days and seven nights. He didn't die, but he lost his faith in humankindness and became a Baptist first and a banker second.

The house was boarded up, and it held its breath.

In 1923, after a racehorse called Eurythmic was put

grandly out to pasture, a publican from the town of Geraldton bought the house without ever seeing it. He thought perhaps he'd retire to it in style sometime in the future. He was forty years old. Twenty years later, men were reading his Last Will and Testament to a small gathering of sunburnt people in the Ladies' Lounge of the Eurythmic Hotel, Geraldton.

A House on Cloud Street

Sam Pickles couldn't believe it, and the way everyone started filing out of the Ladies' Lounge without looking him in the eye, it was clear that no one else could, either. The pub was to be sold and the money to go to the local branch of the Turf Club, except for two thousand pounds which was willed to one Samuel Manifold Pickles. And there was a house, a large house down in the city, left to the same Samuel Manifold Pickles with the proviso that it not be resold for the next twenty years.

Rose Pickles wandered through the quiet halls, along musty floor runners, into newly vacant rooms where only last month jockeys and sailors had lived. She tugged at her plait and smelt the sea on her flesh. After these weeks of hopeless waiting and expecting the worst she couldn't decide whether she was happy or sad. She couldn't help feeling that her life was over.

A few days later, the Pickles family packed three cardboard suitcases and a teachest and caught a train to Perth. That was the end of Geraldton. The bay, the pub, the Norfolk pines, the endless summer wind. No one cried; no one was game to.

It was evening when they reached the city and they caught the first taxi of their lives, to Cloud Street. Number One Cloud Street. When the driver piled them out they stared at the shadow back there in the trees. Somewhere, a train whistled.

Oo-roo!

Sam walked up on to the timber verandah with his mouth open in the dark. He put the key in the lock and felt Rose pushing him from behind.

Gwan, dad.

The door opened. A dozen cramped smells blew in their faces: lilac water, rot, things they didn't recognize. Sam found a switch and the long, wide hallway suddenly jumped at them. They stepped inside to the grind and protest of the floorboards, moving slowly and quietly at first to open a door here, to peer there, exchange neutral high eyebrow looks, gathering boldness as they went, the four of them getting to a trot with their voices gathering and gaining, setting doors aslam, and moving to a full gallop up the staircase.

It's bloody huge! said Sam.

Bloody strange if you ask me, Dolly muttered.

Where do we sleep tonight? Ted asked.

There's twenty rooms or more, Sam said, just take your pick.

But there's no beds!

Improvise!

I'm hungry.

Here, eat a biscuit.

With all the upper floor lights on, Rose walked through drifts of dust, webs and smells from room to room. She came to a door right in the centre of the house but when she opened it the air went from her lungs and a hot, nasty feeling came over her. Ugh. It smelt like an old meatsafe. There were no windows in the room, the walls were blotched with shadows, and there was only an upright piano inside and a single peacock feather. Not my room, she thought. She had to get out before she got any dizzier. Next door she found a room with a window overlooking the street, an *Ann of Green Gables* room.

Well, she thought, the old man had a win. Cloud Street. It had a good sound to it. Well, depending how you looked at it. And right now she preferred to think of the big win and not the losses she knew would probably come.

In a day or so they had the house on Cloud Street clean enough to live in, though Sam privately swore he could still smell lilac water. It was a big, sad, two-storey affair in a garden full of fruit trees. The windows were long, buckling sashed things with white scrollwork under the sills. Here and there weatherboards peeled away from the walls and protruded like lifting scabs, but there was still enough white paint on the place to give it a grand air and it seemed to lord it above the other houses in the street which were modest little red brick and tin cottages. It was big enough for twenty people. There were so many rooms you could get lost and unnerved. From upstairs you could see into everyone else's yard, and through the trees to the railway line and the sea of sooty grass beside it. The garden was gone to ruin. The fish ponds were dry; orange, lemon, apple, mulberry and mandarine trees were arthritic and wild. Creeping rose grew like a nest of thorns.

Rose explored and found creaks and damp patches and unfaded rectangles on the walls where paintings had hung. There were rooms and rooms and rooms but it wasn't the great shock it might have been had she not already lived at the Eurythmic all last year. She liked the iron lace in front and the bullnosed verandah. Some floors sloped and others were lumpy and singsong as you walked on them. Each of the kids had a room upstairs and hers looked out on the street with its white fences and jacarandas. It was musty, like the beach shack at Greenough Uncle Joel had let them use every Christmas. She knew she would even forget what Uncle Joel looked like in a year or two. She had loved him and she understood that she had to love this place too, despite how glum it made her, because it was his gift, and if it wasn't for him they'd have nothing.

Rose cleaned the dead, windowless room herself because she knew that all the books from the beach house were coming on the train with the furniture, and this would be the library. She loved books, even to hold them and turn them over in her hands and smell the cool, murky breeze they made when you birred the pages fast through your fingers. A house with a library! But she got halfway through the job and quit. There were bolt holes like eyes in the walls where shelves had been, and the old piano groaned, and she didn't like to think of being in there with the door closed. No, it wasn't for books. The books could come in her room, and this room, well it could just stay closed.

Rain fell sweetly on the corrugated iron roof all morning, and in the afternoon a truck pulled up out front.

From her window Rose saw men bringing boxes in off the truck. She went downstairs like a wild thing, stirring the others out of the gloomy silence of scrubbing. Teachests and crates came in through the door, a fat old sofa from the Ladies' Lounge of the Eurythmic, brass vases with the star of David on them, a cuckoo clock, mattresses and beds, a huge stuffed marlin, golf clubs, sixteen black and white photos of Eurythmic, each as big as a window. Rose opened crates and chests to find curtains, towels, sheets. Five crates were full of books. She dragged out an armful – *Liza of Lambeth*, *Jude the Obscure*, *Joe Wilson's Mates*, *Hints for the Freshwater Fishermen* – they were greensmelling and dusty, but Rose was exultant.

Well, her mother said, appearing beside her, this old stuff'll at least make it look like we're not squattin here.

Look at these books! Rose sighed.

There's nowhere to put them, said Dolly.

The old man came alongside. I'll make some shelves.

Rose saw her mother's eyes travel down to the stumps on his hand and back away again, and they went on upacking in silence.

Next morning they had their gear unpacked and the house was theirs, though they rattled round in it like peas in a tin. The cheque arrived from the trustees.

We're rich! Sam yelled from the letterbox.

But next day was Saturday. Race day. And there was a horse called Silver Lining. Sam had great faith, what, with the shifty shadow being about with such goodwill and all. But the horse was legless.

Saturday evening they were poor again. Sam got home sober, in time to have Dolly push him down the stairs. He went end over end like a lampstand and put his head through the plaster wall at the turn. He pulled his head out, took the last few steps on foot, and shrugged at the kids who went outside without even bothering to shake their heads.

On the back step, Ted muttered. That's our friggin luck. House and no money.

Ponds and no fish, said Chub.

Trees and no fruit.

Arm and no hand.

Rose turned on them. Oh, yer a pair of real cards. Real funny blokes.

Reckon it's a friggin *house* o cards, I do, said Ted. The old girl's the wild card and the old man's the bloody joker.

Sam surprised them, coming up behind. There was blood dripping from his nose. They moved aside to let him by. Rose watched him walk all the way down to the back fence where he stood in the grass. From somewhere near came the roar of a football crowd. The old man just stood there in the wild grass with his hands in his pockets, and Rose went inside when she couldn't watch it anymore.

Nights

The Pickleses move around in the night, stunned and shuffling, the big emptiness of the house around them, almost paralysing them with spaces and surfaces that yield nothing to them. It's just them in this vast indoors and though there's a war on and people are coming home with bits of them removed, and though families are still getting telegrams and waiting by the wireless, women walking buggered and beatenlooking with infants in the parks, the Pickleses can't help but feel that all that is incidental. They have no money and this great continent of a house doesn't belong to them. They're lost.

At night Dolly hears the trains huff down the track loud enough to set the panes a-rattle in the windows. All night, all day, people seem to be going someplace else. Everyone else somewhere else. Some nights, even as autumn thickens and the chill gets into her, she gets out of bed and walks down the track to the station where, from the dark shelter of the shrubbery, she can watch people getting on and off trains; men and women in uniform, sharp-looking people who laugh and shove at each other like they don't care who hears or sees. She hears their voices trailing off in the streets, sucked into the noises of steam and clank. Not many of them look as though *they* belong either, like the Yank marines honking their accents and tossing fags and nylons about, no, they don't belong but they don't give a damn.

Look at her, crouching there in the bushes.

Dolly always gets back in bed cold and angry and more awake than she was before. They're poor, dammit, still shitpoor, even with a house as big as a church that they can't bloody sell and maybe just as well. God she misses the wind and the flat plains and the bay and the dust. And that Catalina pilot, worthless bastard. No, she doesn't really miss him; just the idea of him. She misses the idea of herself as well. Back in Geraldton people knew her. They all whispered behind their hands, all those tightarsed local bastards, behind their sniggering looks and their guts in their laps, but at least she was somebody, she meant something.

Now and then in the night, only some nights, she leans across Sam, lets her breasts fall on his back and kisses his neck to taste the salt on him. He still smells like home, like other times, better times, and she feels everything tighten up on her and hurt just a little. But he never wakes up.

And Sam?

Every night when his wife lies there sighing, as he pretends to be asleep, or when she runs her breasts and lips over him before giving up and creeping out, he just sets his teeth and holds onto himself and knows he doesn't deserve what he's got. Now and then, if he stays awake long enough, he can feel the floors move, as though the house is breathing.

He has to think of something, but he thinks of all the

wrong things. All the useless warm memories. Like those Greenough summers. That summer Dolly and he left the kids asleep in the afternoons and swam across the river with a cold bottle of beer so they could pull each other down on the hard sand between the paperbarks and lick the salt away and peel cotton from each other without having to keep quiet. Sam Pickles remembers the heat of the day, the drumbeating of cicadas, her breasts in his fists, her thighs vising his ribs and the shellhollow smell rising from her as he bunted her into the sand, bucking them along as all the muscles of her pelvis clamped on him until they were almost in the water when the finish hit them like a hot wind down the valley. He poured beer down her back, cold beer between her breasts so it gathered in her navel so she laughed, shivered, went taut again and drew him down to suck his tongue from between his teeth. With her teeth in his flesh he knew there was a heaven and a hell.

Sam remembers. He feels a hot jet of sperm on his belly in the dark. Always, he thinks in disgust, always the wrong things to think of.

There they are. The man and his bung hand and the disgusted look, the darkhaired woman with the hips and the nervous racehorse gait, the two crewcut boys asleep, and the little girl looking prissy and lost. In the middle of the night she's there poking her head out of the window as if to get her bearings.

Sam's Big Idea

On the way home from school Rose walked ahead of Ted and Chub along the train line to be free of their stupid boys' talk and just in case anyone thought they were her brothers. As she came into Cloud Street she noticed the place had started to look familiar: the long line of jacarandas, the rusting tin roofs, and the sagging picket fences. The first thing she saw, as always, was the big ragged front lawn and the gable peak of Number One nesting right up there in the treetops by the rail embankment.

She walked down the side path beneath the rotten canes of a grapevine and came upon the old man out in the backyard with a stranger who was hammering nails into a great sheet of tin. Down the middle of the yard, from the house to the back pickets, was a tin fence which cut the yard in half. The wooden frame was jarrah; it smelt of gum and was the colour of sunburn. The old man was holding a big green sheet of tin while the other man hammered clouts in. Rose cocked her head to read the red lettering that ran diagonally across it. LIVER. The whole fence was built of tin signs.

The old girl sat on the back step in her dressing gown with a smoke in her mouth and a look on her that said she didn't want to know about any of it anymore.

Where'd this come from? Rose said, to the old man.

Aw, it just got there, he said with a grin.

Who's this? She looked at the tall, darklooking bloke who paused in his work to smile at her. She hated his guts.

Now, mind yer manners. This is a bloke who knows a lot about horses –

Rose turned and left him. She ran past her mother who looked aside. Some strange kind of murderousness lifted in Rose Pickles and she just didn't know what it meant.

She heard the boys coming down the long hall from the front, and she went to duck into a side door to avoid them, but the door was locked.

Hey! Chub called from the other end of the house. All these doors are locked.

She met the boys in the middle and they looked at each other.

They're all locked, Ted said. All this side.

The three of them went out the back to watch the old man and the stranger nailing up the last of the tin sheets. There were two yards all of a sudden, the trees divided, and a big ugly fence with stupid writing on it.

He's had his idea, their mother said. Someone's given him his idea.

Rose Pickles ran upstairs to her room. The door was locked – they all were, on the sunny side of the house. She

44

crossed the landing and found her things piled into a room across the way. With a snarl she kicked the door closed so hard the knob jumped out of the door, rolled across the boards and stopped, tarnished and dented, at her feet.

Next day, Sam Pickles came up from building the second privy. He'd built it out of more of those tin shop signs and Rose didn't know what the hell to think as she sat on the back step with the last of the sun in her eyes, watching him come up from the back with little silver twists of tin filings on his trousers. Birds picked off the last of the muscats in the vine above her; she heard them quietly feed.

A tin bog, eh? She tried to sound casual, but there was fury in her voice.

Bet you've never seen anything like it, Rosebud.

He waved in the direction of the little tin shed. The door said NO WADING.

A person like you shouldn't even say the word 'bet', Rose said.

Her father pulled out a shilling and held it silverpink in the dusk light.

Heads I win, tails you lose.

Rose Pickles knocked it out of his hand and got up quick, ready for a hiding.

Even the Only Miracle that Ever Happened to You

From the flat bed of the old Chev with the tarp over him and his sisters, Quick Lamb saw the old sheds sink back into the grey maw of the bush. There was a big blue winter sky hanging over everything and it made him sick to see how cheerful the place seemed. There was dew on the flaccid wires of the fences and magpies were strung along them like beads. The truck shook and all the junk stacked on it quaked and rattled like it'd collapse on him at any moment. As they pulled out onto the limestone road, Quick saw someone else's truck parked by the gate with the driver's head averted politely. Their name was gone off the old kero tin letterbox, and as the place disappeared from view with the first wide-hipped bend in the road, Quick remembered the threepenny bit he'd left in the lightningsplit base of that old blackbutt tree by the gate. He'd stuck it in there one morning the week before he first started school, just to see if anyone'd find it and pinch it by the time he was grown up. Too late now, he thought. And anyway, it's probably not even there anymore. I'm such a dumb kid. And he'd lost his postcard from Egypt, the one he got from his dad's cousin, Earl. Back in '43 he wrote a letter to cheer up a digger. He addressed it: Earl Blunt, EGYPT and it found him, just as he assumed it would. And a card came back, an exotic picture from another world. He'd stuck it somewhere secret and had bamboozled himself with his own cunning. He left it to the house, the farm, his old life.

As the mountain of limestone dust rose behind, the world went away, and there was only him and the wind flapping at the tarp and his sisters just not looking anyone in the eye.

Fish Lamb is flying. The trees pass in a blur as he glides low, and the glass is cold against his cheek. On the back of his neck, his mother's hand feels like a hot scone.

Oriel Lamb says nothing. Her son Fish coos and turns an eye at her. Little Lon is asleep already in the other arm. Lester Lamb whistles an old church chorus and it seems, to Oriel Lamb, less than necessary. She turns the pages of the *West Australian* and finds the classified section.

When they roll down through the main street, no one even pauses in their business to wave. Some taffy kid is teasing a horse outside the post office. There's a truck piled with spuds parked near the Margaret River bridge. But the Lambs pass on through without a wave given or got. There they go, someone mutters; the silly bastards.

You can't stay in a town when everything blows up in your face – especially the only miracle that ever happened to you.

All day they travel. Their bones brittle up with the jolts. Limestone dust flies into the trees. Out of Capel, the smoke from a bushfire comes downwind in a spiritous column, like a train passing. Past the emaciated glitter of creeks, into the heat ahead, the bluewhite nothing of distance, they travel. The Lambs do not speak. For each of them, some old nightmare is lurking, some memory of flames or water or dark wind, the touch of something sudden. Upwind the land is black and bare, the sky bruised with smoke and the oil of eucalypts. No one says a damn thing. The tarp flaps, the junk rattles, and it goes on and on, me in Oriel's arms, smelling her lemon scent, seeing the flickers in their heads, knowing them like the dead know the living, getting used to the idea, having the drool wiped from my lip.

There we are.

The Lambs of God.

Except no one believes anymore: the disappointment has been too much.

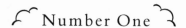# Number One

Right at the end of the day, at the very end of their choices, and at the bottom of the classified column, the Lambs roll into a street by the railway line and look about dejectedly. It's Number One, says Oriel. They idle down the street, look for some scabby little bungalow until they're running out of numbers: five, three . . . one. Number one? Number One is an enormous, flaking mansion with eyes and ears and a look of godless opulence about it, even now. Oriel Lamb flings the battered newspaper down and suddenly everyone's talking at once.

Shut up!

The whole truck goes quiet.

Down on the tracks, a freight grunts along in the twilight with a spray of steam and smuts. They coast into the side of the road. From up the tree–lined street there's the sound of someone booting a football into a picket fence. They hear water on lawns, the slap of a screen door. As it cools, the old Chev ticks and grumbles.

Go in, Lest.

Up on the second floor a blanket shifts at a window.

Quick leans around from the back. Looks flamin haunted.

Well, Oriel says without a smile, we'll be hauntin it from now on. Go on, Lest, go in and tee it up. Tell em what we want.

With a sigh, Lester Lamb gets out and clutches his hat to his belly. He swallows the thick in his throat and stumps up to the gate, pauses, takes a breath, and goes all the way to the teetering verandah. Makes a fist. Knocks.

The door is answered by a woman. Lester Lamb takes a look and a step back, and he punishes his hat sorely. She's got curls and lips and hips and everything, and she looks at him as though he's a prop seller or just some other street hawker rubbish from nowhere, and when she says, Yeah? with a hip on the jamb, he's looking for a way to get a word out.

Umm . . .

Jesus. Sorry mate. We're poor, and stupid too. Try up the street a bit.

Lester takes a step forward, moving his hands.

You're white as a ghost, she says, moving back.

The house.

She's got a deep vee between her breasts, big as a drinking trough, and it makes him feel like a dumb animal.

Oh, you've come for that. I'll get the hubby. Sam? Saaamm?

It's limestone dust.

What?

The white on me. We came up from the country. Margaret River.

48

Knew a bloke from there once. Had hair growin out his nostrils.

Oh.

Saaam? Come down here, Sam. Stop buggerizin about!

My name's Lester Lamb.

She bunches up her lips to make a hard little flower and just looks at him. From behind her, a small muscular man in a singlet appears. His blonde hair is ruffled and there's a day's growth on his jaw.

His name's Lester Lamb.

There's a moment of confusion as they're forced to shake lefthanded. Lester sees the pink stumps and reads grief in the man's face. He knows what it looks like. He only needs a mirror.

Come an have a look. You get half the house, half the yard, yer own dunny. The corridors are no man's land, same as the stairs. Big bloody joint, eh.

A couple of boys stand at the head of the stairs, about the same age as Fish and Quick.

I got six kids, Lester says.

Cathlicks, eh?

No. No, nothing.

Can yez pay?

We'll pay.

You'll do.

Lester hears Lon crying out in the truck.

Mays well bring em in, the man says. My name's Pickles. Then he guffaws. It's gunna sound like a counter lunch – Lamb and Pickles.

Lester hears Oriel shushing them up out there, and he stands quiet for a moment in this big sagging joint, gives himself a second before calling them in.

Rose Pickles and her brothers saw them unloading the dust-white truck. They made a crowd standing about down there, and they looked so skinny and tired. They carried a big jarrah table in but no chairs. There were teachests, a clock, shovels

49

and hoes, a couple of bashed old trunks. They all struggled and heaved up the stairs with that little woman barking instructions.

Cripes, Ted said. And I thought *we* looked like reffoes.

Rose opened the door a crack to see them piling gear into her old room. There were three girls, mostly older than her; the oldest looked bigknuckled and tough, the middle one walked around like she was dying slowly of some disease, and the youngest one looked pretty and mean.

Ted shook his head. Three more sheilas.

There's three boys too.

One's a slowbo, dja see?

Is not, said Rose.

Betcha.

If yer yer father's son yull bet on anythin.

They listened to the thump and scrape of things moving in the other half of the house until their father came in.

Who are they? Rose said.

They're called the Lambs.

Ted fell on the bed laughing. Gawd, we're living with sheep!

The old man smiled. That's their half now. They pay rent, so keep away.

Why dja do it? Rose said.

We've got no money, dick, Ted said.

The old man was by the window looking down at the truck. People across the road were peering from between curtains. He ran his puffy knuckles over the sill.

Time for youse to be in bed. You got school.

I hate the new school, Chub said.

It's not new.

I hate it.

Get to bed.

Chub followed Ted out the door and they banged it shut.

You shouldna done this, Rose said.

I'm your father.

That night Rose Pickles lay and listened. A little kid cried, and one of the girls as well. Trains rolled thumping by. Lightning flared now and then, but there was no thunder.

A long time after the house went quiet, she heard a door open across the hall. She got out of bed and pulled the door the tiniest bit to see a boy in pyjamas at the landing window looking out at the starless sky. In a moment of light she saw his face turn her way. His eyes were black. He was beautiful.

Across the Corridor

That autumn the street seemed full. There were always Pickles kids and Lamb kids up one end of the street throwing boondies or chasing someone's dog. Sometimes they squared off at one another like opposing platoons. Most times they acted as though the other group didn't exist. Everywhere they went they made a crowd, albeit a quiet one considering neither tribe spoke to the other. People stared at them from passing trains. Neighbours winced in anticipation of gang fights.

The war got bogged down in Europe.

Oriel Lamb supervised the digging up of their half of the backyard and it was a sight to see all the Lambs down there on their knees in the black dirt planting seedlings of onion and cabbage and the withered, shoothairy fists of old potatoes. Lester Lamb tied rags and bottle caps in the almond tree to keep the birds away. Wire was unrolled to fence off a back corner and Quick Lamb built a fowlhouse from broken teachests and an old forty-four gallon drum he found under the house.

Fish Lamb stood beneath the almond tree and watched the rags fluttering on the frame.

Down the street Oriel Lamb met a neighbour who had some pullets for sale. They talked friendly for a while and Oriel Lamb came home with four hens and a rooster for the price of a smile.

Fish Lamb put his fingers in the wire, hooked them in as

51

though it was all that held him up, and watched the white hens fatten and flutter in the warm sand.

In the park at the end of the street the flame trees and the Moreton Bay figs covered the grass with their broad, brittle leaves that Dolly Pickles kicked up in drifts as she walked alone when the children were at school and she was waiting for the copper to boil in the laundry or she just couldn't stand to be in that big old place anymore, avoiding the plain gaze of that little Lamb woman as she went stiffbooted about her neverending business. Just the sound of those boots coming her way was enough to get Dolly looking for an exit. That woman was plain. Plain and plain bossy, and under Dolly's roof.

During the day, with the children at school, the house on Cloud Street became relatively quiet except for Lon Lamb playing on the stairs and the occasional hissed quarrel from either side of the corridor.

The evenings were the most difficult because there was only one bathroom in the house and twelve people to be washed. Then there were children shouting and complaining and the halls were full of dark looks.

There was an uneasiness about the whole place. The Lambs sat around their table on fruit crates and stools eating the food that Oriel cooked on the gas ring by the bucket they had for a sink. Sometimes in the quiet before a meal, when Lester Lamb stumbled quickly and uncomfortably through Grace, the house went quiet enough so they could plainly hear the crack of wood in the stove across the corridor. No one looked up. They'd just go on with their eyes grimly shut until the old man got through his halfhearted thanks so they could eat and talk and fill up the space that seemed to loom at them from all about. Across the way the Pickles family ate their chops and mashed spud quietly and it often looked as though they cowered at the cattle noises from across the hall. It was like an invasion had taken place. Sam Pickles shook Worcestershire sauce about and tried to be jolly, but the others brooded, sculpted their potato, raised an eyebrow.

It went on for weeks.

The Knife Never Lies

It's a circle of silver blur on the table, almost solid with motion so that you'd swear you could see their laughing faces reflected in it as it spins. They drum their hands on the tabletop, the girls screaming and elbowing each other, Lon bouncing up and down on his chair, Fish clapping with a roar of glee as Quick closes his eyes and moans in dramatic apprehension. At the head of the table, Lester Lamb holds up his finger.

Remember, this is for who washes up tonight.

And this week! Red says, getting her pink elbows up in the air. All this week.

The knife never lies, you know, Lester says. It always knows best.

You shouldn't teach em such heathen stuff, Oriel Lamb murmurs with a smile. The room smells of gas, lamb stew, mildew in the wallpaper. A fire of rotten pickets snaps and quavers behind them, beginning to warm this back bedroom that's become their kitchen. Jars and bottles stand on shelves made from packing cases, and dented pots and baking dishes stand about in order.

It's slowing down! Lon cries.

Now you can see the round ended old butterknife blade and the browning bone handle – hear it whirr.

Slowing.

It's you, Hat.

Nah, it's got plenty in it, yet.

Gaw.

Quick knows it'll be him; he can almost feel the metal against his skin.

It's you, Dad.

Nope. It's gunna be Quick, Lester said. Lookit im. He's gettin out the teatowel already, aren't you, mate? Here it comes again.

Elaine!

Wait. Waaiit!

Oh, Gawd! Quick thumps the table.

Quick! Arrr, Quick gets the dishes!

The knife never tells a fib, but it can make a bib for a squib. Here's one. Who's got a pimple up their dimple?

Lester! Oriel turns to the stew.

They rollick and niggle and shriek and giggle and the knife goes round in the centre of the table. The fire has a hold on the room now and there is warm light between bodies and noise.

It's . . . aaagh . . . it's Eee-laine! Arr, pimple up ya dimple, Ee!

Is not.

Carn, Ee, fair cop, says Hat.

Yeah, says Quick, the knife doesn't lie.

And the knife spins again and again, for Who is the Smartest, for The Ugliest Feet, for The Next Prime Minister, and when the knife predicts that little Lon will be the first to marry, they rock back in their chairs until the room is ready to burst with the racket.

Orright, Lester Lamb says. One more while Mum's dishin up. Who's gunna win the war for us?

Plates come steaming with stew, and cutlery chinks and chairs are all a-scrape, so no one but Fish sees the blade pointing at his chest in the moment before the old man snatches it away into his lap.

Say Grace, Lest, Oriel says as she finds her place.

The old man looks away from Fish and his face goes tough.

Good food good meat gettin late let's eat.

Hat guffaws.

Lester. Oriel looks sideways at him.

I'm grateful. To you, love. It's good food.

Oriel looks about to give him a lecture, but her heart isn't in it.

I suppose the Lord understands, she says, picking up a fork.

Hope He does. Cause I don't. I'm damned if I do. And neither do you, so let's not be hypocrites and thank God.

No one is shocked. It's been coming, this talk. Everyone just eats on until Lon regurgitates a long string of fat onto the

54

tablecloth setting up a groan of disgust around the table.

Swallow a snake, mate? Lester says.

It's the pimple from me dimple, Lon announces soberly.

When the kids were asleep, or at least bucketing around in their rooms, Lester and Oriel had only each other across the table and the quiet was unnerving. Here they were again, a little square box of a woman and her plank-lanky husband. They looked each other up and down.

Well, he said. We're makin somethin here, I can feel it.

We need things, Oriel said.

Plenty.

Don't smile me down, Lest.

There's money left, love. We're not hungry.

You need work.

I've been thinkin.

She sighed and folded her arms. I thought I smelt burnin rubber.

Thinkin about this place.

We need our own bathroom, we need a stove, the kids need clothes – they go to school like they haven't got a mother. This place is temporary.

Yeah, I know.

Lester dropped a hunk of antgutted fencepost onto the fire. From above came the thumping of feet as the children got in and out of bed.

But I've cottoned onto somethin, he said. There's no corner shop this side of the railway line.

I know, I've carried the groceries back from Subi – I should know. She held the needle to the light. It was a wonder how something sharp came down to nothing like that. She looked through the needle's eye. So that's the Kingdom of Heaven, she thought. So that's all there was.

I've brained it out. We could do it.

What're you talking about?

A shop. Our shop.

Oh, don't be a fool, Lest. We can't pay rent on a shop.

We already are. Right now.

55

Oriel put down her darning and raised herself in her chair. What've you done?

I've used me noggin.

She sighed and squinched her eyes shut. Explain.

The front room, we'll use the front room out there for a shop. Gawd knows, there's enough room. It won't hurt us to use some of it for enterprise.

That's a good word that sounds weak on your lips, Lester Lamb. Across the corridor, they'll chuck all whatsername about it.

They're broke, darl. They're poor as us. And lazy – look at em, waiting for the boat to come in. They need the money.

Oriel Lamb pursed her lips. It wasn't such a bad idea, though she knew well enough who'd have to see it through.

We'll pray about it, he said automatically. We'll take it to the Lord. No, wait on . . . the knife never lies. Lester picked up the smeary butterknife and sent it spinning in the centre of the table.

If it points to me it's a yes. To you and it's a no.

She wondered if it wasn't really the way things were, everything just happening by chance in this sorry world. That knife spinning. She thought about her poor dead brother and the ashes and bones of her mother and sister, of Fish, the farm and every other bad turn that led to this night in a strange street and a makeshift kitchen. The knife turned over slower, flashing like her thoughts and it was no surprise to see the bone handle toward her and the blade aiming at him.

How do you know it never lies? she asked, taking up the darning again. But he was off in the next room rummaging. The needlepoint broke her skin but she didn't flinch. He'll be off the idea by bedtime, she thought. He'll be back onto the old vaudeville idea again, launching the Lamb Lyric Co., and the Lamb Family Octet onto the stages of the world. And out came Lester with a cap on the side of his head and the maw of the squeezebox hanging at his belly. She felt a great jam of confusion in her as he stood there smiling like an oaf.

What'll it be?

Something I don't know. Play me something I don't know.

56

Dolly Pickles left it till the last seconds of closing hour before she scratched on a bit of lipstick and went downstairs to see for herself. People had been sidling past all day. They'd worn a track across the weeds since dawn, and the cratchety tinkle of that little bell had driven her spare, but she wasn't going to go down there early and give her tenants the satisfaction of gloating. She didn't know why she should loathe the Lambs so much; they'd been polite and friendly, but they were pushy and beelike, the lot of them, and that little woman spoke to you with her blunt fingers nearly pecking at your tits. She couldn't help telling you how you should be doing things, what was a better way, a quicker way, the right this, the proper that. Not that she ever got personal, she was always talking general things, but Dolly felt it all get specific somewhere between the lines, as though that little magpie was letting you know what you could do to fix your life up. Oriel Lamb mouthed off a lot about work and stickability until you felt like sticking a bloody bility right up her drawers. That woman didn't believe in bad luck the way Dolly did.

The house was dark as she went down the stairs and along the corridor to the front. The door was open. Kids were pushing billycarts in the street. Dolly Pickles strode out onto the verandah and looked back at the Lamb side of the house and laughed. The huge livingroom window was gone and a shutter stood propped open in its place opening up on a view of that grand old room full of pineboard shelves bowing with jars and jugs, the fireplace bristling with hum-bugs and bullroarers and toothbusters. Crates stood on the stained floral carpet loaded with second grade fruit and vegetables and the air was thick with midges and fruit fleas. A big Avery scale stood like a lighthouse in the middle of this fog and behind it Oriel and Lester Lamb. The sign along the counter said:

LAMB SMALLGOODS
quality nice – best price
They watched her laugh. She straightened her hair and

lit a smoke to calm herself, leaned against the verandah post.

Well, how's it doing, ducks?

Lester Lamb began covering the fruit with damp hessian bags and doing other closing down kind of things while the little box woman lit on her with that steely stare.

A shillin and ha'p'nny, Oriel Lamb said.

You'll get rich if you keep it up. Dolly had meant it to be more friendly, more comradely, but she heard ridicule in her tone and watched Mrs Lamb brace up. Geez, I'm makin a friend here, she thought.

And *you'll* have an income, Mrs Pickles.

Lester Lamb smiled weakly as though he was neutral in this, and he put the shutter down apologetically in her face.

WE'RE LOCAL.

it said:

WE'RE HONEST,

it went on,

WE'RE HERE.

And there wasn't a damned thing she could do about it, that was for sure.

Stickability

It wasn't long before everyone on Cloud Street and anyone who lived near it knew about the Lambs' new shop, and not long before they started to spend as much as they gawked. At dawn you'd see the little woman out there sending Lester and Quick off to the markets across the rails, and the whole still street would be full of the coughing of the truck and the reverberation of Oriel's instructions. Nobody was ever left in doubt as to how many stones of spuds she thought necessary for a day's trading, or how to feel the ripest watermelon or what to tell that man Boswell when he started trying to fence bad tomatoes onto them again. Even if you couldn't see those meaty little arms and the sexless ashen bob and the sensible boots on her through your bedroom window and your morning blear, there wasn't a chance you'd escape the sound of her sending the family about its business. People started to call her the sergeant-major and they observed the way the shop came to life at the sound of her drill yell.

Soon the place was a regular feature of the street, a pedestrian intersection, a map point. It was where you came to buy a *West Australian* and talk about the progress of the war with your neighbours. It was where you could smell that daft beanpole husband of hers baking his cakes, though, fair dinkum, you had to hand it to the coot, he could bake his way to Parliament if he set his mind to it. Though *he* thought gettin a rise was only what happened inside an oven. Kids mobbed in on Saturday mornings before the footy to buy up the pasties he made. All the Lamb girls would be there, rattling the till, climbing on ladders, shaking out tuppenny measures of jubes. They'd blush and scowl when their father came to the counter singing a loopy tune.

> *Whacka diddle di-do*
> *How the heck could I know*
> *She wanted my heart*
> *for a billy cart*

He accompanied himself with a jar of humbugs or a feather duster, and said whatever came into his head and changed the tune from verse to verse. Nothing seemed to suppress his good spirits in those weeks. Nothing could stop him singing except the sound of Oriel's boots coming through the house behind the shop.

The house on Cloud Street took on a wonky aspect. It was still a big, old, rundown eyesore, but it seemed to have taken on an unbalanced life with all that activity and foment on the Lamb side, as though the place was an old stroke survivor paralysed down one side. The Pickleses didn't seem to go out much, and if they did they got swallowed up and lost in the picture. They were weak in numbers and all the activity seemed to cause them to fade from vision.

Oh, you're from next door the shop, love? people'd say to Dolly. You'n yer hubby rentin offa them, are yez?

Neighbours somehow got it into their heads that the Pickleses had come after the Lambs, and that stuck in Dolly's guts. Locals took pity on the crippled hubby and all, but they couldn't help but feel that the Pickleses weren't made of the

same stuff as their tenants. They didn't have stickability.
Now that was a word that moved camp along Cloud Street
quickly that autumn. After a month or two no one could
remember its introduction. But then neither was it easy to
remember Cloud Street without the shop. After a time the
shop *was* Cloud Street, and people said it, Cloudstreet, in one
word. Bought the cauli at Cloudstreet. Slip over to Cloudstreet, willya love, and buy us a tin of Bushells and a few
slices of ham. Cloudstreet.

The Dance

Quick Lamb tries to get on with his life. It's been a happy
one, being part of a mob, having farm fun and long dreamy
days free of things. But it's tough now, anchored to half a
house, being a glorified boarder in a city he's never even seen
before. Maybe if he could get out into the paddocks more,
out where air is stronger than memory so he could at least
sometimes get shot of that terrible noiseless moment when
he is walking along and Fish is just gone. He'd just kept
walking and his brother, Fish – the handsome kid, the smart
kid who made people laugh – Fish was under, and the net
was just floating across him like the angel of death. He knows
it should have been him, not Fish.

In this new house Quick has a room of his own for the
first time in his life, and he's not real sure how he likes it. The
girls are all bunched together in a room the size of a dance
hall down the front, and he knows they'd rather split up,
being girls and all. He feels their looks in the corridor and
gets the guilts. Besides, he's not sure how he likes it, being
alone. He wonders if maybe it's a banishment, his quiet
punishment for the Fish thing, but he reckons if it was that
they were after, they'd bung him in with whiny little Lon.
It's a good, big room that he has, though he's got nothing
at all to fill it with. His iron bed stands like an exhibit in the
middle with enough room to train a footy team on either
side. It takes time to get the feel of it, what with his lonelysick
wakefulness and the rumble and quake of the house going on

60

all night like the bellyaches of a sleeping whale.

Down the back when he's building the chookhouse, Quick finds a pile of newspapers and magazines someone's tied up and thrown over the fence. Now and then he opens a paper and sees a blinded prisoner of war or a crying baby or some poor fleeing reffo running with a mattress across his back, and he'll tear it out with care, take it up to his private room and pin it to the flaky wall to remind himself that he is alive, he is lucky, he is still healthy, and his brother is not. When he works on his spelling assignments he looks up and sees the gallery of the miserable; it grows all the time and they look down at him, Quick Lamb the Survivor, and he knows he deserves their scourging stares.

Now and then Fish comes into his room and looks about, wide-eyed and humming. Quick stiffs up with guilt, with sadness but sometimes he'll touch his ruined brother just to hear his musical giggle. It's the same giggle. It's still Fish Lamb, his brother.

Fair dinkum, Quick Lamb hates himself.

But at night those cripples, the reffos, the starving weeping wounded on his walls wait till Quick is asleep and then they dance in their ragged borders, buckle paper and sag on their pins as they throw themselves into a weird joyous tumult over his bed. They never make a sound and he always sleeps through, but it happens all the same – men throw off their mattresses and soldiers tear away bandages and the dead rise out of the ground, inheriting the lonely quiet of the room until near morning, when they're exhausted by happiness and freedom, and they resume their places for the dawn so that Quick Lamb might trap them again with his sorrow.

 Props

Lester was closing up the shop amidst the long verandah shadows when a blackfella appeared on the step. It took him by surprise. He turned from the bolted shutters and the man was there. He was tall and thin, the colour of a burnt kettle, and he had a shoulderload of long dry branches.

Wanna buy props, Mister?

Oh. Oh. Props.

The black man's hair stood like a deserted beehive. His feet were bare. His toes splayed on the ground like he was as much bird as he was man.

Gooduns. Not too much. Cut em meself.

Wait a minute, I'll ask the missus. Lester turned and went to go in, but stopped. Listen, you might's well come through yerself. She'll be out the back. No use standin about out here.

The man hesitated.

Can leave the props just inside the door here, if you like.

The black man nodded. He unshouldered the sticks and stepped inside. Lester saw his eyes suddenly widen. The whites were porcelain and they seemed to vibrate. Something clicked in the man's throat. Lester, stunned, watched him hold his pink palms out like a man with his hands against a window. He went back carefully, as if moving back in his own footsteps, his eyes roving about all the time from wall to ceiling to floor, and as soon as he was back over the threshold he turned and ran. Lester watched him go with his heart punching. The house grew quiet around him.

The props stayed just inside the door for two days until Oriel seized them and shoved her washing lines up with them.

The Lamb Girls

The time it took to fold a lace hanky, that's all it took for Hat Lamb and Elaine Lamb and Red Lamb to know that they liked the city better than the farm. Cloudstreet was like somewhere out of the movies. All of them loved the staircase; they'd never even imagined a place with landings and banisters before. Hat liked sliding down with her skirt up around her ears, but Elaine wouldn't contemplate that kind of activity, even though she was Hat's twin. Elaine imagined sweeping down with hoops in her skirt and a bustle, to a cologne-smelling beau with his hat in his hand. Red, who was only twelve, just liked to spit from the landing and hit the sad little cactus in the terracotta pot in the hall.

People came into the shop and there were the Lamb girls, the unmistakeable Lamb girls with their dresses sewn from the same conglomerate of scrap material their mother seemed to tack together in bolts, and their severe hairdos and priceless complexions, their efficiency and sharpness. All of them knew how to count, and the twins had begun to take other forms of arithmetic as well, especially when soldiers came into the shop, bored and fatheaded. Sometimes Yanks came in flashing their big teeth, slapping on the accent thick as bread. They were boys with the voices of men, and it sent the Lamb girls absolutely troppo. Hat had a broad smile and she was starting to look like a woman. Elaine was already prone to 'spells' and she never smiled much for fear of seeming young and simple. Red was just a tomboy, she didn't think about smiling or not smiling. There was a gap, now that Fish wasn't being the ratbag of the family, and Red was out to fill it. She beat boys at cricket and she terrorized the bike sheds at school with the way she could throw a punch.

The Lamb girls didn't speak to each other much, but when they did they all agreed that things were on the up.

Medicine

By May, when a chill had come into the nights and the street was subdued and indoorsy after dark with the Lambs' chooks racked along their perch like mumbling hats, and the air so still you could hear the sea miles off and the river tide eating at the land, Lester and Oriel went to bed bonesore but grateful. It was a time when they talked like the old comrades they were, the way they'd bedtalked in those early farm years before the Depression when the kids hadn't yet crowded them back into reputation and role.

You know what I miss? Lester said. The singin, that's what I miss.

Talkin church again. Lester yull always miss singin, army, church or school.

63

Worldly songs are pretty, love, but the old church songs, they're beautiful, you gotta say it.

Yairs, she said, it's true enough. But we shouldn't talk about it. It'll only upset us.

Strike, we hold a grudge, Orry.

My oath, she grinned in the halfdark.

The house shifted on its stumps. Their new rooster crowed itself stupid ten hours short of daybreak.

Quick's lookin blue, said Lester.

Well, Oriel murmured, that's natural enough.

Blames himself, thinks we blame him.

Don't we?

Lester turned onto his back to see the ceiling mottled with streetlight. I don't know. I know it's not his fault. Why would it be? It's just what happened.

But do you blame him?

Lester said nothing.

We blame him, she said. And I blame you. And God.

It scares me, he said, hearin you think like that.

Me too, she said. I can't help it. I'm a sinner, Lest.

Do you ever wish you were like her next door?

Oriel sniffed. Mrs Pickles? No. I couldn't take ten minutes of it.

She's hard as nails.

Hard as lard, you mean. I'm the one hard as nails.

Lester coughed out a laugh.

We can't help it, Oriel said vaguely, none of us can.

You always said people can help anythin and everythin.

That was once.

What about Fish?

Least of all Fish.

No, no, I meant what are we gunna do with him?

We'll give him the gentlest life we can, we'll make it the best for him we know how.

Lester agonized. How do we know what's best? How do we make him happy? What does he think?

Oriel thought about this. It's like he's three years old . . .

You know, Lester says, almost giggly with relief, we've

64

never talked about him like this since it –

Lester be quiet, I'm thinkin.

He waited. Lester thought about poor old Fish, that skylarking ratbag turned brainless overnight. There'd been times he'd thought the kid was better dead than to have to live all his life as a child, but he knew that being alive was being alive and you couldn't tamper with that, you couldn't underestimate it. Life was something you didn't argue with, because when it came down to it, whether you barracked for God or nothing at all, life was all there was. And death. Oriel began to snore. Lester gave up waiting and went off himself.

Having both watched parents hurried to the grave by medicine, Oriel and Lester weren't chuffed about doctors. Neither had stepped inside hospital or surgery since childhood. The children were born wherever they were. Hat and Elaine in the kitchen at Margaret. Quick in the lockup of the police station, Red in the saddle room, and Lon was born at the side of the road in the shadow of the broken-axled Chev. Hard work and plenty of food, that kept the quacks away. And a bit of care, Oriel would say. She could fix most ills with a bit of this and that. She conceded that doctors were like governments: it was possible that they served some use though it didn't pay to put them to the test.

But the ache of their doubt about Fish got hold of them and besides, it looked like victory in Europe and they were feeling optimistic, so they found themselves in a surgery across the tracks that week telling a quack their story.

He was a waistcoat and watch chain type and he spoke like the pommy officers Lester remembered from his days in the Light Horse. He put a light down Fish's throat and then in his ears. It got old Fish giggling. The doc looked puzzled and amused. Oriel munched her lip. Lester kept his hands on the boy. Fish stood there with his shirt open and his eyes flicking all about.

What's your name, boy? the quack asked.

Fish Lamb, said Oriel. Samson.

Fish, said Fish.

Mrs Lamb. I'll ask and *he'll* answer.

Very well.

Why do they call you Fish?

It's the name, said Fish.

Hm. How old are you, Fish?

Nine.

Ten next month, said Oriel.

Mrs *Lamb*.

Can you count to nine?

Nine, said Fish.

Yes.

I'm big.

Indeed, said the quack. Fish, where do you live?

In the family. With Quick. Lestah.

Who is this? the quack asked, pointing to Lester.

Fish grinned. Lestah! My da.

And who is this, Fish?

The bright look stayed on Fish's face, but it became a look of suspension.

Who is this lady?

Oriel set her teeth in a smile, her jaw tight enough to break.

Fish?

Lester, he doesn't see me.

Who is she, Fish?

Please, Doctor, this –

Fish looked past her into the wallpaper, his features bright and distracted.

The water, said Fish.

On the wallpaper there were waves and jumping mullet and sails.

Queer, said the quack.

Oriel got a hanky out for the eyes.

How long was he under the water, you say?

Lester shrugged. A few minutes. He was caught up in the net and my lamp went out –

Yes, yes. And you revived him Mrs Lamb?

Oriel looked at Fish but couldn't get his gaze. Yes. And I prayed.

The water, said Fish.

And you didn't take him to a doctor, or a hospital?

We thought he was better, said Lester. A miracle, you know.

Hmm. Like Lazarus, eh, the quack muttered; Jesus wept.

But he's retarded, said Oriel, it's like he's three. We had to potty train him again, start from scratch.

You mean he's improved?

A bit, yes.

A boy would have more than this regression after an experience like that, said the quack. He shows no spastic tendencies at all.

He blacks out.

No speech impediment. He seems alert, aware, sane. This is not what happens. Now I –

Are you saying we're liars? Oriel growled. Do you think we'd come here not telling the truth?

Mrs Lamb –

Because I am a woman whose word has been respected as long –

Oriel! Lester's voice was shaky with momentary authority.

This boy seems traumatized. There's nothing physically wrong with him. Are you sure he hasn't been through a great shock of some kind that would explain his obvious . . . retreat?

He's been alive and he's been dead, said Lester. One of those was bound to be a shock.

Perhaps he was under a few seconds, enough to give him –

Minutes, said Oriel. No heartbeat. Another minute, two even, before I got him back.

You could think about a psychiatrist.

Lester swallowed. If his . . . his brain is damaged, can a shrink fix it?

No. He might help hysteria, trauma and so on. You could think about a specialized home for him . . .

Oriel picked Fish up in a swoop. There's no home as

specialized as mine, Mister!

Lestah! Lestah!

Mrs Lamb, sit down.

Come on, Lester.

Fish, asked the quack, where do you want to go?

The water, the water!

Oriel crashed through the waiting room like a fullback.

Fast! said Fish. Fast!

 VE

While they slept, Sam Pickles nursing his tingling stump, Oriel Lamb snoring beneath her eyepatches, the house stumps grinding beneath them, the wallshadows flitting and dancing and swirling up a musty smell in the darkness, the war ended in Europe.

Before dawn, word was out at the Metro Markets where Lester heard it, dropped what he was doing and drove home, punishing the old Chev across tramlines and through stop signs until he throttled it, smoking and steaming, into Cloud Street. He went through the door like a stormtrooper.

Victory in Europe!

And the wireless was on somewhere.

Unconditional surrender!

VE Day.

Lester barrelled into the kids' room. No school today! VE Day.

What? said Red, always snaky when woken.

VE Day!

Violet Eggleston? What's she done, that dag?

Who?

What?

The war. The Krauts are out.

Oh.

What about the Japs? said Quick from the hallway.

The Japs are still in.

We'll get em, said Quick.

Anyway. Hitler's dead.

68

Hitler didn't bomb Darwin, said Quick.

Tokyo'll go, said Red.

Gawd, said Lester, what a mob of glumbums.

Wait'll Violet Eggleston finds out, said Red, she'll think it's for her.

The kids climbed back into their beds. Next door the Pickleses were laughing. Well, thought Lester, that's that then.

Fish Forgets

Fish hears the winter rain hissing on the tin roof. When lightning flashes he sees the fruit trees without leaves down there in the yard. On still nights, cold nights, clear frosty nights, he hears the river a long way off across the rooftops and treecrowns. That's something he does remember. But he forgets so much. He doesn't remember being a real flamin character. He's forgotten all his old ways, how people loved him, people's names, his daily jobs. Before, he'd likely as not tie your shoelaces together while you weren't noticing, but nowadays he can't even get his own shoes on, let alone lace them. School learning has evaporated in his head, horse-riding, stone-skipping, fartlighting, limericks, stars, directions, weather, rabbit trapping, beetle racing. From the outside, those are the things you *can* tell about him. Mostly, he just forgets to grow up. Already Lon is thinking of Fish as the baby of the family.

He knows Quick, Lester, Lon, Hat, Elaine and Red, but he can't seem to place Oriel. Either that or he sees her and ignores her. He just looks through her like she's not there, like she's never been there.

It's like Fish is stuck somewhere. Not the way all the living are stuck in time and space; he's in another stuckness altogether. Like he's half in and half out. You can only imagine and still fail to grab at how it must be. Even the dead fail to know and that's what hurts the most. You have to make it up and have faith for that imagining.

Fish is still strong and beautiful. That Rose next door

69

sees it. She watches him. Mostly Fish is quiet. He talks, but not much. He likes to stand around in the yard and see birds. He likes the way things move in the wind. Wind excites him. When he feels breeze on his face he smiles and says, Yes. Winter days now, he stands out in the westerly that blows down the tracks from the sea and it closes his eyes with its force.

Hello, wind!

He loves to sing. He knows 'The Old Rugged Cross', 'Blessed Assurance', 'Bringing in the Sheaves', whole strings of them. Lester brings out the accordion some nights after tea and Fish moans along. Music seems to make him feel good. Music and spinning things.

Knife never lies! he yells as Lester spins the butterknife. Fish claps his hands wide fingered.

Lester shows him how to spin a soup bowl, send it rocking across the table, standing up of its own momentum, whirring and blurring, making wind and sound for him. Fish becomes an expert at it. Quick and Hat and Red and Lon stand and watch him spin two, three, four at a time.

When he's frightened or angry he falls down. He cries like a man. It makes the Lambs crazy with emotion to hear it.

Oriel doesn't realize it, but she begins to dress Fish like an idiot, the way people clothe big sadfaced mongoloids. She hoiks his trousers up under his arms with a belt so long it flaps. She combs his hair straight down on his brow and shines his shoes till they mock him. The reason Oriel doesn't notice is that Quick gets to him early after breakfast and drags the clobber round on him, messes him up like a boy, normal and slouchy. It makes old Fish giggle, Quick tugging at him.

Yer a boy, Fish.

Big boy.

My oath, says Quick.

Kitchentalk

Sometimes after tea there was no shopwork to be done so the Lambs'd loiter round the kitchen table, talking above the hum of Fish's soup bowls with the new range all roar and glow. Hat at the sink. Oriel pulling out the darning. Lester picking the flourbits off his forearms.

Fine sink, this, Dad.

Yeah, but what about the other five? said Oriel.

A job lot, Lester said.

Your father has a nose for a bargain, Oriel said rolling her eyes.

We could make dunnies out of the rest, said Quick, a five holer.

Quick, stop that.

Lester laughed: We used to have a sixteen holer when I was in the army. That's how they got the idea for the Lancaster bomber for this war. Saturation bombin.

What'd you do durin the last war, Mum? said Quick.

Oriel kept darning.

Hat raised her eyebrows: Mum?

Hm?

The Great War. What'd you do?

Waited. I raised six kids and waited for one of em to come back.

The kitchen fell quiet, all except for Fish's whirring bowl. Lester tapped scum from his chromatic harmonica.

I didn't know you were married before, said Elaine, lips aquiver.

Eee–laine, you nong, said Hat. 1914 to 1918. She'd hafta start havin em at age twelve to get six out, not to mention one off to war. She was born the year of Federation, 1901.

Well, said Lester. Margaret River School obviously taught Hat more than groomin and deportation.

They weren't my children, said Oriel.

Well, I figured that, said Hat. Whose were they?

My father remarried after my mother died. His new wife already had a boy, Bluey, and they had a whole squad of babies after they married. Half-brothers and sisters. I brought them up. *She* taught at the bush school. She wasn't much older than me, you know. And I wanted to be a teacher, but I never finished school. I raised her family.

Why?

71

Because, Quick, I loved my father.

Did he love you?

When I got burnt one day in a bushfire, in 1910, he killed his last pig, and took out its bladder and put it on my legs to heal the blisters. A whole beast, just so I wouldn't scar. Not only was it his last pig, it was the last living thing on his farm but me.

I wouldn't have wasted pork on *this* family, said Lester with a creasyfaced wink. Slice of polony, maybe. Pound of tripe, yeah.

Garn, Dad, yer all bluff.

Did I tell you about me and Roy Rene?

Arr!

Did he Mum?

Oriel finished a sock and threw it at Lon whose foot belonged to it. Yes, Yes. The Les and Mo Show.

At the Tivoli, said Lester, and then The Blue Room. Ooh, I was a lair then. All the best people'd sing me songs. I wrote for the best of em.

He was good, said Oriel, not dirtymouthed like Roy Rene.

Old Roy's the best, said Lester.

Quick looked at the old girl. She caught him looking.

What? she said.

The one who went to war. The half-brother you were waitin for. Did he come back?

No.

Died of wounds in Palestine. The Holy Land. Shot by a Turkish airman at a well. He was a signalman. He was waterin horses. He always looked good with horses.

Did you know him, Dad? You were there.

I was only at Anzac, said Lester.

He was a genius with horses, said Oriel.

Horses were geniuses with me, said Lester. That's why I was in the Light Horse. They were always lighter after they bucked me off.

You were a hero, said Quick.

Lester pumped the old harmonica to break the quiet, and because he knows, well as Oriel knows, that it's just not true.

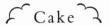
The day Quick turned twelve his father baked him a cake and wrote his name in icing and stuck twelve candles in it, and when the evening rush at the shop was over, the Lamb family came through from the counter to the kitchen to sit around the oval table and sing 'Happy Birthday'. They'd just finished the singing and were into the three cheers when the cowbell rang up front and Oriel went to serve in the shop. She came back at a jog.

Lady wants a cake, Les. She's desperate. She'll give us a quid.

It's too much. We haven't got one.

Quick looked at the candles, still smoking.

It's too much, said Lester.

Quick watched as his mother whipped out all the candles, smoothed the icing over with a knife and gathered the cake up under her arm to charge back down the corridor.

Birthday, Quick, said Fish.

Yeah, said Quick.

Suddenly, they all laughed – even Quick. It started as a titter, and went quickly to a giggle, then a wheeze, and then screaming and shrieking till they were daft with it, and when Oriel came back in they were pandemonius, gone for all money. But they paused like good soldiers when she solemnly raised her hand. She fished in her apron and pulled out a florin. Happy birthday, son.

You want change from this? said Quick.

That set them off again and there was no stopping them.

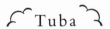 Tuba

Quick Lamb was surprised when his father joined the army. He was even more surprised to know he'd joined the army band. The old man came home one day with a full kit and tuba and spread it out in the bedroom behind the shop so they could all see it.

I thought I'd do my bit, Lester Lamb said. They wouldn't take me in '39.

All the Lambs looked at it in wonder. Quick worried about the old man sometimes. They were bombing Tokyo. There couldn't be a few weeks left of the war. Deep inside Quick knew his father was liable to do anything at all.

I used to be in the Salvos, Lester Lamb said. I'm orright on the old tub.

The tub? Quick said.

Tuba. Chew-ba.

Lester took up the dented instrument and sat. He honked out a couple of notes. It sounded like a tune, right enough. Like elephant farts.

Oriel said nothing. Lester let out a strangled oomph and the rooster down the back started screeching. Lon giggled and Fish smiled.

More, said Fish.

Don't worry, said Oriel, there'll be plenty more. More than plenty.

From then on, the old man was at band practice every afternoon and as the year got on towards Christmas Quick saw him less and less and he wondered more and more. His mother ran the shop and said nothing about it. The girls served. Hat and Elaine had finished school for good now. They were old enough to work for money. The shop went on. Quick went to school and did badly and came home. Sometimes he'd lie on his bed with Fish and just look at the ceiling and feel Fish against him. He missed the old Fish, especially at school. With Fish, people noticed you. But without him, at this new school, he was just a country kid whose shorts were too long, whose feet were horny from barefootedness. He was slow and dreamy and the teachers gave up on him quickly. When he came home and lay on his bed and looked up, he didn't know what he saw; he couldn't decide what he felt. Fish might come in and say Hello, Quick, and stand at the window watching the motes in the late afternoon sun, or maybe slouch in beside him on the bed and say, It's the roof you're looking at, Quick.

One afternoon, when they were lying there in the socksmelling heat, Fish dug him in the chest and asked: Are you happy, Quick?

Quick turned his head to look at those black eyes. For a moment it occurred to him that Fish might have been pretending to be slow this whole year and the thought made him sick and angry. But he looked close at Fish who began to giggle and he knew it wasn't pretending.

I don't know, he said. What about you?

When I feel good.

What about now?

Fish skewed his lower lip and considered. Aw, yeah.

When are you sad then?

When I want the water, Fish said.

What dyou mean?

Fish watched the motes diving and whorling.

What water, Fish?

The water, the water.

Fish got off the bed and went to the window. Quick watched him stand there with his yellow hair sticking up all over.

⌒ Science ⌒

Sam Pickles started the day with a smoke on the back step before he went out walking. You'd think he was a one-handed brain surgeon the way he concentrated on the task. The walk started out in July as the daily job hunt, but after a few weeks it just became the thing he did, the shape of his day. It kept his blood cool, eased the itch he slept and woke with. Luck was out there waiting on him, puckering at him. Joel always said that hard work makes good luck, but any man who made his fortune on a horse like Eurythmic was deeper into the mysteries than he knew. There was no work in that. A winner like that had the weight of the whole bloody universe behind it.

No, there was a change in the air by August, and Sam

knew it; the winter sky the colour of sixpence, steady rent coming in from those tubahonking Lambs, the electricity in the stumps of his fingers. Walking, he held his crook hand in his good one and tried to read its message. Hours he walked, to clear his head of Dolly's stormcloud humidity and Rose's new hardset stares. The house vibrated with hustle these days, groaning laborious as a ship with those Lambs going at it night and day, singing, working, laughing, shifting boxes and furniture morning and night and their blasted rooster going off like a burglar alarm at all hours.

Those Lambs. No joke, it took his breath away to see them go at it. You'd think they were carrying the nation on their backs with all that scrubbing and sweeping, tacking up shelves and blackboards, arguing over the situation of jars, tubs, scales and till. Stinking dull work, the labour of sheilas at best, with all that smile and how do you do, sir, but you had to admire them for it. They were just scrub farmers green to town, a mob of gangly, puppet-limbed yokels but they moved in like they'd designed the house themselves. Making luck, the hardest donkey yacker there is. With that little woman pushing and harassing and haranguing. They'd never go hungry, that lot, but neither would they have it high on the hog. Their way was alright if that was as far as you could see, but Sam had his father's blood. He was no donkey worker, he was more of a scientist. Not the kind to yoke himself for the long haul like that, he saw himself as the kind of man who read things on the wind, living from divining the big wins and taking the losses as expenses on the way. No guts, no glory. He could feel it in his wheezy old lungs, in his stumps. There was science in it, and science always wins through. His time would come. Hadn't this subletting bizzo been a gamble and a win?

Alone in his room of an afternoon, Sam'd get down his two-up pennies and hold them in his palm. Dolly took the rent personally and she didn't even let him get hold of enough to buy baccy. But, by crikey, his time was coming, she'd see.

⌢ No Wading ⌢

God, how she hated winter. Dolly Pickles stood in the weak sun of the backyard looking at her feet. Two flaky hens scratched nearby. Today, again, she felt angry for no reason. Sam was out looking for a job, the kids were at school and the place was quiet. She was waiting for the copper to boil so she could finish the washing.

All she needed was summer, and some sweet, healing, nipplepricking sun. Short of a good time, that's all she needed to get by.

Green tufts of wild oats rasped at her shins. The sun'd make her young and hopeful and it wouldn't matter that she was married to a crip. She wanted to be brown and oily on some beach, to feel the heat slowly building in her skin until she couldn't bear it and had to run down to the shore and flop into the gutter between surf banks and have her flesh fizz and prickle with chill. But all she had was this winter feeling, this shittiness, this anger that she couldn't place. And washing she hadn't done on wash day. Herself next door always had the washing out at dawn washing day, as though she did it to shame everyone else, especially Dolly.

She wandered down through the long weeds of her yard and beneath the lilac tree to where she could see down the embankment to the railway. She heard someone next door straining in the little tin dunny. Up at the house Lester Lamb was singing and Dolly could see the slow kid with his nose pressed to a second floor window, so she knew it must be the sergeant-major who was on the privy. A thrill of mischief sparked in her. Here's a lark. Hello wash day. She stuck her head over the pickets.

There sat Oriel Lamb with her knickers round her bumpy knees and her skirt hoiked avast. The little woman stiffened and closed her mouth.

I'll go and get the ranger, Dolly said with a wicked grin.

Why's that? Oriel Lamb asked, mustering some dignity in tone if nowhere else. She grabbed for the door.

Smells like something's crawled up inside you and died.

The door slapped shut.

No Wading.

Dolly Pickles laughed until there wasn't even any bitterness in it. And she was sober as a saint.

After the kids are asleep Dolly stands at the window with only her stockings on. There is no noise from next door, and the whole house is quiet. Sam lies on the bed, rolls a smoke, watching her. She looks out at the moon that rests on the fence.

We aren't that old, she says.

Anyone with an arse like that isn't real old. He licks the paper, tamps, then lights up.

Dolly rests an elbow on the sill. The grass is shin high out in their half of the yard. Bits of busted billycarts and boxes litter the place beneath the sagging clothesline.

I dunno what I'm doin, she says.

Do you ever?

She shrugs. Spose not. What about you?

He takes a drag. I'm a bloke. I work. I'm courtin the shifty shadow. That's what I'm doin.

This is another life.

It's the city. We own a house. We got tenants.

Do you remember Joel's beach house?

Sorta question is that?

That was our life.

The late train rollicks up from Fremantle. It sends the long grass into rolling gasps and sighs on the embankment in the moonlight, and Dolly watches as Sam comes up behind her to fit snug against her rump. She feels the heat of his fag at her neck and his hand and his stump on the cold porcelain of her nipples, and the hot, glowing end of him getting up into her, making her twist and feint, grip the sill, see her nails bending in the wood. Dolly can smell the charge in him, it hisses against her stockings and bows her legs until it's him that's holding her upright, and so it goes, on and on, until out there in the moonlight she can see the river and the dunes and Joel's shack, and the two of them on the beach rubbing the flesh of oysters into each other.

When Sam is asleep, Dolly gets up and pulls on a coat and creeps out of the house. The mob next door are long asleep. She goes down to the tracks and looks at them gleaming in the moony light; she can see her face in them, almost. She remembers riding out to the siding when she was a girl. She rode on the back of the saddle behind her father. Oh, she worshipped that man. He was strong and sunbrown and quiet. There was a way he had of laughing that made her feel like the world might stop right there and then, as if that laughter was enough for everyone and everything, and there was no point in anything else bothering to continue. She must have been six or so on that ride out to the siding where the great tin holding bins stood bending in the heat. The ground was blonde and rainstarved and after Dolly's father had fixed up his business with the rail men he saw her standing by the buckled railway lines.

Those rails go all over the world. They go forever.

And she felt it was true. It was like they were electric with all knowledge, all places, all people.

Dolly squats by the cold rails here in the winter night.

She never did get to try those rails. She just got to be goodlooking and cheeky and by sixteen she found herself out on her back under the night sky with a long procession of big hatted men, one of whom, the youngest, the fairest of them, was sleeping up there in that saggy great house with his arms up behind his head, and his fingerless fist on her pillow. No, she never did find out about those rails. But nothing ever turns out like you expect. Like how your father ends up not being your father, and all.

Dogs get howling all down the way. Somewhere a bicycle bell rings. Somewhere else there's a war on. Somewhere else people turn to shadows and powder in an instant and the streets turn to funnels and light the sky with their burning. Somewhere a war is over.

Bells

Rose woke up to the sound of bells. She opened her window and the world was mad with noise: church bells, tram bells, air raid sirens, train whistles, a rocket going up, klaxons and trumpets, dogs howling nutheaded at the sky. Cloud Street was filling and below, the shop was bursting with huggers and clappers who were opening bottles and crying out on the lawn where she could see them. The house shook and a thousand smells whirled through it with a bang of doors.

The war is over!

Ted came bursting in: The Japs! We creamed em!

It's finished, listen to the wireless.

Rose rushed to the landing. Downstairs she saw that Mrs Lamb giving her mum a roast chook and a plate of fruit. The old man was breaking open a bottle of grog he'd got from who knows where. There were a couple of Yank sailors out in the hallway and that wet eyed Mr Lamb squeezing his accordion fit to wring blood from it.

She went down into it and couldn't help but have a smile cracking her chops. She danced a barn dance with a Yank and got a smack across the bum passing the old man on the verandah.

Here, said Quick Lamb, holding out a jar of humbugs.

She went elbow deep for them.

Mum'll kill us, he said.

Me! said the slow kid, the goodlooking one who was on the front step spinning a butter knife. The blade pointed at his chest. It's meeee!

IV

Break in the Weather

THAT'S it, Sam thinks; that's bloody it. The streets are still full of revellers as he heads for the station with his pennies in his pocket. This is the break in the weather, Sam my man. Come in bloody Spinner.

His teeth ache. His hair buzzes at its roots with power.

Wherever it is, I'll find it.

Whoever it is, I'll find em.

And I won't be back till I do.

A couple of days after VJ Day, when everyone was still crazy with peace fever, and the old man still hadn't turned up and the old girl was getting vicious, Rose walked home from school with her booklumpy bag, wondering if he was gone for good and how she'd have to tough it out with the old girl. It was torture. Other kids swept past on junky grids, pulling wheelies and skids in the dirt, startling clumps of gossiping girls and sending small boys up trees in fright, but Rose walked straight and sensible as though nothing could touch her. Up ahead she saw the Lambs shagging along under the Geraldton wax that burst over the fences beside the station and hung full of bees and fragrance. Somewhere behind her, Ted was shouting at Chub not to be such a wanker and that he could flaminwell carry his own bag.

If the old man was gone another day, she reckoned, that Mrs Lamb'd be over with some advice quicksmart. She knew the fast, cheap, clean, sensible way of doing everything and she'd be dishing it out like the Salvos, and the old girl'd be pukin.

Rose stopped by the Geraldton wax. Geraldton. Already it seemed like something she'd dreamt up. She pulled a waxy blossom off its stem and took it with her.

Kids were milling round Cloudstreet buying penny-sticks, freckles, snakes and milkbottles in little white paper bags. Rose pushed through the congregation on the verandah, heaved open the big jarrah front door and went inside.

And there he was. Arms akimbo, like General Douglas-flamin-MacArthur, the old man was sitting at the bottom of the stairs, polishing his stumpy knuckles and grinning fit to be in pictures.

You look like you lost a penny and found a quid, she said.

Sam held out his two-up pennies.

Where you been?

A bit of scientific work.

Oh, gawd. So what are you grinnin about, then?

I got a job.

A job! How?

The shifty shadow, Rosie.

Arr!

True as me word.

How?

He rattled the pennies.

Two-up?

That's right.

You gotta be jokin, Dad.

Plus a bit of the foldin. Sam slipped a pound note down the front of her pinafore.

Rose shivered, ready to burst from excitement, anger, disbelief, something.

I put a bloke so far in the red he had to pay in kind. He's the union boss, Blackie Stewart. He owes me a job. Start Monday. I'll be makin money.

Don't get beyond yerself.

No, fair dinkum, I'll be makin millions. It's a job at the Mint.

I hope they don't find out that you count on yer fingers, Rose said.

Sam started after her and she ran giggling through the door into the rangy mob of kids outside.

Cheeky blighter!

Rose stood in the yard and looked back at him and it didn't seem so strange to love him.

Monday. Rose ran home from school and waited for Sam to show. Even the old girl seemed nervous, up there cooking his tea.

He came swinging his gladstone bag into the yard.

Well? she said.

They're for water, Sam said.

What do you do? Rose asked as they went up the stairs.

Push a broom. Take turns looking for duds. Not a lot a fella with one hand can do, love.

They came into the kitchen.

Rose looked at the new penny he'd just taken from

85

under his tongue. She couldn't imagine money being made.

They just cook it, like yer ole lady cooks a batch a scones. Cept more regular and a bit softer.

Dolly hissed at him without malice.

Out they come, pennies, zacs, deaners, shillins. The place stinksa money. Ya feel it in yer hair and on yer clobber. Spend all day breathin in gold dust. Fair's fair, the place is like a cake shop and the smell always gets ya hungry.

Chops are done, said Dolly.

They sat down to eat, and Sam told them all about the noise and the machines and the heat of furnaces and the bars on the windows and the colour the limestone had gone on the outside. He described the wheezy press and the smell of kero and the way all the blokes thought he'd lost his fingers on some secret mission in an unknown archipelago instead of from sleepiness and bad luck while carting birdshit. They called him Sam and got all serious in his presence. He saluted with his thumb and half finger and they didn't laugh.

Rose saw it all as clear as if she'd been there herself. After dinner she worked on her geography, colouring maps and diagrams at the kitchen table while her parents smoked and talked in short, low bursts. Ted and Chub disappeared outside for a while. Everything was normal and right. There were dishes in the sink and the sound of kids playing in the street and the trains passing smutty wind. Something settled over the kitchen. Rose kept the colours inside the lines and all the patterns were proper, sensible and neat. Happiness. That's what it was.

 Winning

In spring Sam Pickles went back to the September races and started winning. All through October, and into November he bet on a gelding called Blackbutt and saw him place or win every time. Sam knew it didn't make any sense at all that this horse should keep winning. But luck came from some other place, bringing weirdness and aid into the world and he didn't question it. He kept every winning ticket in the hat band of his Akubra. He bought binoculars and a grey suit and you could spot him there amidst the soldiers and sailors and women, despite his smallness, because he looked like a punter, and more importantly, a winner. When they thundered around on the last turn, filling the air with sods and dust and great creaturely gasps of horsepower, Sam Pickles stood still with his teeth set and his blue eyes clear to see Blackbutt come home the money. His blood was charged, he felt the breath of magic on him. He came home with his pockets stuffed, his stump aching, and the kids grabbing at him on the stairs to feel success.

We've come a long way, he said to them. By crikey we have. Eh? Eh?

One afternoon when she got home, Rose found a desk in her room. It was dark and compact, built from jarrah, and in every drawer there were sharpened pencils, ink, paper and books. She stood there, smelling the wood and the varnish, the newness and shock of it. When she turned around he was at the door. Rose began to blubber. He laughed and knocked on wood with his fingerless fist. The boys ran in with their airguns and it was like an early Christmas.

All spring it went on. They had good shoes and black market meat, sly grog and shop toys. The Pickles kids looked out across the fence and saw the Lambs digging noisily in the garden in their patched clothes, their square ordinary bodies dark with sweat, and they felt they had gotten back the edge. Rose and Ted and Chub slept and only dreamt of more.

Dolly sat up in the evenings and drank stout with lemonade. When Sam came out of bed to get her she'd be soft and warm and quiet and she kissed him like she was sucking at something he had. He felt her legs fasten around his waist and her teeth in his neck as they ground up the bedclothes. Her breath was sweet and she cried out enough to make him breathless and frantic. He could have wept with triumph. But when he was asleep, skewed off on his own side of the bed with his arm across his eyes, Dolly would get up again with his mess coming all down her legs, and she'd go out and open another bottle and sit in the dark alone.

Rose heard it first. The old man was coming in after work. The steak was spitting on the stove and the place smelled of pepper.

Fair dinkum!

Rose looked at her mother. It wasn't the old man's voice, but it sure was his gait they heard coming down the hall. They were his boots alright.

Fairrrrgh! Dink. Dinkum.

He's drunk, Dolly said.

Rose saw a ladder in her stocking.

And then in he came with a damn bird on his shoulder. He looked radiant and proud and prettywell sober. The bird was just an ordinary pink cockatoo with those clear side-winding eyes behind a beak like an ingrown toenail. From Sam's shoulder, the bird looked down at Rose and Dolly with an expression of hauteur.

Say hello to Stan, girls! said Sam, dropping his gladstone bag to the floor.

Gawd help us, said Dolly.

Fair flamin dinkum! said the bird.

Rose laughed and Stan lifted a clawed old foot in her direction.

I won im, Sam said.

What in, a mugs' lottery?

Just a bet.

He's a beaut, said Rose. What does he eat?

New pennies.

That'll be cheap, said Dolly.

We can shake him out at Christmas, said Rose. Like a money box.

Fair dinkum! said Stan.

They laughed and laughed, but little did they know. Two days before Christmas Stan crapped out three ha'pennies and a shilling, enough to buy seed for months.

When those coins dropped out of him onto the kitchen table two days before Christmas, he cocked his head at all present. He fixed his eyes on them with irascible turns of his head.

Eh? he said. Eh? What?

Stan always paid his way.

In time the house absorbed the bird, though it could never fully absorb his irritable shrieks. Even the neighbours winced at it. Whenever he was about the house Sam took Stan on his shoulder. The rest of the time the bird side-stepped up and down the fence, cocking his head and dodging the honkynuts Lon Lamb shot at him with a rubber band. Sam Pickles liked to feel Stan's claws in his shoulder. It made him look a little taller. Rose said it made him look like a pirate. Dolly said it made him look like a perch. Ted and Chub didn't care. Stan bit them and they lost interest.

Stan's wing was never clipped. He could always have flown away.

Quick Lamb's Sadness Radar

Quick Lamb reads the paper every day and sees the long lists of the missing believed killed, and the notices in memorium for sons and fathers and brothers. The war's over, he knows, but he picks up sadness like he's got radar for it. The whole world's trying to get back to peace but somewhere, always somewhere there's craters and rubble and still the lists and the stories coming home as though it'll never let itself be over. There's families on this street who've lost men, and while they remember the war will still be on.

We're lucky, he thinks; the old man was too old and I was too young. We've got food, coupons, a full ration book. We're gettin away light.

Quick sees kids at school who are poor. The Lambs are patched and barefooted, but at lunchtime their mother always brings warm pies and pasties to the gate. Quick and Lon and Red meet up wordlessly and eat together. Through the winter Quick notices Wogga McBride sitting with his little brother Darren. Wogga McBride is in grade six, one

below Quick. They have a queer way of eating their sandwiches: whatever it is they bring wrapped in vine leaves gets
eaten under cover of their hands in a way so quick and deft
that it's impossible to know what it is they have. Maybe it's
Quick's misery radar, but he can't let it be. He watches
them every day from the corner of his eye until it's almost
October, and by then he knows what he's begun to suspect –
Wogga McBride and his brother aren't eating anything at all;
they're just pretending. Out of pride, they're going through
the motions of unwrapping, passing, commenting on, eating
food that doesn't exist.

Quick lies awake that night with shadows vibrating on
his wall.

Next day at lunchtime, Quick leaves Lon and Red and
takes a pastry over to Wogga McBride.

I'm full, Quick says. Want it?

The skinny blue kid takes it with a nod and Quick leaves
it at that. From then he resolves to take food to Wogga
McBride every day, but most days he forgets.

The McBrides live further down the tracks towards
West Perth but they cross at the walkway just below the big
house on Cloud Street. Quick gets into the habit of falling in
behind Wogga and Darren McBride and following them
until they jump the tracks and head down toward town to
their place.

Not long before the holidays, Quick is behind the
McBrides, straining to hear a bit of their rare conversation.
He doesn't know what he finds so fascinating about them.
True, they have blue-mottled skin and legs like hinges, the
way they fold inside the knee. There is a kind of weariness
about them. Their hair lies flat against their birdlike skulls.
To Quick they look like ghosts.

Quick tails them down Rokeby Road, through all the
food smells and the odour of newness seeping out of the open
doors and shopfronts. They skirt the football ground. Quick
can't hear them saying anything. A truck clatters by loaded
with pumpkins. Quick has the feeling he should catch up
with them, just bust into their ghostly tight aura and say
g'day, but what if they don't want him? They actually look

like they don't care about the world, not what people think of them or wonder about them. And yet there they'll be at lunchtime palming pieces of nothing – of air – into their mouths. Aren't they pretending so that others won't think they're poor? Geez, Quick understands that much pride. Or are they keeping up the fantasy for themselves? Do they feel less hungry, less lean and hopeless, if they pretend their bellies are full? This kind of thought bothers Quick in class and it's on his mind this afternoon as he sticks close enough to hear the voices, but not so near that he can understand what they're saying.

And they hardly ever laugh, that's another thing, though it isn't until late tonight that he thinks of it, and by then it won't help to think at all.

Quick climbs the bank behind West Leederville Station with the wild oats parting before him. Wogga McBride and his little brother are at the top and heading down into the cut where he loses sight of them for a few moments. When he gets to the crest of the embankment he can see Railway Road and the date palms in front of the rich people's places. A train is hauling out of the station going his way and he sees down the track, behind the wobbling carriages, the slant of his own roof. A dog is barking. Someone has the flag flying in the front yard across the tracks, there's a war over somewhere. Quick feels the breeze coming up behind him, cool and southerly. He'll never catch up with Wogga McBride today. They'll be across the tracks in a moment. He's twelve years old and primary school is almost over. Smuts rise and the rails groan. Down there Wogga McBride is fooling with the dog, some carpetbacked stray that's got a hold of his school bag and he's laughing. Laughing! The two boys prance around the brown dog up on its hind legs, twisting and feinting with the leather strap in its mouth. Quick can hear their virulent laughter. He wants to go down there with them and run that dog ragged with them. Oh, the laughter, even over the sound of the train.

And then Wogga McBride tears the bag free of the dog and sways back, shrieking with glee, and the sleeper catches his heel and he staggers and the engine smacks him with the sound of a watermelon falling off the back of a truck, and he's gone.

Everything is screaming. The train punishes itself to a halt. Down there, Wogga McBride's little brother stands with his mouth open and train noise coming out. There's men jumping out and down, there's screaming, alright. Screaming, screaming.

Quick hoists his bag and goes home and gets into bed and pulls the sheet over his head and stuffs his ears with notepaper.

Fish Waiting

What can you tell him, Fish? Right now, while you're down there on that side of the water with your strange brain and your black, wide eyes. What do you understand enough to say? You stand there in the morning and the afternoon and see Quick all closed, white and hard. Motes rain down. The sun is alive. The whole house is shaking with sound. Why won't he look at you? How do you bear it? How can you just stand at the end of his bed like that, with the patience of an animal? It's like you're someone else down there, Fish. Or does it just hurt me to think it's not so?

Debts

Every morning the old man came up to see Quick and sit on the end of his bed and sigh. Quick lay under the sheet, smelling all the trapped stinks and odours, and through it he could see the shadow of the old man moving in front of the window.

How'd ya be, son? the old man said quietly. He seemed to know something was wrong, but he was stuck for some way of fixing it.

Quick was glad it was him coming up and not his mother. She'd be too busy getting the shop open for the day and anyway, she'd be liable to just hook him out of bed,

kick him in the ring and send him on his way. He didn't
know why he was staying here in bed anyway; he just knew
he didn't want to get up and it had something to do with
Wogga McBride.

The second day Lester had a better idea of what was
wrong. Quick heard him rustling a newspaper theatrically,
walking up and down, stopping now and then to say: It's
a flamin tragedy, Quick, an honest-to-the-Lord flamin
tragedy.

Quick didn't think about that wet teatowel snap of
Wogga McBride disappearing. Neither could he let himself
imagine what had happened after, how Wogga would have
been dragged and ricked and torn and wedged and burst and
broken. He thought about nothing like that. Quick thought
about nothing at all. He listened to the grinds and groans of
the house. Flies went about their mysterious business. Ticking noises came from in the walls. The cocky next door
squawked and quipped. Below, the bell clonked on the shop
door. Sometimes, when the hunger drifted over into dreaminess, he forgot he was Quick Lamb at all. It excited him to
discover how quiet he was inside.

On the third day the old man came in and rustled a
newspaper, and then Quick heard scissors going, hissing
through paper.

A lot of sad people on the wall, Quick. What're you
doin with em? What's it mean?

Quick said nothing.

Knocks me round to see you like this, boy. You'll starve
to death. Look at these poor sods – you don't wanna be like
them. You don't need to be. You've got a roof over yer head,
family – well, we're not much I know, he chuckled. But,
strike. Here –

Quick saw the shadow cross him and hover. He heard
him thumbing a couple of tacks into the wall.

There. Another one. That's yer schoolmate, if you really
wanna feel miserable. They're buryin im in Fremantle
tomorrow. Be dressed by eight. After that we'll go down the
wharf for some fish and chips.

Quick set his jaws. He realized suddenly that he was

93

aching; he was sore and tight in the guts and he stank.

No.

It's for Fish. He's worried.

No.

Quick heard the old man cross the room and slam the window down.

Christ Almighty, boy, if you care that much about someone from school, why don't you care about yer own blood? You know damn-well your brother is busted in the head and he'll never grow up right. The least you could do is let him be happy. Don't torture him, Quick. And us. You don't need to be like this – it's a lie, a game, and yer not helpin anyone at all. Yer feelin sorry for yerself and it's making me sick. Don't pretend to Fish. And then the old man's voice got quiet and dangerous. You and me understand about Fish. We were there. We were stupid enough to drown him tryin to save him. You remember that. We owe him things, Quick. We got a debt. All we can do now is let him be happy, let him be not too confused. I can sit here and talk and get nothin back for as long as it takes to get angry enough to swat your arse and send your mother up to deal with you. But Fish, he'll wait. He'll wait till you say something to him. Don't you forget about Fish, boy. Not as long as you live, or your life won't have been worth livin.

Quick heard the old man go out then. The door closed, and it was like the room was roaring. He'd never heard his father say words like that.

In the dark that night, Quick tried to pray, but nothing came. He knew it wouldn't come for any of them anymore. He felt the hunger raving in him.

He woke and saw it. The people in all the pictures on the wall – they were dancing and there was Wogga McBride jitterbugging along the tracks. They were laughing, all of them. He'd never known such terror as coiled in him right then. He got out of bed, ran into Fish and Lon's room and climbed

94

into bed with Fish. He lay awake there with his brother's sleeping body beside him until dawn. When the sun came up he began to weep. Fish woke.

What you laughin for, Quick?

The Kybosh

It was strange that Lester should get up before her on a non-market day. Oriel Lamb found a bowl and a teacup on the kitchen table, and that's all. She sat down with a sigh and rested her head on the wood. It could only be bad. To be up early, to have gone somewhere without a word, to have taken the truck. The fresh summer sun tilted at the window. She saw the pale blue promise of heat out there. An engine whistle blew. Oriel looked at her hands. They were farmer's hands. Women told her they were men's hands. She watched the way they squared up to make fists. She rested them on the table. Her knuckles were like dirty blocks of ice.

There was something wrong with men. They lacked some basic thing and she didn't know what it was. She loved Lester, but a lot of loving him was making up for him, compensating. He was never quite up to anything. She knew he was a fool, but it wasn't the same thing. Her father had been the same. He was a kindly man, big and thin and softlooking, but without enough flint in him to make his kindliness into kindness. As a child she could tell that he thought well of people, but he never had the resolve to make his feelings substantial. He never did anything for anybody but himself. Like when he remarried. Oriel's mother and sisters died in a bushfire that razed the farm and the house. Her father was so broken by the event, that after she was dragged alive from the half-collapsed cellar almost mad with fear and shock and guilt, and after he'd killed his last pig to fix her burns, it was *she* who nursed *him*. She always had the feeling he would have just faded away, had she not mothered him as they moved from property to property on neighbours' charity until she'd earned enough from kitchen work and dairymucking to buy them a moth-eaten old tent to take

95

back to their place and start again. She made it a home for them until the darkness stemmed in him long enough for him to think of going on with his life. And when he remarried he told Oriel it was to give her another mother, though she knew perfectly well it was to give himself another wife. Her stepmother was a strong girl, and though she hated her, Oriel knew she couldn't help being strong when she had such a weak man to live with. Oriel continued to love her father, but she knew that loving a man was a very silly activity; it was giving to the weak and greedy and making trouble for yourself.

Even Bluey dying in Palestine. Killed because he was careless, the swaggering underage horseman from the colonies showing how young and fearless he was, and in her bitterest moments Oriel thought of it as a betrayal, that for Bluey there was loveliness but not love. If he'd loved her he would've come back made sure of it.

Lester came back alright. She danced with him at the Woodanilling victory dance, another strange boy gaunt with malaria. He laughed a lot, seemed bemused by the way Oriel fastened herself to him. That's what men had, those bemused grins. She'd seen it in him all along, from courtship to the farms, the police force, the oddjobs, oh, the endless trail of oddjobs . . . she'd known it right along. But what could you do? Be like that poor wretch of a woman next door?

These days she wished she could take it to the Lord in prayer, but there was nothing there anymore and there was no choice but to grit and go on. She didn't mind the army. The army was the nation and the nation gave her something to believe in. Him, too, that's why he joined up again so suddenly when there wasn't even a war on. But on a Saturday morning before anyone was up, he wouldn't be at band practice, he'd be somewhere he shouldn't be.

Elaine came downstairs with a headache already.

Where's Dad?

He's out on business.

To be sure, Elaine smirked.

Don't wrangle with me this morning, my girl, or I'm

liable to put the kybosh on your Saturday.

I've got a headache!

These days you are a headache. Put the kettle on.

Oriel Lamb tromped out the back to the privacy of the dunny and latched the door with great care. Whatever was going on with that husband of hers would need the kybosh put on, too. But today she wasn't sure she was up to men.

Like a Light Shinin

The night before.

It's dusk when Sam Pickles sees his tenant and neighbour come down from the back step into the yard. He's been standing here a few minutes smoking and easing up. His clothes and his skin smell of metals and kerosene. These days after work his mouth tastes of copper. Out the back here by the splintery fence near the mulberry tree that towers on the Lamb side, it's pleasant and cool and except for the muffled shouts of children in the house and the faraway carping of a dog, it's quiet. Sam sees the other man stand still a moment with his hands in his pockets to look up at the pumpkin-coloured sky, then to spit and regard the ground at his feet with what looks like a great sobriety. He's tall and thin; he's beginning to stoop a little already, even though Sam guesses him to be about his own age. Maybe older, he thinks, maybe he's forty – yes, come to think of it he'd be at least that. He looks like that cowboy cove, Randolph Scott. Since the night they arrived Sam has hardly spoken to his neighbours. They're always working too damn hard to talk, and they're not the sort of people to waste much time having fun.

Sam leans his elbows on the fence.

Gday, he calls.

Lester Lamb looks up from the ground, straight into the crown of the mulberry tree and then along the fence. His face changes when he recognizes who it is.

Oh. Gday there. Thought I was going daft. Sounded like you were in the tree.

97

Too tired to get up there.

Lester is coming down to stand beside him on the other side of the fence.

A man aches all over, Sam goes on.

Ah. Know how you feel.

Cepting I get all the ache down one side, you know, cause of this. He holds up his pruned hand. Lamb squints at it and murmurs a sympathetic sort of noise. See, Sam continues, I favour the other arm all the time. Makes it ache like buggery. Used to using both arms.

Lamb gives the stump a careful look.

They say you feel the pain, even when there's nothing there. Told me that in the army.

Yeah. No lie. More an itch you get now and then, if you catch my drift, and a man goes to scratch it and there's nothin to scratch. Sam sees his neighbour moving his mouth as if making up his mind whether or not to ask something, so he answers it anyway; a winch, says Sam. On a boat. Just bloody stupidity. And bad luck. You believe in luck, Mr Lamb?

Can't say. Dunno. Didn't used of. Anyway, call me Lest.

Orright, Lest. Call me Sam. Or landlord'll do, if yer stuck for words.

They laugh and there's a silence between them a while. So you do a lot of physical, then? Lester Lamb says, more confident now. Work, I mean.

Yeah. Well, not like before. This's only from last summer. I've been on wharves and boats all me life. Funny, you know, I was a butcher's apprentice four years and never even nicked meself. Now'm at the Mint. He laughs. Makin quids for everybody else.

Sam sees the look of respect come onto Lester's face.

I'm a sort of utility man there, if you know what I mean. Lester clearly doesn't and Sam feels chuffed. His neighbour seems to be reappraising him all of a sudden. You were in the army?

Last war, Lester says. I was a young bloke then.

Ah, I've got the asthma.

Right.

98

And the war wound.

Exactly.

You don't believe in luck, you say.

Can't say I've been persuaded by it.

Everythin's easier to believe in when it comes a man's way.

That's true enough, I reckon, Lester says.

Sam pauses. He thinks about this. He feels like there's gold in his veins but he's not sure whether to tell.

I'm on a run, he says in the end.

How d'you mean?

Like I'm winnin. Luck. It's like a light shinin on you. You can feel it.

Lester Lamb doesn't look sceptical – not at all. He's a farmboy, you can see it on him – honest as filth. The sun is gone and there's only the faintest light in the sky, but Sam can still see the other man's features. Cooking smells seep down to them, the sound of screaming kids, a passing train down the embankment.

I'll show you, Sam says, with his heart fat in his neck. If you like.

Before dawn Rose heard the old man wheezing as he passed her door; she was suddenly awake. She lay still and listened. Her father's boots on the stairs. Some whispering. She heard the front door sigh back on its hinges down there and she went to the window. Below, in the front yard, two silhouettes moved toward the Lambs' truck, one short, the other tall. She knew who they were. Now they were pushing and shoving at the truck to get it rolling a little and it crept along flat old Cloud Street to the corner until it found the incline of Railway Parade and got up a good roll and was gone. Rose waited a few moments, heard the motor hawk into life and went back to bed. Whatever the old boy was up to was bound to be stupid, but she wouldn't tell. Oh no. She'd been dead asleep the same as everyone else.

The smell of horses reminded Lester Lamb of a dozen things at once, almost all of them good. The worst thing he could associate horses with, apart from seeing rats eating up into their arses in Turkey, was having a stallion bite the back of his neck once when he was mending a fence. He turned on it and gave it a good whack between the eyes with the claw hammer and the damned thing fell on him and crushed the blasted fence for his trouble.

The track was quiet and dew-heavy in the early dawn, muffled in by the empty stands and sheds. Small lights showed in and around the stables. Horses neighed and spluttered. Timbers creaked from their weight. Men laughed quietly in little blear-eyed clumps and lit cigarettes. Sam Pickles led him down the soft dust of alleys between stables. Behind one shed a soldier and a woman were kissing. Lester saw a great swathe of flesh as the soldier slipped a hand up the woman's leg. Sam whistled and the couple laughed, but Lester went prickly with embarrassment.

Sam stopped at a small tin hut and knocked. A little blue-chinned man opened up.

Gday, Sam. Pushin yer luck another furlong, eh?

Gis a coupla brownfellas, Macka, and somethin for the flask, orright?

Early start. Macka went in for a moment and came out with two big bottles of beer and a smaller bottle that could've been anything. Sam slipped him some money and they headed back down the alley. You could hear the gentle thrumming of hoofs on dirt. Out on the track a couple of trainers had horses just rolling along with a relaxed gait. Like men tuning cars, they had their heads cocked sideways or pressed into the great dark cowlings of flank, listening as they rode.

Never been here before, Lest?

No. Can't say I have. The only time Lester had been at a racecourse before was back between the wars when there was a revival meeting out in the open one night. Families had driven and walked in from miles around to hear the gospel story and the man up front had shouted like an angel and glowed in the face as though he might go to flames any moment. They'd gone up the front, him and Oriel and the kids too, and the man had laid hands on them and Lester had felt the power. But that was a long time gone.

I've never really done any bettin before, neither.

Oh, you won't be bettin today, old son, you'll be investin in success, you'll be baskin in the glory. You religious?

Lester looked out at the brown rising of the sun. No. Not really.

Shame. They have this sayin about getting tenfold of what you give. That's what we're gunna slip into today. This day, cobber. You and me.

Lester looked at the little husky fellow beside him. He'd never seen him so animated. Before, around the house, he'd just been this beaten down ghost of a bloke who looked like a loser from day one, with his bighipped wife brooding over him. He was a different man here, and Lester felt wound up in some kind of new excitement as he sucked on the beer bottle and felt the stuff go cold and brassy all the way down. Yeah, it was like having a light shining on you; it suddenly felt like everything was possible and none of it mattered a damn.

By noon they were drunk, which meant Sam was lucid with luck and laughter and Lester just couldn't tell where his feet were anymore. They'd toured the stables. Sam had done some whispering and a lot of careful listening, and they'd spent an hour outside one door solemnly observing the equine snafflings of a horse called Blackbutt. He was a big haunchy stallion with eyes like cue balls, and he frightened the hell out of Lester.

This is our boy, Sam said. At the end of the day everything goes in his name.

Come on home, old Blackbutt! Lester said.

I only believe in one thing, Les, Sam solemnly uttered. Hairy Hand of God, otherwise known as Lady Luck. Our Lady, if she's shinin that lamp on ya, she'll give you what you *want*. There's two other things people say are worth believin in – the Labor Party and God, but they're a bit on the iffy side for my money. The ALP and the Big Fella, well they always got what I call a tendency to try an give ya what they think ya need. And what a bloke needs most is to get what he wants most. Ya with me?

Reckon so, Lester murmured, though he wasn't sure. It sounded like baiting the Lord to him. Maybe he didn't go along with it anymore, but he sure as shillings couldn't get out of believing in it. You think we've drunk too much?

Ya still standin?

I think so, Lester laughed. Those big boats down there're me shoes, unless I'm wrong, and I'm higher'n them, so –

Then he was on the ground and in horseshit. The clouds were cantering by and Sam Pickles was gargling with laughter, peering down at him.

You trip me?

Nope. Ya did it all on yer own. Never ask a flyin man whether he's flyin or not.

Will I chuck up now?

If ya feel it's important, Les, yes I spose you'll get round to it.

Never drunk liquor before, really.

Yer feelin chunderish?

No. Well. Praps.

Think you'd like to get up out of the horse patties, Lest?

Yes, I think so.

Lester listened to him laugh a while as he planned by what means he'd get standing again. He didn't feel a million quid, and he couldn't comprehend how people made a life out of this sort of thing. He could feel the roll of tenners in his coat pocket, family money it was, and he was ashamed. He felt like a thief.

But in the afternoon, and all afternoon, Lester Lamb felt like a winner. It seemed the worst he could do was back a horse that'd only come in with a place and a close call, but after midday, with food in his belly and Sam Pickles beside him, wildeyed as an anchorite, bleeding tips from every well dressed passerby, Lester couldn't lose. His pockets were bloated with money and he felt a kind of delirium coming on towards the last race of the day when Blackbutt burst from the barrier with the rest of them and was, for a moment, swallowed up in the flailing and dirt-spraying melee of the start. At the opening of this last race, Lester's pockets were empty. It was all or nothing. It was the real test. He was sober now and it took all his will to hand over those solid little rolls to Sam who counted them out to the bookie. Men kicked in the dust and he heard women laughing and the bookie looked at them with one eyebrow cocked, only smiling after he'd given them their tickets.

Won't be seein youse blokes again, today.

Reckon you will, mate, said Sam.

That's a tired horse.

That's a winner.

You know the odds.

I'm a punter, mate, Sam said with a smile. And I'll be back with these, he held up the tickets, and I'll see you smilin on the other side of yer face.

So when the heads and forelegs and riders' arms explod-ed onto the track in a great solid mass of desperation, Lester Lamb had his lungs full and his fists closed. The mob surged and spread by the first turn. Grass sods and whip hands thickened the air.

For a while Lester couldn't see who was where; he couldn't even understand the gabble of the race caller over the PA. Out on the long stretch on the far side of the track, the mob was lengthening. Beside him, Sam Pickles was smiling beneath the binoculars. Lester noticed a lone seagull lazing in some curly updraft over the track. He knew he should have been home with his family. As the lead horses came into the turn, he began to yell like a lunatic. The horses' eyes were like stones, their legs beat the ground. He heard their tortured grunts, the bellows rush of air in and out of them. Their manes sprayed and slapped. The knees of jockeys rode high into their necks and Lester heard the little shouts of riders goading one another. Three horses shouldered their way into the open and reached out with their great long shining bodies, their heads down ploughing wind, straining forward until the sound and heave of them infected the people at the post with a crazy, dancing abandon. Lester laughed and screamed and felt the crowd beating at his sides, and as the horses passed with a sound like a back alley beating, he heard the reedy cackle of Sam Pickles and little else. As the stragglers stumped past the post, the crowd was already sighing and it felt to Lester Lamb like the last finishing moments with a woman where heat suddenly turned to sweat and power became fatigue. It was like sex, alright, and he was thrilled and ashamed and he couldn't have stopped laughing for all the love in heaven.

Blackbutt! the man with the PA yelled. It's Blackbutt, by crikey!

Quick stands in the dusk and stacks pine crates on the verandah. He's forgotten all about Wogga McBride's funeral by now and what he's wondering about now is where his old man is. It wasn't eight o'clock this morning when his mother came roiling and spoiling upstairs to get him out of bed with the persuasive front edge of her boot. She had him yelping and hollering and on the banisters, laughing with fright and relief before he was even awake.

It's not your fault you'll grow into a man, Quick Lamb, she was saying all the way down, but it's not mine either! Pull an oar or get off the boat!

Fish seemed delirious with joy at breakfast. The moment he saw Quick slide cowering into the kitchen, Fish set an empty bowl going on the table so it roared and rattled, rose and fell, like it was laughing at him.

And so here he is, pulling oar, even now it's nearly dark and the old man still hasn't turned up. Somewhere upstairs Fish is singing and the girls are talking low amongst themselves. Back in the kitchen, the old girl is thrashing a few shirts, drowning them in Velvet suds, wringing their necks and beating their headless bodies on the table, singing

'Throw out the Lifeline' in the sweetest voice. The whole place is like a bomb ready to go off.

Rose pushed through the grey and khaki trouser legs of all those sour, stinking boozers in the public bar who shouted through their noses and made wings of their elbows and holes of their mouths, and she found the door and shoved against it.

Come back in five years! one of them yelled.

Geez, he's not fussy.

Not a touch on her old girl, I reckon.

It took another heft against the door for it to swing open and let Rose Pickles out into the cool, clean night air, and when the door swung to behind her, the noise and smoke of the pub stayed inside.

She sat down against the wall, below the ugly roses in the leadlight window to feel how all her teeth met perfectly, jaw to jaw, and how, if she set them firm enough and kept up the pressure, little lights came into her head.

Damn her, damn her, damn her to hell and shit and piss and sick! She's drunk again and loud and vile with her eyes full of hate and meanness, but I'll get her out in the end. I'll drag her home. I'll kick her shins, bite her arse. I'll get her out.

Dolly was rooted to her soft chair in the Ladies' Lounge with all those wrinkled, smokefaced old girls who laughed like a flock of galahs and fluffed and preened and looked about with their black, still eyes, cold as anything. They rattled and prattled with gossip and rubbish, and yes, even their mouths were like horny beaks, and their tongues like dry, swollen fingers. Rose hated them, and she hated her mother with them. She should be home, heck someone should be home. Rose didn't even know where the boys were – they'd shot through early on, and when her mother had gone off at opening time this morning, Rose had sat alone in her half of the house and listened to the Lambs blundering about nextdoor in the shop and in all the rooms, and after a while she couldn't bear the way they just went on and worked and whistled and chiacked around as though nothing was up, so she went walking. It wasn't far to Kings Park. The grasses were all brown with summer, nuts and seeds lay popping with the heat on the ground. Birds scratched around in the trees. Rose walked into the raw bush and found a place in the shade and just sat thinking nothing until the sun got so high it just drilled down through the leaves and into her skull. Sometimes she hated being alive.

But right now, out in the cooling street with no one coming past, she just felt all hard inside. She'd get the old girl out, even if she had to wait till closing time. She was hungry and angry, her heart felt like a fist, and she knew that if she took her time she was strong enough to do anything at all.

It was stone quiet when Sam and Lester got in. On the Pickles side it was quiet because Dolly was out like a bag of spuds on the bed, and the boys still weren't home. Sam took one look at the blue anger in Rose's face and went to run himself a bath.

Fair dinkum, said his bird.

Yeah. Fair dinkum, said Sam.

On the Lamb side no one was absent, but neither were they speaking. Lester came in with dinner in progress and barely an eye lifted to acknowledge his arrival, though Fish giggled, as if under instruction not to. Lester found no cutlery at his place and no plate warming in the oven. He put his rolls of money on the table and heard an intake of air from the girls.

In the till, Oriel said, wiping something off Lon's chin. Money has no place at the dinner table. And so he left and had himself a shower, listening to the roar of the gas heater in the sleepout that had become the bathroom.

All night Cloudstreet ticked, but it didn't go off.

106

The River

In the morning Quick discovers that the old man is full of whistle and laugh. The shop's closed and he's scrounging recruits for a trip to Fremantle.

Carn! he's yelling, Carn, let's go! We'll drop a line from the wharf, we'll buy fish n chips, we'll get sunburnt, we'll let the harbour know we're there! Carn, we'll absolutely Lamb the place!

Fish is at the breakfast table, spinning the knife.

Knife never lies, he says, and five times the blade comes to a stop pointing at him, and he laughs with wonder and looks at his distorted reflection in the blade. Hah, knife never lies!

Yeah, Fish, but *you* never ask it any questions, says Quick.

Ask no questions, get no lies, the old man says.

The girls sweep in and the old girl turns red-armed from the spitting stove and looks them all over.

Carn, Orry, the old man says to her.

Oriel levels a bristler of a stare at him: You gunna grace us with your company today?

Geez, love I'm gunna be fair bountiful with the company today. If it wasn't Sunday you'd be wearin a new dress an silk stockens before lunchtime, so you'll have to make do with a fambly day with only fish, food and fun to keep you from black despair. Whaddayereckon?

She says nothing, but she's in the truck with the rest of them when they pull out with the gearbox squealing.

All the way down, they race the train to Fremantle, sky-larking along in and out of traffic to bob over hills and see the engineer give them the thumb. The sky is blue as gas and the wind rifles through the holes and cracks that the Lamb truck's made of. You can see this mob coming a long way – all hands and open mouths and unruliness.

Quick sits on the tray with his back to the cab. He can smell the salt as they pass Cottesloe. With one arm he holds

Fish steady and he sits on the other hand to soften the jolts that go right up his bum every time the truck hits a hole in the limestone road. Quick feels himself today. His father is honouring the promise after all. They've missed the funeral, but they're going to Freo all the same. For a while there he wasn't sure what it'd mean if he didn't.

The water beneath the wharf is green. Lank strands of algae lift and settle in it, staying fast to their roots on the wetblack piles that stretch to blurring like a forest away to beyond sight. The Lambs sit or scurry on the network of footways and landings that sit just out of the water, their light gut lines taut with lead and watersurge. Lon tortures blowfish and lets them inflate full and prickly so he can stamp on their bellies and hear the pistol shot it makes and the way the girls hiss at him for doing it. Lester plays a jig on his noseflute and doesn't catch any fish. Red fools with the sinkers in the plywood box. Hat hauls in gardies and skippy, keeping a ruthless count. Elaine has her feet in the water and feels a headache coming on. Fish lies face down, cooing, peering through the plank cracks at the way the green mass rises to him and stops at the final moment. Quick takes a herring now and then and watches his mother who baits and casts with a determination that's kind of frightening; she scowls at bites and sucks air in through her teeth as she jags and pulls in, spooling line neatly in her lap. There's a tin bucket drumming with fish at her side. Now and then she clips Lon over the ear or looks flat at the old man who grins like a lizard and goes on looking happy and useless.

At noon the old man disappears and comes back with a great, sweaty parcel of fish and chips which they unravel and guts down with the cordial that the old girl has cooling in her bucket of fish. They're all squinching the butcher's paper up and dipping their hands in the water to wash off the grease when their mother addresses the old man in a quiet, level voice.

How much did you win, then?

The old man takes up his noseflute and starts into 'Road

108

to Gundagai'. His eyes bounce, his big flat feet clomp on the boards and then he stops.

A hundred and six quid.

What about him?

Sam?

The old girl's eyes bulge as if to say 'so it's *Sam* now, is it?'

The old man grins: Two hundred.

She just baits up a hook and casts as if they haven't even spoken.

In the afternoon the old man buys a boat. He walks up to a bloke in the fishermen's harbour and offers him money. The old girl is still as a post. They've just been strolling – the lot of them – now that the fish have gone off the bite with the new tide, and he just comes out with it. The whole mob stops dead and watches. No one moves the entire time it's going on, and when the old man goes off to get the truck they still don't move.

The boat is a good sixteen foot, clinkerbuilt and heavy as hell. A big skiff sort of boat, and it takes about a second and a half for it to be obvious that it'll never fit across the tray of the truck. The man who's just sold the boat laughs and slaps his legs. He's fat and red and his scalp is flaky. He's not mean about it, he's just a good humoured sort of bloke. Everyone stands around and looks at everybody else – except Fish who's looking at the water, and the old girl who's looking at absolutely nothing and no one, and in a moment the old man turns to Quick and says:

What about you row it home, boy?

Dead quiet.

On me own?

You can take someone.

Up the river, you mean?

The old girl goes and gets in the truck. The door slams so hard bits of rust fall off it.

Yeah, you could put in at Crawley. That's not far from home.

109

Hat spits. It's miles, Dad. Don't be daft. She's looking at him like he's the most dickheaded human she's ever encountered and it hurts Quick to see.

I can do it, he says.

Right. Good bloke, Quick. Who's goin with him as first mate?

Fish, says Quick. I want Fish.

Quick sees the panic in the old man's face and he knows he's pushing it here, but he knows he'll win. It's man on man.

Orright. If he wants to. If yer careful.

And Quick smiles up a storm.

It was hard to believe how big the ships in the harbour were when you were creeping by at water level. Quick could see that it wasn't lost on Fish who sat in the stern with his jaw halfway to his chest, the shadows of cranes and winches falling across his brow. The boat felt good to Quick. It sat well in the water, was dry inside and he felt it cut along just fine. In the rowlocks, the oars chafed quietly in a reassuring way. The truck and everybody was out of sight now and it was just him and Fish. He felt the blood running crazy in him. He was scared. Packin em, pooping himself nearly, with all that fat, green, dredged water and the walls the wharf and tankers made high above. He rowed and kept his eye on Fish and it was a surprise how soon the bridge came over them with its restless, chunky channel water bumping underneath. It was cold under there. Fish giggled as a train roared across and it took Quick's mind off the confusion of tide and flow and how hard the water felt against the oars, how it was like rowing in gravel all of a moment. Then they were through into the afternoon sun again, with the river wider, gentler, with boats moored at the shallow edges of the channel where grass came down the banks to sandy beaches littered with wrecked bikes and prams amid upwashed mussel shells and tidal hedges of weed.

Orright? Quick asked Fish.

The river's big.

My oath.

Quick watched the whorling wake behind him and felt good at how straight it was. He wasn't too worried now; his bum felt good on the seat, the handles of the oars weren't too big for him and he liked how they stretched out so far and kept balance right there in his palms.

Cracker boat, eh?

Yeah.

It's ours Fish.

Whacko! yelled Fish. A gull dived across the stern, slapped the water and was gone.

Oriel Lamb shoved her hands into the dishwater and didn't utter a sound. It was hot enough to cook in but she went ahead scouring and scrubbing, letting herself absorb its heat into her own until she felt fire behind her eyes. It was even making *him* sweat, she knew, *him* standing there dumb against the kitchenette, waiting for her to say something. She slapped dishes onto the draining board. Her hands were the colour of crayfish. He can wait, she thought; he can jolly-well, flaminwell, he can *damn*well wait. But now that he was wiping sweat from his face with the teatowel there was a stubbornness coming on him. He was getting ready to wait and that twisted the heat up in her still more. She thought: people murder each other. Yes, it's possible that you could just take up that meatskewer there and ram it into his lungs. Lord, she never thought it likely that he'd hold out like this, defy her, defy the whole burning rightness of her. And then he began to sing:

There's a track winding back to an old-fashioned shack along the road to Gundagai –

She hefted the big china gravyboat and swung it with a backhand sweep that caught him square in the belly hard enough to beat the wind out of him, hard enough to knock him back against the kitchenette and slip and hit the floor bum first. Oriel put the gravyboat down on the draining

III

board and the handle came away, still round her fingers.

Has my life been a waste? she said in a flat, still tone. Has it been that useless?

But Lester said nothing. He sat there. It looked like he was making plans to get some air into him somehow and it gave her no satisfaction at all.

It didn't feel so bad to have sore hands when you knew that you'd left East Fremantle behind and passed Rocky Bay, with all its puking foundries and limestone cliffs, for the long stretch through Melville and the sugar factory whose pipes came down to the water to send rainbows out into the channel. Quick saw yachts moored in flocks over on the Mosman shore and the great, long scar of the sandspit. Shags sat high on channel markers to watch them pass.

It's a long way, Fish said. Is it a long way, Quick?

Yeah, mate. It's a fair whack, orright.

Quick was starting to wonder if the old man was the full quid. He wasn't sure if even a fullgrown man could do this. It was late. The sun was sitting low now, right back where they'd come from.

Can I do?

Do what? Quick asked.

Do the sticks. The rowers.

Quick rested a moment and felt the boat glide along upstream.

Orright. We'll share. Then we'll go faster, eh.

Fish damn near rolled them out of the boat in his excitement to get up there and it took all Quick's will not to yell at him.

It was lucky they were headed in the long bellied arc around the Mosman spit because that was the only direction they were ever likely to go in, the way Fish was rowing. Quick pulled hard, but Fish seemed bent on digging all the water out of the river, hauling and grunting so they heeled around to port. Quick hoped Fish'd get bored by the time they needed a straight run, though he figured it'd be dark by then anyway.

Lester sparked up the truck in the dusk and pulled out into the street. Down on the tracks, an engine was hammering up from West Perth with the city lights behind. No one saw him go, he was sure. He felt prickly with nerves; his mouth tasted like sand.

Passing through Subiaco he dodged the late tram and heard the town hall clock ringing the hour, and then he steered the old rattler down along the sombre wall of bush that was Kings Park towards the University and the river.

Down at Crawley there were lights out on the river and fires on the beach. Lester parked the truck and went down through the boozing parties of prawners with their whinge-ing kids and boiling drums of water to where the grass ended and the peppermints gripped the bank above the sand and the thick stewy smell of the river was strong and plain in his face. He walked up and down, staring out into the darkness. Now and then he could see men in the water wading with nets, or kids with Tilley lamps and spears in the shallows hunting cobbler, but no sign of Quick and Fish. They had no light, no real idea. They could be anywhere, and it was his stupid fault. Panic was acid in his throat. Lord, what a fool he was; he wasn't fit to have children, she was right.

He began to jog.

Out past Claremont, out past somewhere – Quick doesn't know anymore – he just stops. He sits back and ships the oars and gives it away. Fish is curled at his feet, sleepy.

Well, Quick says. He sits a few moments. In the star-light he can make out Fish's features. He has his eyes open. What you thinkin?

I can hear the water.

We're on the river, you dill.

I can hear it.

Yeah. Quick twists about in his seat. Up on the hills there's houselights and even the dimmed lamps of cars. You cold?

No.

I'm knackered.

You wanna sing, Quick? Let's sing.

It's quiet for a few moments and then they begin to sing, and once they start it's hard to give it up, so they set up a great train of songs from school and church and wireless, on and on in the dark until they're making them up and starting all over again to change the words and the speed. Quick isn't afraid, and he knows Fish is alright. He lies back with his eyes closed. The whole boat is full of their songs – they shout them up at the sky until Fish begins to laugh. Quick stops singing. It's dead quiet and Fish is laughing like he's just found a mullet in his shorts. It's a crazy sound, a mad sound, and Quick opens his eyes to see Fish standing up in the middle of the boat with his arms out like he's gliding, like he's a bird sitting in an updraught. The sky, packed with stars, rests just above his head, and when Quick looks over the side he sees the river is full of sky as well. There's stars and swirl and space down there and it's not water anymore – it doesn't even feel wet. Quick stabs his fingers in. There's nothing there. There's no lights ashore now. No, there's no shore at all, not that he can see. There's only sky out there, above and below, everywhere to be seen. Except for Fish's giggling, there's no sound at all. Quick knows he is dreaming. This is a dream. He feels a turd shunting against his sphincter. He's awake, alright. But it's a dream – it has to be.

Are we in the sky, Fish?

Yes. It's the water.

What dyou mean?

The water. The water. I fly.

Lester punishes the truck up and down the bays and bluffs, getting out to blunder along shelly beaches and call out to his sons, but all he flushes out are soldiers and openbloused schoolgirls who leap up and advise him to fuck off before murder is committed. It's a warm night. Sweat gathers on him and the old truck is overheating. Lester's making promises to himself now: he'll never play the ponies again, no more grog, no more foolery and toolery. Street lights are out now and the prawners have long gone. The city is asleep and the quiet infuriates him. Up on the bluff over Claremont, he aims the headlamps out over the river across the masts of moored yachts and the bowed backs of sleeping shags. At Freshwater Bay he stands on the sand and listens to the sound of mullet jumping and prawns scattering before them. You'd think I'd learn about rivers, he thinks; you'd swear a man'd get smart. He remembers the sound of Fish thrashing under the net, how he was forcefed river until he was still and dead and trampled on by his own frightened kin. That funny, skylarking kid. That Fish.

God Almighty, it was hopeless. Now look, now he's weeping; he's on his face in the sand and he's bawling.

Quick knows the planets from school but he can't tell one from the other as they blur past like stones someone's chucking at them. Fish sighs and tilts his wings in the bow. The boat's vibrating the way it'd hum if they hit rapids and went chuting down over snowy water between rocks. Quick'd swear Fish is steering them. Even the anchor's rattling against its little length of chain. Quick feels fatigue coming to claim him – he aches all through – but he strains to stay awake, to see, to see. Fish is up there gargling like a nut, talking to himself or something, and then in a moment he's quiet and the boat is skimming, full of hiss and bounce and Quick knows straight away they're back on the river.

The water! Fish cries in distress.

The river, Fish. We're back on it.

Where's the water go?

We're on it, mate.

No. It's go.

Fish begins to whimper. Quick pulls him gently back into the bottom of the boat and holds him. Like a baby, he thinks, and he's as big as me. He feels Fish's head against his chest and the big, sad jerks he makes sobbing. All the excitement disappears. Quick knows the old misery again but he doesn't let himself break. He gives in to sleep.

Lester found them at dawn, asleep and aground in the shallows along the foreshore at Nedlands. Old men, retired officer types, were smoking pipes and walking their great ugly hounds back on the grass, and the river was flat and without blemish. Lester pumped along the beach, seeing only the boat, and his vision started to blotch with fear. He wanted to pray, but it felt like vomit rising in him so he held it off.

When he came to the boat he saw them. They were wrapped in each other on the boards between the seats, all knees and elbows and skewed shorts. The oars were shipped, the rowlocks stowed. They'd damn near made it all the way to Crawley. Lester stood ankle deep in the cool water and let out a great roar of relief and wonder. Quick twitched and sat up. He looked about him. Then he looked at his father.

You orright? Quick asked.

Lester opened his mouth, but all he had was laughter. He couldn't help himself. He was dancing in the sand. Fish woke and he and Quick exchanged glances. The old man chiacked on the beach and the sun hauled up over the hills.

They got home at nine. After pushing the truck through Nedlands, Shenton Park, and Subiaco.

Oriel met them on the verandah. It seemed the whole street knew they were coming up Railway Parade, and when they heaved in, she saw the three of them were singing. The Pickleses were looking from their windows and the early customers in the shop came out into the yard to watch. Quick and Fish and Lester came up chuckling and nudging and she felt the pit between them. They were foreigners, they were her blood but they were lost to her. Oriel hid her fists in her apron and felt ready to die.

No juice, love, Lester said. No juice, and no money.

She seized the boys and hooked them into her breast. She felt their blood, their breaths against her. She spoke over their heads.

No brains, Lester Lamb, she said. And no wonder.

Blisters had risen like fruit on Quick's hands. She saw them. She pulled herself erect and looked about at those who'd gathered to watch. Her little green eyes sighted on them and the spectators shuffled, looked at their boots, looked back again to see that she hadn't let up, and a couple moved off. No one spoke. The rest began to file away. Lester stood with his hands clasped together like a child. His daughters began shutting down the shop. Even the Pickleses above pulled their heads in.

I'm hungry, said Fish.

⌒ Burning the Man ⌒

Rose Pickles saw the bonfire out of her window with its rippling yellow mass making silhouettes of the Lamb girls as they tossed fruit crates onto the great spitting blaze to the sound of an accordion. Guy Fawkes night. She heard voices in the hall, the parade ground barking of Mrs Lamb becoming suddenly lowpitched and friendly enough to make her curious, so she went out to the landing and hung over the banisters.

Oh carm on, Mrs Pickles – look I'll call you Dolly an be done with it. Lester's gone out and bought all the gear for the kids – they'd love it. Carm on over. There's spuds to go in the fire and cakes and everywhatall.

Mum? Rose called down. Her mother looked confused and embarrassed. She only had on a dressing gown and her hair was set beneath a tartan scarf. She looked awful, like anyone's mum. It made her angry to have a pretty mother, but when she let herself go it was worse still.

Guy Fawkes night, said Dolly. I forgot.

Carm over to ours, eh?

Mum?

We haven't got any crackers.

Rose got the boys off the floor of their room where they were making a wingless fly dance with a piece of matchstick and had them hammering down the stairs after her. Their mother stood there with one of her legs showing and watched them go out the door.

Firelight softened everyone's faces as they stood around, poking at their scorching potatoes and singing to the accordion Mr Lamb strode around with. The boys fiddled at the fence, setting up strings of fizzers and penny bombs and Catherine-wheels until sparks leapt up into the clear black sky. Mrs Lamb brought out cocoa, lemonade, and leftover pasties with Rosella sauce. Mr Lamb organized a mass whistling of 'God Save the King' while he ate a lemon, right under their noses. The last one to plug on to the end was the winner. Chub hardly noticed the lemon, and though he whistled like an emphysemic lung he got the prize which was a box of broken cake pieces and half a jar of cream.

Rose screamed and giggled as the crackers went off and everyone gasped at the colours and the noise. She could hear her mum and dad laughing as the Catherine-wheels got going. She couldn't remember when she felt so happy before. The yard was full of kids, full of shouting, full of orange light and smoke. The Lambs yelled a lot. Their boy, the slow one, bellowed with laughter and grabbed anyone's hand who went past. Hens laid eggs in fright and a dog somewhere down the block barked until it was hoarse. The older Lamb girls were friendly even though they talked to Rose like she was much smaller, and even the redhaired one she didn't like much was sharing things and cracking dumb jokes. The eldest boy, the one they called Quick, was alternately shy and boisterous and he kept asking which parent should be burnt first.

When they brought out the Guy Fawkes Rose clapped and exclaimed. It was stuffed with wild oats and dressed up in motheaten flourbags (because Mrs Lamb didn't believe in wasting old clothes) and he had a pipe Mr Lamb had whittled from pine. Everybody yelled and cheered when Rose's father helped Mr Lamb put the dummy on the fire, but when they sat to eat their black potatoes, the slow boy Fish began to cry and then to scream.

No. Burn the man. Don't burn him. He's the man.

At first they laughed. The Guy Fawkes' head was tilting and one of his arms was gone. Flames shot out of his collar and he seemed to twist a little as the flourbags caught. But when Fish went crazy Quick Lamb and his mother took him inside and everything went quiet and strange and the party died.

Oh, you remember that alright. You see lights buzz and whizz up bangcrack. Everyone loving. Taters black an eaty. Here, Quick, look here! Lady and Lestah's laughing with fire up they chin. Lon come runs with fizzer things laughing up he hair. Tummy full with laugh and taters. That girl, she laughs. Right up, the sky big an black, nightime after darking an not in bed, you know, not even close to bed.

Whacko! Quick say.

Whacko! Lestah say.

Whacko! Lady say.

Fish wants a whacko but out come the Man with arms out Jesus arms, stiffy an funny. But no! No, Lestah! Noooooo! They get him on the hot, gots him on the fire. Lestah, you burnin the Man, Quick you burnin the Man an now theys fire out his mouth and eyes. Now he's head off alright. No. No. No. No. Quick? Yous burning He, the water Man. Ah, Fish mouth all black with hurt an they pullin an hookin on me and there cry tears an mess in me eyes. Legs hurtin up the stairs in the dark. House full of breathin. An Fish he cry like littles, like baby Lon in the truck. Theys pull me up goin hard in the hands. Everythin hurt. Theys open the door. The handle sees me in the dark. Fall down.

Quick drags his brother up the stairs. He can feel tears and snot and spit on him and he wishes he could just go to bed and die. Fish is still going, his voice busting with pressure, and his mother is pushing from behind.

It's only grass, Fish, Quick says. It's not a man.

You burn tha maaaann!

I'll give you a hidin if you don't slack off, son, his mum says, but Quick can tell there's none of the usual iron in it.

The piano, Mum. Give him the piano.

I hate that room.

Let him in. He likes the piano.

They got Fish to the landing and steered him round to the door at the very back where no one went much, and as soon as the door was open and that sweet musty smell came out, Quick felt crook to his guts and his mother let go of Fish and stepped back. Quick held Fish by his belt and took him across the stained boards to the piano that stood against the wall. There were no windows here and it was the kind of place you'd rather not be in. Fish flicked up the cover and put his fists on the browning keys. Quick watched him beat out a horrible noise with his eyes all busted looking and wet and then left him there with the lights on behind the closed door.

Outside, on the landing, his mother was crying. She had her brow on the banister looking ugly and red so he put his hand on her back. But it was like she didn't know he was there, and he didn't say anything, so, after a while he went back downstairs. The thumping music drifted down over the flames and Mr and Mrs Pickles looked bored and edgy.

Quick's dad did animal impressions for an hour and though the Pickles girl laughed, he felt shame and embarrassment.

That night, as they all lay in bed, tossing, askew, asleep, awake, the piano rang on. Middle C droned through the house, and though they all heard it, no one said a word.

↶ Down into the Light, Samson Lamb ↷

Sink and glide to where the light comes down like a vine. It's all calling, softbottomed and the colour of food, the rich saucy look of a meal you'll feast on forever, Samson Lamb, so down you fly, to the sky beneath, we are the firmament below and can't you see the light coming up from the darkness, it seems to say. Cool goes to cold, but now there's a heat to it, a joy here you didn't expect, growing in you all the time so the thrashing back up there where the night sky growls down doesn't matter anymore, and the true faces are smiling. See this, boy. The fish are coming to you; they are letting you aside. You will pass. This is joy. You don't struggle. Go down into the light. Soft fat bubbles tickle you now. You begin to recognize. Oh, boy.

Oh.

Oh.

No. Not back.

No.

The Hand Again

School ended for the year, but even so, Rose sharpened all her pencils and kept her writing desk in good order. Each drawer was neat as a diagram inside: paper, nibs, clips, crayons, blunt scissors closed like a body in repose. It was the way she'd have her whole kitchen, if she ever had one to herself; her whole house. Maybe it wasn't such a fantasy. She was learning to cook these days because the old girl was always too drunk and the old man was always late home. When they were home they were always fighting and tossing things at each other so dinner never got cooked. Rose knew how to grill chops and fry up eggs and bacon. She learnt how to boil cabbage till it looked and tasted like wet newsprint, the way the old man liked it. The boys always ragged her and took the piss these days, but they let up around six every night until she'd cooked them their chops and cabbage and mashed spud. She knew they couldn't help being dills – they were boys. That's why they were mean and clumsy. She knew they'd go hungry without her. Maybe they'd even starve. Rose felt tough sometimes. She felt best when she slapped the spud on their plates like it was mud and looked down at Chub and Ted like they were just helpless animals.

Now that the holidays were here, the three of them just mucked around in the house or out in the yard. There was always the river, so often they walked down to Crawley to the baths for a swim. The old man was at work and the old girl didn't seem to care much what they did, these days.

Down by the tracks, the three of them dug a cubbyhole. Well, Ted and Rose dug. Chub just sat round looking like he might do something any moment. It was a kind of alliance forged in boredom, but they got the long trench dug. They made a rectangular chamber at the end hacked into the side of the embankment where trees grew and shielded them from view, and they roofed it with tin from dunny roofs in back lanes and shovelled sand back over so the whole thing was invisible. Ted was good at building things, Rose had to concede. He was good at pinching things, too. They pulled nails out of other people's fences, knocked off the odd fourbetwo from wood heaps and even copped a shovel. It took a week. The final touch, a trapdoor, was the oven door from an old Kooka stove, and it opened out on a hinge and all. Inside, the sand was blackpacked, and Rose thought it smelled of chook feathers. It was quiet in there, and even with a candle you could only see a foot or two ahead. Rose could barely believe they'd done it. In the whole week there wasn't a quarrel or even a bad feeling. Ted was funny, cracking bum jokes and teasing. He loved to make things join up. It made him happy, and Rose wondered if this was the first time she'd really seen him happy. They got on so well they didn't even mind Chub walking up and down, pressing his lips together and doing absolutely ringall.

But it all went to the dogs in a hurry. The day it was finished Chub went in the trapdoor and climbed straight out again and wouldn't go back in.

I don't like it, he said.

Well if you'd done something to make it better, you wouldn't need to complain, Rose said.

I don't like the sand.

Shit, said Ted.

Then Chub ran off. Ted and Rose climbed in and lit candles and sat in the dead quiet of their bunker. Ted showed her the tin of Capstan tobacco he'd knocked off from a shop in Subi. She was outraged, but she wanted things to go well so she watched him take out his Tally-Ho papers and open the tobacco tin crouched down on his haunches with his loose shorts showing that revolting little thing of his hanging down. Then it was all over. Someone banged on the door, Ted snapped the tin shut in fright and screamed. The roof started caving in, and they spent an hour in Mrs Lamb's kitchen watching her try to get Ted's dick out of the Capstan tin. Some grownups stomped the cubby in, and Ted snarled at everyone that came near. Every time one of the Lamb kids passed they'd laugh their boxes off and Rose knew there'd be no fun before Christmas.

The old man lost big at the races. Things started to disappear from the house. Then the old girl disappeared from the house.

It's the Hairy Hand, the old man said.

Rose couldn't speak to him.

Poison

Dolly followed the rails. It had been a long time since a train had come by. The moon lit up the steel so it looked deadly cool, and now and then she had the feeling she could just lie down there and go to sleep and the whole world, the complete fucking mess, would just evaporate. She was drunk. She was stinking putrid drunk and she didn't care, though she'd like to know where her left shoe was. Her mouth tasted like burnt sugar. They could all go to hell.

Remember those hot buckling rails up there, up north where childhood lived? Remember that? Coming back from that ride with your father who was, after all, not so much your father as your father's father-in-law. Remember all your sisters hanging off the great long gate as it swung open to let you in? Can you still see your big-boned sister watching you pass, her eyes narrowed in the dust, the diamond engagement ring plain obvious on her hand? How far it was from the rails, that blanched stretch of dirt where you got down off the horse, and with your fingers in the wire, climbed up on that gate, to look her straight in the face and say absolutely bugger all. Remember the groaning of cows? The sound of your grandfather leading your horse away, the other sisters climbing down all quiet. Oh, God, there was poison in you, Dolly. Right then, if you'd spat in her face you'd have blinded her, killed her. So why didn't you? Well, that's the question, old darling, that's the wonder.

It only took Dolly's body a second to decide that it couldn't go on. She dropped in the dry grass, even as she walked. The moon hung over her like a dirty Osram globe. She watched it till it was a sure bet it wouldn't fall on her, and then she passed out.

Rose knew she'd be the one to find her. She set out early with this fact sitting on her back, and an hour down the rails towards Karrakatta she came on her. At first Rose didn't know what to think. There was dew on her, and she *smelt* like she'd be dead. Rose stood and looked a while. The old girl's feet were black and bare. Her skirt was twisted, foul. There was a pile of chunder next to her head, some dried like the glaze on a teapot, along her cheek.

Rose thought: If she's dead, then I won't have a mother.

She stooped to touch. Well. She still had a mother. But the old girl couldn't be woken. Rose shoved, poked, slapped. In the end, she walked up to the station, and with the money the old man had given her, caught the 7.15 home.

Oriel Lamb had never seen anybody throw up like Mrs Pickles was throwing up. Yesterday she was hitting the wall and erupting into the air and Mr Pickles was cracking nervous jokes about her being an old geezer after all, but today it was black-green stuff coming up and no one was joking. Oriel poured water into her and sponged her down and left the shop to Lester. The poor woman's flesh was the colour of pastry and cold to touch. It was like she'd been poisoned. The Pickles kids came and went. Mr Pickles was at work. The house was dim and in need of scrubbing and airing. Everywhere there were saucers full of fag ash, dirty clothes, unwashed plates and dust. Oriel Lamb sat at the foot of the bed to wait. It went on all day like the law of diminishing returns, Mrs Pickles puking and moaning, until in the end there was only her heart and lungs to eject before it could logically cease. But late the second day, Mrs Pickles eased back into sleep and Oriel knew it was finished. She got up and looked at the place and decided to finish the job.

Rose walks in and it smells different. Windows are open and curtains thrust aside. She goes into her mother's room to find her sleeping. The room smells of phenyle. There is no dust on the dresser. The big tilting mirror is free of specks and splats. Down in the kitchen the dishes are done and there are nine fresh pasties on the draining board. The floor is still damp. Rose thumps upstairs and puts her head in the boys' room. Their beds are made; their dirty clothes are gone, the window is up. The rug looks beaten within an inch of its life. She goes next door to her room and looks at the brushes and ribbons rearranged metrically on her dresser; she regards the remade bed and feels her jaw harden. In one movement she rips the bed clothes back and tosses them across the floor. Her eyes fatten up with tears, fury, shame.

Downstairs the old man is stamping around, back from work.

Four weeks to Christmas! he's yelling. How's the old girl?

Rose kicks the door shut and begins to destroy her room.

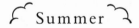 Summer

Summer came whirling out of the night and stuck fast. One morning late in November everybody got up at Cloudstreet and saw the white heat washing in through the windows. The wild oats and buffalo grass were brown and crisp. The sky was the colour of kerosene. The air was thin and volatile. Smoke rolled along the tracks as men began the burn off on the embankment. Birds cut singing down to a few necessary phrases, and beneath them in the streets, the tar began to bubble. The city was full of Yank soldiers; the trams were crammed to standing with them. The river sucked up the sky and went flat and glittery right down the middle of the place and people went to it in boats and britches and barebacked. Where the river met the sea, the beaches ran north and south, white and broad as highways in a dream, and men and babies stood in the surf while gulls hung in the haze above, casting shadows on the immodest backs of the oilslicked women.

Cloudstreet did a bottling trade on icecream. Lester Lamb half wore his arms off turning the churn and lifting the tombstone hunks of ice inside from the truck. Kids mucked around along fences; they sent dogs and grownups bellowing. They were mad with the nearness of Christmas. Oriel baked and served and held up trams getting all her children on, while Dolly Pickles, weak and gloomy, watched everyone pass in the street below until evening when Sam would come home with pennies behind his teeth and the dust of money in his skin and there'd be early watermelon and hot bread and open windows.

As the days cannoned on, and the heat got meaner, everybody did things crazier than normal. They bought things, they said things, they heard things, they moved things, they lost things, they joined things and left things. They were mad, loony, loopy with summer.

Red's Method

Red Lamb the tomboy got sick of blokes swimming under the girls' change sheds at the Crawley baths. They dived in around the piles like randy seals and merged in the shadows where all was green and perilous with barnacles, and they floated along silently, eyesup, to get a fisheye view of naked bums and boxes. Hat and Elaine were bigger and had hair on theirs and they did pretend to be outraged, but Red could tell their hearts weren't in it. Climbing into her scratchy wool costume which stank of her own hammy crotchpong, she heard their half delighted screams of disgust and she knew boys were headed her way, so she spread her towel on the boards and stood quiet with her nose in the air until shrieks came from cubicles on the other side and she was safe.

As the heat grew that summer, so did her rage. She devised a scheme and took great delight in employing it, so much so that when it started to get results, when word got around and the boys backed off, she was kind of crestfallen. It worked very well, Red's method. When she was changing in her cubicle and heard the trail of squeals coming her way, she'd whip off her bathers, squat on the boards, take good aim and build up a head of steam in her belly so that when some frecklefaced pair came sidestroking along beneath her she could piss right into their awestruck faces while bellowing her war cry 'Death to Pervs!' She could pee through the eye of a needle, Red Lamb.

Hat and Elaine went to their parents about it but did not get satisfaction. Lester and Oriel had always measured an eye for an eye.

Everything in the world seemed to happen just before Christmas.

Dolly Pickles decided never to speak to Oriel Lamb again.

Sam Pickles won a pig in a pub raffle and donated it to the Lamb family in gratitude for nursing his missus back to health.

The cockatoo bit Chub on the lip, got a taste for it and began an offensive that lasted all week. Chub took to wearing a box on his head. Here comes the Cardboard Kelly Gang, people said.

Ted Pickles kissed a girl on the sand at Pelican Point and she showed him a thing or two. It changed his life.

Rose Pickles read *Jane Eyre* and decided never to give it back to the public library. She scraped and rubbed to remove all signs of ownership from it, but each morning she woke to see the stamp still bright on the endpapers: CITY OF PERTH. In the end she cut it out, but it always grew back in her mind's eye. She took it back and her old man paid the fine. They cancelled her membership.

Next door Fish struck up a friendship with the pig.

On a bad tip from Sam, Lester Lamb bought a clapped out racehorse to pull his new delivery cart.

Elaine had a migraine every day.

Hat became unofficial marble champion of Cloud Street. By Christmas Eve no one would play her because there were no marbles left to lose. Her mother said she was too old to play doogs in the street, but Hat loved to be a winner.

Red Lamb saw Ted Pickles with his hands inside Mary Modine's bathers, and it didn't change *her* life one bit.

Over the fence, Lon Lamb saw Chub Pickles being pursued by the pink cocky, and he laughed so loud he was wearing a bucket on his head within hours.

Quick caught nine dozen tailor out in the boat at Nedlands one day, and came back so burnt that he couldn't chew, bend, sit or stand. He saw Rose Pickles watching Fish in no man's land and knew she was in love with his brother.

Oriel Lamb went out and bought a tent. She bought a steel box and a padlock for the till and the accounts book and took to hiding them.

The Pig

The pig is down the back in a pen that's just been tossed up for him by Sam and Lester, and Fish is standing there to look, to look. It's late in the afternoon and all the birds are crashing back into the trees and the great summer sky is disrobing in swirls. The pig is pink and hairy with smart little eyes and a nose like a wet light plug.

He's all yours, Sam says.

Preciate it, Lester says.

Better butcher im quick, I reckon. The council wouldn't like it.

They wouldn't like Cloudstreet beginnin to finish, says Lester.

Fish looks. The pig turns and looks back. The two men wander back up to the house and leave them alone. Fish scratches inside his shorts. The bristly animal flexes a shoulder. Shadows from the lilac tree, the lemon, the almond, fall across him like camouflage. It's quiet.

Give us a squirt with the hose, wouldja? the pig says.

Fish looks at the pig and giggles. Orright.

He gets the hose, fumbles with the tap, and with his finger over the nozzle, he sprays the pig up and down until the ground in the pen turns miry and the pig is streaked with mud. From up the house Lester bellows.

Turn that water off, Fish! There's a drought on!

Thanks anyway, cobber, says the pig.

Fish regards the pig a good while, forgetful of the hose water that drills into the dirt, bubbling up sand and sticks. The runoff makes a long spewy black rivulet that proceeds down the yard into the strawberries and the early corn.

Fish! Oy, Fish!

The pig winks and rolls in the bog. He kicks his legs up and his trotters clack together. The sun is low over the roofs of the neighbourhood. There is the smell of oncoming night, of pollen setting, the sound of kids fighting bathtime. Lester comes down, waving his hands.

Don't drown the pig, Fish. We're savin him for Christmas. We're gunna eat him.

No!

I'll drink to that, says the pig.

Lester stands there. He looks at Fish. He looks at the porker. He peeps over the fence. The pig. The flamin pig. The pig has just spoken. It's no language that he can understand, but there's no doubt. He feels a little crook, like maybe he should go over to that tree and puke.

I like him, Lestah.

He talks?

Yep.

Oh, my gawd.

Lester looks at his retarded son again and once more at the pig.

The pig talks.

I likes him.

Yeah, I bet.

The pig snuffles, lets off a few syllables: *aka sembon itwa*. It's tongues, that's what it is. A blasted Pentecostal pig.

And you understand him?

Yep. I likes him.

Always the miracles you don't need. It's not a simple world, Fish. It's not.

The pig grunts, as though this fact is self evident. He heaves onto his side and regards Lester and Fish with detachment. He sighs and the sky squeezes out its last light. Mosquitoes are out already. Lester stands there in the twilight. Fish comes close and puts a finger through Lester's belt loop. The pig clears its throat and begins to hum under its breath.

I won't have the proceeds, the dividends of gambling in my yard or on my table, said Oriel, and she got down her notebook to quote at him.

If the rich gamble, they do it with money filched from the wage earner. If the poor, they play with their children's bread. Where, indeed, is there a class that may gamble and rob none?

Mary Gilmore, she said.

Who?

Never mind.

We have to keep the pig, said Lester.

Why, pray tell?

It was a present. Sam's grateful to you. Besides, Fish has taken a shine to it.

He shouldn't have been put in the situation where he'd –

Oh, just be reasonable! Lester yelled, scaring himself with his boldness. The boy thinks the pig's his friend.

Reasonable! You call that reasonable?

Oriel. Love.

Don't you Oriel Love me.

There's another thing.

There'll always be another thing.

The pig talks.

Oriel put down her pen and closed the account book. She looked at him with an expression that signified that she'd reached the last knot on her rope.

It talks some foreign lingo.

Get the torch. Show me this pig.

The pig opened an eye at them when they came tromping and flashing lights down his way. He snouted up some dirt and sighed.

Gday, said Lester to the pig.

The pig sniffed.

Lester, if this is an old vaudeville joke your life won't be worth seeing to its natural end.

It's no joke, is it, me old pork mate?

But the pig said nothing; he just lay there with a bored and irritable look on his face and eyes like Audie Murphy.

It talks in tongues, Oriel.

You've been drinking. Let's go inside before we strike up a conversation with the chooks. The pig goes.

But in her bed that night Oriel lay awake thinking of the pig her father had butchered to heal her burns as a sign of his love and it troubled her sorely.

The Horse

The animal world didn't let up. A racehorse came to Cloud-street on a sure tip from Sam Pickles. It was a big bay gelding with feet like post rammers and a history of depression and emotional disturbance. A few days before Christmas Lester bought himself a hawker's cart and harness to go into the delivery side of the business. He saw himself clopping through the suburbs ringing his bell, swinging his scales, rattling his blackboards, the cart laden with fruit and vegetables and his songs and jokes drawing women and children into the streets. It wasn't the commerce of it that got his pea rattling (though he sold the idea that way to Oriel), it was the performance side of things; the singing and shouting, the jokes, stories, the eyes of the crowd on him.

He planned to hobble the horse on the grassy embankment at the side of the house, perhaps with a lean-to against the fence. Oriel gave him money and rolled her eyes, preoccupied with stranger things than him, and when he bought the horse he truly believed he'd backed a bargain.

But Lester, old lighthorseman that he was, should never have assumed that a depressed horse was a slow horse. The delivery business didn't live a full day.

He harnessed the horse, loaded the cart with the best of Cloudstreet's fare, and had only dropped his bum on the driver's seat and taken up the reins when the horse took to the idea of liberal and rapid food distribution and took off for the streets of Subiaco with its head up and its tail down. Lester braced out the long, slithering ride down the embankment, the spinepowdering jolts of the wheels clearing the rails, and when he hit the street on the Subi side his hat was low on his brow and he looked indeed like a Randolph Scott. But at the first turn, when the cart got up on two wheels behind the slavering lunatic of a horse and the harness thwacked and twanged like a man's braces he looked like any ordinary projectile waiting for gravity to have the last word. He landed in the dickey seat of a Packard parked outside the Masonic Hall. The horse went on without him and he followed its trail the rest of the day. Kids sat on fences eating apples, the occasional letterbox gripped a carrot in its teeth, and there were cauliflower sludge marks here and there, a Hansel and Gretel trail of lettuce leaves, beetroot and orange rind so thick that the city's birds and half its scavenging children couldn't obscure it. In the afternoon he found the horse grazing on roses in a yard near Lake Monger. It looked at him placidly with sated, longlashed eyes. He took it to the knackers and got two quid for horse, cart, and ten pounds of pureed tomatoes. When he got home, he found Oriel out the back, pegging a tent beneath the mulberry tree. The pig looked on, mute. A headless turkey hung from a hook on the fence. Water boiled on the kitchen stove.

Quick came up and stood beside him: I think the pig's got away with it. How's the horse?

The horse wasn't so lucky.

Mum's not happy.

They watched her hammering in pegs and tightening ropes on the tent. A bed stood endup against the trellis of the grapevine.

Can't see why, Lester said. She likes turkey.

Quick looked up at his old man in wonder. Behind him

132

three heads poked from the second floor window. Pickles heads.

Gday, Quick said.

Gday, Rose Pickles said.

The pig's for *next* Christmas, Quick said.

The Pickles kids cracked up laughing.

Oriel Lamb straightened up, axe in hand, and everything went quiet. There was sweat on her upper lip. Somewhere inside, Fish Lamb was singing. He sounded like a colicky baby at midnight.

Fark! said the cockatoo in its cage.

Quick Lamb looked at his toes and pressed them tight together. It was no time to laugh.

The Tent Lady

On New Year's Day, 1949, people gathered to watch Oriel Lamb move her things out to the white tent beneath the mulberry tree at Cloudstreet. They crowded into the second floor rooms overlooking the yard, and found cracks in the scaly picket fence; they climbed trees in yards all around and perved through pointed gum leaves at the little woman carrying bedclothes and fruitboxes out through the bewildered half circle of her family. No one missed the sight of Quick Lamb helping his mother out with the jarrah bed and the umps and bumps they made getting it in. There wasn't a noise to be heard otherwise except for Fish Lamb slapping away at the piano in the centre of the house; everyone looked on in wonder, missing nothing. She had a desk, Tilley lamp, chamberpot, books, mysterious boxes. People gathered at the fences. When she had it all in shape, Oriel Lamb tied off the door flap and went back into the house to organize her family's dinner, and the crowd went away murmuring that surely this was a day to remember.

She's ad enough kids, said the women of the street.

She's caught him out, said the blokes.

But the real reason remained a mystery, even to Oriel

Lamb. It wasn't actually one thing that'd moved her. The pig, the sound of middle C ringing in her ears, the sudden claustrophobia of the house, the realization that Fish didn't even know her, and the feeling she had that the house was saying to her: wait, wait. She didn't know, but, whatever else she was, Oriel wasn't the sort to argue with a living breathing house.

Combustible Material

BY the time he was sixteen, Quick Lamb was taller than his father. He was a fairskinned, melancholy boy, slim and a little cagey around the ribs but robust in his own way. He loved to walk and to fish, to be out on the water in the shadow of the brewery or anchored out from the Nedlands jetty. It was so much more peaceful than the teeming house where there was always some fit of yelling, some quiet tussle, some jostling spectacle in progress. The sun tended to turn his skin to bark in an hour, so he rigged up a longshafted umbrella he'd found in a bin outside the university and fixed it to an old rod belt strapped to his waist and it gave him the feeling of rowing with a small cloud always overhead. He smeared his face and arms with zinc cream, and the overall effect failed to render him inconspicuous.

The river was broad and silvertopped and he knew its topography well enough to be out at night, though the old girl would have had a seizure at the thought. He never got bored with landmarks, the swirls of tideturned sand, armadas of jellyfish, the smell of barnacles and weed, the way the pelicans baulked and hovered like great baggy clowns. He liked to hear the skip of prawns and the way a confused school of mullet bucked and turned in a mob. From the river you could be in the city but not on or of it. You could be back from it out there on the water and see everything go by you, around you, leaving you untouched. Cars swept round Mounts Bay Road beneath Mount Eliza where Kings Park and its forest of war memorials presided over the town. With an easterly rushing in his ears, he often watched the toffs picnicking by the university. He saw their sporty little cars, their jingling bicycles, and he wondered what they were, those university people. They came into the shop now and then on a Saturday, stopping for some forgotten thing for the picnic hamper, or seeking out the icecream the old man was known for. Quick looked into their faces and wanted to know how they could bear so much school.

School just gave Quick Lamb the pip. He was too slow to get things right the first time and too impatient to force himself to learn. For a while he was an army cadet, a soldier under the command of mathematics teachers who exchanged the steel rule for the brass ended baton and who liked the sound of both on a set of knuckles. In the cadets Quick learnt to shoot and also to crap with the aid of one square of shiny paper. He loved the khaki serge of battledress and the smell of nugget in the webbing, and he loved to shoot because he was good at it. He could see a long way, pick things in the distance that others couldn't, and the two hundred yard target seemed close to him, only a barrel length away. In the end, even Quick knew the only reason the school kept him on at all was to win rifle trophies for it. Sometimes, after a shoot, he'd see the whole world through a V. There was only ever one teacher Quick Lamb could talk with, but he was the sort of man who winced when you brought up your shoot scores, or rolled his eyes when you spoke warmly of a Bren gun. His name was Krasnostein and he had a limp. He taught history and he liked to have the class in an uproar of debate and discussion. He had the sort of dandruff that found its way into your books and papers and his teeth were like burnt mallee stumps. When he breathed on you, there was no telling how you'd behave.

Quick almost never spoke in class discussions. He could never get out what he wanted to say in time. Mostly he felt breathless and confused, sometimes furious with Mr Krasnostein who baited them all about the Anzacs and the Empire. Yet there was laughter allowed, even out-spokenness. After one class Krasnostein kept Quick behind. Itching with dread, Quick stood by the little man's desk.

You have lovely handwriting, Mr Lamb, but I'm afraid your essay is anything but lovely.

Sorry, sir.

The teacher sucked his moustache and smiled. You must remember that the *West Australian* and the *Western Mail* are not final authorities on history. Nor is what you hear over the back fence. Do you know any Japanese people?

No, sir.

No, I thought not. They really are more than just combustible material, Lamb. Do you know any Jews?

No.

Well you do now.

Quick looked him up and about. He felt his chin fall.

Here, Lamb, take these and read them over the week-end. If you'd like to change your essay afterwards let me know.

Quick went out lightheaded and he didn't even glance at the two bundles until he got home. In his room he opened the crumpled old magazine, a *New Yorker* from 1945. The whole thing seemed to be about Hiroshima, which he'd mentioned in his own essay. Between pages were loose photographs of what looked like burnt logs or furniture, but when he looked close he saw the features of people. He put it down and picked up the small pamphlet. It was called *Belsen: a record*. He picked it up without thought. Inside were long lists, and photographs of great piles of . . . of great piles. Quick went downstairs and out the back where the mulberry tree had stained the old girl's tent the colour of a battalion field hospital. Fish was out there talking to the pig. Corn stood chest high down behind the chicken wire. Next door Mrs Pickles was laughing drunk again.

After dinner Quick went back upstairs. He looked at the brittle, faded pictures he'd stuck on his walls years ago. He'd forgotten about them. Years ago he'd thought them the saddest, most miserable things he'd ever seen in his life and he kept them there to remind him of Fish, how Fish had been broken and not him. But even that punishment had worn off. Now he sat with pictures in his lap that were beyond sadness and misery. This was evil, like Mr Bootluck the minister used to go on about at the Church of Christ. Here were all those words like sin and corruption and damnation.

That night Fish crawled into his bed and Quick felt him like a coal against his skin.

Mr Krasnostein was not at school on Monday. In his place they had a strapping blonde man called Miller who looked like a wheat farmer. His eyes were the colour of gas and he read to them from the *Yearbook, 1942*. Mr Krasnostein never returned. Quick kept the magazine and the little stapled book in his bag, tucking them inside the loose skirting board in his room when he got home. As he came out onto the landing he saw Rose Pickles by the window at the head of the stairs, and it struck him that her silhouette was just like something out of Belsen. He'd noticed she was getting thinner every week, and now, as she turned, her eyes stood out in her head enough to make him feel repulsed. Somehow it struck him as sickheaded for a pretty girl to starve herself like that.

Oh, it's you, she said.

Quick said nothing at all. He was too choked up with disgust. He went down the stairs four at a time. He'd quit school – that's what he'd do.

Rose watched him thump down the stairs, then she turned back to look out across the mulberry tree, but she couldn't recall what it was that had caught her attention in the first place. Maybe it was just the yards, the fences containing other families, more secrets. She went back to her room and looked at herself once more in the mirror. All her bones stood out. Her eyes crowded her face. She gave a grim smile and went down to cook the dinner.

Rose didn't mind the sight of food these days, and she managed to cook for the family without trouble. But whenever she ate more than a few mouthfuls she vomited it straight back again, just like she knew she would. She cooked at six, regardless of who was there, and if no one came she left it on the table till morning, taking a carrot for herself and going upstairs to her homework or to lie on her bed planning ways of escape.

She didn't go to collect the old woman from the pub any more. She'd stopped that a couple of years ago, when she was fourteen. No more sending messages through to the Ladies' Lounge, never again the screaming and slapping out on the pavement, the leery beerwet grins of old men turning on their stools, the hands on her backside, the food thrown in her face. The night of her fourteenth birthday Rose went down to the Railway Hotel to collect her mother for the little party they'd arranged, and when she got to the nicotine sheened door, she just stopped and turned around and went home, knowing she didn't care if the old girl came to her party or if she went to hell in a hurry.

Rose learnt to cook, wash the laundry and to clean the house. If the old man won at the races she didn't have to mend her tights on the trolley bus to school – she'd wear perfect new ones – but in three years of high school there weren't a dozen times she went with tights that didn't need darning.

She poured every bottle of liquor she ever found in the house down the sink and she knew it was worth getting thumped for. She didn't do it to curb the old girl's drinking

– she did it in glee, out of spite. It gave her the most marvellous, tingly feeling to see it going down the gurgler. If the boys and her father were home in time for dinner they'd often have Dolly lurching in the door for a scene, though more often than not the four of them would hear her coming, sweep up their plates and rush upstairs to eat in their rooms. If she still had the legs, Dolly might seek them out, bash at doors, and turn a meal over in someone's lap, but mostly she'd get no further than the kitchen where she'd sit staring at whatever was available to be stared at until she fell asleep, mumbling.

Now and then Rose tried to see the whole business as hilarious; it was like being in the first chapter of a fairy tale about a sweet girl with a nasty but beautiful step-mother. But the pleasure wouldn't stay with her more than a moment or two. There was too much shame, too much cowering under the neighbours' eyes, too much agonizing embarrassment going to school with a black eye or a fat lip – no, it was too real.

Ted and Chub were lazy and careless like boys were, and they were no use at all. Ted was the old girl's favourite. Rose often saw her patting and stroking him when she was half shickered. Ted didn't seem to care what she did at all. And the old man – well the old man was the same as ever. He'd come home tired and quiet from the Mint and shrug his shoulders. On Saturdays he'd go out to Ascot and lose the week's pay. Rose was clever enough to steal a bit of his pay each week, going through his shirts for the laundry, but it was never really enough. She bought groceries from next door and small household things in Subiaco, but the money never went far enough to buy the boys and her new things for school, or clothes, or small treats. If the old man had a win there'd be plenty for all, but mostly it was the bookies who had the wins.

This summer Rose had started to get thin. She went dark in the sun, and on the holidays she'd caught the train to Cottesloe Beach nearly every day and gone without lunch to pay for it. She looked light and lithe and the old man joked around about it.

One Sunday noon in the new year and the fresh decade when the summer days were cooling off toward autumn, the old girl surprised her in the bathroom and she had to grab for a towel to cover herself. Her mother was bleary and sore headed.

Yer gettin skinny. Look like a bloody skeleton. I hate it. People think we starve yer.

Rose said nothing. It pleased her somehow to know that it annoyed the old girl. She watched her smear on all the makeup she needed these days to look halfway decent. Dolly was getting old and puffy. Smoke was curing her brow and cheeks and she had to try very hard to look her best.

Their eyes met and Rose smiled menacingly before leaving the room.

From then on, Rose got thinner every day. The old woman went into rages and the old man bit his lip. She was sixteen and scaring herself.

A Desertion

At first Oriel Lamb thought that vaudeville was undignified. Since way back, since the Bible-believing days, she'd defended dancing and music, but getting up to make a fool of yourself and sing nonsense songs seemed morally dubious. It was hard to shake off the idea that Lester's vaudeville act would somehow bring disgrace to them all. But when she saw how the old diggers loved it, how they stomped their crutches and held their bellies and sang along, she couldn't see the harm in it.

It was hard to remember how he'd got into the whole business. Someone from the army band had been recruiting, or drunk, and suddenly Lester was up there on stage, one Saturday night, starting in on his noseflute before they'd even finished 'God Save the Queen'. And now it was 1950, and the Anzac Club had Lester Lamb on the bill almost every Saturday night. Though she'd never let on, she was proud of him. Vaudeville was something he was good at, something legendary from his past that was actually true. Most Saturday nights she'd hear him from the club kitchen where she kept the urns boiling for tea and buttered pumpkin scones and set fresh Anzacs out on the club china. She could hear Lester on the Jew's harp, comb and paper, the noseflute, and nowadays the ventriloquist's dummy he'd bought in a pawnshop for a mysterious sum.

He's a right card, the other women would say, a real bonzer.

A real dag, love. Oh, to have him round the house.

Oriel rolled her eyes. Women!

People knew the Lambs now, were a little afraid of them even. With or without the children they travelled to and from the club in a Harley and sidecar. Pedestrians always looked twice at the dummy whose jaws flapped alarmingly in the wind.

The Anzacs were what the Lambs believed in, the glorious memories of manhood and courage. The nation, that's what kept the Lambs going. They were patriots like no others. The thought of World Communism put fear in their hearts. Oriel had dreams about Joe Stalin – she knew what he was about. They weren't political, Lester and Oriel, but they were proud and they offered themselves to the nation.

It was at the Anzac Club one night that Quick came into the kitchen and told her he was leaving.

Go over to the sink and wash your mouth out with soap, Mason Lamb, she said, not pausing from kneading the oatmeal mixture for her next batch of Anzacs.

Quick leaned against the laminex counter and saw the gold flecks in it.

I'm going bush, Mum.

There's a bar of Velvet just beside you.

I didn't think you'd appreciate me doin a bunk and not explainin.

Up on stage, Lester was singing:

Chicory-chic chala-chala-

You've got no money.

Mum –

No trade.

– in a binanaker bollicka wollicka, can't you see –

144

Mum –
We not good enough for you?
– chicory-chic is me!
I'm going.

Everyone was laughing and clapping, and now they were headed for the counter for tea and cakes. Oriel rushed to the urn and felt the steam in her face. She wanted to grab Quick now, swallow him in a hug and pin him to the floor. He couldn't go, he was one of hers, he wasn't old enough, he wasn't ready. Men with broad-cracking grins and hat lines in the oil of their hair broached the counter and made clunky, well-meaning jokes to hurry her along. She was trapped.

I won't have a scene, she said, turning to the urn again.

But Quick was gone.

Hat, Elaine and Red came in to help pour the tea. They were all giggle and guffaw, teased by old soldiers and a few not so old. Oriel brought up trays full of cups, each with the Anzac insignia, to be filled, and she went into a trance of composure.

Somehow the seven of them stay connected to the Harley as the old man sends it through the Terrace, whumping up onto the flat stretch along Kings Park Road and then sending them all blank with terror as he hangs a right into Thomas Street. Their collective wailing sounds like a siren. The wind burns Oriel's eyes. She squeezes Lon between her and Lester on the pillion, and hears Fish laughing. The girls scream, cowering around Fish in the sidecar. As they hit the railway line the vibration silences the lot of them. Oriel feels like her bowels have suddenly risen into her ribcage. Lester's already gearing down for Cloudstreet. The dummy's arm rises in the wind. They look like an army in retreat.

Quick hears the piano thundering as he half falls, half runs downstairs. It's not music, only noise, and it scares the hell out of him. He has a duffle bag on his shoulder which beats his back as he goes, and as he swings into the bottom hallway, Rose Pickles, coming out to see what all the noise is, takes it full in the face and goes down cold on the floor.

He's almost to the back door before he realizes, but as he turns to go back he hears the Harley gunning down Railway Parade, and so he stops and gets out the door to the yard and runs. Past the redspattered tent, the vegetables and chooks, up over the back fence and down the embankment along the tracks. The wild oats whip his legs and he bolts, sobbing in the dark.

Rose Pickles had herself almost upright before the Lamb mob came brawling in the door, fanning out like infantry, room-by-room, upstairs and down and she was trying to slip back in the kitchen doorway when Mrs Lamb finally noticed her and seized her.

Good Lawd! Les, get the medicine box. What happened love, quick tell me what happened. Oh, Quick.

Rose felt the little woman's square head on her shoulder and then her whole boxy weight against her. She just wasn't strong enough to support her, and Mr Lamb came downstairs the moment Rose teetered back into the kitchen with Mrs Lamb weeping on top of her.

Sam Pickles came running. He saw Rose and Oriel on the floor in the doorway. There was blood and both of them were bawling, but he couldn't make any sense of it. Lester Lamb was there, too, standing like a man to whom feeling helpless is no great surprise. Their eyes met.

What – the bum dropped out of the world?

More or less, said Lester. More or less.

༄ And the Pig Won't Talk ༅

Fish goes down the back to the pig but the pig is saying nothing. The chooks pick and scratch in their sandy run. The ground is dry with the end of summer and the big house is quiet. No Quick. He's gone. He didn't say. You should say. A boy should say. He feels sick right in his middle. This is sad. Lestah says it's the sad that makes the sick. It makes him hungry for the water again. Some nights he can't sleep for the

146

hungry in him, and in the mornings he just wants to be bad and put poo on the walls and eat sand like a baby. He doesn't like the sound of them crying. He wants Quick. He doesn't care what they want. He just wants to be bad. And the pig won't talk.

That Ted Pickles

Sometimes Dolly Pickles looked at Ted and saw Sam, Sam from a long time ago, in another place. Ted was blonde and small with loutish good looks that girls fixed on in the street. Oh, she saw them looking, saw his arrogant nonchalance and the way it got them all biting their lips. And sometimes she felt a sting, just in watching, a spike in her throat, jealousy. Those firm, fresh-titted girls down there, hanging off the verandah cracking gum and looking sideways at him, Ted Pickles, who couldn't give a stuff.

Yes, he was the young Sam alright, but harder, meaner. Maybe that's what she'd always wanted from Sam – a little less understanding, a bit more steel, something in him with a fearful edge. Oh, that Ted. He was killin em.

Battalions

Oriel Lamb, being the sort of woman who resolved to *do* things, decided to make a recovery. She was off her food and nothing gave her the disgruntled satisfaction it once did, so in the weeks after Quick shot through, knowing that not even she could conquer grief by force of will, she decided on a lesser conquest. She would wipe out local competition.

No one had taken much notice of the big shop on the main road since it opened its doors after last Christmas. Certainly none of the Lambs. Business hadn't dropped off at all. None of the neighbours mentioned the newcomer. But walking past one day, on one of her expeditions to buy cheap eggs in the neighbourhood, Oriel walked by the big, bright shop and saw it properly for the first time. She stood back and regarded the gaudy sign.

```
┌─────────────────────────────────┐
│    G. M. Clay – Ex 2nd AIF      │
│           BUY HERE              │
│                                 │
└─────────────────────────────────┘
```

Ex-AIF indeed, she hissed aloud. A tall woman, unknown to her, passed with raised eyebrows and Oriel decided to keep her thoughts more to herself.

It's a disgrace, she thought, to grovel to the customer
like that, to wave your service to the King like it's a flag.
A good man's above that kind of rubbish. Lester could paint:

```
┌─────────────────────────────┐
│        Lester Lamb          │
│     10th Light Horse        │
│         1st AIF             │
│     Gallipoli, 1915        │
│       Six children         │
│          Hernia            │
│     Ingrown toenails       │
└─────────────────────────────┘
```

He could wheedle just the same, but I'd be ashamed
I would. You wouldn't get me over the threshold. Why, Mr
Pickles could have on his letter box:

```
┌─────────────────────────────────┐
│   Samuel Pickles, one-handed    │
└─────────────────────────────────┘
```

to conjure sympathy. He's not much of a man, Mr Pickles,
but he's enough of a man not to stoop to that. Why, she
could have a sign herself:

```
┌─────────────────────────────────┐
│           O. Lamb              │
│   Family Incinerated, 1911     │
│     Bereaved of Palestine      │
│      Bereaved again, 1945      │
│        Married to fool         │
│         Please help            │
└─────────────────────────────────┘
```

148

Oriel swung her basket on the other side. She looked at G. M. Clay's establishment, its nice window of tins and bottles, the clean glass, the cream and green painted bins of flour and sugar, and she knew that G. M. Clay had to be wiped out. Good Lord, she'd lost a brother in Palestine, and every Saturday night she served tea and swapped smiles with men who'd lost limbs and mates in New Guinea, been robbed of their health in Changi, lost their wives to Americans right here in Perth, WA and she wasn't going to tolerate the presumption of a G. M. Ex-AIF-Clay.

Oriel recrossed the street and stepped into the shop. The bell tinkled sweetly on the door and the interior smelt orderly and hygenic. Shelves lined the walls. A brass set of scales stood on the counter, and beside it, a modern, enamelled Avery.

Oh, gday madam, a tidy looking man in a white apron said, coming from another room. What can I get you?

A dozen eggs, please.

Righto.

She counted out her pence and noted that they weren't bad looking eggs.

Anything else?

No. Thank you, no. Where did you serve, Mr Clay?

Beg pardon?

In the Australian Imperial Forces. Where did you fight?

Oh, he laughed. You must be Mrs Lamb.

That's right.

I hear you're a friend of the Anzacs.

I believe in my country, she said, a new creed on her lips.

I was in the second AIF. Bougainville. New Guinea.

Infantry?

Signalman and runner, Mrs Lamb.

Oriel felt her resolve weakening. He was no pretender. Unless he was lying. The Kokoda trail, no soft spot. He was a well kept man and he had a well kept shop. He'd served his country.

What unit did your husband serve in?

Cavalry. The 10th Light Horse. At Gallipoli. Oriel said

it with a hint of breathless pride, like a priest uttering an unassailable truth.

No, no, I mean this last war. I heard he enlisted before the end. Brave man, with all his kids and family responsibilities. What battalion?

There was a smile on his well-shaved face as he said this and Oriel Lamb felt the hard tissue of hatred under her skin.

He joined as a bandsman, Mr Clay, good day.

Oriel swung on her toes and headed for the door.

Thought it might have been the tentmakers platoon, she heard him whisper to someone else out of sight. The Padre's Brave Twelve.

A woman's laugh it was. From the back room. The bell jangled on the door. Outside Oriel shuddered with rage. She wanted to throw Clay's eggs into the bin on the pavement, but nothing, not even war itself could induce her to waste good food.

The Good Are Fierce

That woman had Lester waking, raking, caking, and baking at all hours, and he knew she meant business. He couldn't really see the harm in advertising that you were an old soldier. He couldn't help suspecting that he would himself if he didn't have the shadows of history at his back. Only a man who was a liar or a bloke who'd acquitted himself well in the field would dare though. And Lester knew he was neither.

Out in the kitchen he rolled dough on the marble slab and heard the old girl bellowing commands. The girls were pulling their end, but he knew they wouldn't stay with it long. His wife was a good woman, and he understood that. But he remembered what the minister at Margaret River used to say – the good are fierce. She'd outlast them all – she'd make damn sure of it. That'd be the way she'd want it. Half the bleedin day out finding the biggest eggs this side of the river, figuring out prices and margins, hammering the reps that sold to them, working deals, inventing pies for him to make, flavours for icecream, strategies for the coming winter campaign. She planned to stretch it right through spring and finish Clay off in the summer with Lester Lamb Icecream. And he knew she'd win. That was the best part, in his mind, that they'd clean Clay up with Lester's own recipe.

It was hard, relentless work, though, and he always knew he'd rather be out fishing with Quick or spinning the knife at a lazy dinner table. His act was getting stale at the Anzac Club, and sometimes he thought maybe the fun had gone out of him. Fish was miserable and would hardly come out of his room some days.

There were nights when he went exhausted into his room to sit on his bed alone just to think about Quick. He knew Oriel'd be still shuffling in the shop up front or the light would be burning in the tent outside as she went over the accounts. Often, the only thing he could think of was that old Bible story of the prodigal son. Now he knew what it felt like to be abandoned and left hurt and confused. He wondered what it was he'd done to turn Quick away. He secretly hoped for an end to it like the return of the son in the story and it made him wonder if he wasn't still half believing. Those Bible stories and words weren't the kind you forgot. It was like they'd happened to you all along, that they were your own memories. You didn't always know what they meant, but you did know how they felt. He still remembered a night back in the last century when his own father had carried him on his shoulders across a flooded creek. He could see the swirling darkness, hear the crashing of trees, and the fearful whinny of a horse. Rain fell. It beat his back. He felt his father's whiskers against the bare flesh of his legs. He couldn't remember where they went or who they were with or what happened before or after – only those seconds. The truthfulness of it tightened his bowel. Whatever it meant it was true, and he had the same pure, true feeling in his fantasy of Quick coming home and Lester himself killing a fatted calf and asking no questions. It's not as if we have any friends, he thought. The kids are all we've got; they're what we are.

Dolly couldn't stand the noise of the house. Day and bloody night it went, all through winter as though they were working shifts across there to wipe out Gerry Clay. No one walked down the big corridor, they always bustled. Things were shunted to and fro, and that Godawful woman'd be shouting and hissing to get things moving. Now it was spring and her hayfever was terrible. Her nose itched and her eyes swelled. At times she could do no more than spend the morning in the bath, just lying back in the tepid water until the vibrations in the walls next door drove her from the house.

Dolly was shaky and fragile with headaches, most mornings. She felt older than she was, and she could see it in the mirror the way the smoke and the grog were curing her, making the flesh on her face puffy and shredded with lines. Her teeth were yellow. Her bottom lip had begun to hang. It'd looked so good a few years ago when she could let it slip to a murderous pout that was rarely wasted. And her voice, she was going croaky. She didn't sound like Lauren Bacall anymore. She sounded like an old mother, a copper boiler, a spudpeeler with a fag on her tongue. It wasn't so bad in a crowd with a couple of beers under your girdle but, nowadays, with Sam losing and losing and losing on the horses, there wasn't a lot of money to be drinking on. Dolly had to keep up the wit, the sass, the fun; she was singing for her supper, alright. She'd be happy, crack jokes, catch blokes looking her way. When they came her way she'd have a snappy line for them, she'd knock their hats sideways and shriek when their palms stung her backside on the way past. The blokes behind the bar always had a good word for her – What'll it be, Doll? – though the barmaids narrowed their eyes a little against her in caution.

Hell, she didn't care what anybody thought. Well, not everyone. She liked to be liked, and didn't anyone? No one wants to be forgotten, have eyes glide past you without even seeing you there. No, she didn't care . . . but bugger it . . . well she didn't know. It was all too complicated. Everything was. Unless you were full as a goog. Then it was simple, then all of it was straight in a girl's mind.

Now and then she'd find herself out the back lane against the fence with some sweetmouthed bloke whose name she could almost remember, a cove who wouldn't mind if she kept talking while he ran his hands about. She'd press his head to her and feel how young she was, how hungry they were for her.

By spring it was the same bloke she'd weave out leaning against, come closing time. He was dark haired and hard jawed and handsome. He was a little pigeontoed, but there was muscle on him and she liked the way his hat brim snapped down over his nose. And there was something else exciting about him – he was a Catholic and dead scared of going to Hell.

Yer a bottler, Doll, he said the first night, pressing her up against the cool bricks. Bet yer old man's a millionaire, the way you look.

Him? He hasn't got a pot to piss in. Give's a kiss, love.

He give you a good knock, now and then?

She felt his fingers up the back of her legs. If he did I wouldn't be here. You've got a foul mouth, sport.

She felt her own mouth covered by his and his breath was hot at the back of her throat. He was after her, this one, and all the weights of boredom, the trying, the pushing out smiles were gone, and she had a happy, dark world to live in. She was always a little more sozzled than him, or maybe it was a lot more, she couldn't tell and why should she care, and he always seemed a good sort when he came in late to the Railway Hotel. By the end of spring he started getting later, until he was hardly leaving himself time for a round before they went out the back, or down the embankment to the whispering grass. She saw him nearly every night of the week, and though she didn't much think about him during the day, if she got stuck in the same room as Rose, that filthy-pretty skeleton, she'd bring him to mind to fight the sight of her off.

Rose looked frightening now, like a ghost, with those big eyes. Her wrists looked like twigs and she did nothing but stare. Dolly knew what it meant, that stare. You're old and clapped out, it said, and you're getting fat and your teeth are bad and you don't do a bloody thing, and here I am, young and clean and sweet and I'm doing your jobs, old girl, and I'll die from it and you'll suffer. Dolly tried not to think about how she hated Rose these days. It was a wonder that it could happen, that a mother could turn like that from loving to hating. But when you find yourself getting more and more looks like that, those bland stares that set off cruel, guilty things in you, when you know all of a sudden that someone of your own flesh and blood can't find a spark of worth to your name – then you harden up. They have to be blotted out. Rose was the enemy. It wasn't the sort of thing you let yourself think about, but you knew.

Because she didn't go anywhere except the pub, these days, it took Dolly a long time to know that Gerry was G. M. Clay – Ex AIF whose shop was only three blocks away. Sam and her had an account with the Lambs for their groceries against rent, so there was never any need for her to even step inside the shop that opened in the winter. Once she did know, though, she kept well away. G. M. Clay had a wife – she knew it from overhearing Oriel Lamb. If Dolly went anywhere at all in the day, she caught the train into the city where people were all strangers and a woman could go about without running into smiling neighbours.

By the beginning of summer, Gerry was looking crook.

Those bastards are king hittin me, he said, down by the rails. They couldn't even drink at the Railway anymore, now that blokes were yacking about them, and it was hard to get a shout out of anyone at all.

And yer drinkin the till dry, Doll. This is a mug's game.

That bitch. Oriel-bloody-Lamb.

She's a fighter, orright.

Now and then a train came punching past to shower them with smuts and the smell of the ongoing and outgoing. Dolly felt the lack of grog, it was a heaviness on her. Gerry seemed weaker now, panicky, done in.

You know someone's gunna spring us, dontcha.

Bloody hell, what're you sayin, then?

I'm sayin I gotta be realistic. You too, Doll. We're gunna get burnt sooner or later.

Oh, you can always toddle off to confession, she said, squeezing his leg.

Don't chiack around about it. I'm serious.

She's beaten you, mate.

Don't even think she suspects.

No, not yours. That Lamb sheila. She's got you busted and bleedin.

Jesus, Doll, she can't lose. She's got an army behind her. It'd be easier for me to pull up pegs and try somewhere else. Never thought I'd be shunted out by a woman running a place from the front room. And she lives in a friggin tent.

You sound frightened of her, said Dolly, lying back furious in the drying grass.

Aren't *you*? You could toss her out of that place, you know. Aren't you the landlords?

They're what we live off. Their rent is what pays our way. We can't.

Well, I'm flat out like a lizard drinkin and I can't beat her. It's got me buggered, Doll.

Dolly saw the stars spangled across the sky. The moon hung sallow in their midst. Something was shifting, she knew it. Any moment now, one of them'd go ahead and say what it took.

Across the Rails

Right that moment, on the other side of the rails, in a sea of wild oats, Ted Pickles tears a girl's brassiere aside and lays his hands on her breasts. He's thinking she looks like Martha Vickers in that flick *Alimony*, and she's looking at him with narrowed eyes, a fag on her lip and her sweater up under her chin.

You're a bastard, she says.

You've got nice tits, he says back.

A train comes squealing into the station and he kisses her neck, feels her go soft under him. Her nails dig into his arms and the grass flattens over them both in the train's rush of wind.

All Money Down

In October the basic wage went up a quid, but the union wasn't satisfied, it being way below the claim, though Sam couldn't get angry – a pound was a pound. He knew that bastard Menzies would keep the screws on them as long as he lasted, and he looked like lasting forever. Anyway, the big knobs of the union didn't seem much different from the enemy these days. You'd never pick em for workers, not in a month of Sundays, and a man'd be a fool to trust em an inch. The hell with em. It was spring and he'd be taking home a quid he didn't have last week. And he needed the money. These days at the races, everything he backed came home hanging its arse like its back legs'd been sawn off. He hadn't taken a win or a place since Christmas, though he figured it was all money down against the pot coming his way.

Sam didn't mind the Mint work so much. It cheered him up to be around the money and he wouldn't pretend it was otherwise. The whole place filled with the stink of melting and burning, the thump of the presses and the whang of steel gates. He oiled machines and wiped them down with cotton waste. He stood on the belt line spotting for duds and took the trollies back and forth. He had no enemies there, and though they were a foulmouthed bunch of bastards, he thought they were decent sorts. Everyone had little perks but no one'd tolerate serious diddling. Any dinkum thief found himself ushered into the shadowy part of the courtyard where a few words of advice would be delivered.

It was clear enough to Sam that the other blokes were uneasy about his stumpy hand. It wasn't just their good nature that kept them off his back, they were frightened of having his luck rub off on them.

Sam took to sucking big round peppermints at work, and he always had one stuffed in his cheek when it came to going out through the gates each afternoon. The security bloke frisked them all and the gates opened for them, two by two. There weren't many coins bigger than a peppermint and it was easy to take something out now and then for the kids, though they were getting old for it now. One time he came out with a Snowy River Scheme Commencement Medallion. It was a hell of a peppermint to be sucking, but he turned it appreciatively in his cheek as the security man checked his pockets.

Now the days were getting longer and the light was lasting, he'd walk up Hay Street in the evenings and hear the clock on the town hall toll the hour. He liked the walk in the warm five o'clock breeze better than the closepressed tram to the station. People would be hurrying along the pavements, calling, whistling, dropping things, skylarking. Pretty women would be spilling out of Bairds and Foys and Alberts. In Forrest Place, in the rank shade of the GPO, old diggers sat bathing in the breeze and swapping news pages. European fruit sellers, Balts and Italians, would be haranguing from the footpath with their sad faces weary as unmade beds, and along Wellington Street trolley buses would haul full loads of arms and legs up the hill. The sky would be fading blue. The station was sootrimmed and roaring with crowds. When a train came Sam swung up and stood in the doorway with his gladstone bag and hat in hand and he waited the three stops knowing he was young enough to be walking it, lazy enough, though, to know better.

The day the basic wage was upped a quid, he got out at his stop and a tall, thin, long-jawed woman stopped him on the platform.

You Mr Pickles? Sam Pickles?

Yeah. Yes that's me.

Passengers faded from the platform, the train heaved itself round the bend. Two date palms down on the street waved solemnly.

You don't know me, and I really don't know you, and I've got nothin against you or anythin, but I think you should try to control your wife. She said it in a gaspy, short winded

157

way, and her mouth was all atremble by the time she finished, but Sam felt so black with fury that he wasn't in the least bit sympathetic.

And I think you should mind your own bloody business, lady.

He stuffed his Akubra on his head and went on, his bag butting against his knee.

Well it's my business, too! she called out, thickthroated with sobs. It's my husband I'm talkin about. I've got youngens to look after and she's got no right. It's a mortal sin!

Sam went down the stairs with the fury going out of him. He walked along Railway Parade where the dandelions moved in the jaded light and by the time he had reached Cloudstreet there was only a dull soreness in him, something inevitable, something he knew he'd been resigned to for years.

Now Black Now White

Rose loves that weird boy, she knows it. She leaves the spuds boiling on the stove and the snags spitting on low heat to go upstairs to listen to him tinkling on the piano. If everything was like the books she reads it'd be sweet, miraculous music coming down from that bookless, windowless library up there, but its just jangly noise though Fish doesn't thump it any more. Nowadays she can hardly get up the stairs without breaks, but she gets up without stopping this time, for fear of missing a look at Fish.

Breathless and giddy she stands at the half-open library door to watch him with his back to her, pushing the keys gently as if marvelling at the difference in them still – now black now white, first a finger, then a full hand spread. It's horror movie music and she thinks of some poor sad movie monster hearing bittersweet music.

He's big now, Fish. Fourteen and growing like a man. His hair is fair and long, half obscuring his little ears. These days his feet are on the ground when he plays.

Rose can't see the look on his face. She'd expect it to be a glowing, rapt expression, but it's grim and hardset. She listens to the thang-dung-dim-tink of his music and wants only to touch him, to be friendly, and yes, if she's honest, to get a kiss. It's ridiculous – she's too old for him and he's a slow learner and a tenant and a Lamb, for gawdsake, but he's just the grousest looking boy, and his hot blue eyes make you go racy inside. Rose steps into the room and Fish stops without looking around. Just inside the door the sickest, foulest feeling comes over her. She knows it from before, the taste of that horrible rotten smell that comes not into your nose, but straight into your mouth, onto your tongue, sliding round on you, curdling your spit till you're ready to vomit.

She races out and stumps downstairs, sick and hurting.

The old man is in the kitchen, turning his hat over in his hands like a man at a wake.

I turned the snags off, he says. The spuds look ready.

Sorry. I haven't got any greens ready.

Don't bother. Where's the boys?

Dunno.

He doesn't even enquire after the old girl. She watches him put his hat on a chair and roll his sleeves up in a distracted sort of fashion. Then he settles on her, looks hard at her. She blushes, still a bit shaky from the upstairs feeling.

Jesus, Rose, you look like a corpse these days. It's a crime you know, he says quietly, a bloody crime.

I get fat.

You haven't been fat since you were hangin off a tit. He smiles. Now you've grown yer own.

Rose turns to the stove and shakes the dark sausages round in the pan, seething with shame.

You have to start eatin again. It's not a joke anymore, love.

I can't, Dad.

Christ, you must be starvin hungry!

I am. But I can't any more. I just toss it up again.

Bullshit, you've just talked yourself off yer tucker. Siddown an eat some with me. Carn, it'll help. Some warmth comes back into his voice, as if he's trying hard to hold himself back. Come on, love. You'll bloody die if you don't eat.

Dad, I can't.

Rose gives him his snags and spuds and goes back to the stove.

Give yerself some.

Dad.

Put some on your plate. Go on.

Really, Dad, I –

Do it.

You don't –

Do it, bugger you!

Rose comes to the table, puts her plate down shaky and frightened. It's not like him, it's just not him. She can't smell grog on his breath, just the peppermints.

Eat it, he says. I'm not havin you starve to death in my own house. I didn't go through a fuckin depression and a war to see my children turn their nose up at food –

Chub and Ted eat enough, those fat bastards –

Eat, Rose.

His fist is set on the table now, his fingerless chunk. Rose sees the pulse in his neck.

She spears a snag and bites it in half, chews recklessly and feels it slip down greasy and fine tasting.

All of it.

She can't see him for waterblur now, but she eats and lets her cheeks run.

All of it.

But she's up and running for the door with it all ramming upwards in her before she can even think about it. On the back step she feels her whole guts jerk and crank. White burns in her eyes and blood roars in her ears.

The house claps with the slamming of doors. Rose wonders if it was the food or the feeling of the library, or maybe both. She just wants to disappear.

You orright, love?

It's Mrs Lamb coming up from the tent with a basket of beans.

Lord, you look like a shadow, Rosemary. Let me take

you to a doctor. Mr Lamb's got the truck out the front.

No, Rose gasps. No, it's orright. Just the curse, I get like this when me time comes.

You look like your time'll be here sooner than you think. Wait here and I'll organize the truck.

Mrs Lamb.

Don't move.

Rose waits till the little woman is gone right through the house and out the front before she bolts. She runs like a scarecrow, and it feels as pathetic as it looks.

Dusk

The library is empty. The walls flicker with a black, gleeful flinching of shade. A smell of shit and corruption rises out of the wood, causing the air to go fluid with sickness as the last notes of the departed boy ring in the room. And then the air stiffens. The shadows press in against themselves all of a sudden and dust motes freeze immobile in the air.

Down on the street, looking up with bloodshot eyes, a dark, woolly man stands with a stick, beating it slowly against his knee, humming under his breath until the dusk claims him and the library goes back to being vile and dark and fluid.

Night After Night

Sam Pickles walked the neighbourhood as if defying them all, daring someone to come up and try it on him. He'd kill them, he'd kill anything the way he was. Rose kept clear of him, dying before his bloody eyes. The boys had that arrogant chemical sense about them, as if they smelled a loser. And Dolly. Good old Dolly. Well the shadow was on him, the Hairy Hand of God, and he knew that being a man was the saddest, most useless thing that could happen to someone. To be alive, to be feeling, to be conscious. It was the cruellest bloody joke. In the dark, night after night, he raised his mangled fist to the sky and said things that frightened him.

ʄ Not a Brass Razoo ʅ

The warm weather came with November and Rose was glad of it. No more shameful holey tights, no more sleeping under old greatcoats for want of a decent blanket. The sun levering in through the kitchen window cheered her up so much she could hardly hear what the old girl was saying. It was noon. Dolly was up early. She had the look about her of a person who'd just been making grave decisions. It made Rose want to giggle, the way the old girl's breasts slapped together like applause under her cotton nightie.

You know you'll have to leave school, don't you? Dolly was saying.

Rose felt the dreaminess evaporating.

What?

We haven't got a brass razoo.

I wonder why. What you don't drink, the old man gives to the bookies.

Don't backchat me, girl, or I'll give you one.

Rose sighed and looked out the window. She loved school. When she could avoid the humiliations of being poor, when she could sink back into the anonymous mass of the class, she did love it. She wanted to be a clever woman, to know poetry and mathematics, to go to Africa and discover something. She didn't do too badly, either. Her marks were good, though they'd been slipping all year as she missed more and more days as the weakness came over her. It would have been easier if she had friends but she frightened kids off with her intensity, the hardness of her that no one would understand. A friend had to be true to death. Rose didn't care for chums, she wanted sisters in blood and loyalty. She never went to the socials they organized with the boys' school. Boys thought she didn't laugh enough and her prettiness was turning to caricature the more she lost weight. Sometimes

162

she thought she was dying and the thought strengthened her, cheered her up. It gave shape to things.

You'll have to get a job. It'll help us all out.

Oh, anything to help out, Mum. Should I still do the cooking and the cleaning, or will you be getting someone else in?

Dolly rose and came at her with a swinging fist and Rose felt a giggle coming up in her.

Leave off! the old man yelled from the doorway.

The old girl stopped.

Don't you touch her, Dolly. Don't you put a finger on her, or –

Or what, you weak mongrel?

The old man had his doublebreaster on, and the hat with the feather in it. The room smelled of shaving soap all of a sudden. He was dressed for the races.

Or you'll be out on the street where you fuckin belong.

Rose got ready for a full tilt brawl. In a way it was a relief. There'd been a silence in the place for the last year or two, an aching, torniqueted quiet, and now it felt like coming to something. But Dolly just went past him and out the door. In the room next door the bedsprings groaned.

The old man smiled. Thought I was gunna get snotted, for a sec there. Get some clobber on and come to the races with me, eh? You can have a bet. I'll buy ya bag a chips.

Rose shook her head. The old man shrugged.

Bag a lettuce leaves?

Carn Fish

Carn Fish, says Lester. Hop up and come out. It's a nice day. You can take your shirt off and get some sun. Can't lie on that bed all day. Carn, yev got legs and arms. And ears Fish, are you listening?

It's a worry to see Fish like this, hardfaced, flat on his back, looking at the ceiling in a way you can never be sure about. He's getting big now, and Lester can't help but

163

wonder what it'll be like in a couple of years when the boy's as big as him and brimming with all that aimless strength he's storing.

When he can be got out of the room and downstairs he'll sit at the kitchen table and spin a china bowl wah-wah-wah on the table with a joyless sort of concentration that draws all attention from around him. If you're standing at the sink or stoking the stove or even going by the door, that wah-wah-wah, the science, the balance of it, the way he can do it like that, it draws you over, and you stand and watch, see his big fingers wrap on the china and send it topping across the polished jarrah surface. But he can only do it when he's not upset or agitated. When the boy is angry or frightened he can barely walk straight. It's a sight, an awful sight, to see him bellowing mad. He actually looks blind with rage. He'll stagger and stumble, lurch into doorframes and walls and not find his feet again. He'll lie there kicking and rolling like a bull in a bog with the most bestial, furious, hurt noise a body could imagine.

It frightens Lon and even the girls get scatty when it happens. Oriel turns into a pillar box, and Lester feels his teeth trying to force each other back into his jaw. It's a hard and unlovely thing to see, and they're not alone in flinching from it. From out of time and space, those long glass planes of separation and magnitude, it's impossible to witness again and again without grief and wonder. Across the planes all things still play themselves out, all fun and fear, all the silliness and quaking effort, all the bickering and twitching, all the people going about the relentless limited endeavour of human business, and the sight of your body rolling like that, bursting with voice and doubleness, reminds you that the worlds are still connected, the lives are still related and the Here still feels the pangs of history. Those who've gone before do not lose their feelings, only their bodies. I stare out from behind the sideboard mirror and see you there, Fish. I don't forget.

Fish! Lester says down there. Fish, get up. Come on, boy. Please?

Wanna go in the boat with Quick.

Lester sighs and sits on the bed beside him.

Quick isn't here, boy.

We see the stars. Up in the water.

Thank God he's old enough still to take himself to the outhouse, Lester thinks. I couldn't bear it if it was worse than this.

Quick's gone away for a while, Fish.

I want the water, Lestah.

I'll take you down to the river sometime, son, when your mother's finished drivin Mr Clay off her mind. But even as he says it, it tastes like a lie. He knows Oriel will never let him near the river again.

In the boat. Up in the water.

Hey, listen. I know. You can have a boat in the back. That's it, I'll get you a boat to have here. Dyou like that, mate? With oars and everything. You can even go fishin. Waddyasay?

Fish looks at the ceiling.

What's your name? Lester prompts.

Fish.

Fish who?

Fish Lamb.

What's your proper name?

Samson.

Who's your Mum?

. . .

Who's your Mum?

. . .

Your Dad?

You, Less.

Sisters?

Red and Hattie and Lane.

Brothers?

Quick Lamb.

You forgot one.

. . .

You forgot one.

165

Fish Lamb.

One more. Small.

Lon. That Lon. The baby.

He's eleven, Fish. Where dyou live?

Cloudstreet. The big house.

That's right. You're clever enough, cobber. Wanna sing a song?

The house sad, Lestah.

What? How dyou know that?

It talks.

Lester can't suppress a chuckle.

Fish rolls onto his side and puts a hand carelessly across Lester's thigh. The veins in his arm are dark and dense.

It hurts.

Lester kisses the boy.

Carn, I'll spin the knife if you come down.

The knife never lies, says Fish.

Downstairs in the cool kitchen Lester spins the butter knife and watches the light of it in his son's eyes. Oriel is banging up and down in the shop up front and Hat and Elaine are laughing at something.

This is for who'll see Quick come in the door first, Lester says.

The blade turns and turns, slow, slower and Lester thinks – is this all there is to it? Just chance, luck, the spin of the knife? Isn't there a pattern at all; a plan?

Me! Me! Lestah, it me!

Lester laughs without effort. He slaps Fish on the shoulder.

Okay, this is to see who'll be Captain of the boat.

Me again.

Don't count your chickens before they hatch.

Ah?

Just watch the knife.

The knife never lies.

Lester can't help but wonder.

166

Sam's surprised to find himself sitting on the lip of the bath tub opening and closing the razor like this. It's amazing to him that his face should look so far past him, and all the tan gone out of it, his flesh looking like a patch of sand that seagulls have walked across. It's cool in here, and he can smell the mortuary stink of phenyle on the floor. No, this is the big surprise, finding himself here, looking down the blade, snapping it back together like somebody altogether different. It's odd what people will do, and what they might do, what he might do. He watches his Adam's apple rise like a plum bob in his neck. Now look at that neck, he thinks.

Sam knows he's not the sort to go round and put the frighteners on Gerry Clay. Well, that's what he's telling himself. Maybe I'm just too bloody gutless to go down there and beat the piss out of him, he thinks. But, Jesus, I'm hardly the onefisted cyclone, am I? What'm I gunna do, stump the bastard to death? Hammer im with ghostly sensations? Oh, but there'd be ways, no doubt.

A picket with a nail in the end.

A sock full of sand.

Acid, any amount.

Running the bastard over, only Sam doesn't know how to drive a car.

Rat poison.

Arson.

Hired help.

There's some manly comfort in knowing there'd be means and ways, but they're the sort of comfort you get from knowing a bloke can always go back to Mother when life fails him. It's there, alright, but the consequences will get you by the nuts.

And anyway, the anger isn't there. That's not what he feels. It's more the hopelessness of knowing, some elemental, inevitable thing about it. It's loss, that's what. Not like losing money and friends and fingers. Geez, he thought, losin's nothin new. I graduated with flying colours from that fuckin

167

school, after all. But this, *this* losing hurts. The surprise of it, the absolute shock of it. Not to have her . . . doing all that, but for it to hurt like this. That's the nasty part.

He looks at his bewildered white face in the mirror. He loves his wife. He's forgotten all about that bit, and he looks like a man who's woken to another century. The blade is open. He can see it through the blur of water, see it shaking, coming his way like a ray of light.

Rose stepped into the bathroom with goo on her hands and there he was. She stepped back a little to let her mind catch up. She saw the mirror tilted a little and peppered with flyspecks. Towels rammed moist to the edge of fermentation through the towel rack. A bar of Velvet like hard cheese in the basin. The old man wore a singlet and tufts of blonde hair feathered from beneath it. His grey trousers wrinkled. Stockinged feet catching lint at the heels. There was real silence here. The open blade of the razor had a cheery gleam, poised there at his unlathered neck wet from tears.

Time, he said. Time.

Rose pushed the door closed behind her and a ball of dust wheeled across the floor to his feet.

She saw the naked knuckles of his stump whitening in their hopeless effort to make a fist. He set the razor down with great care and began to breathe long and ragged.

A man needs to keep his whiskers down.

You need lather, Dad.

Rose went by him to the basin and washed her hands. She made a fair production of it; it took less time to shower. When she wiped her hands, she put her back to the wall and looked down upon him. She felt the blood doing its clockwork in her limbs. She got his direct gaze in passing and held it until it was clear he couldn't look away. He looked small as a schoolboy, hopeless and frail like she'd never seen a person before.

It's just that you feel sorry for yourself, sometimes, Rose. I'm a weak, stupid, useless bastard and that's, that's . . .

168

Rose grabbed his head and pulled it to her breast, felt his sobs like another heart against her ribcage. She felt pity and misery and hatred and she knew this was how it would always be.

He was right; he was all those things and worse, and he probably didn't have much reason to close that cutthroat.

What are we all sposed to do? he said.

I dunno, she said, furious. I don't know. I love you, Dad. You can't do it to me. You can't. I'd piss on your grave, I tell you I would.

Oh, you're a hard bastard, he said with a sobbing laugh. You're the fuckin business you are.

My oath, she said, kissing his head, steeling herself against tears, against weakness, against the great blackness behind her eyes.

You're the one, he said, getting himself back. You're the one, orright. You're a good girl.

Yeah, Rose thought, I'm sixteen and I don't eat and I fall down dizzy twice a day and now I'm pulled outta school. Oh, I'm the one.

You've grown up in a hurry, he said, pulling back from her and wiping his eyes on his singlet.

I wasn't *in* a hurry.

But you've grown up.

Keep me in school.

There's no money, love. We haven't got a nail to hang our arses on.

It was warm in there now and the afternoon light had a twisting traffic of motes to bear.

Don't hate me, he said.

I don't. I pity you, Dad. Because you still love her.

And you don't?

Oh, I stopped that years ago. It wouldn't be myself I'd use a razor on.

Rose. People are . . . who they are.

Then they should change! People should do things for themselves, not wait for everyone else to change things for em!

You can't beat your luck, love.

169

No, you have to be your luck. There's nothin else, there's just you.

Sam smiled, shaking his head. You'll go a long way.

Yes, she thought. Africa. Paris. New York. A long way from this stinking old house and the smell of death and sick. Like a shot. One day.

The Vanilla Victory

Late in January, as summer got its teeth in and the front lawns of Cloudstreet turned the colour of underfelt and the stretches of new macadam began to bubble and boil, Oriel Lamb wiped out G. M. Clay with vanilla icecream. His morale was shot already, but she sent him packing with Lester Lamb's Amazing Vanilla Double Cream. She hounded the ice man till he began to think he was on the payroll himself. She bought in supplies of milk like a company quartermaster. No one rested in the evenings as mosquitoes crowded against the screens in the breathless dark. They turned the churns, skimmed, sluiced, measured and poured. The girls bitched over whose turn it was to be at the ice chest stacking the tins to set. Hat was having time off to go dancing with a bloke up from the country and Oriel was working her hard to pay for lost time. Oriel Lamb liked the idea that their icecream contained a few parts sweat to each gallon of milk. Lester tested and tooled about, touching up his Amazing Vanilla Double Icecream signs. He'd rather not have been at war, but it was nice to see his name in print at any rate, and the nervous thrill it gave him to be backing a winner was enough to egg him on.

The people of Cloudstreet and beyond bought the stuff before it had time to set. Even before Christmas they'd gotten a taste for it and you could see people walking beneath the jacarandas in the cool light of morning unrolling their *West Australian* with the deliberation of people trying to keep their minds off icecream. Neighbours would pass in the street, nod and grumble about Menzies and Korea, careful not to look each other in the eye and give away what they were really thinking. The Subiaco Junior Cricket team could not be found one Saturday morning, forfeiting a big match, and no one needed an explanation if they lived within a mile of Cloudstreet. Oriel Lamb began taking orders a week in advance. Every gallon of icecream bought entitled customers to tuppence off the price of sliced ham, a penny off the price of spuds, and a discount on cornflour to be personally negotiated.

Lester Lamb found himself bringing two truckloads of goods back from the metro market each dawn. Cloudstreet became an official tram stop out on the main road, and ladies swung down with wicker baskets right outside G. M. Clay-Ex AIF to walk down the blistering street and join the queues. They paid in advance, they fainted on the verandah, they pleaded. Lon sold lemonade to those waiting in the sun, and the Pickleses' cocky shrieked Fair Dinkum regular as a timepiece.

When Oriel Lamb saw a woman buy eight quid's worth of icecream one morning, a husband's full weekly pay, she knew that the battle was over and it was time for law and order before looting broke out. G. M. Clay closed up shop and Lester Lamb tried to scale down production without immediate success. The iceman wept, as though he'd been relieved of his post. Angry letters, unstamped and nasty as a note from a church elder, turned up in the mailbox. But in the end Oriel called a halt and put up signs: NO MORE ICECREAM. CHEAP HAM.

It was January 19, 1951. The Lambs slept the sleep of the victorious.

In the morning Oriel went down to Cambridge Street, picking her way past enquiring shoppers, to see G. M. Clay. She'd decided to let him stay on. After all, he had a family to feed. By way of reparations, he would be compelled to paint out the Ex AIF part of his sign, and thereafter no more need be said. But when she knocked on the doors, only Mrs Clay was there.

What do *you* want? Mrs Clay looked at her in disbelief.

171

She had the eyes of a weeper, and the morning light was not kind.

I came to talk to your husband, factually.

Well, e's gone. That'll deprive youse all of a laugh.

Where's he gone to?

It's a big state. Anywhere he likes, I'd say. He's got all the money that was left. No flies on him, eh. Mrs Clay gave out a bitter little laugh. Her hands shook in her apron pockets.

I was here to offer him a settlement. What's he left you to live on?

Nothin. Not a bent penny.

How long'll he stay away?

Oh, he's off for good. Told me to marry Father O'Leary if I needed a bit of –

The children?

Mrs Clay sobbed. She sounded like a dog choking on a string of bacon fat.

You need a job, Oriel Lamb said. She shifted on her sandals like a fighter. Come and work with us. There's room in the house. You could bring the children.

Mrs Clay sagged against the door jamb and a squadron of sweaty kids hauled by on rattling bikes. Oriel Lamb watched her shuddering and sucking in breath every now and then.

Go away, said Mrs Clay. Just go now.

I'm offering you a job, a home.

And I'm telling you to go to Hell!

I'm . . . I'm sorry, said Oriel Lamb who had not said those words since 1911.

Go to Hell! Mrs Clay slammed the doors to.

Oriel Lamb walked home the long way, taking it in. Not for a moment had she thought . . . not by a long way . . . There was the offer and it was refused and a grey shame settled on her in the hard summer morning light.

There would have to be food parcels delivered daily.

A weekly allowance.

She'd see to it right away. She'd not let it pass. This was

a sin. It was her, because of Quick. This was what the heart did to you. This was what happened when you lost a son, another son, and now she knew how it must have felt for that Sam Pickles waking one morning to see the bandages, to feel the tingling but know that there was only a space.

By the embankment, as the trains swept by, Oriel Lamb wept the sound of a slaughteryard and the grass bowed before her.

Mrs Lamb Weeps

Rose Pickles sometimes thought maybe she'd steal Fish Lamb and run away with him. She thought of the places they could hide outside Perth, little fishermen's shacks behind dunes and estuary curves that they could sneak supplies into to live a quiet life in love. She still watched him out in the yard as he rowed the old dory hull with two sticks and looked up into the sun as though it was a pool of water. She'd meet him on the landing and breathe a kiss onto his ear in passing. She'd watch him standing at the window snapping his braces against his chest. He was gentle and soft and . . . But she knew it was a stupid, silly dream she had. Fish was barely more than a baby in the head and his looks were going as he got older. In a couple of years he'd be big and fat and brutish. Yes, he'd make terrible scenes in public places and have to be locked in his room, maybe even strapped to his bed. She wasn't stupid enough to think it wouldn't happen.

But look at him down there on the front fence with the hot easterly in his long hair. Didn't it take half your sense away and all your breath?

Rose saw Mrs Lamb come blubbering down the street. Crying. Like a person. Mrs Lamb crying. Rose saw her fall against the gate grabbing at Fish who didn't move, who just looked across the road where no one was, straight as a board with his mother's arms around him. Oh, it hurt to watch, even after the surprise, it hurt to see.

Rose went downstairs exhausted with emotion, tired,

brittle with feeling. She sat in the kitchen for an hour looking up jobs in the paper.

And then her own mother, missing all night, came in dressed to the gills and bleeding.

Bad, Worse, Worstest

Dolly stood at the sink and ran the water. She put the dishrag to her face and set her teeth. That was something, still having the teeth. Through the kitchen window she could see, with one eye at least, the fruit trees and the shadeless brown stretches, the tin fence and the powerful calm.

Good morning, she said to Rose.

Rose rustled her *West Australian*.

Dolly felt the hard chill between them. She turned, wringing blood out of the rag, and let her daughter see what Gerry Clay had given her as a parting gift. The whole side of her face was the colour of a stormcloud and rising angrier by the minute. Even now her left eye was closed. Her nose and lip bled a little still, and the knuckles of the hand holding up the rag were skinned raw. Rose looked up and took it in without expression. She didn't even seem suprised, and in a way Dolly was grateful that there'd be no hysterics. There wasn't much of a girl left in Rose, she knew. Dolly didn't know whether to be proud or ashamed.

Want some ice?

Hngh! Got any icecream? Dolly felt tears coming and she was burning with a wild, unfocused hatred.

Rose went to the icebox and Dolly saw the brown sticks of her legs as she chipped at the block.

Ta.

She wrapped the ice in the rag and held it over her eye and before long her whole body seemed to have cooled, while all the time Rose looked on without moving. The old man's cockatoo screeched out on the back step.

Ah, what a mess.

Rose said nothing. Dolly made her way to the table and

174

sat down. It was no great shock that things should go from bad to worse to worstest. Right now, she couldn't feel a thing, and this had to be the lousiest day of her life.

I used to wish you wouldn't grow up to hate me, Rose. That's what I used to think.

Rose's lips were set together, as though she was exerting great control over herself.

And then you grow up an hate me anyway. Well, yer have yer hopes.

Rose folded the newspaper, then folded it again.

Hoping is what people do when they're too lazy to do anything else.

People can't do everything they wanna.

They just want some things more than others.

Dolly sighed.

Okay, so you hate me, let's leave it at that. I'm sore.

Did you hate *your* mother?

Dolly got up. I need to lie down a while.

You didn't answer.

Me whole face is fallin off.

I'm gonna love *my* children, I swear to God.

Lookit this. This is what you get from men.

Some men. Other men!

All men!

Dolly didn't have the fight in her. Any other time she'd have been across the room, tearing and slashing, but she felt weak and giddy.

You shouldn't hate me, she said, turning for the door. It doesn't help. Ya shouldn't do it.

Like you say, people can't do everything they wanna. Anyway, I'm used to it now, Rose said, as Dolly went out the door, and then suddenly she was shouting: And besides, I've gotten to like it. Hating you is the best part of bein alive!

Climbing the stairs, Dolly had the old question come back. Bad mother, or no mother at all? Christalmighty, she should know the answer to that one by now.

Closed Shop

The Lambs closed up shop and stayed indoors. The house was quiet. Outside cicadas rattled and the grass burnt in the summer sun.

We'll go crabbin, said Lester, that's what we'll do. Down at the river.

River! said Fish, dropping his spinning bowl in a splintering crash.

Carn, love, said Lester. Orry? A feed of crabs'll cheer you up. And the girls could do with a break.

Carn, said Hat.

Carn, said Elaine.

Carn, said Red.

Oriel poked dead limbs into the fire and sparks rose in the air like stars being born. Fish had cried himself to sleep tethered with a dressing gown cord to an old Moreton Bay fig and she could see the side of his face in the firelight. Whiskers had begun to show on his jaw. She smelt river mud and mothballs in the blankets spread on the grass. Mosquitoes hung around whining like an electric current. Out on the water Lester and the girls were laughing and the lamp swung wildly with the city lights steady behind.

She knew this scene. Her life always came back to the river. A long time ago she'd been baptized in a river. She'd kissed Lester Lamb by the river the first time long before that. And that night, that long, horrid night by the estuary at Margaret, when her men had walked on water and the lamp had gone out, that's what had brought them here to this life with one son gone and one missing and a feeling in your chest that you didn't know yourself anymore.

Whacko! Lester yelled, hoiking another crab into the tub. This is livin, girls.

The water was only shin deep. It was cool and the sandy bottom was ridged with tidal corduroy across which the big

176

blue mannas were manoeuvring. Out here you could smell the fire on the beach. The sky was like a reflection of night water.

One more, Dad, and that's it, said Hat, you're fillin the tub.

Lester turned and saw in the light Red held up that it was true. The tin bathtub he had floating behind, tied to a belt loop, was nearly down to the gunwales and alive with the groping and grovelling of claws.

Orright. Last one.

I'm tired, said Elaine, shouldering her scoop net.

Red moved up alongside him with the lamp and Hat moved vigilantly with her elbows out, scoop ready. Lester was proud of the way he could bluff a crab one way and scoop him neatly in a back-handed gesture and send it flying into the tub.

The last crab of the night was a big gnarlclawed job, and Lester was caught off balance by all the competition. He scooped deep and tossed wide and Hat got the crab on the chest, its claw fixing firmly to her nipple beneath the old blouse. Lester could never have been prepared for the words she had to say. She jogged on the spot brushing at the squirming brooch of a thing until Lester swung the scoop to hit her fair in the chest. Hat went back in the water and the crab went back home.

When Red and Elaine and Lester got her upright, the four of them stood and listened to Oriel bellowing from the beach.

That crab was a rapist, said Red.

Red! Lester was shocked.

It's disgustin, Red said. Even they're the same. Ugh, males!

Hat rubbed herself and said a word that Lester would not repeat.

Oriel broke dead wood over her knee and threw it onto the flames. There was bread and butter, brown vinegar, chopped onions and tomatoes, and a drum steaming with boiled

177

crabs. They ate, crushing glossy red claws, dragging long strands of meat from legs, and they laughed and watched the fire until Lester broke into song.

> *In Dublin's fair city*
> *Where the girls are so pretty*
> *I first set my eyes on sweet Molly Malone –*

Oh, here he goes.

> *She wheeled a wheelbarrow*
> *Through streets broad and narrow*
> *Crying 'Cockles and mussels alive alive-oh'*

Lester –

> *'Alive, alive-oh*
> *Alive, alive-oh-oh'*

Fish called in his sleep. Quick? Quick?

Wherever the River Goes

With the cord of her dressing gown she ties you to the tree, Fish, even while you sleep because she knows what you'll do. You don't even see her, do you? But she sees you, boy, and she knows what you'll be dreaming of here by the river, the beautiful, the beautiful the river. There's always someone with their fingers in the belt loops of your pants. You're aching with it while those dark angels laugh on the water without you. The river. Remember, wherever the river goes every living creature which swarms will live, and there will be many fish, for this water goes there, that the waters of the sea will become fresh; so everything will live where the river goes.

A dark man comes flying by your tree, you see the white of his eyes and tingle with rumours of glory. The city flickers and warbles along the banks of the Swan and in their homes, along their bars and fences the people go at it as if now is all there is, grabbing, holding, loading up for the short run, others before them, millions behind, not knowing that now is always and never, as from and to will be always and never.

I'm behind the water, Fish, I'm in the tree. I feel your pulse and see you dreaming of Quick out there in the wheat, and I see you coming. Your time will come, Fish, you'll have a second of knowing, a man for a moment, and then it won't matter because you'll be me, free to come and go, free to puzzle and long and love, free of the net of time.

They're eating, Fish. And Quick is shooting, and back home, tingling himself at the black man passing overhead like an owl, the pig is singing.

The Dark, the Dark

The pig lay in his grovel hole with the full darkness swimming over him. Up at the house on the lights out empty side there were flickers at the windows. The filthy porker stirred and caught the scent. His limbs quavered and his head went up. Curtains swished up there and that stink forced itself out through the cracks in the weatherboards. The hens shook and shat, shifting on the perch, and the rooster threw himself at the wire. A dog howled somewhere away off across wind that went slushy with the sounds of birds flying. The sound of choking and laughing up there in the empty Lamb side of Cloudstreet. The pig got to his feet and went quietly but unflaggingly: *Keethro mutila gogma seak seak do, asra do, kum asra do . . .*

The rooster crowed uncertainly and a Pickles slipper came lobbing out of the dark from across the fence, landing with a crash against the dunny door.

Girl on the Switch

Rose Pickles discovered that she really could talk. The moment the big rumplebosomed lady conducting the interview finished her question, Rose knew she had it in the bag. She was off like a shot. The talk that came out of her mouth was like a spiritual inspiration: she was snappy, polite, discreet, accurate and cheerful. Around her she could hear the emporium's turbine hum. Even as she spoke she knew she'd be joining that sound, and she'd never felt so capable in all

179

her life. After the interview she excused herself, fought her way through a battalion of naked mannequins and threw up in the toilet.

She started in the morning.

You should start as an office girl, said Mrs Tisborn, work your way up. But you can talk and you can think, and I'm prepared to try you out on the switchboard. Don't be grateful and don't be late. You may learn to be grateful in time, but you may never learn to be late.

Each morning, before the heat had hold of the day, Rose got up and lit the rocket heater in the bathroom, ate a piece of toast or a carrot, and took a shower. Next door was quiet that first week. Normally there'd be the drag of chairs and the little woman's shouts, the whole crew thumping down the stairs to a dawn breakfast, but this week they were subdued. The shop was open again but things were calm. At the steamy mirror Rose nicked odd dabs of this and that from her mother's makeup box and pulled on the only decent skirt and blouse she had. Her shoes were scuffed and daggy and she had no stockings to wear, but no one was going to make her wear those awful black tights again with the darning scars all over them like the swamp plague. The first morning she thought she looked fair, but the moment she walked into Bairds she knew she looked like a sick dog's breakfast and she'd have to crack hardy till pay day.

She got the train into Perth station. In the cramped carriages men smelled of serge and peppermints; their hair was all at the top of their heads and their ears stood out like taxi doors. The women smelled of cologne and stale sweat even this early and they seemed tired and distracted. Rose saw the veins strangling in their calves, saw how their dresses dragged up, and the way the older women's feet seemed gnarled and disturbed by shoes whose platform soles looked better suited to knocking in nails than walking on.

West Perth rolled by and then the dark verandahs of Roe Street. From up on the rails the city looked choked. Cars, trolley-buses, surging workers, the elbow to elbow clutter of commerce. It didn't have the plain, windy spaciousness of Geraldton's main street, but Geraldton was barely a town compared to this. Rose liked the idea of sending herself into this furious movement every morning, and besides Geraldton had just become a childhood memory.

She crossed into Forrest Place where all the men with pinned-back sleeves and crutches and RSL badges were gathering to bitch and sigh together. The GPO was sombre and imposing. Murray Street bristled with commencement of business. As Rose went into Bairds the overhead fans were turning already and floor staff were flurrying to beat the supervisor's opening hour walk. It was a great womanly adventure, it seemed.

Behind the Staff Only door Mrs Tisborn was waiting. Rose went in and surrendered gladly to her training.

The switchboard was a fearsome altar of a thing that first week. Mrs Tisborn stood behind and hissed instructions while Rose searched for the right jack, the right hole, the right cord, the right number, the right moment. The headset clamped her skull and the mornings went on as though time was fiddling the books, but Rose learnt quickly and it wasn't long before Mrs Tisborn's violet breath was receding. Near lunchtime on the second day she could relax enough to comprehend who else was in the room, and at the break she met the Girls on the Switch – Darleen, Merle, and Alma.

Ole Teasebone given yer the runaround this mornin, love? What wuz yer name again?

Rose.

Yull be right. Yull put a hurdle in er girdle, won't she loves? Eh, girls?

Rose found it difficult to distinguish Darleen, Merle or Alma by voice alone because they sounded so alike. They spoke with a cackling kind of pegnosed lilt and laughed like they were being dug in the ribs by a shovel. They were roughmouthed and irritable, with the eyes of rouged cattle. They showed her where to get the best pie and chips in Murray Street, the very thought of which kept her off lunch in general, and they introduced Rose to the addiction of listening in. They were silly, dizzy scrubbers, and she liked them. They were the grousest ladies she'd ever met.

On the train home that Friday, she missed her station because something awful had come into her mind. The switchboard girls reminded her of her mother. The only thing that helped was their bovine bad looks and the fact that they laughed a lot. Just plug em in an shut up, Rose, that's all yer need to know.

Yeah, she thought. That's all I should need to know.

On pay day she gave the old man half her pay and he laughed and gave it back. On Saturday morning at teabreak, Rose bought herself a pair of Nightingale Seamless Stockings and a jar of Helena Rubenstein's Estrogenic Hormone Cream. On the way home, the train carriage wasn't big enough for her.

Geoffrey Birch Came Calling

Geoffrey Birch from Pemberton came calling for Hat. He was handsome and dull, with knees as big as soup plates, and Hat thought he was simply gorgeous. He took her to dances in his FJ Holden. He laughed at all of Hat's wisecracking jokes. He loved her.

It disgusted Red, who imagined them smooching in that FJ down by the river. Elaine was sad and jealous. She liked having Hat around and she wanted a man.

Oriel flicked the shop lights off and on at midnight Fridays so Cloudstreet looked like a ship beacon and the FJ looked like a marauding enemy vessel.

Lester started putting a few bob aside for a wedding. He wondered if Geoffrey Birch knew he was courting the marble champion of the world.

And Hat? Hat was away with the fairies.

Jacks and Jills

Shove the jacks into the jills, says Alma at the switch. Rose blushes and laughs.

Good morning, Bairds, can I help you?

Bairds, good morning, sir, can I help you?

Can I help you?

Bairds.

Hello? Hello?

One moment.

I'm sorry, this is Bairds. Oh, you want *beds*!

Putting you through.

Jack into Jill! yells Darleen, and they all crack up.

Gawd, love, why don't you feed yerself Good morning, Bairds.

Merle's in love with a dwarf Bairds, good morning.

Good morning, Bairds yer a liar, she's lyin.

Putting you through he's shorter than Mum's pastry!

Short ones've got fat thingies Good morning, Bairds.

Well she's hardly the eye of the needle One moment madam.

Youse sheilas are gettin fouler every year Can you hold?

He's never asked me, thank you, sir.

Disgustin Bairds.

Bairds.

Bairds.

Exhausted from not laughing, Rose ploughs through every day with a crazy happiness. She takes home pay and the pavement smell of the city. She puts on a bit of flesh. She eats. The world looks different.

Two Old Girls

One night at the Anzac Club while Lester was going dispiritedly through his routine, Oriel met a widow. You could tell she was a survivor, a leftbehind, by the far off look in her eyes and the way her tall, gaunt frame bent forward. Oriel could spot weakness and need a mile off.

Do you believe in Hell, Mrs Lamb? said the woman filling the urn.

Oriel gasped. It was like being struck in the face. Who are you?

183

Beryl Lee, Mrs. Hubby went down with HMAS Perth.
I come down here to –

You're lonely.

Beryl Lee subsided like a folding chair. Tears rolled
down her face from her wild fargone eyes. Oriel held her
close, felt the woman's eyelashes against her shoulder.

You strike me as a Christian woman, sobbed Beryl Lee.
That's what I thought. That's what they say.

If ever I should strike you Beryl, you'd think different.

Oh, Lawd, oh, Lawd.

People stood and watched. Even Lester gave up and
stared from the stage. Two old girls, short and tall, hugging
like kids.

Hell?

Hell is like this. It's this cowering in the bottom of the cellar
far from the smouldering trapdoor, between pumpkins and
tubs of apples. It's the smell of a karri forest rising into the
sky and the bodies of roos and possums returning to the earth
as carbon and the cooking smell falling through the dimness
like this. Trees go off like bombs out in the light and the
cauldron boils and spits all about. Hell is being six years old
and wondering why you're alone in the dark and no one else
has come down yet. It's the sound of your own breathing,
the salty stink of your bloomers, the way the walls have
warmed, the flickering cracks, the screams like a thousand
nails being drawn, the hammering, throttling noises, the
way the rats are panicking and throwing themselves against
things. Hell is that shallowbreathing trance you slip into, the
silence that goes on and on until it's grown outside you and
fallen on the world. Hell is when you hear noises in the world
again, though nothing in yourself, and men's voices make
your throat cry so raw that light bolts into the cellar with
a gout of ash and charcoal and the burning taste of air. Hell is
when you're dragged out past the black bones and belt
buckles that are the others who never came down, out onto
the powder white earth beneath the sky green as bile and

swirling with vapours. Hell is the sight of your father's face streaked with the ride, the twitching cast on him, the registration of facts. Hell. It's only you left, and you're awake.

Oriel woke and it wasn't quite dawn. She lay there in the dimness until her heart settled back a little. With the edge of the blanket she wiped her eyes. Without washing, without making out her daily work plan, she left the tent ungowned and ran to the house, gumbling along like a spud crate to go room to room in the dim house checking that all of them were still there, that it wasn't only her left again. All of them breathing in their beds, helpless and sweet in sleep. And Quick's empty bed where she sat thinking while Fish snored.

Oh, how she hated to be a survivor, to be left. It had been a lonely girlhood for Oriel, even when her father remarried. She was a leftover from some other time, an embarrassment to him, a rival for her stepmother who wasn't much older than her. But she learnt to be strong; she grew it in herself. When her halfbrother Bluey, who she loved like blood, left her on the dock at Albany, climbing the gangway and shouting back over his shoulder: Don't worry, Or, I'll bring a Turk back on the end of me bayonet! she knew she was pushing further into the kingdom of survivorhood. Her father was often away buying horses and there'd be only Oriel and her stepmother and the children. She grew steel in her.

Or.

Either, Or.

She could never find the choices. Even when Lester came by, there was no alternative. Things had gone so far, so much had not been said, the smouldering silence of the house was not something that could be chosen any longer. Besides, he made her laugh the way Bluey had. He was a character, a dag, and pretty soon she loved him.

Oriel went downstairs to where Lester slept. He snored like a teachest being dragged across an iron roof. There was no malice in that man, you had to give him that. She still loved him, the Randolph Scott look of him. Oh yes, yes, there was a Hell, there were Hells abounding, and if there wasn't a Heaven then there was this, the sleeping, the helpless, those that were your own. She was a sinner, she knew, and proud, and angry at God to the point of hatred, but she knew that she'd made a fortress for her own and for whoever sought shelter there, and that it was good, worthy, and priceless.

Which gave her an idea.

Beryl.

Ted Shoots Through

Ted Pickles shoots through. He takes nothing with him but a comb and all his hormones. His mother weeps and puts a bottle of muscat through an upstairs window. Girls in tight sweaters and heels come by and Dolly screams at them.

Chub doesn't notice.

Rose doesn't care.

Sam doesn't say.

And Then Comes Autumn, and Behind it, Winter

And then comes autumn, and behind it, winter when everything happens without anyone expecting it.

Beryl Lee moves in. Oriel senses that Hat will be gone soon and she'll be shorthanded, so she offers Beryl a job. There is no shouting, no refusal. Oriel moves her into Quick's room, moves Fish downstairs with Lester. Beryl mutters Hail Marys at all hours and it sounds like termites. She tears down Quick's horrid magazine pictures, but at night they come back through the walls and dance.

Some nights Dolly wakes to the strangest hum in her ear.

Rain comes with winter.

A postcard comes from Quick. I'm alright, it says, Love Quick. The postmark is smudgy. The picture on the card is of Wave Rock, that grey curling wall like a petrified lava breaker. The Lambs stare at it and keep their thoughts to themselves.

Lester adds up his age one evening and is surprised how old he is. I'm not young, he thinks. My whole life isn't ahead of me. He buys a camera off a Balt at the growers' market to make a record of things.

Chub Pickles announces he wants to be a jockey. At sixteen he weighs fourteen stone already. He likes to eat pork fat before it's cooked, and he often casts a hungry eye at the pig across the fence.

The pig grumbles and shits irritably.

Geoffrey Birch pops the question and Hat goes spare.

The house sighs in the night but no one lets themselves listen. Except Fish.

The Man Who Came Knocking

Sam watched the flesh grow back onto his daughter. It was something to see, truly something. She looked like Ingrid Bergman with her woollen suit and that little cocked hat. It was the shadow coming good on him. When you were losing races like he was, with a kind of awesome genius for it, when you handled money all day, watched it go out by the bale smelling like schoolbooks and then had all weekend to distribute your own, magnanimously, to every bookie and crook on the track, you knew you had to be truly gifted with bad luck. Lately he'd surrendered to the notion that his would be an unlucky life, unlucky in epic proportions, and that any turn of good fortune would be a bolt from the blue. Expect bad luck, was his new creed, and now and then you'll be surprised. It saved him from a lot of disappointment, and when he saw things like Rose these days, he went as silly as a two bob watch.

Things were quiet and uneventful in a losing way that winter. And then some big, hairy bastard came knocking. Sam thought it was a bookie's man come to collect a debt, one of those minor outstandings he had brooding here and there. He stood there inside the flyscreen door and watched the way the fella's gut rolled like a floundering zeppelin across his belt. The man who came knocking had a blue singlet on and wiry black hair growing down from his back along his arms and hands. Sam wondered if maybe it was the union but he couldn't recall the last union man he'd seen who looked like a worker. He felt the rush of wind. The screen door snapped back in his face and he sat abruptly to watch the blood pour into his lap.

My daughter's up the duff, Pickles, and your boy's gettin married. Orright?

Widge wum? Sam said, pinching off his nose.

I've only got one.

Boy, boy. Widge boy are we talkid about?

Ted, Todd, whoever.

You bedder get the righd wum.

Sam felt himself rising by the lapels. The flywire was floating free of the door.

Don't play funny buggers with me, mate. Don't try comin the raw prawn here an now, orright? I'm not askin you any questions an I'm not makin requests here, get my drift, you cop my wallop?

That's wod id was. I'll lie down now.

Next door Sam heard thumping. He'd have a word

about it tomorrow. It was eight o'clock at night already and still that Lester was thumping about. Or maybe it was his own headache starting up.

Sam crashed against the coat-rack and it toppled to the floor with him. Doors started opening and heads appeared. Even the thumping stopped.

You're comprehendin me import here, I take it?

Well, he was from *somebody's* union, talking like that. Sam saw the Lamb door open and bring forth Lester Lamb with his bloody meat cleaver.

Shite! the man who'd come knocking said. Let's go easy in this particular vicinity. Shite!

Sam's brain bubbled into life: He's a mad bastard – be careful. Look at this, for Chrissake! Sam held up his stump and the man's eyes grew in his face.

You just tell me where you live, add I'll be roud wid my boy. We'll sord it out.

But the man who'd come knocking had already backed through the hole in the screen door and was shuffling back across the verandah in his workboots. A wind was blowing. It seemed to sweep him away into the night.

He a friend of yours, Sam? Lester asked.

No, but you are, sport. Take a week's free rent from me.

Pardon?

What would you've done with that hacker there? I mean if you were hard put.

I'm choppin ham bones, Lester said. For soup. If I was hard put for what? It's cheaper than a bone saw.

Sam guffawed. Must be me with the brain damage.

The door'll need fixin, said Lester.

Yep. I reckon so. Listen, can I borrer that cleaver sometime?

Course. What you cuttin?

Thinkin about what them Jews do. You know. Bar miss fart, whatever it is.

Circumcision? Lester went yellow. You?

No, not me, cobber. My eldest. And I tell ya, me hand'll be none too steady. He'll be sittin down to piss.

Lester wiped the blade on his apron.

Don't have children, mate. Whatever you do.

No, Lester said, turning to leave. What?

The Big Country

All day Lester's been remembering a small thing from childhood. He can't think why, but it sets his limbs tingling. In his
head it plays through and through. It's dark and his back
is pelted with rain. He holds onto his father's ears and grips
his neck between his knees. Water swirls all about, invisible in
the night. His father hums above the torrent and a light
swings somewhere ahead. Out in the darkness a voice is crying.

Lester goes back to breaking up bones for tomorrow's
lunch-time soup special. Fish comes in singing:

I woke, the dungeon flamed wif light,
My chains fell off, my heart was free-e-ee
I ro-o-ose, went fo-ororth, and
fo-o-ollowed Thee!

He walks round the kitchen putting his hands on things
and looking at nothing in particular. He sings on to the end
and begins again. Lester watches the gone look in his son's
eyes and finds himself joining in.

My chains fell off,
My heart was free,
I rose went forth and followed Thee!

Fish lapsed into silence.

Hello, boy.

Can I cook?

I'm busy makin the soup, Fish.

I wanna.

You ready for bed?

Nup.

You washed?

Nup.

You better get ready then.

Lemme cook?

I can't stop. Listen, I'll give you a recipe and you go
from there.

Fish looks blankly at him.

Lester flusters up over the big soup pot: I'll draw pictures. The pictures . . . here, come here, where's that blasted pencil. What's this?

Egg.

This?

Bottle.

Milk, alright. *Jug* of milk.

Milk.

This?

Bag.

That's flour. Here, this white stuff.

Do the picture. Fish do the picture. Like yous.

That's right, like I do it every day.

Lester gives him a bowl and a whisk and tries to leave him to it. Fish sings, tuneless and quiet, concentrating on the pictures. He fluffs flour about, gets butter all over his shirt, can't keep his lips away from the milk jug. It's me, thinks Lester: he's being me. He's watched me all this time.

Fish gets a big greasy dollop into a heart tin and looks back at Lester who's forgotten the soup.

It's a bonzer, says Fish, taking the business right down to Lester's habitual finishing words.

It surely is, boy. We'll put it in the oven while you have a bath.

Do stories?

I used to be crippled with stories, Lester thinks, loaded and hopeless with em. Now I can't work up a decent joke.

Cmon, then, I'll tell you stories while you're in the bath.

The farm ones, Lestah.

Lester wipes his hands on his apron and pulls it off. He tidies down the bench, leads the boy down into the bathrom. He doesn't remember the farm, he thinks sadly; a shame to have been robbed of it. He runs the water, throws busted packing cases into the fire box of the heater and undresses the boy. Fish smiles in his face. There's bumfluff on his cheeks now. Lord, he's nearly a man. There's pulpy flesh growing on him; he's fatting up and needs bigger trousers. At least he's in long pants now. It's less awful than it was.

Fish giggles in the water, balls afloat. The water barely reaches his waist. Any deeper and he'll try to get under it. He can't be left alone. Lester kneels by the tub with a bar of Velvet and a backache.

Stories!

Orright. Well. Well. Lester sighs. The skin on the back of his arms is flaky with cancers. He can't think of anything.

Lest! Lestah!

There was this boy –

Lessst!

Orright, there was this boy. And he lived on a farm. Actually, this is me, it was a grape farm –

Lestaah! Fish juggled in the water. Lester soaped his pink chest and felt the tension in him, the impatience.

Orright, there was this boy called Fish.

Hah! Whacko!

And he lived on a farm with only his brother –

Quick! Whacko, Lest!

Yeah, with Quick. Everyone else was gone on holidays. One night it started to rain, see, and it came down like all of Heaven was tryin to get in the roof. It rained and rained and rained until the creek bust it banks. Pretty soon there was water in the kitchen an water in the lounge an water under the beds. So Quick wakes Fish up and tells him they gotta go. They have to try and make it into town. Now Quick is bigger than Fish. He helps him into his clothes and holds his hand as they wade out into the water. There's rain peltin down and it's dark. Quick puts Fish up on his shoulders and he strides out into the water. It's a swirling torrent –

Yeah. And the water. Yairs. They go in the water. To the big country. Yeah.

Lester loses his breath. Fish leans back with his head against the end of the tub looking dreamy and gone. No, thinks Lester, that's not what happens.

An people there for em, says Fish. There's people there.

Oh, God.

Fish looks smiling upon him.

VI

Down Among Them, Killing

IN the barely dimpled surface of country, the wheat is its own map, neat and dogmatic in its boundaries. You can see the sun in it, the prodigal rain, the magic tons of superphosphate. From ground level, the wheat is the whole world, but in the air, or beyond air and sky, the wheatbelt is just that, a strap of land surrounded by the rest of the world. Beneath the clouds of crows it's hard to find a feature, unless you see a gravel pit now and then, like this one here, with its stubborn island of stonefed trees which cast puddles of shadows about them like shoals. Where the man is still sleeping. Now you make out his vehicle, an old hoodless ute, already rippling with heat, and his dog which snaps at flies and rests its head on its paws. There's dog hair on the old army blankets, some dried blood, and a smattering of roo ticks. The bends in the air beside him mean there is still some heat in the smokeless remains of the fire. Across the treefork a Lee-Enfield is slung, its scarred butt looking like old pub furniture. Now in the shadow you can see an arm, and a rough chin, a boy's chin really. If you were me, you'd want to climb in under that blanket and spoon up by him, to take what time you could to smell him and hear his breath.

In the end it's the flies that wake him. They cluster on the feed sacks in the back of the ute, sucking at the dark honey of thickened blood. The traffic sound of them gets him rolling on his side.

Gday, Bill, he says to the dog.

The dog stands and then sits back morosely. Bill is the saddest dog ever to find water, but he's companionable in his glumness. The young man leans across to a blackened pot and hauls out a meat twined bone. He throws it to the dog who gazes from it to his master as if truly insulted.

What, you sick of roo?

The dog closes its eyes.

Well, give it back then, I'm hungry.

Bill gets up and retires beneath the shade of the ute. The young man throws back the blankets, gets up and fills a jam tin from the waterbag in the tree. He sets the tin on the fire and surrounds it with white tree limbs snapped across his knee. In his duffel bag he finds an old linty piece of damper and hunkers down by the fire, resisting the need to pee. His skin is raw with sunburn. He has the square, aged hands of his family, and his legs are so long that in a squat his knees have to be peeped over or looked between. With a pocket knife he scrapes dirt from beneath his fingernails. His unlaced boots rest beneath him like luggage.

Who's gunna do the dishes after brekky, dog? he says as he spins the knife on the back of a skillet. The blade turns, flashing sunlight, and finishes pointing at his boot. Well, the knife never lies, he says with a laugh. I shoulda flamin known that.

196

This morning he'll pull a few gilgies out of some farmer's dam and boil them up for lunch, he'll sight the gun in with the vice on the back of the ute, and he'll have to start priming his own shells again. If he can find some shade in the afternoon he'll drag out a penny dreadful western and read till he's asleep. The dog will sit beside him in mournful attendance. Barely a thing will move all day in the wheat except the insects and the odd rambling snake.

Quick loaded up the ute when the sun was low on the land. With the mutt beside him on the seat, he drove to the rocky pool and parked in beside the smooth monolith furthest from the water. He laid his ammo along the roof of the cab, stood the rifle against the window and sat back with a smoke to wait. He fiddled with the cable that connected the spotlight to the battery. The dog sat inside, looking at him through the rear window. Quick was learning not to think much at these times, only to listen. Already he could hear them out in the wheat. The sky became the colour of billy tea as the sun disappeared. The motor ticked with cooling. Quick was glad tonight was Friday – he needed a bath something terrible.

When he heard them close he saw old Bill tense up and he got up and rested his elbows on the roof. He slipped a mag into the three-oh and worked a shell into the breech. He let them come on in to the sandy clearing, to the spot where the slopes fuzzed with grass close to the water. The pool was only the size of a double bed. With the faint sky behind them, the roos were easy to see. He counted six, a couple of big bucks among them. He held off, knowing that unless he'd been doing his job better than he thought, there'd be plenty more to come yet.

The pool was shoulder-to-shoulder with them when he switched on the spot. They went rigid and opened their eyes to him. Quick worked from left to right without haste. Shoot, load, aim, shoot. The roos stood there, unwillingly, but unable to tear themselves away. Their necks curved richly, their ears stood twitching. Haunches ticked with muscle and nerve. The sound of the Lee-Enfield was honest

197

and uncomplicated, always leaving enough space in the air for the sound of the bolt clicking in a new shell, as the roos fell, snouts flicking up like backhanded drunks. When finally the survivors began to stagger away, Quick took fast shots, moving the spot with his elbow, until he was taking them down in their stride. And then his sighting eye gave out into a watery blur so that he had to rest. Around the pool the fallen animals lay like a new stone formation, the colour of granite. Some heaved with breath or blood. Even with the whine of sound shock in his ears, Quick could hear the scratching of paws in the sand. He loaded up again, left the light on, and went down among them, killing. He didn't get too close, for fear of catching a hind leg in the nuts. He shot those still moving, only a few. Then he let them settle while he rolled a smoke, hunkered down by the water, his eyes closed against the spotlight. He took hard drags and spat now and then until his ears cleared. Well, there's a quid or two, he thought.

With a machete he took the tails and threw them into the tarp on the back of the ute. It took the better part of an hour to do this and to drag the carcasses into a heap away from the water. Old Wentworth, the cocky, could do what he liked with them.

He wondered for a while about going on to a dam and setting up there, because it was early yet, but he felt sluggish and lazy, and after all it was Friday night and he'd had a gutful.

He finished up his smoke. Now he could hear them all out in the wheat again, trampling, eating, swishing through. Lord, they were eating up the country! People told him that further south, and right across to Sydney it was the rabbits they were knee deep in, and emus too. It was like the Egyptian flamin plagues. They'd started dynamiting them, laying baits. Some blokes, even one over by Bruce Rock, were making double money by selling the meat for petfood. But you needed to have partners for that, and Quick was glad to be alone. He got skins most places, but some cockies, like Wentworth, paid enough on private bounty, roo for roo, that it was only necessary to take tails. He took shire bounty on foxes most green months and did all kinds of skins some time or another, but this time of year he was just culling.

He listened to the sound of a bird nearby, a sort of gasping noise at the edge of the wheat. He'd never heard it before in all the time he'd been living out like this, five nights a week. Bill was standing firm all of a sudden, and whining under his breath. Quick held the dog's head and felt the damp, loose flesh beneath his jaw. The bird noise was a little cough out there now. He took up the rifle and cocked it.

It's orright, boy. Looks like I missed one, that's all. Poor bugger's out there chokin.

It was a good fifty yards out across the roo-battered fence to the edge of the crop. Out of the spotlight now, Quick could only follow the outlines and contours of things, but he could see plain enough where the wheat was moving. A long way out, on the faintest rise, he could see the heads of other roos grazing in the quiet. Once he saw the wheat moving, he strode out beyond the spot and took the safety catch back.

He felt the hind legs in his chest before he even saw the darkness of it rearing, paws out, and within a second all he could see was the Southern Cross up there, clear as a road sign above the tight blonde heads of wheat. There was the cracking echo of the three-oh as it fell to the ground beside him – or was it the crack of his head on a stone? – and in the quiet afterwards there was the slow, strangling sound of the animal only an arm's length away. The whining of the dog above. The sound of blood marching across him, establishing a beachhead on his chest.

After a while, the kangaroo died and gave out a stinking evacuative snort. Bill turned circles. Time proceeded. The light from the spotty on the ute began to fade as the battery juiced out. Quick watched the Southern Cross melt into the great maw of darkness.

Light comes across the sky, a great St Elmo's fire of a thing, turning and twisting till it fishtails towards the earth and is gone.

Quick feels the blood setting like Aquadhere in his nose. He wonders where the light went. If he can't walk he'll die out here. That's a dead ute, now. In a moment he'll have to try. No use putting it off. Bound to be able to walk.

Out of the slumber of giants he comes, and there in the waking world with the Southern Cross hanging over him is his brother Fish rowing a box across the top of the wheat.

Quick pushes the sound against his teeth. Fish?

HARVEY ORANGES says the box. The oars are tomato stakes. Fish's body is silver with flight.

Fish?

Carn.

Quick stares. The box comes to a halt a few feet out from him and Fish is leaning out, causing it to rock precariously. It's floating up there. I'm under it, thinks Quick, I'm under water, under something. God Almighty, I'm gonna drown.

Carn, says Fish. He lowers his hand.

Quick lies still. That's not his brother that's a man. That's a man's arm.

Carn, Quick. Let's go fishin.

Fish?

Yeah?

Am I orright?

Fish widens his eyes a moment, then closes them to let out a long crackling laugh. Quick squints at the sound of it, cowering. When the laugh is all emptied out, Fish rests his chin on the gunwale of the fruit box, looks down dreamily.

Carn, Quick.

Quick looks up, uncertain.

Carn, Quick.

I can't.

The dog is whining, turning circles.

Quick?

I can't, I *can't*!

Ya love me?

Yes! Yeah, Fish. Quick struggles to keep the panicky

200

weeping out of his throat. But, I just can't move.

Fish is looking at the dog now. Bill looks back, agitated.

Where you goin, Fish?

Fish leans down, slouching the box over till you'd expect the sound of water or night sky sloshing into it and arms the dog up into the box. Quick feels a bead of saliva fall on his brow.

You goin home, Fish?

The Big Country.

The box rights itself again and Bill barks in excitement as it pulls away a little. Fish holds the dog between his knees. He's too damn big for a fruit box. He looks bloody stupid, that's what, a man rowing a crate. Across the wheat. Across the still waters of the sunburnt crop wherein lies Quick Lamb breathing without help, with the Southern Cross hanging above, rippling now, badly seen, beyond the surface.

He took my bloody dog.

Goanna Oil

Old Wentworth found him unconscious under a mound of boisterous flies in the afternoon, roasting like a pig at a party.

Yer bloody lucky a man wuz goin by on the orf chance! the old farmer shouted over the sound of the FJ whose gear box was shot to bits already. Yer woulda died sure as shit I reckon.

Quick watched the gravel ahead. The dog was gone, but the three-oh was beside him. He wasn't sure about himself at all. He went to sleep.

Late at night he woke headsore and stiff under a sheet on a cot. He looked about. It was Wentworth's place. They'd lately turned the verandah on the shady side into a sort of sleepout with flyscreens and an old chest of drawers with boyish graffiti scratched into it. It was a cool evening, though Quick could feel the heat radiating from his skin. His chest was taped and there was a bandage across his nose. He could hear them talking in there, Wentworth and his missus. And the girl, their daughter. They'd had the doctor out, he knew.

Well, that took care of the week's pay, the quack and the board they'd charge him. Wentworth had been the one to give him his first shooting job, a break alright, but the old boy was a mean bastard, tight as a noose. He didn't give anything away, not even kindness. But I'm orright, thought Quick, I'm orright, and he sank back into a blank, over-heated sleep.

Quick woke again and there was Wentworth's daughter, Lucy. She was rubbing his blistered skin with goanna oil. He'd never really spoken to her before in all his coming and going from the homestead, and here she was, smelling of horse, her hair a dirty blonde colour, her jodphurs feasting on her.

Is that really your name? she said. Quick Lamb?

Yeah, he said as she slipped a finger into his bellybutton.

Because you're fast? Her hands were ducking and diving under the waistband of his shorts.

Nah. No.

Quick had never been rubbed by a girl before. He'd never even kissed a girl. At school he was too sad and slow for romance. And now he looked at the short and bottley Lucy Wentworth and knew he wasn't interested even now, but he couldn't bring himself to object about her slipping her grabbers into his boxers.

You're blushin.

How can you tell?

You just went red in the white bits.

He felt her grip on his dick. He was glad he'd put on clean undies last night. It was a bit of home-thinking he couldn't shake off. Lucy Wentworth had the grip of a crop duster pilot.

I'm going to live in Perth, she murmured.

Oh? It was all he could manage in the circumstances.

I'm gonna have a flower shop. A floristry.

Mmngh?

My Dad's gonna set me up.

Hhhyeah?

He just doesn't know it yet.

Hhhhow long have you planned to do that?

Oh, she chuckled, I just thought of it. Only three minutes ago. I just got it all figured out. She squeezed and put him through a few manoeuvres that ended in a long, stalling climb which had Quick Lamb shuddering at the point of blackout. Then she abandoned the controls altogether and left him dusting crop at high revs.

As Lucy Wentworth went inside with a slap of the screen door Quick was contemplating a victory roll, though he thought better of it. His skin was so tight it was hurting now to breathe, and he could feel his pulse stretching him at points all over. Then he felt sort of guilty in a way he didn't understand. For a long time he listened to the shifting timbers of the homestead, the clink of dog chain out in the yard, the cicadas dozing in the wheat.

Sleep, Quick, and smell the water leaching. Can't you hear the boy in the boxboat calling? I'm calling, brotherboy, and you won't come. And the waters shall fall from the sea, and the river shall be wasted and dried up. And they shall turn the rivers far away and the brooks of defence shall be emptied and dried up: the reeds and flags shall wither, be driven away, and be no more. The fishers also shall mourn, and all they that cast angle into the brooks shall lament, and they that spread nets upon the waters shall languish. From me to you, the river. In me and you, the river. Of me and you, the river. Carn, Quick!

Safety Off

In one week five cockies sign Quick Lamb up to protect their crops. They know he's the best shot the district's ever seen and there's no reason why they should give a stuff about rumours. Lucy Wentworth is not their problem. Roos are. Coming on toward harvest time, as if it isn't enough to worry about early rain, the boomers are moving in from the desert – reds, and greys alike – eating their way overland. Mobs of blokes hurtle around the paddocks at night with shotguns and crates of Swan Lager doing more damage to the crop than the plague itself and blowing each other's ears off in a regular fashion. Quick Lamb buys an old Dodge with multiple spots, fixes himself a cage on the back to shoot from, and starts earning dinkum money.

Summer is on the land like fever. Pink zink plastered on him, Quick sleeps the day away beneath the tarp on the back of his truck. He misses his dog. Now and then he'll spend a morning burning rooticks out of his flesh with a red-hot piece of fencing wire, then lapse back into the stupor of a western. And at night he drives to water and shoots. The bed of the truck becomes varnished with blood until the weekends when he goes to town to scrub out, cash in and sleep up. Saturday nights he sees Lucy Wentworth, or various moonstruck parts of her, in the cab of the truck, parked up some dwindling road behind a decrepit grove of salmon gums.

You've got a huge whanger, she says. That's what I like about you, Quick. A head like that, it'd be eligible to vote.

He never thinks about her much, though he doesn't object to wrestling her round the cab. He figures he's along for the experience, and mostly he doesn't feel that guilty at all. He looks at himself naked in the mirror. It isn't *that* big. Time just goes along. It proceeds. The summer hardens.

Then a strange thing begins. One night by a dam, as he waits for the roos, he hears the familiar bashing in the wheat and raises the rifle with the spotlight ready. He hears the hacking of breath and sees the crop swaying in the dark. In comes the first silhouette, a leader, so far out in front of the rest that there's no sign of the mob behind, and when it cracks from the dry, heady mass of wheat Quick hits the spot to get a look at the monster. But it's a human, a man running raw and shirtless in the light. His face is tough with fear, there's a sweat on him, and he runs right past and out of the light to the dark margins of bushland. Long after the runner is gone and the light turned out, Quick has the face burnt into his retina, because that face is his. It's Quick Lamb barrelling by right before him.

He doesn't call out, he doesn't go chasing him. He rolls a smoke and thanks God that he didn't shoot.

Coming up to harvest, it happens now and then. He'll be sighted up by water and he'll hit the light and see himself tearing out into the open, right in the sights, right under the first pressure of trigger, safety off. And it scares the skin off him. It starts to affect his shooting. He waits too long now, he lights up too early and loses half the mob. Quick never knows when he'll see himself in their midst. He thinks about Fish coming in the fruit box. Am I orright? he thinks. Was he telling me true? What was he saying? Was I delirious?

The Florist Shop

Quick drove slowly through the great flat plain with her hand on his leg. The Dodge murmured away, sounding deceitfully healthy. The cab smelled of Brylcreem and old blood. Now and then, a ute passed, bellowing toward town for Saturday night, for beer and dancing. Quick wound down the window and rested his elbow on the sill. He didn't know where he was driving – he just drove.

What's up with you tonight? Lucy asked. She had on a small waisted dress that was unkind to her. He saw her bobby sox on the dash in the corner of his eye.

Nothin.

Make a killin this week, didja? she said with a mirthless guffaw.

Nup. I didn't.

Must be losin your eye, Quick Lamb, crackshot.

Quick said nothing. That thing had been happening all this week, too. Seeing himself breaking out of the wheat into his sights. That made it a month, and he hadn't shot a week's worth in all that time.

Crackshot. Make you think of anything?

You don't have to talk like that.

Oh, Quick. I forgot you went to church. I bet all you do is look at those old ladies' bums.

Some of em have better bums n you.

205

You bastard.

Quick felt his throat tighten. I'm sorry, Luce. You shoulden push me like that. I take a lot of crap from you.

And plenty more, you get plenty more, don't forget, crackshooter. What other girls you got in town like me?

Quick laughed. What others are there, full stop? Geez, ya haven't got much competition.

You're so dumb, Quick Lamb.

I believe it.

Spose you feel sorry for me.

Spose I do. A bit.

Well, you shouldn't.

Quick shrugged. He'd slowed the Dodge so much they were barely moving. It seemed like a fine pace to him.

You think I'm a, a conquest? she said.

Nah. Nope. I never went after you. He thought: no you're not a mountain I'd choose to climb without havin the idea put in me head.

You come by every Saturday night, mate. Isn't that comin after me?

You asked me to, once.

Oh, you're just obedient then?

Reckon I am. More than I should be. With you.

So it's just you takin orders. Whip me pants off, Quick. Get me knees up, Quick. It's just you bein obedient? She was starting to snarl now. Quick let the Dodge ride to a stop on the gravel shoulder.

Well, you have a nice way of askin sometimes.

You bastard. I taught you everything you know!

Who taught *you*?

You bloody bastard! You thought your dick was for cleanin your rifle before I took you in.

Did you take me in?

What do you reckon?

Quick looked at her face, green in the light of the speedo. There was always going to be something waiting for him at the end of this, and maybe he deserved it, going along without any feeling at all. Maybe he was a bastard. But things had just gone along like this without him caring

206

either way. She was around, he was around; he got used to it.

Trouble is, she said, I got to like you.

Quick felt a hot blur of embarrassment. He opened the door. The air was warm and breadscented. He turned the motor off and got out.

Hey Quick, you're not . . . are you?

What?

Leaving me here, I thought you were gonna leave me out here.

She got out, stood on the doorsill and looked across the roof at him.

Don't be daft. I want some air, and while I'm out here I reckon I'll take a piss, orright?

She giggled nervously: you're a duck, Quick. A sittin duck. You're dumber than a post.

Quick said nothing. He heard her coming round his side of the truck as he unbuttoned his flies. The sky lit up over the wheat round a bend in the road. A car coming. He tried to hurry.

Can't you go? she said with a laugh, grabbing his arms from behind.

Leave off, willya!

The headlights splayed out across the ripe paddocks, veering through the bend. Quick shrugged her off and felt his stream ease out at last. He forced it along, knowing he was beyond stopping now. He thought he had a few seconds. He tried to be cool, but the note of the motor coming out of the bend wasn't reassuring. There it was, bolting out of him like he hadn't had a leak in his whole life before. Coming out of the bend, the lights hit the top of the cab. Quick tried a complete shutdown, failed, and started crabwalking for some shelter behind the truck, but when he turned round he saw Lucy standing in nothing but her bobby sox. That's how the lights hit them, full whack, him with his dick out, and Lucy with those big breasts in her hands. The car pulled up, brakes snickering.

Evening, said the Shire Clerk.

Well, said Quick.

Quick packed up the Dodge and was gone within an hour. The town was afire with gossip and Lucy Wentworth, beside herself with happiness, began her negotiations for the florist shop at breakfast. Her father, who'd been at the dance when the Shire Clerk arrived, took out his account book to do his sums. His face was the colour of gunpowder. Mrs Wentworth wept. She blew her nose absently on the teacosy and wondered how she could ever go into town again.

Well, thinks Quick as the Dodge runs smooth and unhurried between walls of wheat into the even plain ahead. Well, that's that. That's that, for sure and certain. All the heat has gone out of him now and he's noticing things. Like they'll be harvesting here any day now, any day at all. Like he has a quarter of a tank of juice left. Like he's not sure about himself, what he thinks, what he'll do. He drives away from the dawn.

Outside Bruce Rock, at the beginning of the faintest morning light, he sees a blackfella standing with his thumb out and a gladstone bag at his feet. He is tall, white eyed and half grownover with beard. Quick takes his foot off the pedal a moment, but drives on. A few miles down the road he's out by the gravel shoulder again – thumb out, bag down. Quick, who isn't in the mood to think it through, pulls over and opens the door.

Ta, the man murmurs, getting in. He seems to fill the cab, even with the gladstone bag on his knees.

Quick winds his window down all the way and then begins to wonder.

Wanna smoke?

Yeah. Ta.

Quick passes him the pouch and watches him roll. The road goes on.

Hungry? the black man asks after a few miles.

Yeah, I could do with a bite.

208

From his gladstone bag the stranger takes a bottle and a loaf of white bread.

Whacko, says Quick.

The black man pulls him off a hunk of bread and Quick takes it. Then the bottle. It scourges his mouth. It takes everything he has not to spit.

What is this stuff?

Muscatel, the black man says.

It burns down inside him bringing on some unexpected comfort. They drink and eat, gliding down the road. After an hour Quick feels like he could just start in and tell this blackfella everything, the whole business. About how he took off from his family in the middle of the night, clouting the Pickleses girl with his bag. The jumping trains, the walks along the tracks, the nights he spent in dry grassbedded ditches under the sky. Of the jobs he took on clapped-out farms, and the shoots he went on with shickered country boys, and how he got his name as a crack man with a rifle. The way he started pulling in good money culling roos. And last night's business. Quick gets so that his throat is itching with it, but the blackfella doesn't say anything. He leaves no gaps for that kind of talk the way he sits there erect and shadowy in his corner of the cab. Quick taps the fuel gauge which seems to be on the blink. The wine and bread seem inexhaustible, and he has a good look at his passenger. He's never seen an Aborigine in a pinstriped suit before. The blackfella pulls out a fob watch big as a plate and consults it.

How we doin fer time? asks Quick.

Aw, well as can be expected.

Quick feels warm with wine, and emboldened.

Where you from, mate?

Aw, all over.

I mean where's your family.

All over.

You must have a bit of a job. That's a nice suit.

Bit of a job.

Family business?

Always family business.

Headin for the city?

The black man nods.

Family business, says Quick, smiling to himself. And for the next hundred miles he can't get boo out of him while the petrol tank stays on quarter full.

They roll down the baking scarp into the city where cars are parked outside pealing churches.

Sunday, says Quick.

The river flashes at them between trees.

Where can I drop you? says Quick.

Just follow the railway line.

Quick shrugs and keeps driving. He doesn't know where he's headed himself. South, maybe. His mind keeps coming back to Margaret River. Maybe he'll go and see the old farm, get some work somewhere. Or maybe he'll stay here in town, find a room, get a job, buy a suit. He doesn't know.

They follow the line across the causeway and the river islands till they're in the heart of the city, then beyond, until Quick's palms start to moisten. The streets get more and more familiar.

Any place in particular? he asks uncomfortably.

They roll up Railway Parade along the grassy embankment and the date palms and weeds and fallen fences. Quick sees the great sagging west wall of Cloudstreet and hits the brakes.

Where exactly do you wanna be dropped off, mate?

The man points.

I . . . I . . . I'll drop you at the corner.

At the corner the blackfella takes up his gladstone bag and gets out.

Comin?

Quick Lamb laughs fearfully and guns the Dodge away.

Baulking At Shadows

Quick drove until half a day later the Dodge finally ran out of juice and he woke from his steering daze to see that he had come back to Margaret River. And there was his father's cousin, Earl Blunt, hosing down a truckload of pigs outside the town hall.

Earl Blunt, Egypt, said Quick.

Earl looked at him. Mason Lamb.

You still doin haulage.

You still doin nothin.

I need a bed.

I need another driver.

I'm hired.

Earl Blunt rolled his eyes and hosed pigs.

Earl and May lived in a truckshed by the road out of town. They had been married twenty years now and had no children. They were farmers as well as truckies, and they were rough as guts. Earl could feel no pain and he could not imagine it in others. The Depression had made him hard; war had beaten him flat and work had scoured all the fun from him. He was hard beyond belief, beyond admiration. On a Sunday night Quick saw him apply a blowtorch to the belly of a fallen cow before going back inside to pedal the old pianola for May. The land has done this to them, Quick thought; this could have been us.

Quick moved into a plywood caravan up on blocks behind the shed. The yard smelled of diesel and grease. It was full of rusting crank cases and radiators, butchered Leylands and Fords and fanbelts coiled about like exhausted snakes. In the mornings, Quick woke to the roar of bees out in the karri forest, and all day way beyond dark, he drove for Earl and May: loads of cattle, pigs, superphosphate, rail-sleepers, bricks, to Perth, to Robb jetty, Pinjarra, Manjimup, Bunbury, Donnybrook, all the time wrestling a bastard of a truck with stiff steering and slack brakes and keeping wide of the transport coppers and their safety rules. He rolled up to farms without stockyards and learnt to throw pigs up two storeys by hand. He wrung the tails of steers, he shovelled seven ton of super and did not whinge. Late at night, just for May, he double de-clutched on the pianola and tried to be happy.

After all, it was 1957 and he had his whole life ahead of him. He was his own man.

Some Sundays he took his Dodge out to the old farm and parked on the boundary. The place looked good. He thought about climbing the fence and looking into the gash low in the old blackbutt to see if his threepenny bit was still there. But he couldn't bear to know. There were a lot of things he just wanted to fail to remember. He didn't mind being lonely; he was used to being sad, but he didn't want to baulk at shadows for the rest of his life.

Still, Quick had old habits. On Sundays, he got the newspaper and cut out pictures of those less fortunate than him, and stuck them on the plywood walls of the caravan where they danced in his sleep like everything he ever wanted to avoid. He did not think of home, but home thought of him.

Tho Mine Enemies Rail

For a year or so Quick thought he had hold of himself. He could feel time passing without harm, and though his misery pictures danced on the caravan walls while he slept, they never woke him nor skipped into his dreams.

Earl and May fed him, worked him like a dog and told no one he was a Lamb. Locals still remembered those crazy Biblebashers and their fake miracles.

Winter bored on and he lived an orderly life in his slow, methodical way. He washed every day, cleaned once a week, and managed to see his awkward working hours out by thinking through the importance of every task. You could see it in the way he unlatched the tailgate as pigs pressed against it squealing, how he took his time at the weigh-bridge, how conscientiously he waved cars by him as he hugged the soft edges on narrow roads. And if you met him pulled into the rest bay beneath a stand of white gums along the Coast Road and you shared a smoke with him, he wouldn't strike you as stupid. He'd seem overserious maybe, a little late off the mark when it came to getting a joke. You'd guess he was a bloke who hadn't seen much but who was ageing somehow too quickly. There was nothing exceptional in him but for the fact that he could never seem to be ordinary. He had some mark on him, like a migrant or a priest. You could tell he was trying with you, trying to fit.

Quick Lamb drove without pausing. He caned himself with work and Earl and May could hardly believe their luck. He thought he was coping, but he was miserable, lost, drifting, tired and homesick as a dog. He didn't think about it. He drove. He drove. He just drove.

That winter, some things happened, some incidents occurred.

Throttling the old bus rotten through the bends past Capel, crazy with sleeplessness, Quick lost his brakes on the hill before the rail crossing. The lights flashed red and he could hear the train's diesel engine sounding its bullish horn down the tracks. He had nine ton of super on the back and now that it was mobile it wasn't of a mind to stop. He went down through the gears like a man down a fire-escape, and when he hit rock bottom he could see the snout of the train flashing through the trees. All he had left was the handbrake and maybe the ditch at the roadside. The old knocker was hissing air and shrieking pads. The motor roared with quick comedown.

Thy rod and Thy staff they comfort me, a bit of his brain said, Thy rod and Thy staff . . .

He was slowing, he knew it, he was pulling her back, but in the hundred yards that were left now he couldn't expect a dead stop. He'd be rolling slowly, creeping right into the rush of freight cars.

The diesel snouted through, blurting and roaring, trucks nose-to-arse behind. The crossing lights flared. The lifeless bell tinged and tinged.

Quick hauled over to the scrub strip along the side of the road and felt logs and rubbish clawing underneath retarding him a little. He tried for reverse, but couldn't get a grip on anything. And then he knew that all he had left was the angle he could hold and the fact that the last trucks were in sight.

Thy rod and Thy staff, he thought.

213

Now the wheels snicking along the tracks were all he heard as he dragged on the wheel and veered across the road to the other side where dirt lay in piles at the edge of the tracks. He ploughed it high and wide as the last truck came by and there was an almighty crack like the sound of a man's neck breaking, and when he came back to knowing he was alive, he peered round to see his rearview mirror saluting him all the way down the tracks.

Yea, though I walk, he thought. Yea. Tho mine enemies rail against me.

He was bogged under nine ton of super and he could feel the paddock subsiding beneath him. Earl would not be impressed. Quick got out the shovel and started to dig. Right then he thought how sweet it would be to have Fish come rowing across the paddock to dip the gunwale of his fruitbox and haul him away from here.

Quick got Earl out of bed at four in the morning.

Geez, look at you. You bin sleepin with the pigs?

I just dug that bloody knocker out of a paddock. I want a couple of days off.

To do what?

Go fishin.

Earl yawned.

I nearly killed meself tonight.

Earl sniffed and scratched.

I nearly lost the truck.

It's old. It's insured.

I nearly lost nine ton of super.

Take the week. Use me boat. I'll take it out of ya pay.

 Earl's Dory

At its mooring beneath the trees at the last bend before the river met the sea, Earl's dory dwelt in a state of almost total submersion. It was so full of bird crap that there was less than an inch of freeboard and no gull could even so much as perch on it anymore without having the lot sink beneath the surface. That boat was crapped up to the gunwales, and it took Quick a whole Lord's Day to bail the birdshit out, drag it up on the bank to roll over and scrape till it was clean enough to be tarred, caulked and painted. He spent the week on it, and in the afternoons he fished off the rocks with a bamboo rod and a jar of gents.

Late in the week, on Sunday, Quick took a couple of tin buckets full of overripe prawns and handlines, and in Earl's newpainted dory he rowed round the bend to the great tear-shaped lagoon behind the sandbar. As he came into the flat shoaly stretch of water he met the memory of them all down here at dusk with the fire on the beach, the lantern, the net sluicing along. He set his jaw and kept rowing.

Mullet rushed in mobs across the ribbed bottom. A burnt out Ford stood back from the shore in the shade of trees. The surf rumbled beyond the bar. Quick did a lazy circuit resting one oar and pulling easy on the other. He had the feeling of movement going right through him. Water passed beneath, the trees up the bank rode by, but inside himself he felt something travel, the kind of transport he felt at the beginning of sleep when he sensed himself going out to meet its sky colour and the promises it held. He let go of the oars and just sat feeling queer. Someone walked in the shadows beyond the trees, or maybe it was a roo or just a stray cow turning. It caught his eye, whatever it was, and his insides queered up a little more. Presently, a broad, frisky school of mullet cracked the surface and bore round him, funneling down the tide ribs to the deep seaward slope of the bottom and he watched them go, that uniform mob, and felt cheered by their nerve.

The boat sat well in the water, evenly hipped and clean painted. In their rowlocks, the oars knocked and creaked with business. The working, operating feel of things pleased Quick Lamb. There was nothing more warming than the spectacle of something proceeding properly after a due amount of work. He was like that with rifles, with motors, drum reels, or some fancy roadhouse's new flushing toilet. If you didn't know how they worked, then things weren't worth having – something the old girl used to say.

He pulled across to the narrow point of the bottleneck where the river squeezed out in a cool tea-coloured trickle to the sea and the disturbance of the two bodies meeting caused a roily, chopbroken channel that led out through the surf to the deep beyond. Quick wedged his way into the channel, picked his moment after a set came through, and went like hell. He heard the squeaking and creaking and the airbrake sound of his breath, the bow lifting under him, pushing his bum cheeks together. The sensations were clear and momentous. The sight of foam cracking down the sides and rushing astern, the smell of salt and paint and his bait prawns on the turn. Above him, the sky like a fine net letting nothing through but light and strangeness.

About five hundred yards out, over a wide patch of sandy bottom, he dropped the hook and felt the boat hang back on it. He baited up and then it began. The first bite rang in his wrist like the impact of a cover drive, a bat and ball jolt in his sinews. From below, a skipjack broadsided and bore down on the hook in its palate, sending water springing from the line as it came up. Then he saw another lunging toward it, and when he hauled the fish into the boat, it was two fish, one fixed to the tail of the other. They thumped in the bottom round his ankles, the size of big silver slippers. He baited up again and cast out. He got a strike the moment the hooks hit the water, and then another, and when he saw the upward charge of the mob he felt something was happening that he might not be able to explain to a stranger. He dragged in four fish, two hooked and two biting their tails. He caught them cast after cast, sometimes three to a hook, with one fish fixed to the passenger fish. His hands bled and his arms ached. In his eyes the sweat rolled and boiled. Now the boat vibrated like a cathedral with all these fish arching, beating, sliding, bucking, hammering. In the water they bludgeoned themselves against the timbers, shine running off them in lurches, stirring the deep sandy bottom into a rising cloudbank until Quick was throwing out baitless hooks to drag in great silver chains of them. They shone like money. They slid and slicked about his knees. Quick Lamb's

216

breathing got to be a hacking just short of a cough, and in the
end he stopped casting and lay back in the smother and
squelch of fish as they leapt into the boat of their own accord.

The sun was a penny on each of his eyelids. Fish made
space for him. They embraced him in their scaly way and he
heard their mouths open and close. He felt them slide across
his chest as his head sank into them, against his cheeks, along
his lips with the briny taste of Lucy Wentworth's business
bits. He began to breathe them, stifle beneath them. He
struggled up, began to row, and completed two neat circles
before he remembered the anchor. He pulled the hook, coiled
rope and chain and watched the lot sink into the mass of fish.
He got sensible.

He picked a landmark to row for, and settled in for the
long, methodical pull. Once, when he glanced across his
shoulder to check his bearing, he saw the figure of a man
walking upon the water and it made him laugh. He got
sensible again and had another look.

The man seemed to come closer.

He's on a shallow bar, thought Quick, getting
desperately sensible.

He was black.

But everyone's black at a distance, he thought.

Quick didn't look anymore. He was fished up to the
gunwales with about an inch of freeboard so that a decent
lungful of air would send him under.

Just outside the surf line, the boatful of fish gouted up
blood, died, and sank the boat. For a moment, Quick Lamb
kept rowing because his head was still out of the water and he
still had the family stubbornness in him.

When he got to shore, the blackfella was waiting for him
in a pair of calico pants and a British battlejacket. Quick
could see the waterline on his night blue ankles. The black
man smiled. He seemed to be holding back a belly laugh.

Quick pushed past him and didn't look back.

On the long, impossibly slow drive back to Earl and May's
with the prospect of breaking the bad news before him,

217

Quick kept seeing figures. Along the road every mile or so, some mad bugger would jump out waving from behind a karri tree. Half the time it was that black bastard and the other half it was him. The old Dodge wheezed and Quick abused all comers. He flattened the accelerator but he still could have walked faster.

Nothing computes. Every moment, each vision and image elbows up to the next in Quick's mind, bumping, sliding, rubbing hot and useless in him till he feels like his head is the groanstuffed hold of a ship in a gale. Out beyond the oily dark yard at twilight he climbs up into the plywood caravan, falls on his cot and lies there without knowing how the bloody hell it took him three hours to get back from a thirty-minute drive. He knows he's not crazy, he's convinced of it, and he's right. But he's not firing on all six, that's for sure, because as he lies there, buckled and ready to stop breathing at any moment, he knows he can't decide how he feels – enlightened or endangered, happy or sad, old or young, Quick or Lamb.

Sometime in the night, the misery pictures begin to vibrate above his head. Burnt babies, Koreans, old amputee diggers, a blind nun, they all jig on the wall, roll their eyes, hum like a turbine, sending Quick into an alertness even more discomforting and disabling.

He dreams he is asleep, and that in sleep he's dreaming a dream: there they all are, down by the river laughing and chiacking about, all of them whole and true, with their own faces in a silver rain of light fused with birds and animals. Lester, Oriel, Hat, Elaine, Lon, Red, Fish, himself, and people he doesn't know: women with babies, old people, men with their sleeves pinned, barefoot children, all moving behind a single file of other people the colour of burnt wood. Down at the river where the fish are leaping and the sea has turned back on itself and the trees shake with music.

This Side

I can feel it even this side of the mirror, that's how intense it is, so strong I can sense it this far away, as far as light from a lamp, as time from a clock. Quick's calling out like a wounded bird, seeing, seeing.

And Fish hears it from his bed in Cloudstreet where everyone's asleep except Oriel whose lamp suddenly flickers. Lester is snoring with his teeth on the table and his arms across the boy and beneath his arm Fish stirs, hearing, beginning to hurt.

Fish begins to cry, to cry the best he knows how, and Lester starts awake.

Fish?

The boy goes on and on, teeth clenched, limbs hard as plaster, sending out his note until Lester fears he might smother him with a pillow to keep himself sane.

That cry goes on and on, through walls and walls. Shadows shake and quail openmouthed on the ceiling, the unhappy dead caught like wallpaper and groaning silently at the sound of knowing. It wakes the living and shakes even the happy dead. Even now it makes me shiver.

Load of Pigs

When Earl and May found him next day, Quick was lit up like a sixty watt globe and he wouldn't stop crying. They brought him inside, bathed him and made him drink iced water, hoping the fluorescence would ease off. But by evening Quick's long, bony body was giving off a light all the more clear in the dusk and he wouldn't say a word. A doctor was out of the question with Earl and May – hell, doctors could get you in a lot of trouble, and besides if word got out about him glowing, then people'd know he was a Lamb and they'd never hear the end of it. Earl was all for letting him sleep it off, but by midnight when the boy was burning white hot, May put her foot down. Quick Lamb needed his own. Warm up a truck, she said. We're goin to Perth.

Earl had a load of pigs in the knocker out the front that he'd been hosing down all day while they tried to decide what to do with Quick. He thought of taking just the prime mover, but he couldn't bear to waste a trip. He'd take the pigs and cut his losses.

When they loaded the boy into the cab he lit up the dash and sent the swine into a shitting frenzy. May held him and Earl drove. Night deepened. Passing cars flashed their lights in alarm.

And a black angel, said Quick, a couple of hours north. It was all he said that night.

That woman'll be angry at us, Earl said.

Doesn't matter, love, said Mary.

She'll be all over us like an angry wart.

What can we do?

She'll think it's a way of gettin an invite to the weddin.

She's a mother, Earl.

Now doan start cryin.

At least she's a mother.

They looked at each other in the glow of their relative and tried to stay calm. The old diesel hammered them in their seats. Quick saw everything in the headlights – every-damn-thing.

VII

Madhouse

SEVEN o'clock and the place is like a madhouse! Since five, when he woke up, Fish has been laughing like a bird, and now Lester's trying to dress him while the women fight it out in the next room. Oriel turns her lamp out and comes inside to supervise the dressing. She's weary and can't make herself any excitement for the day. Dew drips from the flaccid gutters, catching the first hints of sun now and then as it falls to the grass. Dogs and roosters stir and territorialize on the westerly. This morning Cloudstreet looks like a scabby old steamer resting at her moorings in the quiet time before the seas quicken and unsettle her.

Out in the garden, the pig is muttering in tongues: *Gwalia logoreemi muluth dooloomoos speptie* . . .

Rose Pickles, freshly showered and peering at the steamy mirror, pens on the Dawn Heat lipstick with plenty of speed and nerve as Sam fries bacon and eggs for himself down the corridor, and over the sound of spitting fat comes Dolly's straighteight snoring.

The floors rumble across the way. It's a non-opening Saturday today. The Lambs are killing the pig, that's for sure. Well, not literally. The pig is as safe as parliament, but they're bunging it on for young and old because today Hat Lamb's marrying that handsome dill from Pemberton, the one who always wears tweed and whose brogues could house a family. Today they're giving one away, and Rose Pickles could spit, she's so cheesed. It's something she wouldn't miss for quids, but there's a morning at the switch to be got through, there's Mrs Tisborn to be borne, there's more than she can stand to think of, and she's gonna miss it.

If you hook me again, Elaine Lamb, someone yells next door, I'm gonna knock your block into ya frock, ya hear me?

Someone begins to sob.

Rose pauses, strains to hear.

Settle down!

Rose stifles a laugh to keep listening. It's like they're all in the same room.

You be careful, and you show some patience or the whole cricket match'll be cancelled!

You can't –

We're payin for it if we're stayin for it, so you button your lip and let your sisters dress you. You're not playin doogs now. This a weddin for grownups. Anymore gripin and you're not invited.

But it's my wedding!

Bumslash! It's *your* marriage. The weddin belongs to us. Behave yourself.

Oh, maarm!

You look beautiful, now shut up.

The sergeant major's at it again, thinks Rose.

Rose! Brekky's ready.

Coming.

Rose snaps her makeup case back together and straightens herself. She catches a whiff of something terrible.

In Lester's bedroom, Fish stops laughing and Lester thanks God or whoever for ending it before it killed the boy. Fish is all got up in a serge suit, dark as a bagman, and now his father can straighten him up and comb his hair, glad that he shaved him last night.

It's Hat's big day, Fishcake. She's gonna be married.

Quick.

What?

Quick, Lestah.

No, it's Geoffrey Birch, from Pemberton. He's a timber man.

There's the snort of airbrakes outside and a sweet gummy pong.

Whew.

Quick.

Oh, Gawd, there's someone at the door. Stay here boy.

Lester goes through the shop and meets Oriel at the front door. Sam Pickles is halfway down the stairs.

Let's hope it's not the groom, Sam says with a chuckle. Oriel levels her martial look at him until he goes up again.

Open it, Lest.

Morning light pours in on them and for a while they can't see who it is backlit in their doorway.

Lester. Oriel. We've brought him home. Hello? It's Earl and May. From Margaret.

Oriel barges past like a half back and sends them whirling out onto the verandah. There is fierce morning light in the cab as she climbs up to the door of the pigstinking cattle truck with house windows and doors cracking open behind her. She hauls on the handle, swings the door out past her hip, sees Quick Lamb in there, wedged between the seats asleep and glowing.

Lawd, he's glowin like a lamp, says Lester behind her. Hala-bloody-lujah!

225

Oriel turns on him: Get your mouth outta gear and help me get him inside. You're a pimple of a man, sometimes, Lester Lamb.

Oh, but you love me.

She snarls and he gets helpful.

He's thin.

He's home.

He looks terrible, and don't smarm up like this.

They carry him in, long and bony, before the gathered crowd. Up in the house the piano jangles but Fish is out on a second storey windowsill leaping and kicking like a squaredancer.

Rose Pickles snaps her handbag closed and passes on the verandah.

Good morning, she says brightly.

Damn right, Lester replies.

Hold him up, Lest, for pity's sake!

Upstairs, Hat is bawling: That's it, then, that stabs that in the guts.

Oriel rears: Leave off with that racket and make up your bed for him. Where's Beryl?

Asleep still, like a Cathlick!

Get her up. Get dressed. Get ready and get married – we need the space.

Tell me you're happy, Lester says halfway up the stairs. Tell me you're happy to have him back.

He could have timed it better, don't you think?

I couldn't give a damn, you know.

I'm happy, I'm happy, just lift your end. We've got a weddin on.

The Do

At a quarter to ten that Saturday morning, with the sun streaming across in a dockside farewell that lit up every peeling, rusted surface, each brushed jacket and bleached blouse, the Lamb family climbed into the truck to follow father and bride who led billowing on the Harley and sidecar.

They proceeded at a stately pace to an Anglican church in Shenton Park, a venue of committee compromise, and were met by a fidgeting group of inlaws-to-be whose jaws dropped like eggs from tall chooks.

Oriel marshalled her children inside and left Lester and Hat scuffing their toes on the pavement outside. Black swans came low across the sky, searching out the lake. Children rattled by on larrikin billycarts. Earl and May pulled up and parked the seven tonner in front of the church, pigs squealing and stinking.

I'll miss yer, love, Lester said, looking at his tall eldest daughter. You're a fine girl an I never saw a better marbles player in me life.

Oh, Gawd, Dad, let's go in and sign on the line.

You can always come home.

Think we shoulda done it in a real church? You know, without the stained glass and the chessmen?

Lester shrugged. Well. Your bloke's from that kinda family.

Yer a dag, Dad.

Let's go in. Looks like an overpainted gin palace.

Hat went in with the giggles, and, without the dignified snooting of the pipe organ, the whole business would have turned into a footy match.

Oriel sat up front with her rank and file, peering discreetly at the statues and the lantern slides the stained glass made, trying to muster up some silent thanksgiving for this day. Fish began to hum a beefy descant across the anthem as Hat came down the aisle sending everyone up out of their pews, reverent and neckcraning. I have a son at home who is glowing, thought Oriel, as Hat came past looking tall and proud. Oriel felt the centripetal pull of the old things and she felt lonely the way she never had in her life. The words rolled out, the prayers proceeded like rote school poems, she upped and downed with the rest of them and kept her eyes off the Christ pictures, the ones that really set her teeth. It was like fighting off a toothache – you had to concentrate and will, overcome, pretend, become another thing.

Before she was ready for it, Oriel saw Hat and Geoffery

Birch from Pemberton going back up the aisle with the organ snuffling in their wake.

Mum, yer crying, Hat said out in the sunshine.

No, it's just sweat.

Oriel hugged her daughter till the whole lampshade and gauze construction went askew.

I'm losin children.

And yerv gained a son, said Geoffery Birch from Pemberton.

Yairs, Oriel said, without feeling.

They drove off in a pale blue Humber festooned with toilet paper and lipstick and Oriel thought glumly of the feast ahead. Should have cooked for it myself, she mused; it's a lot of money.

Lambs!

They gathered round her. Fish looked into the sun, his tie the shape of a pig's tail already. Lon scratched at the bumfluff on his chin. Elaine squinted, a sulk coming on.

I want some behaviour at the do, alright?

Orright, said Lester.

Lester.

Yes. Yes.

I want an example set. There'll be alcohol there. I want Lamb behaviour. Remember, we're Lambs, not sheep.

There was a stenchy gust of airbrakes as Earl and May's truck pulled out. Fish waved to the shitpaddling pigs who steamed in the sun and lurched into the turn.

They're not a bad pair for relatives, said Lester.

They'll see us in Heaven, dear, said Oriel. A smile slipped in under her nose and the whole mob went silent with happiness.

Country

Seven days they nurse Quick Lamb who says nothing but goes on glowing quietly, taking a little water but no food at all. The colour of his skin is strange; like mother of pearl it

changes at every angle, pale but somehow riddled with
rainbows that catch at the edge of vision. He's cool to touch,
and sweet smelling the way a man rarely is. Morning and
afternoon they take shifts sitting with him, while Beryl Lee
and Elaine run the shop. Fish stays all day, sitting on the bed,
humming, watching. At night they let him climb in beside
Quick. Fish holds onto his brother as if he expects him to
float away at any moment, and the room is lit by Quick's
candlepower. The walls crawl with shadows.

On the fourth day, Lester and Oriel sit out on the back
step alone the way they haven't for years now. The night air
is cool and heavy with dew. A train always seems to be
coming down the tracks. A wireless murmurs from an
upstairs window.

How sick is he, you think? Lester asks. It's times like
these he wishes he'd never given up smoking and drinking.

Oriel sighs. He's not sick.

He doesn't look that good to me.

I just don't think he's sick.

I wondered if . . . if he hadn't lost his marbles. He looks
like he's gone someplace else, you know?

You're not as silly as you look.

I'm sillier and you know it. I'm an old fool and I don't
care at all. I just wish I knew what to believe in. Life throws a
million things, good and bad, at me, but all I really care
about . . .

What?

I just wish I knew what to believe in.

You believe in what you like, Lester Lamb. That's one
thing I can't show you.

You've got mean, Oriel.

She sniffs.

Is it the war that's done it to you?

It's all war, she said.

What is?

I don't know. Everythin. Raisin a family, keepin yer
head above water. Life. War is our natural state.

Well, struggle maybe, said Lester.

229

No, no, it's war.

Ah, things come along. You take the good with the bad.

Oriel rears with sudden passion: No you don't. *You* know about boats. You can't steer if you're not goin faster than the current. If you're not under your own steam then yer just debris, stuff floatin. We're not frightened animals, Lester, just waitin with some dumb thoughtless patience for the tide to turn. I'm not spendin my livin breathin life quietly takin the good with the bad. I'm not standin for the bad; bad people, bad luck, bad ways, not even bad breath. We make good, Lester. We make war on the bad and don't surrender.

Some things can't be helped.

Everything can be helped.

You're a hard woman to please, Oriel.

That's what I tell myself, she says with a sudden drop of tone. She sounds almost lighthearted.

Aren't you happy?

Oriel sighs. Do I look like a winner?

We have a big place to live in. We're three years ahead with the rent, the kids have food and clothes, they go to school and have jobs, and now one has a husband – she's a credit to us, that girl – and there's the shop. People say: There goes Mrs Lamb who lives in a tent, she runs the best shop this side of the river. Gawd, the trams even stop for you. People come to you for advice like you're Daisy-flamin-Bates. You're famous! Course yer a winner.

A winner wins them all, Lester, not just the worldly things.

You've won me, love.

You're a fool, Lester Lamb.

That's what I tell myself.

They're quiet for a time. That train is still promising to come. Lester puts his hand on her leg.

Do you still love me?

I married you before God.

The mention of that character puts them back into quiet.

Oriel?

Hmm?

Why are you in the tent?

230

Oriel cracks her knuckles. Why's Quick lit up like a beacon? Why is Fish the way he is? Why does this house . . . behave?

Strange, says Lester.

Oh, nothin's really strange. Strangeness is ordinary if you let yourself think about it. There's been queerness all your life. I've seen stranger things than Quick glowin, haven't you?

Lester looks out across the crumpled tin fence: I used to ride farm to farm down there at Margaret, and I'd look out across the hills, the karris, the farms and dead crops, and you know the whole flamin country looked sad. All the plants with their heads bowed looking really browned off. And you know, I used to hear it moan. Not the wind; the ground, the land. I told meself it was the horse, but inside I knew it was the country. Moanin.

Like this house.

Come to think of it, yeah. I thought it was just me hearin it.

It's just a house.

You think maybe we don't belong here, like we're out of our depth, out of our country?

We don't belong anywhere. When I was a girl I had this strong feeling that I didn't belong anywhere, not in my body, not on the land. It was in my head, what I thought and dreamt, what I believed, Lester, that's where I belonged, that was my country. That was the final line of defence in the war.

Lester shifts his butt and rubs his knees in consternation.

What're you sayin, love?

Since Fish . . . I've been losin the war. I've lost me bearins.

Lester makes his teeth meet at all points round his jaw. Talk like this makes him nervous. Something's going to happen, to be taken from him, to be shone in his face. It's like walking down a rocky path at night, not knowing where it'll lead, when it'll drop from beneath your feet, what it'll cost to come back.

You believe in the Nation, though. You're the flamin backbone of the Anzac Club.

231

Ah, it's helpin the boys, I know, but I read the news-paper, Lester. They're tellin us lies. They'll send boys off to fight any war now. They don't care what it's for.

But, but the good of the country –

Oriel put a blunt finger to her temple: This is the country, and it's confused. It doesn't know what to believe in either. You can't replace your mind country with a nation, Lest. I tried.

Lester almost gasps. It's one thing for him to say it, but for her to admit such a thing, it's terrifying.

You believe in hard work, love.

Not for its own sake, I don't. We weren't born to work. Look at them next door.

There's always the family, says Lester.

Families aren't things you believe in, they're things you work with.

Don't you believe in . . . love?

No.

No? Lester bites the ends of his fingers.

I feel love. I'm stuck with the love I've got, and I'm tryin to work up the love I haven't got. Do you believe in love, he says. It's like sayin Do you believe in babies. They happen.

What about goodness, lovingkindness, charity?

They're just things you do, you try to do. There's no point believin in em.

So what do you want? says Lester.

I want my country back.

The tent?

I wish I could lace it up an never come out, she says with an unexpected laugh. You could slip food under the flap and I'd never see a soul, never say a livin word.

Lester shakes his head. Why?

Then I could get on with the real war.

You want a miracle, don't you?

I want the miracle finished off. I demand it, and I'm gonna fight to get it.

So you do believe.

Lester, I believe in eight hours' sleep and a big breakfast.

Oriel gets up and goes to her tent.

Lester sits out on the stoop and watches the lamp waver into life inside the tent. The scabby arms of the mulberry tree reach around it so that from the upper floors Oriel's silhouette looks like it's moving about inside the ribcage of some sleeping animal. From where Lester is, though, it's just a woman going through her drill before bed. I'll bet she even prays, he thinks. But the light goes out, the sight of her diminishes in the gloom, the dew chills him.

Keeping Watch

Day by day Quick began to fade, until by the end of the week he had no light in him at all, and he slept thirty-two-and-a-half hours with the snores of an explorer. A tall, pale woman he'd never met sat on his bed with a rosary and a hangdog look and took turns with Fish to keep watch.

In the Poo

Sam Pickles came home a week after the wedding with grass on his sleeve, blood on his collar, and a tooth in his pocket. His hat looked abused. One eye was oystered up with swelling. There was bark off his nose.

My Gawd, murmured Dolly who was still in her dressing gown. That's what I call a day's work. What the Christ have you been into?

Me luck's runnin uphill.

Runnin out yer arse by the look.

Sam eased himself into a chair at the table.

You've lost a tooth.

Sam fished it out of his pocket and put it beside the teapot.

Geez, look at the colour of it. That's smokin, doin that. It's as yeller as Tojo.

Pour us a cup.

How much do you owe? Dolly said as she poured him the strong metallic tea.

233

I could make it back on a quinella or just a decent run of luck.

That much.

The stove fizzed and snapped with the kettle working back up to the boil. Next door creaked with the business of closing the shop. That slow kid was laughing; the sound got on your nerves, made you wish they'd put him in a home with his own kind where he'd be happier.

Wincing, Sam drank his tea.

Could you eat a chop?

Sam nodded. Dolly got up and slipped the pan onto the stove. She was in an unaccountably decent mood tonight, he thought.

How many blokes dyou owe?

One fella who owns all the fellas. He's a nasty cove.

What're they gunna do?

Work it out of me, I spose. There's plenty of shonky jobs they'll want done.

Oh gawd. Haven't you got some union mates to back you up?

Sam smiled: They are the union.

Jesus.

When he was eating, Dolly took his gladstone bag and shook the *Daily News* final out of it, the horseshoe, the rabbit's foot, the breadcrusts, pennies, watch parts, peppermints and old train tickets, and went upstairs with it. She came back with it full of clothes and shaving gear. He looked at her across the table, pushed the plate away. There was a knock at the door.

Godalmighty.

Sam got up, found the crooked old poker by the stove and went to the hallway door. Before he turned the knob, he looked at her and saw what a handsome woman she still was, despite all. He opened the door with his bung hand and had his good one ready.

Gday, said Lester Lamb. I've got some old caulies. They'd be good for a soup. I had too many too quick and . . . you orright?

Yeah, yeah, come in Lester.

234

Lester put the two greyish cauliflowers on the table. Evenin Mrs Pickles.

Cauliflowers.

Yeah, I just –

Thanks, that's beaut.

Lester saw the open bag on the table. He looked at Sam's face and the blood on his shirt.

You off, then?

Yeah, said Sam. I've got some business to do.

You're in trouble.

The stove spat and swallowed. Someone thumped up stairs.

The bookies?

Sam squirmed against the door. Well –

The union, said Dolly.

Ah, the flamin unions, then is it? That bunch of grovellin bullies. By crikey, I can't . . . He trailed off and went thoughtful. Need to find a bit of tin to crawl under, eh? Listen, gimme ten minutes. Grab some blankets.

Rose came down the station ramp and saw the Lamb truck going. She waved dutifully and then stood there in the little gust of wind it left in its wake. The old man; that was the old man in the passenger side with his hat pulled down over his eyes. And the cocky, the bird on his shoulder and all. Rose swung her handbag and tried a quick trot but her feet were just too sore from dancing. He's in the poo, she thought; he just has to be.

Lester drove out north and before either of them spoke the city was behind them, vibrating in the rearview mirrors.

What's the story? Lester asked.

I gotta keep me lip buttoned, really.

Fair enough.

Sam lit up a smoke. It was something to see, a man with so few fingers rolling and lighting like that.

Your missus clean your face up a bit?

235

Yeah. Gave me the shock of me life, Sam said with a wetlunged laugh.

What you bring the bird for?

It agrees with everything I say.

What's she really like, Sam?

The bird or my old lady? Jesus, I dunno. Like she looks. She's just a rough broad. She used to be . . . I dunno . . . softer. We had a lot of bad luck you know. She used to be easier to get along with. She wasn't such a piss artist in the old days.

Heard from your boy?

How'd you know about that?

Come on, mate, we live between the same walls.

Sam dragged so hard on his smoke, the cab lit up till they could see each other a full few seconds. He's not so bloody stupid as he seems, Sam thought. He's the sort of bloke you'd never know what he was capable of. He might come good in a blue, for instance, though he might be a dobber, too. Didn't he used to be a copper once? A man should never trust an ex-copper.

I haven't heard from Ted yet. Silly bastard. He's gonna find his dick in the wringer before long. He'll end up married to some big bellied girl lookin down the barrels of a shotgun.

Bad way to start a marriage.

Sam snorted. Tell me about it.

Is that your story?

Doesn't it bloody show?

Lester shrugged politely.

He's got Sunday School written all over him, thought Sam.

They drove into the dry, capstone country where ragged banksias showed up in the headlamps and groups of roos stood in paddocks, motionless as shire committees.

Where we goin?

A fishin shack. How long will you need?

A week maybe.

Will it blow over or do you have to blow it over?

I reckon I have to do the job meself.

Trouble is, said Sam, thinking as he spoke, that a bit of

236

action costs money. To get things done.

I can't lend you any, said Lester, the wife wouldn't have it. He thought: he sounds like a little crim all of a sudden.

Wouldn't necessarily be a loan. Rent in advance, maybe.

Well, we're paid up for years already.

Lester turned off towards the coast at a clump of black-boys on a rise. The sky was littered with stars.

You ever thought of buyin it?

Lester sniffed. Cloudstreet?

It'd be a money spinner.

Hardly made you a rich man, mate, said Lester.

I've had a lot of bad luck.

I thought about buyin it once. A long time ago before the old girl moved out the back. But it's too crowded.

Christ, yelled Sam, it's hardly deserted. There's your whole mob and us. And that flatchested Cathlick sheila your missus took in.

No, I mean it feels claustrophobic. Even when it's empty it feels overcrowded.

Jesus. You believe in luck, Lest? You remember that horse Blackbutt? Luck!

Mm.

It's like that lighthouse out there. Pointin the finger, like the Hairy Hand of God.

Lester drove silently until he couldn't bite his tongue any longer. Come clean, Sam, how much do you owe the bookies?

Sam sighed. So the bastard had known all along. Two hundred quid. Some blokes in the union paid it for me.

When was this?

January.

Coo. No wonder they're a little punchy. Will they just take the money if . . . you come up with it?

Yeah. I reckon. But I gotta come up with it.

They rolled down between balding dunes where a small river was dammed up behind the beach. A half dozen tin shacks stood concealed from one another by peppermint trees. No lights showed. There were no other vehicles except a rusty old Fordson tractor that looked like it was used to

237

haul boats out of the water. Upturned dinghies stood beneath trees, with the frames of chairs, kerosene tins, broken rope swings from summer. Lester stopped outside a little corrugated place, left the headlights on and got out to work at the padlock with a bunch of keys. Sam stood out of his light, smelling the sea, wondering how it could all go this far.

There's a coupla crates back in the cab you can bring in, Lester said, getting the door open. A stink of dust and ratshit wafted out.

I didn't know you had a beach house.

It's Beryl's. That flatchested Cathlick sheila you were bein so nice about.

Inside, in the broken beams of light from the Chev, Lester found a lamp, fooled with the wick for a bit, and got it lit. In the sick yellow glow, swimming and bobbing in the uncertain light, the big bed appeared, and the bench, the deal table, the bits and pieces. Sam came in with two boxes.

There's a fuckin revolver in this crate.

Old army days.

Whatm I sposed to do with that?

You got enough fingers to pull the trigger, haven't you?

Yeah. But a gun . . .

I was operatin under the idea that it was a union matter. Keep it here anyway. Shoot rabbits. You'll need the meat.

You goin?

Lester felt disgust come on him in a rush.

I got a family to get back to. I'll be back in a week. No one'll find you out here. Those blokes'll be back, and I'll pay em off and come back for you. There wasn't much camaraderie in his tone, and even he was a little surprised by it. Orright?

Why? Sam said, snaky all of a sudden. What's in it for you?

What's in it for me is I don't have to worry about bruisers hangin round my kids or my house. It buys me some peace of mind.

And a warm feelin, eh, Lester? Sam said bitterly.

Yeah, if you like.

Fair dinkum, said the bird.

Sam swatted it from his shoulder and Lester went out the door to the Chev.

Lester waved and drove off. Sam looked in the boxes. Bread, polony, toilet paper, fruit, vegetables, flour, tea, sugar, a book about John Curtin, a *Reader's Digest* and a Smith & Wesson, six shells.

There's always Russian roulette in the evenings, bird.

Yairs!

Wallpaper

Red Lamb liked Beryl Lee. She was a hard worker and kind. She treated Fish as though he was special. She'd just arrived one day with a teachest of clothes and no explanation. Apparently the old girl had invited her in, and in the weeks after Hat got married Red was especially glad someone had come along. Her mother had foresight, she knew. Right back then, before Hat fell in love, her mother was recruiting a reinforcement.

Beryl didn't say much. She ate with the mob, worked with the mob and on Sundays she went to Mass. Red couldn't tell if maybe it was the changing seasons, but day by day, Beryl seemed to grow paler. It was like seeing someone fade like wallpaper.

That, thought Red, is what happens when you wait for men. Red knew the story. Beryl's hubby had gone down in the *Perth* and no men had looked at her since.

Red thought that Beryl Lee didn't know how lucky she was.

Morning

But no one explained to Quick just who Beryl Lee was. He needed to know because she kept arriving on the end of his bed at dawn to stare at him. One morning she pulled a dandelion to bits and left the petals on his blanket. She was kind of longfaced and horsey, maybe a bit crosseyed even, and when she was around Quick she flounced about a lot, as though she had worms or something. For a couple of days after he came good, he didn't get out of bed, and the days began with this strange woman turning up. He wondered if perhaps she climbed up the drainpipe or crept up through the house while everyone was asleep. Maybe she was a relative. She never said a word and he pretended to be asleep.

One morning he woke to the familiar pressure on the end of the bed but when he peeped through his eyelashes he saw it was his mother. He opened his eyes.

Gday, he said.

Hello.

Quick doubled his pillow beneath his neck. He looked at her. Her square jaw, the arms muscling out of her cotton dress, the bigdialled watch on her wrist. She had long distance eyes. Now he knew where he got his aim from.

I thought you wouldn't speak to me.

I'm your mother, you know.

Geez, how can I forget it.

Not by runnin away.

Quick looked at the ceiling. Great shales of paint hung only by spiderwebs. Waterstains spread map-like across the plaster.

How old are you, Mum?

She cracked her knuckles. I'm fifty-four.

I never knew. You don't look it.

No. But one day I will.

He smiled.

Hat got married last week.

Oh. Good old Hat. Be nice to see her.

She's in Pemberton. Hubby runnin the mill now.

I feel like Rip Van Winkle. Do we fly to the moon yet?

Only on the wireless.

They looked at one another, and then Quick saw business come into her eye.

What did you see? she asked.

What do you mean?

You saw something.

I don't know.

I'm your mother.

I don't know, I said.

240

You broke Fish's heart, Quick. People aren't like furniture.

He closed his eyes.

I'm sorry, she said, I didn't want to go crook.

He felt her hand on his face. He opened his eyes again.

What did you see, Quick?

Why are you out in that tent?

I asked you first.

What's for brekky?

Quick.

I saw myself runnin. That's all.

Well, that's enough I spose.

You bet.

Fatted Calf

Down in the kitchen the old man is at the stove, ducking and weaving as fat snipes at him from the pan. He looks old and exhausted, damn silly with his hair all on end and his lardspattered specs up on his brow. Fish is at the table where two china bowls roar and roll, teetering and toppling as gravity gets hold over motion. His big, soft hands hover over the bowls.

Keep it down, says Lon in his morning sulks.

They're up. I keep em up.

Brilliant, just flamin brilliant, Fish.

Rain falls against the window. Outside looks glum and unavoidable.

Cut yer grizzlin, Lon, says Lester. You'll be late for work.

I'm waitin for me eggs.

You'll be wearin em if you keep that up.

The bowls slide to a stop like pranged hubcaps.

Jesus, Fish!

In a moment Lester is at the table with the lobe of Lon's ear between thumb and forefinger and Lon's squealing like a cut cat. He's small and hoarse, these days, muscly enough, but still no match for Lester who's thin and tall and angry.

241

Lon wriggles and lurches, squinting with pain.

If your mother was here she'd wash your mouth out, boy. It'd be Trusol paste at least. Don't let me hear you talk like that again. Now eat your eggs.

Lester lets go and slides the fried eggs and tomato in front of Lon whose face is lit up red and nasty.

He makes a racket!

It gives him pleasure. Can't you cope with him havin a bit of fun? In case you hadn't thought about it, his prospects aren't as . . . brilliant as yours, you know. If you can't show him any respect –

Respect! He's a Clydesdale. A monster! He should be put away.

Lester expands, you can see his flesh taking on ballast. His arms quiver. He steps out of his crushedheel carpet slippers and puts down the egg slice. Smoke begins to rise from the pan behind him. He's never seemed bigger or meaner than he does now, not to himself, not to the others, not to the room he's in. Lon gets up and backs off.

Don't hit us! calls Fish. Lestah, don't hit us!

Lester turns, startled, and Fish yelps in fear. Lon bolts for the door but Oriel fills it like a Frigidaire.

What's this?

Fish sobs in the corner. Lon barely breathes. Lester looks a kick behind the play, dazed again, incompetent to the moment.

I've never had cause before to feel ashamed of a child of mine, he almost whispers.

The eggs are burnin, Lester.

Yes, I know woman, I know. Mornin Quick, he says, seeing Quick behind his mother. Welcome home.

Quick smiles.

Fish looks up, blotchyfaced and afraid. He's gone out. He's light's off.

No. It's brekky now.

I've gotta go, says Lon.

Take a wrench to your neck, son, says Lester, and get your head off and see if you can't give it a good flush out. A plumber should always mind his own blockages.

242

He's a plumber? Quick asks, when Lon slams the last door in a long line of them.

Apprentice, says Oriel.

You bin gone a hundred, Quick.

Yeah. You've got big, too.

Fish lowers his eyes. He must be six feet tall. He's soft and oafish, but his eyes are still bright as a child's.

Lester comes back to the table with the black-soled eggs, their yokes petrified and split. Hardly a fatted calf is it?

Elaine and Red come in from the shop.

A what? says Red.

Hello, stranger, says Elaine.

Gawd, look at these two!

Where you bin you slack bludger?

Red, you've grown up.

Glad you still know me name.

There's porridge, says Lester.

There's always porridge, Elaine sighs.

Everyone notices Oriel hiding a smile behind her fist.

Yer mother's not well this mornin, Lester says, rolling his eyes. She's havin an attack of smiles.

There's a snort, a sniff, a smirk, and then they're all laughing like themselves from another time.

 Voop

Well, says Quick leaning into the pig pen, I see you're still with us.

The pig grins and rubs his nuts against a stump.

Did you look after Fish, you dirty old cold cut?

Voop, says the pig.

Quick heads indoors shaking his head. I'm surprised you didn't get my bed while I was gone! he calls back, laughing, but the pig just rolls over and farts like a statesman.

In the hallway he comes face to face with Beryl Lee.

Good morning, she says.

Well, hello.

I'm the star boarder.

Pleased to meet you.

I've heard a lot about you, Quick.

How long have you been here?

Oh, quite a while. Your mum's a kind soul.

She's a battalion.

Beryl Lee laughs: nick, nick, nick. It's the saddest laugh he's ever heard.

He stands in the big house and hears it creak.

Matinee

In the middle of the afternoon when the house is quiet, Lester leaves Red and Beryl and Elaine to the rest of the re-stock and steps across the corridor to the Pickles side. Dolly opens the door to the kitchen and lets him in.

Where is he?

Up the coast a bit. He's orright.

She is dressed and made up, and he hears the current in her stockings as she crosses the room for a chair.

Whatm I sposed to do? she says.

Sit tight, I reckon.

She sits and faces him. He can't remember seeing her nervous like this; it takes the crustiness from her features so that she looks younger, more pretty than voluptuous. Lester takes the chair and sits on his hands. A pulse pecks in his neck.

You've got no way of raisin the money, I spose.

I could stand on the corner, she says with a snort. That'd bring in enough for a packet of smokes.

He smiles, uncertain. Men'd pay money, he knows, men'd queue up if she looked every day the way she looks this afternoon. It's something he's never done, hardly even thought about. Thirty years have passed since he was in the company of a woman who would even joke about such

244

things. She grins, as if she reads his thoughts.

Sorry if I'm a bit rough for yer.

Lester fidgets.

What if they come again?

Tell em to see me, he says.

You don't seem the fightin type, Lester.

There won't be any fight.

Dolly pours him a cup of tea. She seems perturbed now. He's never seen her face so different. Until now she's always looked disgusted or just plain nastymouthed.

You can't have this kinda money.

There's savings we've got, he says. We live poor. It's the way we are somehow.

You know it'll be money down the dunny.

Lester shrugs. He feels a continent of trouble sliding his way and sees the flesh of her leg. Where the skirt is slipping back each time Dolly Pickles recrosses her leg.

What else am I sposed to do? he says.

What dyou mean?

Well, he says. We live in this house and we got our shop here and the family. If this thing turns into a proper blue we're liable to find ourselves on the street. I mean, what if you have to sell to clear your debts?

We can't. Not for another ten years. It's in the deed.

Then these blokes are gunna come round and take goods to the value of. Guess which end they'll pillage. I reckon it's worth me insurin against that.

And that's all?

Dolly comes across, takes his cup, and kisses him. The taste of tannin and tobacco are on her lips and her live, moving tongue. The cup falls to the floor, the saucer rolls, and she slides astride his knee and winds her hands into the elastic of his braces. Lester Lamb feels the weight of her buttocks clamping on his knee, the hardware surface of her nails through his shirt, the grate of her heels on the lino, and the speed of her mouth across his face. It's the Saturday Matinee, that's what it is. He can hear the popcorn going off between his ears. His dick begins hydraulicking around behind his flies, as he gets a handful of backside and

245

draws her closer. She comes up for air like a navy diver.

You sure that's all you're buyin? A bit of safety?

He got up, foggy behind the eyes, rearing out of the chair with her still attached to him, and he ran her into the wall so her head hit the flaky plaster and jerked back against his chest. She slipped sideways to the table looking dazed, with her legs still round his waist and her skirt hoisted. Lester felt shock and fury, a kind of gear slip. She had her hand inside his trousers and he took her backside in hand and shoved down onto her. The silver flecks in the surface of the table stung his eyes. She had her hands over her mouth. A shoe dropped to the floor. There was a puddle of tea. The inside of her was firm and strange as sweetmeat. It wasn't the Saturday Matinee anymore. He could hear people passing in the corridor a long way away. Her breasts heaved on her, and in the moment before he felt sick with gravity, he flew his mouth across them and bit down to keep from crying out.

Was that rape, do you think? he asked when he could breathe again.

Dolly pulled her legs down off his shoulders with a wince. I spose not. More a deposit on a hundred quid.

Lester covered his face with his hands.

You bin waitin ten years for that.

And you?

She laughed. I've bin waitin all my life for everything.

We're different.

Yeah, you're gonna go off feelin bad, an I'm gunna go to bed feelin sore. You're not handsome, but you're a nice fella. You've got ninety quid's worth left.

No.

Very flatterin, Lester.

No, not to either of us.

You're a churchy bugger, mate. When you get what you're after you go off feelin awful.

And you just go off soundin awful.

Dolly laughed shakily. What do you want, cobber?

I want you not to use this against me.

I told you you weren't buying safety.

Lester unstuck himself and tried to get organized. The job was beyond him.

ᑫ Disciples ᑫ

Sam woke full of burn and tingle. The stumps of his bad hand seemed to be shooting sparks. The shifty shadow was about; he knew it. Rain beat on the tin roof and he heard the dark, choppy sea rolling restless. He found his matches, lit one and got the Tilley lamp burning, and as he did so he saw a large tweedy rat sloping off, nose up like an Englishman, towards the door. The .38 lay on the deal table by the light. Sam took it up and aimed, saw the rat go stiff and thoughtful in his sights, contemplating a quick sidestep, whiskers aquiver. Yeah, a bloody pommy gentleman, you are, Sam thought. You could be a mine owner or a politician like that rodent Churchill, that nasty little fleshfeeder. The hairy hand is about, rat, so how's your luck gunna be?

All Sam's nerves fizzed and fibrillated. This must be what it was like when the old man could feel water in his rod, the magic of it going right up his arms like a shot from a live fence. The light shinin, the shadow fallin, the seesaw tippin our way.

The rat took a step. Sam spat and hit the door behind the rat which sent it into a panicky spin, a desperate effort to identify its opposition and face off against it. Its eyes were all over, trying to pick an exit.

I could blow your arse out through yer teeth, you little bastard.

He stamped his foot and the rat was off like the Fremantle express.

Sam sat back on the cot, took a coin out of his pocket and flipped thirty-two heads in a row. Then he began to laugh. Pickles, you prize dill, you didn't even call. You dunno if yer winnin or bloody losin!

Heads, he said, and put the florin back in his pocket.

His back hurt again, the way it had all day since he went walking down through the heath country back from the river. He had lumps there, like the beginnings of boils, the kind of boils he could remember having as a kid. Oh, those afternoons over the old man's knee biting into an apple while the old bloke tore clean rags and squeezed through them with his thumbs, pinching the skin of his backside to 'decarbuncle him' quick as could be managed. Be brave, the old man'd say, and you'll be laughing it orf in a sec. A cove only has to be brave for a few minutes of his life. Ooh, I'll bung this on me toast tonight! And he'd laugh across the final lancing scream that Sam, nose deep in apple, came out with.

Boils! he called in disgust, and tossed the florin. Tails it was. Well, it matched. He decided to be satisfied.

A few days of this and they'd be chookraffling him to the nuthouse.

Right then he heard a motor. He looked at his watch – 1:15. He turned out the pressure lamp, reached for the revolver.

Headlamps forked up over the hill and swung down among the trees. Sam went to his knees by the window. Now he'd see which way his luck was runnin. It was hanging over him like a cold dark cloud tonight, and he knew it was momentous, but there was no way of reading it – salvation or his head on the block.

Well, whoever it is, they're comin my way, he thought. A man'd pay coin of the realm for a peaceful leak right this moment.

He ducked as the headlights came swinging his way. With his back to the wall beneath the window, he could see every feature in the shack, the chair and table, cot, shelf, pots and buckets, all with long, tearing shadows from the light barging in through every crack in the tin walls.

Sam? The motor cut short. He heard the handbrake. Sam?

Sam fidgeted. The .38 felt like a laundry iron in his hand. He'd never shot a pistol before in his life. Should he break the glass first and then fire, or shoot straight through the window? He tried to think what they did at the matinee.

The door opened.

Sam? You there?

Friend or foe?

Tenant.

Shit, you scared me.

Get the lamp on.

When the lamp came up Sam looked white and shaky. As he stood there shiftfooted by the door he scratched his back, squirming.

You got the money, then.

What's wrong with your back?

Friggin boils.

When did they come up?

Today.

Don't scratch em.

I'm feelin lucky.

Let's get you packed up.

Sam swatted the bird from his shoulder, but a claw caught in his singlet so that the cockatoo flapped in a fit of squawking and crapping, upside down, suspended from behind Sam's neck. Lester reached out to unhook the bird which took a piece out of his hand the size of a snapper bait.

Dammit to buggery! he yelled.

The bird got free, flew straight into the window and crashed to the floor where it lay groaning like a floored boxer.

You orright? Sam said, laughing.

Yeah, but you aren't. They're not boils you got there. It's ticks. Roo ticks.

Bugger me!

We'll have to get em out. You smoke don't you?

Yeah, what –

Roll a smoke thin and tight and give it to me.

I don't –

Come on, you're wastin time. When you're finished take off your singlet.

What you gunna do, for Chrissake?

Burn em out.

Wonderful. Bloody marvellous.

You won't feel a thing except those little fellers reversin out in a hurry.

Sam lay on the cot while Lester went over his back

finding the little pointed butts of the parasites and applying the fag end.

I've got a plan, Sam said, wincing.

What plan?

For the money.

I thought we'd just drive you straight back to town an you pay em off.

No, I feel lucky.

Oh, you *look* lucky.

Lester rested the glowing end on the tail of a tick and watched it shunt out like a dog from a snake hole. You're gunna look like a flywire door when this is finished.

There's a big two-up game tomorrow.

It's already tomorrow. Where?

I'll show you, said Sam.

It's stupid.

You said you'd get me the money.

I got it. To pay off your debts and keep trouble away from Cloudstreet.

Well I'm gonna do that *and* make us some money.

Us?

Well, it's your money. I reckon you deserve a dividend.

I need a horsewhippin, Lester thought. For this, for a lot of things. You'll lose it, Sam, he said.

Don't bloody talk like that, I know when I'm gunna win.

Well why don't you win more often?

I'm a dill for excitement.

I could do with a little less excitement.

You're gutless, Lamb.

You just remember one thing, mate. I haven't given you the money yet.

I've got the .38.

A man who can't drive a car could never use that thing.

Want to test that little theory? Listen, I'm gunna win. Me stump's bloodynear glowin. I know it.

There was a sweat on Sam's face, and his eyes were bright. Lester didn't know whether to admire or pity him. It was too late to save the money now. In any case, he thought, aflush with shame, you can't deny a man a chance when

250

you've just had his wife on the kitchen table.

Carn. Get up and pack.

You're in?

No, you're in.

Where's that . . . Sam then? said the bird trying to get up. Where's that Sam?

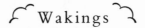 Wakings

At dawn, and the first raw-throated stirrings of hidden birds, Cloudstreet floats soundlessly from the gloom to join the day. Down on the tracks a Fremantle freight creeps past under a limestone sky, and in her tent, towelling the water from her face and chest in a manner so delicate as to be secretive, and to someone who knew her, completely un-characteristic, Oriel Lamb feels the vibrations in the duck-boards. When she's finished washing she applies a little talcum powder and dresses in her floral frock, stockings and hardsoled sandals which look more like work boots with ventilators cut into them. She notes again the ugliness of her feet all distorted with corns and bunions. She still remembers her own bare running feet on the dirt of the home paddock when the world was a place given by God for the pleasures of children, when all that was good was unbroken. Oriel empties her washwater onto the seed pots outside and comes back in to make her bed and tidy the shelves, clear the card table that is her desk. For ten minutes, with the help of the rimless spectacles she needs now, she reads the *Reader's Digest* and makes pencil marks beside instructive passages. The early morning 'quiet time' as she calls it, has proven impos-sible to shake off. But it gives her time to meet the day, steel herself, put on the full armour as she used to say. She finishes up, tidies the table again and feels the mulberry tree hanging over the tent like a cloud. It's still early, she'll give them another half hour before reveille – it's been a hard week since the wedding, what with Quick turning up and keeping them on the lookout like that, and the hole that Hat has left in the company. Another loss. Oh, if she thinks about everything that's been taken from her over the years – Lord, it's like the longest subtraction sum invented. She can't help it, the feeling is on her and she's furious. It's a sickness, selfpity, it'll eat you up, woman, you know it. It'll eat the day and worm into your labour and weaken you. She puts her square, red fist on the table, watches it like it's a paperweight. Up the back the pig snorts like a priest chanting. Fowls begin to scuffle. She hears water in the sewerage pipes beneath the garden path. Someone is up.

Elaine waits till the stove finishes smoking and makes sure it's properly alight before waking Beryl Lee. Back in the kitchen they lay out the bacon and yesterday's eggs. Elaine stands at the back door in the cold morning air and sees movement in the tent. The New Guinea beans Fish planted have overtaken the yard, the great hairy, veined creeper enclosing the chookyard and the pig's den, the whole of the back fence and each side, right through the other vegetables, across the apple and orange and lemon trees, right to the door of the tent itself. Elaine can't think how the thing has been tolerated this long. There's even a tangle of it in the mulberry tree, and in the first sun, a-shine with dew, you can see a bean hanging above the tent the size of a man's arm.

Your father's not in, Laine, Beryl murmurs behind.

Hmn?

The truck's gone. His bed hasn't been slept in.

Elaine turns and is distracted from wondering how Beryl has the nerve to go into the old man's room, by the mystery of his absence.

Probably gone to the markets early, I spose.

He hasn't been here.

He used to be in the army, Mrs Lee. He knows how to make his bed. Elaine isn't used to being firm with Beryl. Sometimes she has the feeling she'll end up like that poor woman, alone, too old, pathetic and dependent, it's the only thing that keeps her from lashing her now and then, the image of herself in Beryl's rednosed maudlin face.

Well, says Beryl, I hope he comes good on the apples today. People are asking.

Here comes Mum, put some wood on the stove. I'll wake the boys.

Quick wakes from a plain wide sleep without dreams to remember, and finds Fish in bed beside him. It brings back more mindpictures than any dream – they could both be boys instead of the men they are. Fish has his head against Quick's chest and his arm thrown over his belly. Quick smells his brother's hair, feels the weight of him against his ribs. It feels like forgiveness, this waking, and Quick is determined not to be embarrassed. He looks around the room and sees how shabby it is. Wallpaper has gone the colour of floor fluff. The bedspread is patched, and he feels the pillowslip against his chest, an assembly of old pyjama tops. The furniture could have come from any combination of shutdown pubs from Beverley to Bakers Junction, the kind of firewood gimcrack he's seen as a shooter and rouseabout and truckie.

Quick?

Hmm?

Lester goed.

What?

He didden come.

Did you get lonely?

He didden.

He probably had somethin to do.

Everyone goes.

Quick chewed his lip. There was more action around the old house than there used to be. It took all your energy just to keep track.

Down the corridor Lon sleeps openmouthed. Pimples break out on his chin and others are plotting. A bomber jacket, new and wrinkled, lies across his chair. Out on the landing, Red gets on with her situps. She has a shine on her, the firmness of green fruit, and wind comes out of her like truck brakes.

On the other side of the corridor, Chub Pickles sleeps like he was custombuilt for it, Rose Pickles writes in her diary with her tongue wickedly in the corner of her mouth and listens to him snoring through the wall. She checks her nails between sentences. She has beautiful hands and they still surprise her.

And then the silly drongo told me my ear tasted like treacle, and that HAS to be the dumbest thing I've ever heard. Still, he's nice enough for his kind. It's hard to believe I come from this nuthouse every morning and go out there into the world without everyone guessing straight off. It's like two lives. Ha, ha. Like a book!

Rose hears the Lamb truck pull in and goes to the window. Down below she sees her mother's arms protruding from her ground floor bedroom. There's Mr Lamb with Stan the cocky, but no Sam. Curious.

Dolly can't catch Lester's eye as he stumps up onto the verandah with a crate of lettuce. She waits, braving the chill in her thin nightie, but he comes and goes as though she's not there. He looks tired and needs a shave. The windscreen of the truck is running with the goo of a hundred exploded bees.

You look like you just lost a quid and found a shillin, she says in the end.

Lester stops, a box of Jonathons swaying in his arms. I'll let you know when I find the shillin.

Are you in the poo, too?

Let me put it this way, Mrs Pickles. By midnight we're probably all gunna be in the poo.

People like you aren't used to it.

Being in trouble, you mean?

Yeah.

She watched him thinking about this for a good while and she could tell that a thousand cruel comebacks were reeling through his mind. She braced herself for it, but he said nothing and she felt ludicrously grateful. It gave her the feeling that there'd be no more visits to her kitchen and she was surprised to find she regretted it.

Lester went to bed with the curtains drawn and slept till noon but instead of getting up to make tonight's pasties and do the afternoon grocery deliveries, he stayed where he was, paralysed with wondering how he could have gotten himself into such a spot. All their cash savings in a two-up game depending on a dud gambler landlord whose wife he had been knocking himself only yesterday. And it wasn't only his own mystification he worried about. He could feel the wonder of the others almost crashing at the door.

He didn't sleep, though he wished he could because he was still weary from the night. He looked around the room, tried to concentrate on its contents. I miss kids, he thought; I miss having children around. To fool with and muck about with. I was somebody with kids – they believed in me, I made them laugh. And now . . . what is it? That they see straight through me? The bloke who's married to the lady in the tent.

He noticed how patched together everything was, everything in the room. What had they been saving for, anyway?

All our clothes are old and mended, he thought; we never buy anything except for the shop, so what are we intending to buy?

He listened to the sounds of lunch being prepared down the hall.

He's probably picked up a wog, said Elaine.

Do the knife, Quick, said Fish.

Quick spun the knife with a grin.

This is for the biggest bloke in the family, and remember, sport, the knife never lies.

Fish hunched over the spinning blade, giggling. It was a strange sound to hear coming from a fourteen stone man whose hands were as big as T-bones. A pale forelock bobbed on him as his head followed the slowing movement and Quick set his teeth against that old feeling of grief and blame. The blade crept around now, and Beryl and Elaine stopped putting out the ham to watch. Lon looked out of the window. Oriel turned from the stove looking blank. Fish's

255

giggle thickened and he barely seemed to need a breath to sustain it.

It's me! Meeeee!

Fish beat his fists on the table and they laughed with him until Oriel put the early potatoes out, steaming in their pale jackets with butter sliding over them and parsley sprinkled on top. There was tea from the urn and fresh bread, a salad with grated carrot and cheese, chutney for the ham.

Before anyone else was finished, Quick excused himself and went down the hall. He knocked at the old man's door and went in uninvited.

How you feelin?

The old man was lying there with his arms behind his head. He looked pale and worried.

Oh, I'm orright.

You crook?

No, not really.

Quick sat in the old reading chair that used to be in the loungeroom before the loungeroom became the shop. He could smell the lemon scent of the old boy.

Good to have you back, son. You get out of bed and I climb in, eh?

You're lucky Red's at school. If you're not crook she'll be onto you. She doesn't believe in sickness. Even if you were crook she'd have you out.

They laughed quietly at this.

She's like her mother.

Quick shrugged. Well, *she* hasn't been in to hook you out, so I gathered you must be on yer last legs.

Well, that remains to be seen.

What dyou mean?

Oh, I'm in the poop. I've lent money to Pickles.

Quick whistled. A lot, eh?

The old man nodded.

Mum know?

She's got a nose.

You're too soft, Dad, Quick murmured without much censure in his voice. Let's go fishin, take Fish along.

Not tonight.

256

They sat quiet for a while. It was like a hospital visit, or what Quick imagined a gaol visit to be like.

You ever dream? the old man asked.

Plenty.

You ever have the same dream twice?

Quick nodded.

I keep having this dream, the old man said, almost in a whisper. It's the first thing I can remember in my life – you know my earliest memory. It's dark and raining and I'm in a storm and I'm in the middle of a creek – I can hear it roaring and see the white. There's lightning but it doesn't show anything up, just blinds me. I'm absolutely packin myself. And I'm on my father's shoulders and he's carryin me across. He's steady and big, and we're makin it. I'm just hangin on, and he's takin me across.

Their eyes met. Quick smiled.

That's a nice one.

I always wake up in tears.

Why don't you come down and make the pasties? Mum'll botch em up.

Lester smiled. Don't ever join the army.

Geez, one army's enough.

She's a good woman, Quick. She's worth two of me.

But she makes a lousy pasty.

Go on, you drongo.

Quick left and saw Beryl coming.

He alright?

Quick nodded.

I'll see if he wants something.

He doesn't want you, Quick thought; you're the last thing a man needs. Regular bedside Betty.

He heard her open the door behind him as he went on up the front to the shop. The bell was ringing.

∫ Promises ∑

Lester was most of the way out of his pyjamas when Beryl broke in, knocking as she came, and he found himself

257

standing like a soldier ready for a short arm inspection. Beryl
had a sweat on her upper lip; her eyes were china white
taking in his kit. She showed none of the disinterest army
matrons had impressed him with, and he felt a fury rising out
of his embarrassment.

Would you like to break a piece off as a souvenir, Beryl?

What?

He hauled up his pyjama pants and sat back on the bed.

What do you want, Beryl?

Oh, strewth, I'm sorry, Lester.

She stood with her back to the door, wearing a faded
bag of a frock and a pair of chunky heels that must have given
her curry all day in the shop. He knew she was a fragile
thing, and he'd seen her kindness to his children and the
gratitude she offered to Oriel for building her back into
someone who could stand in her own shoes again; regardless
of the style. She worked hard in this house and he respected
her for it, but he'd never been able to cipher out why she'd
stayed so long.

As he watched, a composure, a toughness came into her
face that he'd never seen before, and he was about to ask
her again what the matter was when she started talking.

I know about you and Mrs Pickles, Lester.

You must hang off the banisters like a fruit bat.

I watch you.

You don't know anythin, Beryl, he said, a quiver coming to his jaw. How on earth could you know that what you
think happened actually happened?

Well, you seem to know what I'm talking about without
any explanation.

Lester tried to scrape up some form. He looked at his flat
pink feet sticking from his barber's pole jarmies. Well, he
thought, catastrophe hasn't exactly been long in the wings.
Least it hasn't kept me waitin.

She's a low woman, Lester.

That's our landlady you're talkin about, he said with the
feeblest of grins.

I'm shocked, surprised even.

Me too.

You're in trouble.

More than you think, Beryl. You know I've never been in trouble in my whole life – I mean seriously nose deep in the nure. I've kept laws and rules and contracts –

And now you're gunna tell me you feel free for the first time in your life, like Bette Davis or somebody! That's really got to be the living –

Beryl! he hissed. Keep your blessed voice down.

Beryl sagged back against the door.

Are you gunna dob on me, Beryl? Is that why you're here? I haven't got a brass razoo if it's money you're after.

Oh, you . . . bugger!

State your business, Beryl. What have you come to do to me?

Beryl came to the edge of his bed and her proximity forced him back onto the pillow.

I came to tell you to leave off with Mrs Pickles.

Or?

Or you'll ruin your life and break a fine woman's heart. Mrs Lamb deserves better.

Fair enough, Beryl.

What?

I said you're right.

Well . . . well good then.

Go, Beryl.

Lester lay back and felt the cool palms of his hands on his face.

The World Through Beryl

Pausing for barely a second now and then like a motor gently missing, Oriel stopped to watch Beryl, who had grown paler still. That woman will disappear if she keeps fading like this, she thought. What is it with Beryl? Hunger for a man? What man deserves a good honest woman like Beryl? Even as she watched, Oriel saw Beryl fading by the window. She saw the mulberry tree through the tall woman's translucent, veiny arms. The sky moved behind her. You could see the whole world through Beryl Lee.

Take a break, Beryl.

No, I'm right. Truly.

Business

For the better part of the day, Sam stays in Kings Park where Lester left him at dawn. He sleeps in cool shade before the sun gets high, and later he walks down the quiet avenues, along the endless rows of trees, each with its plaque bearing the name of a dead soldier, his unit, his deathfield. The bush of the park comes alive with sweeping birds, the scuttle of goannas and rabbits. All day he wanders, finding a statue, a new road, a landscaped garden, and at the eastern edge, a view of the city with the river leaning its way in and out of the plan below. A ferry pushes its way from Mends Street to the Barrack Street jetty. A rich man's yacht, red sails shuddering like a singer's lungs, cuts in behind it, and children wave. He's come to like the place, he discovers. The autumn blue sky bowls across the whole business and warms his certainty. He feels the notes in his pocket.

Heading down to the big boulevard of eucalypts, past the statue of John Forrest, he comes to the great log the kids call the Toothpick. It's huge and barely weathered, ten feet high and a hundred feet long, on its side like a fallen beast. At its sawn ends he sees the lines that divide its years, concentric markings like the inside of a gobstopper.

There's some floorboards in you, old son, he murmurs, leaving.

Lightbrained with hunger, he goes on down to Mount Street, past the grand houses and the gleaming Buicks and Humbers, into the city. Hay Street is full of trams and beer barrels. Kids are selling the *Mirror* and the *West* on corners, trollies hiss by down William Street, and outside Foys the cashews roasting, the sandwich counter roaring, send him giddy and glasseyed on his way. Afternoon picture shows are finishing with a straggle of squinteyed patrons coming back out onto the street as if stunned by the ordinariness of the day. Men smoke on the steps of the GPO, eat pies and stay wary of their suits. With two hundred pounds in his pocket, he sits in Forrest Place with the gas-crazy Anzacs and mealy whingers who ask for a fag and a florin and look at you like you might be the bloke who caused all their problems in the first place. With two hundred quid against his leg, he sits without food, without a drink or a smoke, looking across the rails toward Roe Street where someone's backyard is being rigged with a tarp and the dirt raked in a flat circle for tonight. All along the street, the tired old tarts are calling sailors and frightening off schoolboys while the trains shunt by spitting steam. Sam feels change in his pocket. Yes, he'll buy a shave in an hour, and after dark he'll go across the bridge, hungry, smokestarved, dry, clean as a monk. And lucky.

⌒ Beryl Fades Out ⌐

Mum, said Red. Beryl is fadin.

Oriel looked at the potatoes in her hand and thought of the things she'd like to tell the spud growers of Australia about taking a little time, a little pride and a little care.

Mum? All afternoon she's bin goin out like a light.

Your father's out like a light today himself. Hasn't been out of bed all day.

I think he's crook, Red said disapprovingly.

Hm.

Then what about Beryl?

Go find her for me.

They're holeing up this afternoon in Cloudstreet. In their beds, their rooms, in their work and their heads they're closing doors and turning keys while the trees lean in against the gutters and squeeze and the nails creak, the boards

squinch together just a notch more beneath a shifting, a
drifting, a lifting sky as Sam Pickles pulls lint from his
pockets, as Fish touches Quick's back leaning into the steamy
guts of the Chev with a spanner, watched by Dolly and
above her by Rose while Beryl goes back in to Lester without
knocking.

I'm leaving here tonight, said Beryl.

Lester sat up in bed and saw Beryl trying not to bawl
and weep.

Going? Lester'd gone beyond fury today. He'd been all
day in a state of silly wonder, and now he didn't know where
else there was to go. He'd spent years arresting people for
things both mild and maniacal. He'd been to war and lived a
Depression on the land, been a father and a husband, and this
week, even an adulterer, but it counted for nothing because
here he was with Beryl Lee on the end of his bed beggin
the question: why was it that he didn't know a thing about
the underlying nature of people, the shadows and shifts,
the hungers and hopes that caused them to do the things
they did?

Why, Beryl? I thought you were happy here, safe.

Beryl unwound her defeated neck and fixed him with a
doleful stare until he could feel his eyes pressing the back of
his skull.

Well, I have . . . I have *feelings* too you know.

Lester sighed. Ah. Quick, is it? I've seen you since he's
been back.

Oh, Lester.

What?

You'd have made an awful copper.

I was.

She fixed him with that significant look again and Lester
groaned.

Me? Oh, Beryl. I'm sorry.

It's just got too much for me.

But you don't have to go.

No, I've been deciding ever since Quick came back.

I . . . hung about him because, well because of the state
he was in when he came home to us, and I wanted to talk to
him, ask him some things. You see there's a house I've been
talking with, a convent –

Oh, come on, Beryl!

And I wanted to pick his brain about a few things. He
has shadows in his eyes, that boy. I'm sure if he'd wanted to
talk to me –

He doesn't know you, Beryl, he hardly knows his own
family anymore.

Well, anyway, I've decided without the benefit of getting through to him. I'm going tonight.

But you don't want to be a nun.

Don't you believe in commitment?

I dunno, Beryl.

Why're you staying here with your wife? Think of the
calisthenics you could have had with . . . other people.

Well, I made some promises in my time.

Beryl smiled and her whole posture seemed to benefit.
And you'll keep them all in the end, Lester. That's you. See.
And I'm the same. I'm a Catholic. I make promises, too.
I love the Church.

Geez, Beryl, it's drastic.

Look at this old house, Lester. Look at that tent down
there. Do a room-by-room and have a look. This has always
been drastic and I thank God for all of it. I'm getting married
again, Lester. Be happy for me.

It's not natural.

Marriage is never natural.

Lester laughed. Oh, Beryl, you're a bonzer.

Beryl Lee smiled the sweetest most crucifying smile and
Lester heard Fish begin to thump the piano upstairs.

And we hardly noticed you, he said.

But you'll remember, won't you?

My oath.

A terrible moaning came down through the floor. Beryl
left him and he lay there like a sprayed insect.

Oriel looked at Beryl and took her in her meaty arms.

Don't pity me, Oriel.

Pity? You've gotta be usin levity on me! You see that tent? You see this non-Cathlick beatin breast? Pity, Beryl? Don't shame a woman. I'm just sad to see you go. I'll . . . probably . . . well, miss you.

But we hardly ever talked.

Talk? Those poor misguided nuns'll teach you the use of talk, love. A woman doesn't need talk. She needs a team. I hope you find it. You can always come back. Always.

Beryl said her bit and stuffed her bags and everyone descended to the kitchen to make a dinner worthy of her. Lester whipped and dipped. There were scrubbers and peelers, stringers and wringers, as the stove bawled and the pots jangled up a head of steam. The big old house heaved and sighed around them. Chooks were still fighting for roosts down the back, and the pig was snoring by the time they finished eating and Lester cleared his throat to speak.

Beryl, as head of the household I think it's time to let you know how glad we are to have had you round. You've worked like a bloke and we'll miss you, I reckon. We wanna say good luck in all you do. He looked at the others, a little uncertain, as though calculating something, and then he grinned. You know we're not a drinkin family, Beryl, and you'll also be aware that Mum here doesn't agree with fluids at meals on account of the science of digestion, so in order to serve you a toast, I'll ask everybody to charge their forks.

And he speared a spud and held it aloft, waiting for them all to follow suit, which in the end they did, openmouthed with amazement. Yes, charge your forks, and here's to Beryl, a jolly good fella.

To Beryl, they all said, lamb, spuds, or just gravy on their forks, if that's all they had left, and they bit and munched, following his lead – even Oriel whose face led you to believe she was eating live bullant.

Nun better for our money, said Lon, who got a blow

264

from everyone in reach except Beryl herself.

Bless you all, she said.

We'll smuggle icecream in, eh, Dad, said Quick.

Ah, Beryl laughed, you'll bring the Church to its knees.

I'm told that is the correct position, said Oriel stone-faced.

In the brief, hysterical silence to follow, Lester said:

I do believe your mother made a joke.

Their eyes were as big as hardboiled eggs.

 Ticking

Sam Pickles opens a gate across town with his stump sparking like a cut cable.

The light goes out of the night sky a moment. The pig hoots and bawls. Fish goes to the window stormbrowed. A man stands in the street across the road with his great timepiece ricking and ticking.

Lester came back from dropping Beryl off. Everyone slumped round the cleared kitchen listening to the queer rattle of the gutters.

I'm goin prawnin, said Oriel.

Thay all just gawked.

Not really the season, Mum, said Quick. November at the earliest.

There's always prawns in the river. There'll always be something.

Brrr. I'm listening to the wireless, said Elaine.

Me too, said Red.

Yeah, said Lon.

In the river? murmured Fish, building something out of his hands.

You'll be in bed, Fish.

265

I'll tell you stories, son, said Lester. He looked darkly at Oriel.

Come on, Quick, she said.

Eh?

Get the net and get your togs on.

It's cold, Mum.

Goin on me own, am I?

Quick stood by the big old wireless and sucked his teeth. It's givin in, he thought; it's too early to be givin in.

And I haven't seen him for two years, Oriel said to Lester.

Quick sighed and gave in. Heading for the door, he muttered: It's just silly.

Everyone else can be silly all day long in this house, so why not me a couple of hours in me lifetime?

Out in the water it was cool but not quite cold. From the shallows outside Pelican Point where all the bigboned birds nested restlessly in sleep, Quick and Oriel could see the lights of Mounts Bay Road, the baths, the party glow of a ferry coming through the Narrows. The whole city seemed to lay itself flat upon the water. In summer there'd be fires on the beach and the sound of children, smells of boiling prawns, the lights of kids chasing cobbler along the shore with gidgie spears. Now there was just the sound of the two wading and the triangular net slushing behind between the two upright poles.

You know, this is the first time I've been prawning since Margaret River, Oriel said.

Since Fish you mean.

Yes, I spose that's what I mean. Do you still blame yourself for it?

How did you know about that?

I'm your mother. Besides, it's obvious. Fish was every-one's favourite.

You mean it's true – he was the favourite?

Oh, people say they don't have favourites when it comes

to children, but you know, son, it's a lie we tell to protect the others.

So you did love him more than the rest of us? Quick's voice was dead with hurt.

Wasn't he your favourite, Quick?

Quick waded. A small fish skipped away from him. All around his body was an aura of phosphorescence.

Didn't you love him more than all of us? Don't you still love him more? Haven't you always had Honour Thy Retarded Brother as your number one commandment? You see, it hurts to know you're not the favourite whoever you are, child or parent. Did you feel guilty about leaving us, or about leaving Fish?

Why do we have to talk about this, Mum?

Because we're family.

Jesus, I hate this family stuff. It makes me sick! I don't need all this.

It's all we have.

What?

Each other.

Oh, come on, Mum.

You're scaring the prawns away.

There aren't any bloody prawns – Jesus Christ!

Don't *say* that.

Oriel pulled the net and tried not to show exhilaration at having him here like this, at the two of them talking like adults together. There was something hard and resistant in him now, something he'd grown in being gone, and she knew it had been worth the hurt.

Why are you so bitter? Because of your family or because of yourself?

What dyou mean?

Do you hate the fact that you come from . . . well let's just say crack troops.

Weirdos, Mum, flamin whackos.

Or is it just the old business of feelin guilty about being a survivor?

Quick almost stumbled at that. It went deep into him.

What the hell would you know? You don't know the first thing about feelings, certainly not mine, and damnsure not about what I feel about Fish.

I know about bein a survivor. You think it's your fault he died. You think it should have been you. You're paralysed with this thing that's eatin you, and you don't know that it's rubbish.

You don't know a damn thing about it, Mum.

She thought about her mother and sisters up in the house cooking like picnic steaks while she lay helpless in the cellar, she saw the bullet torn wallet of Bluey her half brother with its black crust of ink and blood and the King's stamped signature on the slip of paper. And she could feel Fish's chest under her fists as she beat life into him with the sky kiting over her, silent as death. She pursed her mouth with her teeth set behind them.

Have I been a crook mother?

Quick sighed. She was upset now. He could feel the explosion in her.

No, Mum, of course not.

Do I lie?

No.

Do I cheat?

No.

Steal?

No.

Fornicate?

Well, I'll have to check on that with the neighbours. I reckon the tent's a dubious sign. And to his complete surprise, she laughed.

Don't be a drongo, Quick.

He pulled the net. Now they were inside the bay at Crawley where the uni glowed like a cathedral up there behind the peppermints.

What's wrong with me?

Mum.

Carn, what's my problem, Quick?

Quick had never known his mother to be like this. It was exciting and unnerving. He could no longer tell how

268

she'd react. It was like having a dead shark in the boat. A dead shark always *seemed* dead enough, but the buggers had a habit of coming to life and taking your feet off.

You don't have enough fun, maybe, he ventured, a little breathless.

She made a little popping sound with her lips. It sounded ominously slight.

No one takes me to dances anymore.

Geez, Mum, you're always at dances.

Yes, and I'm either organizin them or playin the piano. Your father's always on the stage, and I can't even remember if he knows *how* to dance. I used to dance with my daughters until I lost out to men, and Heaven knows I dance better than every one of *them*. And my sons never stooped to dancin.

Stoopin'd be right, thought Quick. It'd be like dancin with a teachest. But she'd made her mark; she was right enough.

Let's face it, Mum, he said, suddenly reckless with courage, you do everythin better than anybody. It's just that you're flamin bossy.

She laughed. I'm glad you see things my way.

Quick pulled with her to the beach, and helped empty the net of its cargo of jellyfish and gobbleguts and other useless small fish. He had a boyish impulse to kick her in the shins and run, just to have her after him, awful and reliable with it.

The strong are here to look after the weak, son, and the weak are here to teach the strong.

What are we here to teach you, Mum?

Too early to say.

They set off again, down toward the deep end and the baths. Quick was real tired now, and cold. Oriel strode out in her hard little granny shoes, feeling quivery inside. She wondered how far things had gone between Beryl and Lester. She wondered what instruction there was in it for her. Sometimes she couldn't think what jerrybuilt frame was holding her together. It wasn't willpower anymore. She'd gone past that lately. She only had will enough to make everything else work, these days. There was never enough

269

left for her. She was like that blessed truck of Lester's, running on an empty sump.

I'll take you to a dance, Mum. The best. I'll shout you to the Embassy.

Hmm. Their sandwiches are dry.

How do you know? Quick said, miffed.

I sell em day-old bread. There's an arrangement.

Quick guffawed. You *are* bent, then.

No. I'm astute. You ever heard anyone complain about supper at the Embassy ballroom?

No. Never.

Well, there you are.

Quick pulled for a while, and a strange sort of question came to him. The strong can get rich, Mum. You know. What would you do if you got rich?

Get poor again, I expect. I'm surrounded by fools, you know.

Seriously, though.

It's a silly schoolboy question.

It isn't. You just don't want to say.

She surged ahead and forced the pace a little. The water was hard and cold now. He was right; she didn't want to say.

That was when they came upon the wild wheeling mob of prawns that came brawling out of the deep unlit gutter near the baths, and swerved in panic, beating against Oriel and Quick's legs, skipping and bouncing into the net, ricocheting like crossfire, breaking the surface of the water in an unearthly frenzy. When they got to the beach, gasping and whooping, with the net near splitting with its freight, they had to lie on the sand a while before taking off their clothes, shorts, trousers, singlet, spencer, shirt, pullovers, hats, and tie knots in them to make bags because the five gallon drum just wasn't enough. They rode home nearly barebummed through the back streets with the sidecar awash with prawns, and they sprinkled a mist of river as they ploughed through the sleeping streets.

From above, the two-up circle looks like a sea creature, some simple hungry organism in the water of night. A sea anemone whose edges rise and fall as bodies press and spread with two glittering morsels turning and dangling in its maw. Two coins spinning above the pulsating mouth, catching light and shining to tantalize. But they're men down there and the coins' light shines on them the way the sun and moon have never done. A swearing, moneyflicking, beery mob of blokes dancing to the music of the toss, the dance of chance. They call in intercession, they pray and whine and moan as if those two big crosspainted pennies can hear them. See among them the little fella with the stump and the mad light in his eyes, crazy as a crusader, mad as a cut snake, driven as a dog. It's the look men have in their eyes when they go green to war – one eye on duty and the other on the spoils – when they can't wait to step beneath the spinning pieces to see whether they'll be torn in half by them or feel them lob safely and full of promise at their heels. He's not a young man anymore, the little fair fella. Beneath the noise of the crowd he's wheezy and his veins are swollen. His back aches, he's thirsty, hollowgutted, in need of a smoke, but he stays planted to the spot awaiting the certainty of his blessing. And down it comes again like manna. Men hush at the sight of it, though he doesn't even nod. He puts another fistful of notes down and hears the grumbling. He must be the only sober man here tonight, and he tries to decide what this feeling is like, being the lone man, the onehanded man, the man pushing on into the darkness of the rest of them. Like Christopher-bloody-Columbus, that's how it feels, he thinks; sailin out, knowing you're not gonna get to the edge and fall off the bleedin map, at least not before you bump into a whole continent of treasure with the angels on your side. Pennies go up and stay there a heartbeat or two, as men wring their hats and wait. Sam's heart almost explodes with devotion.

From the outside, if you don't share the love of the game, if you don't know these men, it's still cause for wonder. How they love it, how they dance and sing in the dragon's jaws. And Sam Pickles. If you hated his guts you couldn't help but be affected by the sight of him, the prince of losers, winning the bank.

The whole damn cake and candles.

Feast

Dolly grabbed him by the shirt and pulled him close before he'd even got in the kitchen door. She was shaky and sober and ready to scream out of fright and worry and she could barely believe she was clinging to him like this. Drawing back and drawing breath, she saw there wasn't a mark on him. His trousers were stuffed like a mattress. Before anything could happen, Rose came in the door, fresh from the dance.

Well, look at you two.

They peeled off each other selfconsciously. The three of them had the flesh of new people. For a moment.

Laughter echoed from across the corridor.

We could sell them! Elaine said, putting out a huge china bowl of brown vinegar. The table was spread with newspapers, and the first steaming, red pile of prawns was upon it.

No fear, said Oriel, unable to stop a smile.

Be a good few quid, Mum, said Lon, who was the first to shell. The meat was longer than his hand.

No fear, Oriel said again.

Why not, Mum? Red slid a prawn around the vinegar bowl. There's so many.

They're gunna keep jumpin outta me pockets fer years yet, said Quick.

You'll always be comin the raw prawn, said Lester to a uniform groan.

We can't eat em all, said Red through a disgusting mouthful.

Watch me, said the old man.

They're a gift, Oriel murmured. And you don't go floggin off a gift.

Quick and Lester raised eyebrows at one another.

You don't look a gift horse in the mouth, said Red, quoting from somewhere or other.

Yeah, said the old man, laughing, you send it to the knackers before it can take off with your vegies.

Where's Fish?

He'll be asleep.

Go up and check, said the old man to Quick. He might want a feed himself. Hey, an you might's well knock at the Pickles hatch and ask em if they want to join us. I think they're still up.

That raised a few brows and stopped a few jaws, but Oriel nodded. Yeah, fair enough. Share n share alike.

And after midnight the Lamb kitchen was full to the boards with the lot of them. It wasn't till Lester got the broadest, leeringest wink from Sam Pickles that he remembered disaster and discovered that he'd been saved. And then some.

Up in the library, Fish asked the shadow girl why she wouldn't come out, but she said nothing. She was always either crying or angry and nothing else. He played her a tune and she stood beside him, but he couldn't tell if it made any difference.

Quick came calling. The dark girl shrank away.

VIII

Voices

ROSE crossed the nightwet lawn and sat at the edge of the verandah to take off her heels. Cloudstreet was still, the house limping with shadows, and the sky over it all was the colour of an army surplus blanket. She was still damp under the overcoat – taffeta and tulle clung to her, cooling. It was getting pretty late in spring for an overcoat, but she couldn't stand having every bloody dag and drongo on the bus knowing she was coming home unescorted yet again from a dance. A faint smile of sympathy was just as bad as a leer when you were all clobbered up and coming home alone.

She sat there a while in the shadow of the house, trying to fend off the twinges of hayfever she felt in her nose and throat. An easterly tomorrow would be all she needed – pollen like the Yellow Peril.

It was the same blokes at the Embassy tonight, the larrikins in suits, the quiet movers with brandy on their breath and Brylcreem in their hair. The ones with vagrant hands, the ones with bad teeth, broken noses, feet like snowshoes, bellies like baskets. The same old meatmarket with all the girls backed around the walls and the blokes perving in from the doorway. The band cranking up, and the awful rush of blood to the face as they came in to pick and choose for the night's first dance. God, how she loved it! The itch of petticoats, the rushes to the toilet when it was clear there'd be no first dance for her, and the breathless re-entries she made to the ballroom in time for some lottery marble to grab her by the arm and say: Gday, love. Like a spin, wouldja? Oh, she got some grouse dances, and some fine old moments, but it was always Rose on the bus without a bloke to see her home. She couldn't understand why she cared half the time; she didn't really make big efforts to be noticed, and she didn't quite know how she'd feel having some handsome sort bringing her to this particular doorstep, this great sagging joint with its pile of crates out front and the compost stink of aged vegetables. All its timbers were unpainted, grey, flaky. From the front, it had the appearance, with only Rose's light burning and her blind half up, of a miserable dog sleeping and keeping an eye half open for an excitement that was never going to arrive. No, she could hardly own up to some smart love that this was where she lived. Moreover, that her family only lived in half of it.

She sighed and went inside, pausing a moment on the threshold to unhook her stocking from a splinter that seemed to live for this moment every Wednesday and Saturday. Going up the stairs, she heard the whoosh of petticoats and the electric buzz of her nylons.

In bed she listened to the sound of someone crying. There was always someone weeping in this place. So many

278

people lived here it was hard to figure out who it was. Just a quiet sobbing, it lilted in the walls, and willed her to sleep.

Rose Pickles was twenty-four years old and a woman, though she hadn't got used to thinking of herself in this way, and even a stranger could tell this by the girlish look on her face which she wore underneath every other expression she ever had, whether happy or miserable. She had a noticeable face – strong nose, brown unsettling eyes, and a complexion that always had summer in it. She had the Pickles shortness and their cocky way of walking. A man'd be stupid to think she wasn't pretty, but then most men are at least a little stupid. Rose Pickles was proud, and difficult to slow down long enough to get a good look at. She never looked anyone in the eye, and as often as not, she went unseen as a result.

She voted Labor every election because she knew it would break her old man completely to have a bosses' pimp in the family. Still, it didn't do much good because Pig Iron Bob was still there in Canberra queening it up, and no one looked like moving him yet. Actually, she didn't care or know much about politics; she just hated Australians who tried to be English (though she figured it was reasonable for a Pom to try to be an Australian – at least there was a future in that). For years she'd enjoyed working on the switch in Bairds, but she was bored with it now and would have changed jobs years ago if the Depression hadn't hung so heavy over the old man. When it came to jobs, Sam Pickles threw incaution to the winds. Better the devil you know, he'd say. You've got a good job, now be grateful and keep it. And though she had her own ideas, Rose could never bring herself to leave.

Besides, she had fun on the switch. There was plenty of safe mischief to be had, and friends, and talk at tea-breaks. Darleen, Merle and Lyla were older than her, and they weren't the marrying sort, though sometimes Rose suspected that was something they said to protect them-selves. They never seemed to go out with the same bloke twice. They were loud, hearty and big, like farmers' wives, with plenty of clothes and makeup and no one to go home to cook for.

Rose learnt ways to meet men that Darleen, Merle and Alma had been using for years, and she discovered that with a headset and a bank of wires between her and whoever she was talking to, she was as confident as all getout; full of cheek and fun, able to knock up a rendezvous with a Nice Voice in the time it took to put them through to Accounts or Hardware. The trick was to arrange a meeting at lunchtime on the steps of the GPO, to organize the bloke to stand beside the first pillar off Murray Street so you could spot him as you walked past, anonymous in the crowd, and if he was a dag, as most Nice Voices turned out to be, you just walked on and got yourself a salmon and onion sandwich at the counter at Coles till his lunch hour ran out. Still, they weren't always dags. She got friendly with a few decent-looking blokes who took her to the flicks at the Piccadilly or the Capitol and then shouted her a milkshake or a spider before putting her on the bus home. They were always perfect gentlemen, to her vague disappointment, and at the humid discussions that went on in teabreaks between the girls from the office and the girls from the switch, Rose had to lie to keep up with the others. But she hardly had the imagination to compete. Her friend Marge from Mail Order always stole the show.

And then he says to me: Do ya knock? And I says: Not if I'm oiled. Ah, like a motor are ya? Well, I says, I do take some startin. What are ya, six or twelve volt? And I tell ya, he was all over me like a rash. I was lucky to get out of that Buick alive!

Rose could never figure out why blokes never acted that way with her, though she had a feeling about the salmon and onion sandwiches. But she wasn't miserable the way she could remember being when she was younger. At least now she was out of Cloudstreet all day and half the night, and even if blokes did wave her off on the bus from a night at the pictures, even if she came home alone from the Embassy, at least she'd got to do the things she loved – see movies and dance.

The morning after she'd gone to sleep with the crying in

the walls, about a week after the old man came home from the bush stuffed like a scarecrow with money, Rose had a run in with a Nice Voice that got her excited in a strange way.

It was barely nine o'clock when she got the call. The light came on, Rose put down the nail file and jacked in.

Bairds, good morning.

Hmm. Bairds. The voice was male and resonant and the tone wasn't matey.

Can I help you, sir?

It's about Earl Grey.

Does he work here, sir? I'll have to check because the name's not familiar.

It's tea, love, he said drily.

Mr T. Earl-Grey, is it?

Oh, a card, are we?

Sir?

Look, I'm expecting ten pounds of tea from you people and it's weeks overdue.

I'll give you to Mail Order then, sir, said Rose. Gladly, she added as she plugged him through. Earl-flamin-Grey, my bum.

A moment later, he was back.

Heard that, I did. I should report you, girlie.

The firing squad in haberdashery or death by moron on the switch, it's all the same to me, mate. Go look for Earl. And she plugged him through to Farm Supplies. He was back inside a minute.

Now listen here!

She jacked him through to Boys Wear and counted.

Very smart.

There's a ladder in your stockings, sir.

She gave him to Haberdashery and Hosiery, and thought she could feel the old switchboard heating up. When she heard his line back, she waited only to hear him draw a breath before punching him on to Mail Order and his mysterious ten pounds of Earl. She was flushed with excitement and took a few moments to see that the switchboard was lit up like a pinball machine. The last light on the board was him again.

It's me again.

You don't say. Any luck with Earl?

They haven't found it yet.

Dear, dear. Want me to put you through to the Governor-General?

You're a cheeky bugger.

The board was lighting up again.

Well, thanks a dozen, but I've got to get back to work. There's a lot of buggerizing to be done.

She heard him laugh.

Well, I'm going to keep after this tea.

Good luck, Earl.

Rose pulled the plug on him, and went to work on the rest of them before the whole three floors fell on her. Darleen came in and Merle and Alma behind her. Rose glared at them; they were ten minutes late.

Bairds, good morning . . . just putting you through . . . one moment please . . . Where the hell have youse been? I've had the Charge of the Light Brigade on my hands here . . . Bairds, good morning . . .

Gawd, look who's in a tizz this mornin!

I spose we'd better begin, ladies.

Heads on, bums down, I reckon.

But by the time they got their headsets on, the switchboard had cooled off.

You bludgers, Rose said with a smile. What have you been up to?

Oh, a meetin of minds in William Street.

Sailors, I spose.

How'd you guess?

Who else is gunna go you three in a group at nine in the morning? They must've been at sea a good while to pick a pack of rough sheilas like you. Bairds, good morning . . . Oh, it's you again.

Listen, he said on the other end, sounding sort of mature and well-fixed, why don't we meet somewhere? You sound like a smart girl.

Only meet smart ones, do you?

Somewhere close to your work? You're on Murray

Street, right?

That's right.

Righto. What about lunch? Let's meet at the GPO.

First column on the left as you go up the stairs, she said. Twelve o'clock. Bring your teapot.

When he'd rung off, the switch was quiet and the others were quivering with suppressed laughter.

Looks like their mate caught up with them, said Merle.

Whose mate?

The sailors, said Alma. He wasn't in our league. They reckon he only goes for the roughest scrubbers, and I bet he's glad he found ya, love.

Rose smiled tolerantly across their squall of hysterics. The door opened, and Mrs Tisborn came in from the office. They ruffled themselves into sobriety and blushed guiltily.

This is a switchboard, not a fowl house!

Rose had a light on.

Bairds, good morning.

My name's Toby, by the way.

Very good, sir. Shall I put you through to kitchenware?

What?

Rose pulled the plug on him and felt the sweat slipping down the inside of her blouse. Mrs Tisborn was prowling, the great buffer of her bosom aimed here and there.

I'll be watching you girls. And remember, Miss Pickles, you're still not too good for Hosiery.

Thankfully, a light came on and Rose caught it first. When she plugged it through, old Teasebone was gone.

Cor, blimey, whispered Darleen. Straighten yer seams, girls. It's stockins for the lot of us.

Penal servitude, said Merle.

You rude thing, said Alma.

It was him, said Rose. My date.

Geez, love, even Blind Freddy could've put a girl straight on that score. No salmon and onion sangers for you today.

Through the crowd she sees the bloke leaning on the first pillar above the post office steps, and her first impulse is to go on ahead and buy those salmon and onion sandwiches at Coles and forget the whole flamin thing. He's not bad looking. Good suit, nice pair of shoes. Glasses, though he doesn't seem the squinty, limp type. Hatless. A bit of an individual, it seems.

She's too nervous for this. What's a bloke like that want with a shopgirl like her? He's no run of the mill lair. He's the sort of man you pray will come out of the smoky gloom and ask you for a dance.

Rose wheels back for another look and finds herself going up the steps. Now or never, Rosie.

When she gets to him, his eyebrows rise and Rose feels herself being given the onceover. Before he can, she gets the first word in.

Gday, Earl. Haven't strained yourself, have you?

He smiles indulgently.

Hello. I thought you'd be a looker.

Boom! goes Rose's heart.

They stand there a full moment in the spring sunshine with people coming and going around them, posties wheeling past on their heavy old PMG bikes.

You hungry? Rose asks. I am.

Yes, yes, let's get a bite.

They wind up at the sandwich counter in Coles and Rose forgoes the salmon and onion. They eat and Rose swings on her stool like a girl, waiting. This bloke seems different to men she's known. There's no big talk, no flashing of money, no nervous guffaws.

I'll guess and you tell me how close I am, he said, wiping his fingers on greaseproof paper. You left school at fifteen. Your dad votes Labor, you play netball, you'd like to be a lawyer's secretary and you sleep with your socks on.

Rose smiles and knows whatever she says will sound stupid. Patchy, she says, but boring enough to get me right.

What's your name?

Rosemary.

Rose.

284

Yes, she says relieved.

What a talker. You need the switchboard between us, do you, before you can really fire?

I spose I'm used to it. I suddenly don't know what to talk about.

Football? The common cold?

Just ask me out, she says.

Let's go out together. Friday.

You're a reporter, she says. You went to uni, your parents live in Nedlands and you've tried to teach yourself to talk like one of us.

Us?

Friday, she says. Meet me at Shenton Park station. Seven o'clock. Bye.

She slides off her stool, minding her stockings.

She steps out into the sunshine and has to concentrate to find her way back to work, though it's barely a block away and she's walked it every lunch hour for years.

Well, she thinks, hardly believing her cool delivery. Well. She wondered about her guess. A reporter? Yes, she'd seen those blokes around. Fast movers, funny, sharp, always asking and watching. Yes, he'd be right there in the thick of it. He'd know politicians and criminals. He'd be a mover and shaker. Well, well.

Toby Raven

At six-thirty that Friday, Rose was waiting outside the Shenton Park station. He lurched up in a Morris Oxford and nearly took her left hip from its moorings. The first thing she learnt about Toby Raven was that he couldn't exactly drive. He made his way, but that's the best you could call it. Rose climbed in, suddenly twice as nervous, and they hopped away.

Well, well, he murmured, smiling widely at her after a few moments.

Hello, said Rose.

Hel-lo.

285

Toby sent the car in a swoon towards the kerb and Rose prayed that he would never again feel moved to take his eyes off the road.

It'd taken all afternoon to dress for this, and she could barely move for starch; with her nervousness turning so quickly to naked fear, the sweat on her steamed up the tulle and the car began to smell like a laundry. She pulled the wrinkles out of her gloves and tried not to ruin her lipstick with gnashing as they drove beneath the long shadow of Kings Park and beside the river reclamation to the lights of the city centre.

Gawd, she thought, this should be a fabulous feeling – cruising with a beau – if only a girl wasn't afraid of dying. She sat back as Toby swooped and swerved, grunted and grated, and took deep breaths as the colours of the city broke over her; she did a real job of seeming perfectly serene.

They passed through the high class end of town with its grand hotels and ballrooms to cross the railway bridge into shabby streets and boozers' parks. Toby wedged the car up on a kerb with a thud that nearly put Rose's head through the roof. He sighed triumphantly.

Let's go in.

Rose couldn't see anywhere likely to be an eating establishment. There were shopfronts, houses, shadowy doorways. She got out and smelled garlic.

You've gone to a lot of trouble, Toby said beside her. It was hard to tell what he meant, but she smoothed her great full skirt graciously all the same.

He led her to a narrow doorway where a big, bumper-breasted woman met them and took them down to a crowded, smoky room full of tables, chairs, tablecloths, candles, laughing people, chinking glass and cutlery. Great vats of spaghetti were carried past by boys, and jugs of wine that reminded Rose of nosebleeds. People seemed to be speaking all kinds of languages, and some seemed to know Toby.

They sat at a small waxspattered table, and bread was brought. It wasn't exactly the dining room at the Palace Hotel.

Where are we? she said, trying to look pleased.

Maria's. This is where the real people come.

Rose felt her cheeks glowing. Beaut!

How do you like your spaghetti?

Oh, she huffed, like my tea – as it comes.

He laughed. You're not about to let me go on that tea business are you?

Listen, she owned up, I don't know a thing about spaghetti. Or the real people. I'll just have whatever you reckon.

Two carbonaras, he told the boy. And a jug.

Do you come here a lot?

Yes, all the time. Terrific place. It's a hideaway for those in the know, you might say. We all come here. Makes a bit of a change from the old mutton and boiled veg.

Toby smiled at someone over Rose's shoulder and now and then she sensed an eyebrow raised.

You know all these people?

I know who they are and they know who I am. Some of us are friends, associates, old flames. I'm clubbish, you'd have to say; it's my last concession to a bourgeois past.

Rose tried not to panic.

You okay?

Rose strangled out a yes.

You're not nervous? Don't be nervous. I'm quite safe, you know. Not respectable but I am able to restrain myself with a lady.

Rose smiled. She ran her fingers along the checked tablecloth.

What are you thinking? You want to go home?

We're different, said Rose.

You don't know a thing about me! he protested gaily.

Then tell me. What do you do?

Is a man only what he does?

No, Rose said, only what he is, I spose.

Well, Rose, you're dead right. I'm a hack. A journalist on the *Daily*. I is probably what I does.

You've been to university, or something, haven't you?

287

Ah, sharp lady.

See, we're different.

So what?

Rose smiled. You write, then?

Well, you couldn't call what I do writing, though I do scribble a bit in my own time. Do you read?

Yes, she said breathlessly, I read.

Thank God. Thank Jesus, Mary and Josephus, she reads! Rose, you're a lovely girl. The moment I heard your snooty twang on the phone I knew it was love. See, we're not so different.

Rose laughed. Toby was so confident, his face so full of mad expression, his hands seemed to crackle with animation. He fitted the din and swirl of this place.

The spaghetti came with wine and salad. Rose hadn't eaten since breakfast, so she went to work. It was like eating kite string but the wine soon took the awkwardness out of it.

Tell me who you read, he said with a lump of cheese camping on his chin.

Oh, Gawd.

Don't be shy.

I love books. My room is full of them. I read the whole Geraldton library end-to-end when I was a kid.

Name some names.

But Rose didn't know names, she only remembered stories.

You name some, she said.

Toby grinned, closed his eyes: Hammett, Steinbeck, Hemingway, James Jones, Mailer, D. H. Lawrence, Xavier Herbert, Sillitoe, Camus . . .

She let him go on and on in a winy whirl as people brushed by with friendly nods and vats of red sauce. Their duffle coats and minks flapped, their pockets jingled, their laughter blanketed Rose Pickles in, warm as all get-out.

Rose had enough wine in her to keep calm as they jerked their way through the traffic to the Esplanade. The lights of the river seemed more beautiful than she'd seen them. The palm trees along the foreshore cast weird silhouettes.

One of the world's strangest towns, said Toby, aiming them down Riverside Drive.

I wouldn't know, said Rose.

Perth is the biggest country town in the world trying to be a city. The most isolated country town in the world trying to be the most cut-off city in the world, trying desperately to hit the big time. Desert on one side, sea on the other. Philistine fairground. There's something nesting here, something horrible waiting. Ambition, Rose. It squeezes us into corners and turns out ugly shapes.

You must see a lot of things, said Rose, hating herself for sounding so wide-eyed.

Too many things.

Rose thought of morgues, cells, the steps of aeroplanes, the flash of camera bulbs. Her world was mundane and domestic in the high times. In the low times . . . she couldn't even think of those times. The night wasn't big enough for all those feelings.

Toby jacknifed the Morris into a carpark across the river from Crawley. The university clock was lit and it stood above the trees, the lamps, the water.

That's nice, she said.

No, he murmured. This is nice.

Rose took the kiss and was surprised at how soft his skin was. She slid in close to him.

Nice is a terrible, bourgeois word, said Toby catching a breath.

Whatever, said Rose, whatever. She loved the smooching sound of the upholstery. She stopped being kissed and started kissing. She held his head, felt his hands on her back, in her hair.

Just switching you through, she murmured, trying not to giggle.

Rose Pickles, he said.

His hand was between her breasts and she left it there as the river went by and by.

Oh, Rose, you loved me. How you did. And there you go drifting by with the river, out on an eddy in a black, shiny Morris Oxford with a man who quotes D. H. Lawrence with his tongue in your ear and cheese on his chin. How you longed, how you stared at me those thundery nights when we all tossed and the house refused to sleep. It's gone for you now, but for me the water backs into itself, comes around, joins up in the great, wide, vibrating space where everything that was and will be still is. For me, for all of us sooner or later, all of it will always be. And some of you will be forever watching me on the landing.

Back at his flat, Rose falls on the bed thinking: dammitall I'm twenty-four years old, as her acre of tulle comes away and his hands run down her legs to peel her stockings; I want him. She feels the air cool on her shins and draws him down. He slides into her and it's as hard as the recesses of her heart and wonderful, only unlike Rose Pickles' heart it stops beating and lurching and loses its steel and lets her down into a sad melancholy quiet. Well, she thinks, I'm a woman. She wants to cry, but ends up feeling grateful.

By the time summer came, Rose knew she was in love. Toby was clumsy and vague and she quickly discovered that he wasn't the political scribe, the crime-chasing reporter she imagined, but the writer of a social column, a man with a notebook at a charity ball whose family name got him in the door. His real love was poetry and talk. He quoted Rimbaud by the river and Freud by the sea and Rose shut up and listened, let herself be taken along by the sheer force of him. He took her to clubs, to balls at the uni where people were stylish and confident in a way she'd never seen, and though he muttered critically in the dress circle, he took her to the pictures just to give her pleasure. They ate Italian food, Greek and Polish, drank at the Latin Quarter with Toby's friends, and ignored all sports.

The moment she left the yard at Cloudstreet the wide

world fell wonderfully upon Rose. She always met him in neutral places out of shame, and never mentioned the big old house, the squealing, romping, toothy noise of those who sailed on in it. Toby read the London newspapers and talked of escaping Perth for a real culture: Bloomsbury, the Left Bank, or Sydney at a pinch. The two of them drove in the warming evenings with the windows down and the wind in their clothes and always found themselves by the river with lights drifting round them.

Toby talked. Talked day and night about sex, about words to describe it, about how other cultures *did* it, about what it really meant. He gave her a plainwrapped *Lady Chatterley* and dared her to say the words. She dared him to bodysurf with her at Cottesloe Beach, but he stayed in the shade with an Evelyn Waugh. Rose sunbaked in her Jantzens and laughed at his passing commentary. The Norfolk pines reminded her of Geraldton. She dripped icecream on her Cole of California sundress. She read Scott Fitzgerald, discovered Henry Handel Richardson, and in the evenings cooked Toby meals in his flat and took him to bed where he was rarely as good as his word, though helpful enough in his way.

After sex, Rose went melancholy and fanciful. On the pillow beside Toby, she even imagined herself married with children, with a house in the clean new suburbs and all of Toby's clever friends around to make her laugh. She'd wear a cashmere sweater tied loosely round her neck, her hair would always be wet and combed back after swimming, her children would be sweetfaced and adored by every passing stranger.

After lovemaking Toby went quiet, as though he'd suddenly and terribly run out of talk. He wrote poems, she discovered, wrote them in his head while they lay there subdued. She didn't understand them if ever he showed them to her on paper. They seemed ugly and nonsensical, and as he wrote more of them and had them roundly rejected by magazines in the East his moods darkened.

She began to tell him about her life, but there were times when it was no use talking to Toby. With his friends it was no use saying anything at all. Every time she opened her mouth he'd scowl. She'd always put something into a conversation that would stop things dead. Toby's friends painted and sculpted or wrote, though some just came around looking harried and thoughtful and did nothing at all. They knew everybody's name, and certain names brightened their faces. They blew cigarette smoke like they were spitting. They spoke with their heads back and their eyes closed and their accents were Englishy. Rose didn't mind them. Early in the evenings, when she was feeding them all, they showed an interest in her and once a woman painter suggested she go to night school to improve herself. She listened like a kid at a keyhole.

Rose went to work bleary and sullen. The switch girls teased her. She's a bloody inta-llec-shul now! they shrieked, but they let up on her and bought her salmon and onion sandwiches in Coles and fussed over her when she was tired.

In the autumn Toby went into a long period of quiet, and after careful enquiry, Rose found that he was writing a book. He had hundreds of poems, hundreds, and she began to type them. In May, she was still typing. The poems were long scenes in which athletic men whispered Greek words into the ears of virgins.

Is anyone going to buy and read this? Rose asked, late one Sunday, after another weekend of typing.

Toby snorted. Probably not. Look what we're up against. Oh, libraries'll buy it.

Good, said Rose.

Is it?

Isn't it?

He looked doubtful.

In May, one Sunday evening, Rose stopped typing. I'm not a typist, she said. And you're not a poet.

You want to marry me, don't you?

Ambition, Toby, it makes us funny shapes. You said it

292

yourself. Let's go to the football next weekend. Stuff the poetry.

Toby laughed.

Forget it, she said, it was just an idea.

An *idea*!

Yes, the switchgirl gets an idea. Call me a taxi.

I'll call you a lot of things.

I'm going home.

Ah, the mysterious home. I always wanted to see where all these gothic strains come from.

Rose left.

For a few days it's quiet between Rose and Toby. It rains in passionate bursts, usually when Rose is going to or from a train station. The girls at the switch are crazy and loveable, but she feels a stranger to them after these past months. She stays in at night and the house is almost tranquil except for the crying in the walls at night. She eats dinner with the old man and Chub, and with the old girl if she is out of bed in time. The kitchen smells of the pepper on the steaks, and of burning jarrah in the firebox. The Lamb mob seems quiet, subdued even. Sometimes she can hear the slow boy singing.

He's a clever bloke, this fella of yours? Sam asks one night between wireless shows.

Oh, he's clever enough, says Rose.

Gets a fat pocket at the end of the week, I spose?

Well, he gets more than me, Dad. He writes gossip during work hours and drivel in his free time.

Sounds like the life to me.

Oh, Dad, you silly bugger! she laughs.

Rose leaves the room before she clouts him one.

At the window by the landing Rose looks out on the backyard, lit softly by the lamp in the tent and the dunny light on this side that Chub's probably left on, Chub who's never had a job, Chub who eats and sleeps. It's wet and lush out there, wild on the Pickles side of the tin fence, bountiful on the Lamb side. Rose unplaits her hair, and watches the shadow of the little woman in the tent. She's been out there years now, and everybody in the street knows about it. No one knows why she's there. She works all day in the shop and goes out there at night. It looks warm, the colour of that tent, and close and private. Yeah, she can see why a woman'd move out there to have some life of her own. It occurs to her that she hasn't spoken to Mrs Lamb for a year, maybe two.

There's a creak on the boards behind her. She whirls around to see Red Lamb.

It's pretty hair you got.

Rose looks at her. Red is a year older than her, but Rose has always thought of her as some years her junior. Her red hair is cut flat and short, and it occurs to Rose that if the girl waits long enough it'll actually come into fashion, especially if she had a tendency to hang around at the Snakepit and be a widgie. But she can't see it. Red has the look of a hopelessly sporty girl.

Thanks. Thank you.

Red steps up on the landing beside her and peers out through the rainspatter on the window.

Your mum's still up and about.

She's a saint, you know. There's no one else like her alive.

They stand a few moments like that, like two strangers waiting for a bus. Rose smells hard Velvet soap on Red.

Well, good night, says Red.

Yeah, g'night.

Rose watches the shadow in the tent. Rain falls without a sound.

In the night, Rose woke with cramps and had to stuff the pillow under her belly and lie like a baby on her front with her legs drawn up under. It was a horrible pain, the beginnings of a bad period, but she was grateful for it. Any period was a good period. Men had taught her that much. But it was severe alright. She'd get the old man to call her in sick in the morning. It'll shock him, she thought, he doesn't believe in missing work. Except to lie low. Well, maybe it's the same. I'll be lying low.

Some girl was blubbering in the house again. There was no one here anymore as young as that voice. Sorry sport, she thought; I've got my own problems.

At noon, the old girl came up in her dressing gown with a letter.

It's from Ted, she murmured. He's in South Australia. He married that girl who was pregnant. He's a jockey. Can you believe it – he doesn't weigh nine stone. You orright?

Rose nodded. Geez. I'm an auntie.

And I'm a grandmother. Never even knew about the weddin. I love a weddin.

Right there on the bed, the old girl got a weep on, and Rose found herself with an arm around her, patting the back of her head, smoothing the crumpled, smokestained bangs.

I'm old, Dolly bawled. I'm old.

She stayed there until she seemed exhausted by it all, and Rose laid her down on the bed.

What's wrong with you, anyway, love? Why you off work? Dolly murmured beside her on the pillow.

Oh, the painters are in, that's all.

God was laughin when he made women.

Rose lay there and listened to her mother fall asleep. She smelt of Guinness and lemonade. Rose put her hand on the old girl's big arm and then she took it away again.

When Rose woke, it was evening and she was alone. Someone came hammering on her door. The old man.

Rose. Rose! There's a bloke here!

Oh my God.

Says his name's Tony.

Oh, please, she thought.

And then in came Toby himself, wildeyed and lurching.

What the hell are you doing here?

A poem! Someone's taken one of my poems.

Don't spose you're insured? said Sam in the corridor.

Rose Pickles pulled the blanket over her head and laughed.

I'll bung the kettle on, said Sam.

We're invited to the editor's house, said Toby.

Now? said Sam.

Tonight.

Then I will put the kettle on.

Put the bloody kettle on, Dad.

Sam gave an awful wink and went on his way.

How did you find . . . us? she said, trying to neutralize her tone.

Oh, the girls on the switch. They remembered the street, though none of them knew the number of the house. Once I found the street it was easy. Seems everybody knows this place. They were all talking about some woman with a tent? Anyway I found it.

Rose pulled the blankets around her.

You've been dark on me, Rose.

Congratulations on the poem. Who took it, that poonce from the university?

Oh, Rose, show some taste, some decorum.

I said congratulations, didn't I?

You're not the same girl I heard on the switch last year.

Well, I know about Earl Grey tea now and I've read Rimbaud. And his . . . imitators.

Nasty, nasty.

Don't bloody patronize me.

Jesus, Rose, it's my big day. I'm asking you out to a do. I've cracked it at last. They're welcoming us in.

That mob? I thought you were avante garde or whatever.

Cmon, Rose. Be nice.

Nice is an ugly word.

You're a sharp girl, Rose.

And I type like a demon.

Oh, don't sulk. Cmon love. We'll drink champagne and lose ourselves. I'm sorry for barging in on your . . . hideaway. Look pretty for me, alright? I'll be by at eight.

There was a photographer from the *Daily* waiting on the steps of the Dalkeith mansion when Toby and Rose arrived starched to the gills, and the coincidence was not lost on Rose.

Who are these people, anyway?

Oh, uni people, old money, the usual literary establishment.

What's the editor's name again?

George Headley. He's edited *Riverside* since the ivy started growing.

This must be important to you.

Ah, she loves me.

The door opened. Rose felt her shoulders sag in fear.

Toby Raven, said Toby to the big silver man.

And friend, said Rose.

Welcome to our little nest. Come in my boy.

Rose crept in behind Toby. A jazz combo played in the hallway. A buffet table filled the dining room and forced its trestled way into the huge, dark, heavy panelled livingroom. Leather furniture, jarrah bookcases, elephant's feet, hatstands, squirish paintings on the wall squeezed Rose into her dress. From the huge windows she saw the slick lawns, the gleaming backs of cars, and below it all the lightmoving river.

Out in the sunroom men had gone into a huddle, and spotting them, Toby bolted their way. Rose did her best to seem unhurried and unflustered. She found the wives and girlfriends in the kitchen and was immediately loaded up with a tray of beer and Porphyry Pearl.

Run that past them, would you dear? An old pinkhaired woman said.

Rose stood among the men and heard Toby giggling nervously. She wanted to go. She was thinking of ways already.

Ah yairs, someone was saying, Katherine and Henrietta are alright in their way, but what we need is more Tobys, don't you think?

Harumph!

Yairs.

My oath.

I mean I particularly like that bit where you liken the fallen beast to the Korean soldier.

Toby looked ashen: Um?

Ah yairs, and the stuff about the old barbed wire bridle.

Rose looked at Toby and sensed him knowing it. His lips gone almost brown in contrast to his face. He began to giggle. He's never written a poem about barbed wire or war in his life, thought Rose. He's a gossip columnist who writes sex poems.

Thought of a funny, Raven?

Toby tittered in some air: Did you like the bit where he whispers Homer in her ear?

General silence, then a slow rumble of amusement.

That's it, thought Rose, knowing Toby knew it too. It's a balls-up. They've got the wrong man, wrong poem. She wanted to go now. She couldn't bear to see him humiliated like this, but neither could she be seen with him. She felt it so clearly here of all places; she despised him as much as pitied him.

You should let us have some comic work, Raven, said George Headley.

Toby's giggle mounted another sentence: Well, well, well, actually I've been thinking of some very comic, funny, funny material inspired only today. Rose, tell them about where you live. Tell them about the lady in the backyard who lives in a tent. Tell them about the slow boy you used to love.

Rose shook in sick surprise. Toby went on in desperation.

You see, fellows, I'm working up this grotesquerie about . . . well there's this shopgirl and a famous writer and . . .

Short story?

Oh, oh, oh longer.

Sounds promising.

Tell them Rose. Tell them!

Rose dropped the tray, felt the shower of bubble and glass fizz as she went. She went past elephant's feet and dinky triangle sandwiches, through the deep darkness of the house while poor desperate Toby called, Tell them about my poems! Men roared and whaled with laughter and Rose heard Toby's terrible miserable giggle outside the front door, across the glittering lawns and down the street as she went

298

coatless and blank into the cold. The river was down there, black and moving. The river.

⌒ Silhouettes ⌒

Quick couldn't get going again. After he got back with his family, he found that Cloudstreet had a hold on him, and though he couldn't think why he should stay in the place, half falling down as it was now, empty of children and rarely the scene of much fun at all, with the old girl muttering to herself out in the tent half the night, the old man inside telling lies and glooming everyone up by trying to sound cheerful, Lon growing pimples and a snarl, Red with her beak always in a book confirming the frailties of Homo Sapiens, Elaine pinching her temples with a migraine and continuing a five year engagement with some bloke he'd never actually met, he kept his old room and helped out in the shop, drove the Chev which sounded these days like a chaffcutter, and watched the summer come, then autumn, winter, spring.

The kitchen floor kept him busy. One morning, the whole mob came down for breakfast and the floor had a list on it that caused the lighter chairs to slide down the hill into the stovefront and the sink. Quick got under the house with a couple of truck jacks to crank and pack it, but next day the slope was back. He jacked and packed three times, but each time the floor came back to an ideal walking surface for people with short left legs. In the end Red had the idea of nailing blocks on the floor and gluing chair and table legs to them on the down side, no slope, no sliding. In a week the old girl herself had taken on a new gait. She now walked more like a bosun than a sarmajor. The Lambs were a crook bunch to look at once they got their sealegs.

Fish lay on his bed with the crystal set, day and night. He said little. Sometimes he didn't even come down to tea, and not even Lester could get him down. Oriel had lost power over him long ago, a defeat that you could read in her face every time Fish came shambling by.

Late in summer, Quick found the boat the old man had

299

bought years ago, the one Fish and he had rowed from Freo when they were kids. It was still beached and upside down at Crawley, so he scraped it, patched it, caulked and painted it so that in the evenings he could row down to the narrows and put out lines for mulloway, flathead and bream. He was comfortable out there on the water, alone with the city lights and the quiet pressure of the outgoing tide. The river was a broad, muttering, living thing always suggesting things that kept his mind busy. Every important thing that happened to him, it seemed, had to do with a river. It was insistent, quietly forceful like the force of his own blood. Sometimes he thought of it as the land's blood: it roiled with life and living. But at other moments, when a dead sheep floated past, when the water was pink with storm mud, when jellyfish blew up against the beaches in great stinking piles, Quick wondered if it wasn't the land's sewer. The city had begun to pile up over it as the old buildings went and the ugly towers grew. But it resisted, all the same, having life, giving life, reflecting it. On clear nights you could see lights in the hills and the scarp beyond the city. He remembered the wheatbelt, that great riverless domain, and recalled himself charging madly through the wheat. I was looking for this he thought. The river. Quick watched the few old battlers who still netted the river for a living, and it was from observing their silhouettes with pity and admiration that he came upon a job for himself. He'd supply the shop with fish! It was a good mile from Cloudstreet to the nearest fishmongers, and he'd seen all the Balts and Greeks moving in, these past few years, and the lengths those coves would go to just to buy a decent piece of fish. He went home and put the idea to Oriel who claimed it as one of her best, and the next day Quick was buying nets and setlines, looking out for a cheap seagull motor, and feeling pleased with himself. Actually everybody was happy. Quick felt like his own boss again, Oriel felt like everybody's boss again, and everybody bossed. The fish sold. The shop prospered. Late of an evening, you'd see Sam Pickles down there, hat back on his head, gladstone bag in hand, weighing up a couple of pounds of crabs for himself.

Geez, I forgot how much I miss the smell of fish every day, he'd say. I been in the city too long. I'm gunna up an orf one day, he'd say to nobody special. I'll be orf like a shot.

Fish started coming out of his room late in the afternoons to watch Quick mend his nets over the frame he'd knocked up down the backyard. At first it was a surprise to see him. Fish poked his fingers into the mesh the first time, then left the net alone thereafter, but he continued to leave the wireless and come down to watch.

Can I come, Quick? he'd ask, sitting with his chin on his knees. He was big and rolylooking nowadays, and not handsome like he'd once been. Lips wet and turning; a squint of incomprehension that five-year-old boys learn to hide.

Not tonight, no.

When? How many sleeps?

Mum says no, Fish. She doesn't want you on the river.

I like it.

Yeah, I know, cobber.

But I'm big!

Quick looked up from his work. Yeah, that's true enough, I reckon.

Carn.

Carn what?

Carn, take me.

I just told you, Fish.

You did once. You took me one time. Remember? We goed in the stars.

Quick snapped an end off and put the net down. We were kids, Fish. We were asleep. It was a dream. And we were hungry, remember?

Strange, but he'd forgotten about that night. There were so many things he just didn't think about.

We saw.

Nah.

And Quick knew he was lying. God Almighty, the things he'd decided not to remember, not to wonder about. Was it a family thing, this refusal to wonder? There were plenty of things to chew over if you let yourself, if you're the

301

type. Things happen – when you're a kid, or sick or asleep or maybe a bit stupid – they happen, and maybe it's best to leave it there.

Fish would head off towards the pig who slouched up against the fence in his smelly enclosure, and Quick would hear him talking. To a bloody pig.

Some nights the old man would come out with him. Lester was unusually quiet out there on the river. It was a relief to have him quiet these days. At home, in the shop, he was painful with talk. He'd rattle like an Owen gun, whipping off chronic old jokes from his standup days at the Anzac Club, tell stories that couldn't possibly be true or even listened to, but even on the river he got quietly philosophical in the wee hours.

I remember my first ever memory, he'd say. I was on my father's shoulders in the dark. It was raining, and we were crossin a creek that had burst its banks . . .

Oh, Dad!

What?

That's bullshit.

It's not, the old man murmured with emotion.

You tell such lies, said Quick, trying to sound gentle.

I know. Lester began to weep: But that's true. It happened. Even if it's only a dream, I know it happened.

Hey, its orright.

I'm gettin old and stupid. I'm an old showoff and me family's ashamed of me.

Come on, Dad, I'm sorry, orright?

I just miss the playin and singin. I don't tell lies about anythin important. You know, boy, I just like stories.

You shoulda been a poet.

Henry Lawson. No, too sad for me. Old C.J., that's who I shoulda been.

Who?

The Sentimental Bloke.

Oh.

The river ran slow beneath them while Lester blew his nose and Quick thought about his father's life.

No one's ashamed, Dad. Aren't you happy? You've done things.

Yeah, I've done things, boy. And I'm happy when I don't think about it.

About what?

Not measurin up.

To what?

Your mother. Oh, she's good about it and all, but a bloke can't avoid it. You know, I was in the cavalry at Gallipoli, but as a *cook*. No wounds. And she lost that brother. You can't compete with a dead hero. You can't beat the dead.

You don't have to, they're dead.

But they stay, Quick. That's one thing you'll learn. The lost will stay with you.

Quick listened to the water under the boards. It was a strange sensation, having your father talking to you more or less like you were equal.

Dad, why's she out in that tent, then?

Oh, she's got ghosts of her own.

Tired of ordinary mortals, I thought.

Well, people disappoint her.

She's a queer bird, the old girl.

She's a fighter, said Lester. She wants all the answers.

What do you want, Dad?

I just want to be liked. She doesn't care about all that – well she tries not to. I always wanted to be loved, that's all. When I was a kid I wanted to be a hero. Hah! Your mother came along and I wanted to be loved by her. And I was. Still am I reckon. I wanted people to think well of me. And I wanted to be loved by God.

Were you? All those things?

I figured I was. That's how I saw it.

You don't believe in yourself, Dad, that's the trouble.

Does anyone?

Mum, I spose.

No, not even her.

So what . . . what dyou live for?

303

The old man laughed: The family, Quick. Your mother'n me always had that in common. Take away the family and that's it, there's no point.

Our family? Us. Come on!

It's why I don't shoot meself quietly in the head with the old Webley. If I did nothin else in me weak old life, Quick, I know I had a family and I enjoyed every bit of it. Hell, I made youse laugh, didn't I? We had fun, all of us, didn't we?

Quick thought about it. They lived like some newspaper cartoon – yokels, bumpkins, fruitcakes in their passed down mended up clothes, ordered like an army floorshow. They worked their bums off and took life seriously: there was good and bad, punishment and reward and the isolation of queerness. But there was love too, and always there was music and dancing and jokes, even in the miserable times after Fish drowned.

Quick? Boy? Didn't we?

My oath, Dad.

You're wastin yer brains out here on the river, son. You should be usin yer brains.

I like it, Dad. The water makes me happy, lets me think.

You need some ambition.

What big ambition did *you* have, apart from wantin to be a hero?

Nothin. I just wanted to be a good man.

That's all I want.

Well, there's time. A whole river of time, Quick. Easy to be a good man out here – there's no one else to think of. Lester pointed to the lights above Perth water where the city hung and the suburbs began their outward roll. But up there, that's the test.

Quick rowed on the slackening tide while the old man crooned a hymn from times back.

That year Quick worked the river from the narrows, where the bridge was going up, down to Blackwall reach where stolen cars and hot pistols were thrown from the cliff into the impossible deep, and even as far as East Fremantle in the shadow of the soap factory and the foundries where the channels ran full of fish, where now and then on the incoming tide, a body might be found, some wharfie, sailor, drunk and king hit. He got plenty of time out there alone to think, and by the beginning of winter, he knew that he really was wasting his time. The fish were selling, the shop was doing well, but he was operating inside a routine. He liked to be on the water, he liked the business of nets and line and fish, but he knew it was a postponement of something.

One afternoon, he gave in to Fish, smuggled him into the Chev before dusk with the wireless still chirping up in the fuggy room, and enough closing hour business in the shop to confuse things.

They drove down along the cliff at Peppermint Grove where in the last light of day, the great, lazy broadness of the river was exposed to them, turning light in insect movements, pricked white with the slackbellied yachts setting out for a twilight run around the Mosman Spit and Claremont water beyond. Fish gasped.

Haaaah! The water!

That's the stuff, orright.

You good, Quick.

Ah, dry up, Quick said, smiling.

Haah.

You know the rules?

I have to have string.

I'll tie your belt to the seat so you don't fall out, and you have to wear this.

Quick pointed at the bouquet of plastic net buoys, each the size of a man's head, that he'd strung together.

It's like a hula belt.

What?

Just wear it. Not now, you nong, wait'll I get you in the boat. I've gotta park the truck first. It was like being kids again, nicking off and going fishing. They moved east, upstream, working the banks and gutters all the way through Claremont where the houses were shabby and colonial, to Nedlands water where the lawns stretched up from the water to configurations of houselights you'd only expect to see on luxury liners. Just before midnight they came upon a batch of cobbler that were easy spearing in the shallows. Fish lay across the bow with a torch strapped to his wrist, peering down into the water, mystified by its loss of reflection. He could see down into the milling mobs of smelt and gobbleguts and the ribbed sand bottom until the batteries began to give out. Then he found the dark water more exciting and Quick noticed how precariously he hung over the side, was glad he'd made precautions.

You hungry? There's some cold pies in the box. Cmon, we'll take a breather for a while. Get back in the bottom, it's cold. Where's your beanie?

In my pocket.

Put it on, it's cold.

Don't boss!

Who brought you out in this boat? Whose boat is it?

It's our boat, all of us. I remember.

Well, so you do, thought Quick, ashamed.

Cmon, let's have somethin to eat. The cobblers can wait.

Not lookin at them.

Just the water, eh?

Yep.

You're a character, orright.

Fish got down in the bottom of the boat. A wind was springing up from seaward bringing in that chill Rottnest air. They ate cold meat pies, discards from the shop, and drank hot, sweet tea from the Thermos.

What're we gonna do with ourselves, Fish?

Eat pies more. You go to sleep. I'll watch.

You happy?

Yep.

Always?

I get happy sometimes. Not you.

Oh, me, I'm the original glumbum.

I like the water.

You remember what happened to you in the water, at Margaret?

Is it a story?

306

It happened, but it can be a story.

I know a story. The house hurts, you know.

What's that?

A story.

There's someone on the bank there.

Some people cry.

Shut up, Fish, someone *is* crying. It's late to be out. Stay down.

In the story, Quick –

Shut up and stay down! he hissed.

Quietly, Quick punted them in under the shallow of the low wall that held the river back in storms. The keel ground along the shell grit at the edge, losing water. He was right. There was someone up there crying, but out of sight, in the lee of the wall.

Is everything orright up there? he called. There was a startled squeak, and a scrape of shoes on cement. A figure rose from behind the wall. Quick held the Tilley high, but succeeded only in blinding himself. He heard a honk of noseblowing.

Sorry, I didn't mean – he stammered.

Quick Lamb, she said. That bloody house won't leave us alone, will it?

Quick looked at Fish who was smiling fit to sin.

Hypothetical, as the Smartbums Say

She wipes her eyes again and looks at him with his puzzlement plainlit by the lamp swinging at his cheek. The brother is down in the boat, luminous in his own way, huge in sweater and cap.

Well, fancy this.

It's Rose, says the slow brother, Fish, the one she used to watch through door cracks and curtains.

From next door?

She's not happy, Quick.

Any chance of a ride?

Where to? says Quick.

Oh, doesn't matter.

Here, hop in.

And the moment she gets in the boat she can't stop howling. She holds back on it like a carsick kid trying not to toss, but it only increases the tearing in her throat. Now and then she gets a glimpse of Quick rowing and the other one watching her, both looking like they don't know whether to go on fishing, head home, or paddle her around till dawn. Now and then she gets her breath back and composes herself for a bit of polite chat, but she loses the lot at the last minute to end up head down in the stink of nets and pots and the mire of her own hanky. In the end she dozes, exhausted. When she wakes she sees they've been fishing again, but now the slow one is asleep up in the bow under a tarp. Horror-faced cobbler squirm around in a tub beside her, all with white patches where their stings have been torn out. She smells the heat of the lamp behind her, hears the dip of oars, and Quick Lamb's orderly breathing. There's a man's great-coat across her shoulders. Her backside is alive with pins and needles.

Wanna fag? Quick asks.

Thanks, I don't smoke.

Fair enough.

Have I been asleep long?

Oh, an hour, I reckon.

Jesus.

You must be pretty upset.

How many cobblers have you got?

Three dozen, maybe.

Do you catch them on a line?

Nah, we spear em with a gidgie in the shallows. Easy work when a bloke can get it. We're just settin nets now.

City lights drift by, but only the boat and the river move. Rose can hardly recall feeling as awful as this, though it's a surprise that it's not worse.

I've got some Chateau Tanunda in that coat, if you want a swig, he says.

No, it's alright.

308

No smokin and no drinkin – do your parents know about this?

Spose it is a bit of a laugh, really.

Think I'll take a snort meself. Couldja find it?

Rose gropes around inside the pockets with their crusty dried flecks of bait, pencil stubs, pieces of string and chips of Buttermenthol.

Think I'll have a splash myself, after all that, she says.

He takes the bottle from her while she's trying not to cough it all into the cobbler trough.

Well, that's cheered you up, he says with a laugh.

It's beautiful out here, she says, turning round to sit facing him. He stands, punting along with effort.

It's cold.

Where are we going?

I was about to consult you on that. Actually, I'm beginning to wonder meself. This hasn't turned out a regular night, you see.

Your brother.

Yeah.

What's the story with him?

He sighs. The dark water moves by like the black glass of a dream's beginning. After a while she knows she's upset him. God, what a clumsy bitch I am, she thinks.

Sorry. I didn't mean to be so blunt. It's just that, well, your mob and mine never really talked much, did they. I'm sorry.

Doesn't matter.

Is he out with you for any special reason?

Oh, he's been after me forever about coming. Mum an Dad worry. I smuggled him out. He's knackered. Snores like a bugger.

Rose reaches for the brandy again to take another pull, and the Lamb boy lets the oars drag a few moments passing it to her, watching her drink. The lamp is strapped in against the gunwale beside her; she puts a hand to it for warmth.

What are you like, Quick Lamb?

What sorta question's that?

Can't you answer it?

Rose watches his features straighten in offence, a moment, before easing back into the soft, boyish lines from a few seconds before.

What'm I like? He takes up the oars again. Even in a coat and beanie he looks thin. A bit lost, I spose.

The lost Lamb.

Yeah, I feel sheepish about that.

Neither of us is likely to get a show on the wireless, you know.

Oh, I thought my joke was a bottler. It was yours that was on the nose. Gawd, yer smilin.

Nah, it's only a rumour.

Why'd you ask the question?

I don't know. Actually, I was just wondering. We live in the same house, what is it, fifteen years now, and I suppose I don't even know who you are. Hey, I remember that time years ago you clobbered me on the stairs with a bag – knocked me down, you rotten sod, you remember that?

He just rows. No. Don't think so.

Well, you were in a hurry.

You grew up pretty good lookin, Rose.

Ta.

Funny, the way he says it; it's like there's no intention behind the observation, as though he doesn't mean it to be an embarrassing personal sort of thing, but just a general comment. Rose flushes, not because he's said it, but for it's plainness.

How come you do this?

Fishin? Reckon I'd do it after work anyway, if I had a routine job, and seein as I can't figure out what the hell to do with meself, it's pleasant enough and pays me way. I just haven't got any ideas, you know, about what to do. Me old man was sort of restless, goin from thing to thing, the sorta bloke who needed the army but wouldna thought of it till the war came along. Spose that means we're weak.

No, I reckon it's just normal.

You look the ambitious type to me.

You come from a big mob, remember. You've been sheltered a bit.

He nods. Maybe you're right. I never thought about it like that.

Rose can't help but laugh.

What do you think about all day?

I reckon I'm tryin to figure out what I lost. I keep figurin I've lost somethin somewhere.

Something to do with him? She points back over her shoulder where Fish sleeps in the bow.

I reckon my whole life is to do with him. It's a sorta mess.

You really love him, don't you.

Everyone loved him. He was the funniest, stupidest kid in the whole bloody world, an everybody loved him.

Jesus, Rose thinks, there's fire in that hole.

He's my brother.

Geez, I've got two of them, and I couldn't say I even liked them.

You woulda loved him, Quick murmurs.

I probably did, Rose thinks: I reckon that's probably the way it was.

What're we doin out here in the cold, anyway? he says.

Talking.

You wanna go home?

She shakes her head.

Well, how'd you like to work while you talk?

Fair enough.

They set nets with numbing fingers as the city grows silent around them, all the streetlights out along the foreshore, houses darkened beyond. Pelicans flap and stir invisible. Now and then a mullet will jump, a prawn come skipping like a stone. Quick lets them drift along gutters with a handline out in case of a passing mulloway and Rose tucks herself down in the bottom of the boat beneath the greatcoat with small slugs of brandy to keep herself awake. She feels unaccountably happy and she knows it's not just the Chateau Tanunda. For a long time, an hour maybe, they don't speak at all. When she closes her eyes it feels like she could be anywhere. What happened earlier tonight is becoming hard to believe; the whole time with Toby, it's receding

311

so quickly as to be a little alarming. Listen to yourself now, she thinks. You even speak differently. He talks like someone out of *Dad 'n' Dave* and you try not to smile. Oh, you learnt well, Rose. Strange, but she can't feel any anger. All her life she's been angry, and now she can't feel it, when she should feel it strong and hard like metal under her skin. For a while she debates the idea of telling Quick Lamb where she's been, what she's just come through, but one look will tell a girl he doesn't need to know. Actually, he's so damn incurious as to be a bit startling. She watches him with the line in his fingers, the low light of the lamp easy on his jaw, and sees how far back in him his mind is, how he has a strange tranquillity riding across the heat she saw a while ago with that brother business. It doesn't seem like resignation, just some time-biding patience that's new to her, not fierce like her determination to make something for herself, but firm all the same. Like an old, old man waiting for something he's been promised.

Why do you get that look on your mug?

He stirs a little. I'm just fishin.

You reckon we'd be any good married to each other?

Gimme that bottle! he says.

Ssh! You'll wake your brother.

Gissit!

In the end he reaches, grabs and hurls the bottle out across the water.

Jesus Christ! What'd you do that for?

Don't talk like that, I don't like it.

It's *my* mouth, mate.

And yer sittin in my boat.

Rose hauls the smelly greatcoat hard about her. She's still pretty bloody sober, thank you very much.

Just a question, you know. Hypothetical, as the smart-bums say.

You've been around with smartbums – I wouldn't know.

So you know more than you let on.

It's a house, not a –

Walls have ears.

Well, you should know, he says. We're even louder than you are.

Oh, you noticed? It's like living next to a cattleyard.

You've done orright from us.

And you from us, I'd have thought. Well, here we are showing our colours. No civil war, fair enough?

Fair enough.

You're true blue, Quick Lamb.

Thanks, he says, with a sudden smile.

Now answer the question.

⌒ Dwellingplace ⌒

Rose and Quick burst into the empty dark library while the rest of the house sleeps. Fish is down the hall snoring. They close the door and cut into the stale dead air with their excitement. They could be children, they breathe so hard, standing apart from one another lit by only the glow of their faces and the heat of their breaths.

I just stumbled into Heaven, Rose says.

Quick just stands and smiles.

You believe in Fate?

He shakes his head.

This isn't happening, she says.

Not yet.

They meet, two points of light sparking up the dark, their mouths gentle upon one another, shocked into sobriety in seconds. Around them the shades hover and hang, twitching.

I know you all of a sudden, she says.

We're nuts, he said. We're gunna be embarrassed afterwards.

No. We're gonna be something else altogether. Come here, here. Here, Quick.

Then suddenly they're going off like a bag of penny bombs, clawing at each other's clothes, talking into skin and opening up while all about the fretting, bodyless shadows

313

back off, mute and shaken in the face of passion, the live, good, heat of the young.

Rose's shoulders slope sweetly under Quick's hands, and she presses into his belly, finds his nipples at her fingertips as she takes him down to the jaded flowers of the library rug where they roll and warp as though they're in some limitless spring paddock that's heady with petals, and pollen and bellowing with sweet energy.

The girlshadow and the hagshadow go limp and open-mouthed, slipping down the walls torn by their halfness. They see the living find curves and dips in one another and hear electric whispers building in their space. Press against the walls, press against themselves, press against the barrier unseen that holds them here. It's love pressing them, see how it distorts their meatless shadows into swatches of darkness, forcing them against the transparent skin of time.

Rose wraps him in her legs, knots over him with hands and mouth and hair, while Quick sprinkles her with sweat, shaking as he is, finding her just . . . just food for him. Across the knots of their discarded clothes they slide and clinch, he with fishblood and her blood on his fingers, she with brandy on her breath, both of them openeyed with a surprise that turns to recognition, and together they make a balloon of heat inside the cold nausea of that dead room whose timbers twist and creak; a new dwellingplace. Love rattles the wallpaper and darkness recedes into itself a fraction when they shout exultant into each other's mouths.

After they're dressed and gone, hurrying out into the daylit house with news for the world, their sudden love remains in the room, hanging like incense.

.

⌒ Outside Chance ⌒

Oriel Lamb had nothing to say. Her son stood at the flap of the tent in his undershorts with the creeping sun behind him, and she had nothing to say at all.

It's probably a bit of a shock, he said.

Oriel stepped into her boots and took a Bex for the

headache that could only be minutes away. She made her bed while he stood there, set things straight on her dresser, trimmed the wick of the lamp.

Mum?

Aren't you cold?

Yeah, but –

Go inside and light the stove.

Just then someone started to laugh up in the Pickles side of the house, the kind of laugh that'd see a person in the casualty ward if it went on much longer.

Well, I see Mr Pickles has just been informed, said Oriel.

Don't see what's so funny, said her son.

The laugh toned down to a fitful giggle that sounded safe enough for the moment. A window on the ground floor slid up and Dolly Pickles put her head out; she looked truly vile with her hair imploded, a fag on her long bottom lip. She shook her head, pulled it and her dishwater bangs inside, and ground the window down again.

Go inside, Quick. I want to get dressed.

He went, she pulled the flap to, and sat on the bed, wrinkling it in a most unsatisfactory way.

Inside, Lester Lamb was looking for Quick. He knew damnwell that Fish had been out all night with Quick in the boat, and that the old girl would go mad, but he'd seen, too, the troughs full of fish still out on the truck with all the local cats fighting and gorging on them, and he knew he had to get to the boy before she did, because he just couldn't imagine what'd happen if she saw.

He went quietly from room to room in the strangely subdued house which felt like a storm had been through while they were all asleep to leave the atmosphere thick and exhausted, until he got to the back door and saw Quick coming. He motioned to Quick to come quickly, the boy seemed eaten by dread all of a sudden.

You've left the fish out! he hissed.

Oh, gawd!

What's the matter with you?

315

I'm gettin married.

Today?

No. It's –

Good, well let's get the fish in.

The cats yowled and spat as Lester and Quick heaved the troughs down and hauled them inside. The house was waking quicker than usual. Through the shop and into the kitchen they went.

It's a good night's worth, son.

I'm gettin married, Dad. I'm marryin Rose next door.

Good gawd!

The old man threw himself onto a chair which slewed on its joints and collapsed beneath him, sending him onto the floor on his back. Pieces of wood slid down the lino like broken tackle on a reeling ship.

She's so . . . pretty, Lester said without breath. I've hurt me back.

It's gunna be orright, Dad.

Let's wait for the X-rays.

No, I mean –

Good Lawd! bellowed Oriel walking in on them. For pity's sake, let's be sensible about this!

He fell over, Mum.

Sit down over there!

Red burst in. Good on ya, Quick. I knew you weren't completely useless. You don't deserve her.

Elaine followed, white, peaky, outraged.

Well, Lon's asleep as usual, said Quick, and Fish'll be down drectly.

Who's gunna declare the meeting opened, then? said Red, grinning.

I've hurt me back, said Lester.

I'll second that, said Quick, delirious with apprehension.

Get off the floor, Lester, said Oriel.

The floor's yours, Dad, said Quick. The meeting's opened.

Oriel Lamb began to weep. It sounded like trains colliding.

Well, it's a step down from Tony from the uni, murmured Sam, rolling a fag philosophically, but he seems a good boy.

That's all he is, Dolly said in disgust. A good boy.

Rose had never felt so much iron in her. There was this feeling of striding, of invincibility that she'd only ever had in dreams before. She shifted in her stance against the kitchen wall and felt the soreness still. There was nothing they could say, that anyone could say, to take this from her.

You up the duff?

Leave it out, Mum!

They'll think you are anyway. Six weeks is gunna look lovely.

Not that having things look lovely has been your enduring obsession, Mother.

I'm thinkin of you, you silly little bitch.

Good, that makes two of us.

They'll hate it.

You mean you hate it.

That woman'll tear you to bits.

Chub came in.

What's all the yellin?

I'm getting married to Quick Lamb in six weeks.

Oh. There any bacon?

It'll be a bloody dry weddin, Sam said with a look of wonder.

Not if we're payin for it, it won't, said Dolly. No flamin fear!

Oh, murmured the old man. I forgot that. See, I knew I won that two-up money for something.

You mean you've still got it? Dolly looked appalled.

Under the mattress. Lost me nerve there for a while, I did.

This is so funny, so bloody hilarious, said Dolly, not managing to sound amused. She wants our blessin, but she won't ask for it.

She's proud.

Stop smirkin like that, the both of yuz! said Dolly.

What do you reckon, Dad?

Oh, you know me, I'll always back an outside chance.

317

Rose kissed him and felt the urgency of his embrace until she could count the fingerless knuckles in the small of her back.

He'll have to come an see me.

He'll come.

We'll get free fish, I spose.

I reckon it could be arranged.

They're gettin this place off us, bit by bit, said the old girl. We're signin ourselves over.

Give's a kiss, Mum.

Go to buggery.

Grandeur, Almost

In the end, after six weeks of tears and tizzes, Quick stands up there at the front of the church with Fish at his side and the family sweating behind him. In his hired suit, Fish looks like he could run the Liberal Party and make a killing. Quick can hardly believe he got his way. There's organ music, the smell of mothballs and pious bookdust. He catches a glimpse of his mother's magnificent look of forbearance and injury; her hair is bowled over in a frightful series of curls, hardly a monument to straightliving and modesty. It's almost like a helmet she's lowered on her scone for protection against passion. The old man beside her sits reedbent and curious, tie knot resting like a spare Adam's apple at his throat. Quick can't remember noticing his baldness as being so advanced. They look so old, the two of them. The knife never lies . . . should have spun the old knife, he thinks, just for a laugh. Though maybe we could do without predictions today.

The high ceiling reaches into a cobwebby dimness with weak streaks of light blunting themselves against one another from opposite sides of the church. It's almost grand, but a good compromise, he thinks, between pooftery High Church and shoebox Baptist.

You got the rings? he whispers to Fish.

Yairs. Fish pats his pocket.

Need a wee?

318

No. Not yet.

Won't be long now.

Someone's asleep in this house, too.

Ssh, now. They're here. Oh, gawd, they're havin a barney out on the street.

A few Lambs and Lamb customers twist their necks to see a moment of sparring between bride and mother before the organ lets loose with a volley of notes which sound like a call to order.

She's comin, Quick! Fish has lost his shonky statesman composure. He begins to bob and grin.

Orright, I can see. Keep your hair on.

Fish reaches for his hair in surprise, though neither powers nor principalities could move that head of hair, such is its cargo of Brylcreem.

Dolly Pickles plots a course and tacks down the aisle to her seat at the front, great spinnaker of a hat resting at last. Chub rolls up beside her, wearing so much babyfat he might have hired it for the occasion. And then they come. Here they come. All that flaming gorgeous brown hair swinging visible under the veil, and the little nicotine stained man alongside, leading with his arm crooked, crippled hand on his hip.

Cor, says Fish.

Ssh, mate. She looks orright, eh.

Mister Pickles is small like a dog.

Rose comes smiling, wet-eyed and triumphant. She knows exactly what she's doing, and it's what she tells herself every few feet. It seems a ridiculous way to walk, this tightrope shuffle, and if she doesn't take her mind off it for a moment, she knows she's going to keel over. How priestly the priest looks coming down beside Quick with his sumptuous bits and pieces, and how Fish . . . how Fish . . . *how* is Fish making that noise, that sound?

Up the front, before the man in costume, Fish Lamb is singing, or saying, or something. He has the ring box in his hand that he shakes like a maracas and holds high as he sways and bobs, lobbing his head about on his shoulders, eyes closed, with complete assurance he goes on, stopping the bride in her tracks and setting dogs ahowl outside the windows. No one grabs him. They all believe it can't go on. But he goes on, right on, until there's a sweat on him and on everybody else, and he falls silent, then down, and in the end, asleep.

The organist finds his place and gets back on his trembly way. The bride steps up, white as her outfit, to meet the groom who wears a smile that looks borrowed.

They don't exactly fill the RSL hall with their bodies, but some huge, pentup feeling makes the place seem crowded as families and friends, punters, customers, neighbours find their tables by way of chinky giltlettered namecards and sit down to the chook and two veg with gravy, jugs of beer, sherry and lemonade. They get through filthy telegrams, Lester's speech turns into a string of the most awful, wonderful fibs and damnnear gets to the brink of vaudeville, Dolly gets shickered altogether on beerglasses of sweet sherry, while Elaine weeps and mopes; Hat and hubby talk about council rates and renovations; Red dances with strange blokes and swats their hands away heartily as she swoops round the floor. Chub eats. Sam dances with his daughter, nimble as a midget and pinches her back from blokes who cut in. Lon Lamb gets quietly stung by spiking his lemonade with sherry until in the end he's camped down under the tablecloth, too un-coordinated to get off his back and avoid the sight of all those ladies scratching themselves discreetly under the table. At the very end, Quick and Rose lounge together, tired and jubilant with their clobber askew and their hair losing ground, while a very strange thing happens. Oriel Lamb hoists herself wearily from the chair she's occupied all evening at her end of the bridal table, crosses the floor to where Dolly Pickles sits frightening a group of young men with the kind of jokes she knows, and asks her to dance. There's no one else on the floor. The band sits around lighting fags and chatting up girls until Oriel catches the drummer's eye. Quick sees his mother's face: something massive has been summoned. Rose feels his grip on her tighten as her mother sits there losing resistance by the moment. The music strikes up quietly. Dolly puts out her cigarette. The lairs look horrified. Oriel Lamb takes her by the hand and waist and they move out onto the floor in a slow rhythm that sobers the entire place. The short, boxy woman slips around gracefully, holding the old beauty up, and turn by turn something grows.

They look so bloody dignified, says Rose. So proud.

As they wheel by like a miracle, there are spectators weeping.

Outside in the Chev, Fish Lamb is sleeping.

IX

The House is Trembling

CLOUDSTREET was torpid with shock for days after the wedding. The Lambs worked in a strange calm; it was unlike them to be so quiet. Lester forwent the noseflute solos to schoolkids on the verandah. Oriel spoke in a low murmur. The Pickles side of the house, always quiet (except when Dolly was on a binge) became mute altogether. Dolly and Sam found the silence companionable at times and there were moments when their eyes actually lit upon each other in Rose's absence.

But the quiet between them all went unnoticed on Cloudstreet because the Water Board started fooling with diggers and pipes, testing out their new machinery.

The sixties are here, said the supervisor with great enthusiasm.

Yeah, said Lester Lamb, thinking of his age.

You can't turn back the clock.

No, said Lester, but you don't have to wind it either.

Men are outside digging the street. Fish Lamb stands at the window tapping the butterknife against the panes – chink, chink, cachink – watching the black man across the street. A truck rolls by with a load of huge pipes. The black man is gone in the dust it leaves, and from behind Fish, across the corridor, comes the old keening noise again. He sits on Quick's old bed and dust rises from the quilt. The house is trembling.

How Small Our Dreams Are

I want to live in a new house, said Rose. In a new suburb in a new street. I want a car out the front and some mowed lawn. I want a small, neat house that only *we* live in, Quick. I don't ever want to live anywhere old, where people have been before. Clean and new, that's what I want.

We've got no money, he said, as he drove them home from their honeymoon. They'd gone crabbing. Crabbing!

I've been working for years, Quick. I've been saving all this time.

And I haven't even got a job. I never got paid for doin the fish.

We'll see your mother about that tomorrow.

Ah . . .

Don't be gutless, Quick. You should've been paid.

I need a job, he said. Two jobs if we're sposed to have a house.

We'll get you two jobs.

You'll be quittin, I spose.

Rose laughed. She'd married a man who still wore the clothes his mother bought for him. He didn't know his shoe size or what size underpants he took. He read nothing but

pulp westerns, had never had an official job and probably
didn't even know what a union was. He'd never signed a
cheque or had a bank account or paid tax. He'd had women
before – that much a girl could tell – but he never spoke about
them. He was good with his hands, could see long distances,
stay awake for days if he wanted to and he woke at the
smallest sound. He had a beautiful copperplate hand but
wrote nothing at all. He took a girl crabbing for a week
on her honeymoon and on the way home expected her to
quit work.

No, Quick, I won't be quitting.

Fair enough.

You want me to.

Girls like to.

Not this girl. This girl wants to buy a house. When we
get back we're going to State Housing to sign up.

Fair enough. I'll need a job.

Two jobs.

Fair enough.

What'll you do?

Quick pursed his sunburnt lips and peered over the
steering wheel. Join the police force.

Oh, gawd no.

Me dad was a copper, you know. But he was only in it
for the uniform.

Quick, she groaned with all her Pickles blood, why?

Don't you read the paper?

Of course I read the bloody paper.

Evil.

What?

I want to fight evil.

You're not in a comic, Quick.

He grinned: Why'd everyone leave it so late to tell me?
Quick thought of his room at Cloudstreet, the victims
dancing on his wall, all the things there were to be stopped.
Now Rose snuggled against him as if to reassure herself.
What a head of hair. How could he have lived so long in the
same house with her without noticing? She was so passionate, so full of restless energy, and hardheaded – though not

327

nearly as tough as she let on. Still, she was her own woman. He felt dumb around her, but not stupid.

A copper, she said.

I'll sign up after State Housing.

Right.

I feel good about it already.

Small dreams, chuckled Rose.

Just a little bigger than us, I spose.

The Day the Fifties Finished

The day the fifties finished, Rose and Quick found a little flat behind a house in Mosman Park. It was owned by a Mrs Manners who lived up the front, and Rose hated it. It was all they could afford on Rose's pay and the academy's allowance while their little house was being built, but being so busy they were hardly ever there. It was old, and Rose hated old. And it was sharing and Rose never wanted to share again. They worked their guts out to pay for their little dream. At night Quick drove delivery trucks and Rose took in laundry, and on Sundays they drove north in Lester's Chev to look at their sandy quarter acre and the piles of raw bricks. They kept clear of Cloudstreet, though at night Quick often lay awake thinking about it. He'd shake it off in time, he knew. Like Rose says, they're them now, and we're us. It's natural.

At the end of the year, the old Chev truck came clanking down Swan Street to pick Rose up, and though the idea of riding in it caused Rose's cheeks to burn, she knew it was the only way she'd get to Quick's graduation, and that maybe it was the best way, too, considering who Quick was and where he'd come from. Besides she had secret news to buoy herself with, and not even the Harley and sidecar would have been too much to bear.

When Lester came shambling down the path in his five shilling scarecrow suit, Rose locked the door of the bedsit entrance and went out to meet him. He smiled, with his lower teeth in for the occasion, and gave her a nervous kiss on the nose.

Well, love, you right? Let's go an see em stick his number on.

Constable Lamb, eh? It was ridiculous, she knew, but there was a fat fist of pride in her throat even saying the words. She'd gotten to love him in that little two room annexe off the weatherboard house. They worked and saved so hard that they barely spent any time together. They were hungry for each other. They saved their hopes as well as their money and in time they'd be moving to a new life. Sometimes Rose wondered if perhaps she wanted the house too much. Quick wasn't like that. He was a boy really: awkward, flatfooted, naive, but he also had the outlook sometimes of an old man. He was calm, steadfast, longsighted and a little mean with money. She was ambitious all ways, she knew, even in the dangerous way. But Quick had more aim than ambition, and for that as much as the rest, she knew she needed him.

Yairp, said Lester. Another flamin Constable Lamb.

Rose followed the old man up to the truck, noticing how much he stooped these days, his tallness turning on itself.

Did you like being a copper, Lester?

I liked the horses. Didn't like chasin people up, much. I was better with the horses.

You sound like Dad. He's better with the horses than he is with the betting, silly fool.

Well.

Oriel sat fidgeting in the cab, forcing a smile as they came. She shoved over to make room for Rose. Her hair was set, her skin looked raw and scrubbed and she smelt like a faintly mouldy towel.

Hello, Oriel.

The old woman scowled and accepted a kiss. She didn't approve of first name terms with juniors and inlaws, but her son's wife was a stubborn one, and Oriel knew it'd take time to win that battle. Besides, she hadn't liked coughing up backpay for Quick. It went against family principles.

I've plucked three pullets this morning, said Oriel. There's lunch at our place.

329

Lester winked behind the old girl and Rose pressed out a smile.

The big day, she murmured.

To think they knocked him back three times over a rash on his feet, said Oriel. He's got my sensitive skin, poor soul. Well, he's showed em.

They drove down by the river, winding along the cliffs past the houses of the rich and Anglophile. Sun forced back banks of cloud, and the mottled waters of the Swan glittered across its wide, languid course through the city and its hungry suburbs. Rose felt the sun across her knees and believed that there was everything to look forward to.

Yes, Rose thought, watching Quick step up to the dais to have his hand shaken by the Commissioner and the Minister, he looks bigger in uniform, filled out, solid. Quick stood his height, his cap set perfect on his head and the buttons on his tunic winking regimental, and up there beside the other flapeared youths, it was obvious that he was older, more a man. There he was, swearing allegiance to the Queen, the very mention of whom sent his mother into a fit of weeping beside Rose. Rose saw Lester's quivery chin in the corner of her eye, and she wished she could be brave enough to reach across Oriel and hold the old softy's hand.

Did you give him clean underpants? Oriel snivelled.

I even ironed them! Rose hissed.

That's my boy.

No, Rose uttered silently, against her will, that's my boy now.

Well, said Quick on the back step where the smell of roasting chickens and spuds and pumpkin and parsnips wafted, I'm a cop.

Rose leaned against the wall where the gully trap protruded and felt her breakfast rising relentlessly.

Yeah. And a father, too.

What?

Which makes me a mother.

Rose. You're kiddin!

330

No lie. Oh. Here comes the proof of the pudd –

Toast and tea gouted up against the back wall, as Rose leant out, heaving.

Whacko, said Quick, that's fantastic!

Thank you, said Rose, taking a breath and wiping her mouth with her hanky. Just something I learnt along the way.

Flatfoot

After a month of being a copper Quick Lamb discovered that in a shift he'd walk further than a whore, streetsweeper, salesman or vagrant and look more out of place in the windripped heart of the city than any of them. Up and down he walked. People went to work, got off and on trams and trolleys, they parked cars, ate lunch, filled pubs and went home. Evil seemed to evaporate wherever he went. He was left to tidy up brothel queues in Roe Street, clear drunks from shop doorways and help old people to crosswalks. He felt like he'd joined the Boy Scouts. There was no swagger, no truncheon swinging, no Allo, Allo. He just stumped along, marked out for invisibility by his uniform, hoping guiltily for a spot of sin to come his way. On the city beat his only pinch was a drunken football coach flashing browneyes in the Ladies' Lounge of the Savoy.

When he was transferred to Nedlands he thought it was a dinkum shift of his fortunes, but he soon wised up. Nedlands was a political station. The MPs and business barons and the old school boys lived there and the station was open to keep watch on those bludgers' property. The sergeant in charge was a depressed and hopeless man. He sent Quick out in the afternoons down Broadway and the Avenue to show the colours and hear the complaints of the toffs. Those days he just had his thoughts to keep him going. He'd plan the evening: get home before Rose, fix some grub, tell a few silly stories and gloat over her swollen belly. They let her work on at Bairds because on the switch she was invisible and couldn't offend the customers. He'd think of fishing, of all his children and the life they would have.

⌒ The Shifty Shadow ⌒

Sam Pickles woke up before the winter dawn with his stump tingling and the smell of his dead father there under the blankets, and he lay awake, cold and sweaty, knowing that the Shifty Shadow had moved across him, and that today was no day to get out of bed. He turned on the bedlamp. This time he'd be no fool, bloody oath, he wouldn't; not till what was going to come had come. Dolly slept beside him with her hair splashed grey and brown across the pillow, her face crushed and old in the lamp. The house was quiet but for the wind creaking it back on its haunches.

Yer losin yer nerve, Sam, he thought, but yer must be smartenin up a bit all the same.

He hadn't felt it as strong and mean on him since the last day at the Abrolhos, and he knew you didn't need to be a gambling man to know that this kind of luck wasn't about to be wagered on.

Morning arrived, the house came alive with business. Dolly slept on, Sam felt the weight of his head on the pillow. The tingling was gone, but there was still a trace of pipe tobacco and port breath in the room. He lit a cigarette and waited. Whatever it was, it couldn't be good. In the end he slept.

Dolly scrapes along the creaky morning balustrade, wild with sobriety. Out in the street those jackhammers have started again. She hasn't touched a drop in four days and you'd swear they had one of those jackhammers up her like a suppository. No, they wouldn't believe you, no fear, no fear, no bloody fear they wouldn't. You can't get a jackhammer up there, but for God's sake, you know someone's smuggled one in. A drinkless sleep is murder – any friggin thing could happen, you could dream anythin! Forgot bein sober was so dangerous. A night's sleep crawling with dreams like a girl couldn't imagine, truly like you couldn't begin to imagine. Oh, the years she's slept peaceful as the dead with just the sweet purr of static in her ears. Now look at that. What I mean is now look straight at that – the crappy threadbare old rug is slippin in and out of the old library door, like a tongue from a slut's mouth. Lessee, let's!

Dolly throws open the library door to see the rug rolled up and shivering epileptic in the corner by the piano where the room is fugged up with the smell of hot bodies.

She staggers out, needing a drink, and knowing it's no use going on with this stupid sobering up, passes the grey old lady with the firepoker at the landing and turns wondering too late. She goes down the stairs arse over, slopping more than she thumps, like a bag of yesterday's fish, and as she goes, she knows for sure she'd have done it better drunk.

Oriel pulls the tent flap to, and in daylight, with a morning's work ahead still, slips the old King James from the bottom of the drawer. Its brittle gilding comes off in her hands, settles in the hairs on her forearms. She opens it. There they are, all their names:

Lester Horace William, born 10/10/94, Eden Valley, SA.

Oriel Esther (nee Barnes) born 31/12/01, Pingelly, WA.

Each one of them, right on down to Lon, and in pencil, the names of a stillborn and two miscarriages: John, Edward, Mary. There they all are, the Lambs in Lester's lovely old Gothic and it seems right and just. We're here, Oriel thinks, calm again; we're here orright.

She stiffens. There's screaming from in the house. She goes out armed and empty handed. And not quite running.

Waiting in the hallway at casualty, Lester and Sam shuffled, folded arms, watched the pretty nurses go past. Sam lit a fag, coughing his bubbly little smoker's hack, and offered it to Lester who surprised himself by taking a drag on it.

Thanks for bringin us, said Sam.

Ah, we're relatives these days, said Lester.

I shoulda learned to drive a car. Never had one or drove one in me life. There's simple things I just don't know about.

What about women?

Sam chuckled. Women? Reckon I know more about cars.

Lester laughed. Which do you prefer?

Sam pursed his lips, reminding himself that he still had his own teeth: I'm partial to trams, meself.

No, dinkum. I'm askin.

Gimme a horse any day.

Over a woman?

By Christ, yeah.

What about Rose . . . Lamb?

She's not a woman, she's a daughter.

Lester laughed. And yer missus in there gettin her leg plastered? Lester felt reckless all of a sudden as though he might confess an old sin to Sam right here and now. But he held himself. We've already taken his daughter, he thought; I couldn't do it to him now just to clean meself of it.

Dolly? No, Dolly's a woman, orright. She always said she was too much woman for me.

Well, Oriel's always been too much Oriel for anybody.

And when they wheeled Dolly out, plastered up like a swearing saint, Lester was singing:

Give me Oriel in my lamp, keep me burning,
Give me Oriel in my lamp, I pray.

I should be drunk! yelled Dolly.

I should be rich, Sam murmured.

And I should be home, said Lester, herding them out to the truck.

Thank Christ, said Sam. I really thought it was somethin serious.

A broken leg's serious enough, said Lester.

It's a bloody gift.

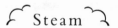 Steam

A long way off, in a cloud of steam like the ante rooms of Hell itself a small man falls naked to the sauna floor feeling

334

his heart stutter. So many women have loved him and suffered him, but none so much as his mother. Sometimes he has dreams about her, the kind he doesn't like to think of. She's just like the girls he chats up and backs up. She's just . . . steam steam steam steam steam steam!

The Blacks and Whites

Look at that, the house's timbers clenching right there in wild daylight. There's no wind, no subsidence in the ground, nothing to resist, but every joint bleats there for a moment as if the place is bracing to sneeze or expel or smother. The river runs louder than a train on the midday air and the lost dead are quaking like sunlight.

Fish Lamb clumps the piano, but all that comes from it is the thick unending drone of middle C and he's not pleased. He knows the sound of his own music, and this is not it. The musty, windowless room is lit like a rainforest floor, the greenish colour shed by the two figures pressed against the wall on either side of him, and in the dimness he sees his own stubby hands thumping the blacks and whites as his fury grows. The floorboards let out a horrible sweet smell. Curling in a snarl, the old rug quivers. Nails vibrate in the walls, and Fish keeps on with some hardfaced determination, while around him the two women bare their teeth at each other, dark and light, light and dark, hating, hurting, hissing silently until Fish, the great trunk in suspenders, heaves up from the stool, whirls and becomes an angry, heavy, menacing man for a moment, and bawls at the walls.

I hate youse you stupids! This is my house!

When he is gone, the two faces are vicelipped, and still, and even the sound of middle C falters a moment before continuing on like an electrical current.

335

⌒ Steel ⌒

The last part of the ride home from the station is downhill and it's the only time the old police bike is any use at all. Quick pedals in a fit of aftershift madness with the wind frigid on his face. He feels so good, it's all he can do not to yell out and yodel jubilantly all the way to Swan Street. He swerves around a milk truck, nips the claws of an ageing labrador and takes the last corner leaning out like a sailor. Some people are at their gates, getting papers and pints, men have their hats on, walking home from bus and train, and the sun is breaking up in the sky. He gives the bell a stiff thumb and coasts down the side of the old brick house where the wireless is on and someone is sobbing. The sound of it shakes him and he's off the bike before it's stopped. It crashes into the empty garage the moment he opens the back door.

Call someone Quick, says Rose, on her knees by the stove. She's dressed for work and white in the cheeks. Call someone. I'm losing the baby.

Mrs Manners! Mrs Manners!

Quick stumbles through boxes and chairs on the verandah on his way to the landlady's door, but she has it open before he knocks. She's a small, startled looking English-woman with spectacles and soft pink hands.

Whatever's the matter, Constable?

Rose's havin a miscarry.

Oh, Lord, I'll come.

I'll go find a phone.

Pedalling uphill with a buckled front wheel and half a uniform on, he can't for the life of him think what to do. A Holden passes, pulls up at the stop sign ahead and Quick has his idea.

Right, he wheezes to the driver who's about to pull away. Police. I'm yer neighbour. I'm a husband. Me bike's busted. Me —

What the bloody hell is this?

Yer car's under arrest.

Rose woke from a doze and they were still there. Her father looked so small against Quick. He hadn't shaved and he was taking it badly enough to make her worry. She was sore, and she could feel a great, surprising bitterness coming on her, but something made her sound stupid and cheerful.

Cmon, you two, you've been there forever. What's the game?

Did yer hear Quick ran over his own bike in the car? said Sam.

Yeah, yeah, he told me, Dad. I laughed.

Good. Good. It's funny, orright. The bloke was a decent sort in the end.

The old man's jaw was starting up a wobble and Quick kept looking about him, as if for somewhere to spit. I wish they'd go home and leave me here, Rose thought, I wish I could sic the nurses onto them and be done with it.

I'll be alright, Dad. You can go, you know. You look terrible.

Quick looked at her and then him, pressing his lips together. Sam mashed his fist into his stump.

What is it, you two? What've you cooked up? You look guilty as gold thieves.

There's somethin I have to tell you, Rose, love. I figure there's no use tellin you tomorrer when you've started to feel better.

Quick nudged the old man: Carn, Sam.

I got a telegram today from Adelaide.

From Ted?

No, from his missus. Ted died yesterday. In the sauna. He was tryin too hard to get his weight down. His heart just went. They reckon he was a decent jockey, though he rode em too hard too early. He's dead, an that's what I had to tell ya.

Well, Mother'll be upset. Thank her for coming in.

She broke her leg, Rose. I didn't get time to say it.

Ah, the Shifty Shadow strikes.

He was a good boy.

No he wasn't, he was a bastard. Go home, Dad, I'm tired. My baby died.

337

She felt Quick looking at her in puzzlement, but she couldn't look him back. She felt like she was made of steel. It was shiny and bitter and it shone all around like starlight. She was steel and Quick couldn't know. No one could know.

⌣ The One ⌢

With a huge and terrible moan, Dolly reached the window and kicked it out with her plastered foot.

My baby!

She fell back on the floor, breaking her nails in the rug, foaming and spitting and squealing till she was hoarse. Her breasts flapped on her, and her nightie rode up to expose her naked, mottled body, her angry slash of a vagina, her rolling bellyfat and caesar scars.

They killed my baby! Him, he was the one I loved, you useless spineless two faced bastards! Heeee was the one. He was the one. He was the one. You can all go and fuckin die because I want him back. He was the one.

In the library the shadows danced. Oh, how they danced. Can't you still see the evil stink coming through the cracks, Fish, the swirling rottenness of their glee turning to gas across the rails, the rooftops, the tree crowns of the city? Take your hands off your ears, Fish, and listen to it.

⌣ Two Florins ⌢

Rose just wouldn't be comforted about the baby, and in the end Quick knew there was nothing he could do. In bad moments he wondered what it was in him that brought these disasters on people. Even his posting to Claremont seemed to bring no relief. For two months after Ted died and the miscarriage, Rose worked on at the switch, getting thinner all the time, looking darkeyed and ghostly when she got home. He cooked for her and she didn't eat. She had little

338

to say as they washed up together, and when he put on the blue for the night's shift she picked listlessly at it as he straightened up.

A whole night of pinchin pervs in the public toilets, he'd say. Maybe I'll get a lost dog or a burgled brooch. It's tough out on the streets, love. Don't you worry about me?

I just worry about how many bikes you'll go through before you make commissioner, she'd say with a weak effort at a grin.

Everythin'll be orright in the end, love.

Yeah. That's what they say.

When Rose quit work and stayed home, Quick knew it wasn't because she'd had enough of Bairds or that the company'd had its fill of her. She was just too weak and spiritless to get through the day any more. He could hear her moving aimlessly all day in the next room as he tried to sleep. She picked up every cough and cold passing through. Clothes hung on her as though she was made of wire. Quick did his shifts glumly, filled in break and enter reports, and rode that mongrel beast of a cycle round and round Claremont until summer came.

When it came down to it, Quick knew he was missing Cloudstreet. There was so much quiet now between Rose and him, and Mrs Manners in the front never made a living sound. The house didn't heave and sigh the way Cloudstreet did; it wasn't restless in any way at all, and there weren't the mobs brawling through, the clang of the shop bell, the rattle of crates and smokers' coughs, the tidal sounds of people stirring up and settling down. This was orderly, calm suburbia. This was merely a list of things missing. And the new house, their dream? Well, it went up bit by bit and Quick sometimes went out just to look at it, the brick box with its red tile roof same as all the other half-finished houses in the street. It looked empty and he'd lost his way with it somewhere. He couldn't imagine them living in it. And Rose just didn't want to talk about it.

One night in December when Quick had the late shift, he was working on the occurrence book at the spanking new Claremont station with only the Sarge asleep in the cells to keep him company, when in walked the old man with a fifty pound mulloway on his shoulder. Quick snapped the big ledger shut and stepped back.

Strike a light!

The old man dumped the great fish on the counter. It was silver and gillheaving, fresh from the river.

I just couldn't wait to show someone, boy. And I knew there wouldn't be another livin breathin soul as'd appreciate it like you would.

Dad, it's beautiful.

Kept me windin a good half hour. Took him at the Brewery wall.

Just then, the fish convulsed with dying, shook scales and mucus all over the joint and coughed up a plug of blood.

Well, that's it for him.

Beautiful.

Think we better . . . get it out, Dad?

Oh, gawd, yeah. Sorry. Back in a sec.

Quick wiped things down with the urn cloth and poured a cuppa for the old man who came back in, excitable as a kid.

Quiet?

Deadly, said Quick. I just wish somethin'd happen.

Wish for somethin nice to happen. There'll be crook things all along the way.

Yeah, maybe. How's Cloudstreet?

Oh, quiet as the grave. Your mother's . . . outside a lot. The girls are seein fellas. Lon – well who knows what he's doin. Dolly next door's got rid of the limp but she's hittin the sauce. Sam's losin again.

How's Fish?

Quiet, quiet. Lies on his bed all day with that wireless goin. Gets a bit rowdy some nights, talkin and singin and things. Says the house is angry. Good old Fish.

Yeah, old Fish.

Miss you, Quick. All of us.

It's hard at the moment, Dad. Rose is so crook still. She's wastin away.

I wasn't meanin to bother yer.

Want another cuppa?

Nah. Lester looked around the smoke stained office with its rows of binder files, notices, mug shots, the old Imperial on the desk, the government ashtrays.

Too quiet, isn't it?

That's what I mean, said Quick.

No, I mean everythin. Cloudstreet, the town, the lot.

Quick shrugged, not understanding.

I sound like Sam Pickles, but I got a feeling. Oh. I almost forgot. Look.

Lester put two coins down on the bench.

Florins, Quick said.

1933.

The year Fish was born.

Have you kept em?

No, I only found em tonight.

Down the river?

In the fish.

What?

He coughed em out with the hook. Out they came, mintfresh. Like a sign. I'll give em to Fish.

He won't know what they are.

Who does? I'll drill holes in em and he can hang em round his neck.

Dad, there's a law against that.

Aw, there's laws against everything and no justice at all. Take it from an old walloper. Look after yer missus, Quick.

Quick was alarmed at the old man's sudden kiss and he was wiping his face as Lester shuffled out.

Weathering It Out

Sam Pickles went to work to earn his pay packet and on the weekends he delivered it faithfully to the bookies and came home broke but not greatly troubled. A long time ago he'd decided that this was to be a straight up and down life of bad luck, and besides the odd shift in the shadow, there wasn't a damned thing he could do about it except go on losing. If anything, he figured there was some strength in knowing the way things were – it gave a bloke security, something to believe in. People knew who he was. At the Mint he was the sentimental favourite – old Sam the Stump who'd been around since the war and wasn't much use at anything except being a familiar part of the place. On the racetrack he was old Sam the Slump, the bloke whose luck was running at a temporary low which began at birth and would probably stay with him to the coffin. Everybody loved a loser, especially a loser of such romantic proportions. He was a cheerful little bloke, always with a wheezy laugh and a fag to give. You knew he was probably right when he said he'd have made a brilliant jockey if he'd thought of it in time, if his father hadn't died, if the luck hadn't gone nasty on him. And at work or on the track, you put up with him saying things like that because he never said them often, and as some lark said, he was too stupid to feel sorry for himself. Dolly was always completely shickered when he got in these days. She drank with a will and an energy he hadn't seen for years. Snoring beside him in bed at night, she gave off a formaldehyde stink that got so bad he moved into Rose's old room. He knew he didn't have a chance trying to figure women out. They were always set on killing themselves. Now Rose was starving herself again like when she was a teenager. He never saw her, and young Quick seemed to be at a loss. One was bloating up like a fat spiritous pile of moans and the other was trying the disappearing act again. He was buggered if he knew what to do. He'd lost a son; it seemed fit that he'd lose the rest of them. Well, there was Chub, but Chub was too lazy to get off his arse and make any trouble; nothing would get rid of Chub. He was apprenticed to a butcher who'd become a depressed man.

By December, Dolly wasn't even home when he got off the train. Some mornings she wasn't even in bed. Things went missing from the house: rugs, silver, even the brass

342

spittoon with the star of David on it that they'd brought down with them from Joel's pub. The times he did see her she was sick and mean and Sam couldn't find the will in him to go at her about all the things she was flogging, the way she looked, what was happening to her. He sat by the wireless, listened to the house cracking its knuckles and decided to weather it out.

One morning, with the hot hayfever easterly blowing in from the desert and whipping the dry grasses against the walls of the house, Sam got the fright of his life. It was light already and he'd finished his breakfast, and had only his hat to find before going off for work. He went through his bedroom, the kitchen, loungeroom, the ground floor hall without a sign of the damned thing, so he went upstairs and looked in Rose's old room, remembering now that he'd left it on her dresser, old fool that he was. But it wasn't in the room at all. There was a thumping in the walls like an erratic heartbeat, the kind he felt with a headache coming on, though when he went out into the corridor he knew it was actually someone pounding and it came from that no man's land room at the end, the one he never much liked. He was getting late for work, but he was curious about that beating in the walls, and besides, he thought, it might be the old girl – there was no sign of her about.

The library door was open a crack and a dim glow showed. Sam went on down, and when he pushed the door open he saw the retarded Lamb boy with Sam's own Akubra on his head, wearing nothing at all else except two silver coins on a chain round his neck. The boy stood against the wall staring back into the corner behind the door, and he was thumping the walls furiously. His nuts swung beneath his belly; his buck teeth were bared and there were tears on his cheeks.

Sam felt a bolt of panic. The boy didn't even seem to see him. He stepped into the room whose atmosphere made his stomach twist, and when he turned he saw the most vicious-looking old bitch he'd ever seen in his life. She was white and dressed in some outfit from another time. There were lacy gloves in her hand that were beautiful, delicate as he'd ever

343

seen. She seemed to be smiling; a sweet, frightening smile. Sure that he might shit himself at any moment, Sam Pickles took the boy by the shoulder. Fish went limp and weepy against him.

She won't let me play! the boy sobbed in his man's voice.

I know how it feels, son, Sam replied, certain at that moment that he'd finally laid eyes on Lady Luck herself. But when he looked back, the old lady was gone, and the only light in the room came from the hallway.

Is there someone up? Sam backed out of the room and called down the corridor.

A door opened. Mr Pickles? It was the Lamb girl Elaine, who always seemed engaged but not married. Fish? She poked her rollered head out into the hall. What's happening? Where's his clothes?

I think he's a bit at sea, said Sam.

She won't let me play, blubbered the boy. He was bigger than Sam and heavy.

Sam felt his joints tingling as if somewhere out of sight there was a small wire shorting.

Whirling Dark

What is it whirling dark across the rooftops and down the streets like a wind, like a hot rancid breath? Cloudstreet suddenly looks small, and the further up you go the flimsier it looks. It could blow away in a moment. All those rooftops could go like leaves, and across the world there's men with circuitry and hardware, men with play lighting their eyes, fellows whose red faces flash like the buttons beneath their hands. All the rooftops of the world become leaves. They quiver and titter before the indrawn breath of brinkmanship and world play right through summer and winter. While down in the streets below their roofs, some people, the people I knew, the people I came to know better having left them behind, fidget before other withheld winds. Dolly

344

drinking and hating up a storm, the shadows bulleting around the library like mullet in a barrel, Fish himself quaking with pent force and worry while across town in the orderly quiet suburbs, Rose Lamb meets the oncoming hayfever season the way she meets the Cuba crisis – with the windows down and the curtains drawn.

Lost Ground

Rose stopped reading newspapers, and put the radio in the linen press. She didn't want to know about Cuba and all the horrors gathering. The world was a sad, miserable place and soon it'd be no place at all. Quick was off deluding himself in uniform, bees hummed mindlessly at the window, the sky was the colour of a suicide's lips so she blotted it out altogether with paper on the panes. Oh, they were waiting for grandchildren over at Cloudstreet but they could bugger themselves as far as she cared. The girls from Bairds called round a couple of times, fat, whorish ignoramuses that they were, calling her Love and Petal all the time. They were gross, sweaty, powdercaked, and their nervous laughter made her want to scratch their eyes out.

The little bedsit was cramped and cheerless, perfect for the hard feeling that had come on her. For the first time since she was a girl Rose felt invincible, as though no one alive could alter her course. The little belly she'd had, which now seemed so gross in memory, was gone, and with it the flesh of her thighs and backside. In the mirror she looked lean and unpredictable; she liked what she saw, though she knew Quick could barely look at her. He despised it, this vomiting food after meals, though he'd exalted over it when there was a baby to cause it. It was puking from emptiness that he hated. Doing it for nothing.

All day she sat inside making and remaking the bed, arranging the cups in the kitchenette so their handles pointed exactly the same way. She boiled and reboiled the cutlery, and on all fours she searched for floor dirt. She didn't touch her books, there was no order in books. When Quick came home she locked herself in the toilet because she couldn't bear to see him deface order.

It was a shock to see the old man at the screen door one Saturday afternoon. He had his hat in hand, smelled of shaving soap, and had a dried out bunch of roses in his fist. She let him in and pulled her housecoat around her.

This is a surprise, she said unevenly. Shouldn't you be at the races?

Well, he said, shouldn't you be out doin somethin?

She shrugged.

You look awful.

Thanks.

You don't have to, that's what pisses me off, Rose.

You'll want a cuppa.

Yeah. No milk.

I remember, Dad. I'm the daughter, remember.

Yeah, I recall right enough. Small here, isn't it? You gunna let me sit down?

Rose wiped a vinyl chair and pushed it his way.

There must be something wrong, said Rose.

I'm here about your Mum.

Aha. Can't you manage a friendly visit?

We don't exactly see you makin a nuisance of yerself visitin Cloudstreet. Besides, it'd be a brave bastard who tried makin a friendly visit on you.

Rose felt the heat of anger gaining on her. Let's just have a cuppa, shall we?

If you can keep a cup of tea down, that'll be fine with me.

Don't harp at me, Dad!

The old man took a seat and slung his hat over his knee. He looked a little changed, as though he'd decided something. And he looked older.

Yer mother's losin control altogether.

She never had any self control. Rats have more discipline than old Dolly.

Jesus, Rose.

Well, what's news?

346

News is she's gettin old an scared. If she doesn't lay off the slops a bit she'll just die.

What dyou care? She's only ever made you miserable.

She's my wife, he said looking at her anew. Looking at her as though she was a snake underfoot.

I can remember a time, Dad, do you remember? When I was a girl, the miserable little girl I was, and I found you in the bathroom getting ready to slit your throat. She drove you that far. You remember that?

I remember, he said, looking at the floor. You came. I stopped. For you.

Rose poured his tea, wiped her hands over and over with an ironed teatowel.

She'll stop for you, too, you know.

So you came for help?

Yeah. Sam let off one of those grins that she hadn't seen since God knows when, since Geraldton and days when there were only air raids and Japs to worry about, and her fury subsided a moment, despite her.

Help? Dad, I cleaned up her vomit, washed her clothes, dragged her home from the pub every bloody night of my childhood. I replaced her, you know. I did her work. My childhood was taken from me, Dad. She hurt me all her life. Don't you think I helped enough? Don't you think you've got a bloody hide even comin to ask?

She's grievin. It's Ted, you know.

Ted, Ted, Ted! She only ever loved the one of us!

Well, for Chrissake, how do you think that makes me feel? You think you're the only one? Nothin can fix that for us, Rose. But show some pity. She lost a child.

Well, she's not the only one!

You never even knew yours. It's not the same. She was Ted's mother.

She was never a mother. She never loved me.

You wouldn't let her, Rose.

Rose stared at him, mouth open.

Sam looked at his cooling tea.

You've lost her, that's why you want me to come.

She's been gone a coupla days.

347

She's left you.

No, she's left herself.

You still love her, don't you?

Sam shrugged, wet-eyed and stiff in his seat. I got used to her. I dunno.

Well, I'm not crawling through the bars of any more pubs looking for her, Dad.

You won't go with me?

Why?

It shames a man lookin for his wife.

Jesus, Dad! Haven't you got used to the shame of it all? She's made an idiot and a laughing stock out of you so often it's like a joke now. Hasn't it worn off yet?

I thought you'd come lookin. Just for me.

I always went for you, Dad.

Don't try to be cruel to her, Rose. She's had her chances, she's nearly finished. Winnin out over someone like that isn't much of a victory. She can only lose from now on in. She's nearly sixty odd. She can only get old and die. You're young. You can have more babies, things are ahead of you. Look at me. Whatever I'm gunna get in this life I've had, and damnnear all that's been lost. You can bear it when you lose money and furniture. You can even grit yer teeth and take it when yer lose yer looks, yer teeth, yer youth. But Christ Jesus, when yer family goes after it, it's more than a man can bear. A man's sposed to have that at least to look forward to.

Rose watched him go out, dusting off his hat, striding down the steps with his elbows in the air and he was gone before the screen door came to with a slap and left her in a shrinking room.

Arrest

Night falls. All down Swan Street the dogs bark and children are hectored indoors. Alone in her two rooms Rose sits on the bed, picking at the candlewick bedspread with a great blankness expanding in her mind. She's hungry, but the feel of food in her mouth just makes her retch. Quick is late off the afternoon shift but she's not thinking of him anymore. For a while there, around five o'clock, when she realized that her flesh had come to feel as though soap had dried on it, she thought that perhaps she should go out and find a doctor because she was suddenly afraid of falling asleep and waking to find herself pinned to the wall by the faint grass-smelling easterly that murmured at the screen door, but the thought petered out somewhere and left her with a fear that seemed to have lost its source. And now, now she's not thinking of anything at all. She's even forgotten to be afraid. The candle-wick bedspread moults under her hands.

She listens to her own breathing. It fascinates her, reminds her of things, so mesmeric. Girls. It's a girl's breath, that's what she hears. And these two rooms don't exist. Something bad is going to happen. All this breathing here in the hallway in front of 36. The Eurythmic Hotel when you're eleven and a half years old. This isn't a memory – she doesn't recall this. The door of 36. Those sounds behind, Jesus Christ, she knows what that is. They're fucking in there behind the door. Who is that? And anyway, what's she waiting for? Listen to them go in there, snorting and snout-ing like . . . but I'm a girl, I don't know this. I don't . . . I . . . my God. Mum? There's been an accident, an accident. Dad's lost his fingers. And she's in there huffing and puffing with someone else. Your mother's on her bed under some stranger and you're turning to steel right there.

A car pulls up noisily somewhere.

Rose begins to weep. I didn't want to remember *that*! I don't want *that*.

And now someone is running, someone close by.

I was a girl, she thinks; I shouldn't have had to hear that. I shouldn't have had *any* of it.

Rose? Rose?

A policeman at the door. He bursts inside like he owns the bloody place.

It's not fair! she yells, Not me!

Rose?

The taxi floats down Stirling Highway. She sees the clock-tower of the uni lit in the far distance.

Rose, says Quick.

Yes?

Are you orright?

Looks like a fuckin scarecrow to me, says the taxi driver.

She's also my wife.

Shit! Sorry, Constable. I thought it was an arrest. Gawd, I'm sorry.

Just drive.

Quick?

Yeah.

You putting me in the hospital?

Quick smiles. He looks beautiful in his uniform: No. Though I probably should. Look at you.

I'm ugly.

Not as ugly as me.

Where we going?

Cloudstreet.

Is everything alright?

We've found your mum.

Oh God.

I don't wanna do this, Quick! Rose pleads, trying to slow him up in the corridor.

From a doorway, a woman's voice comes screaming: You fuckin bastards! Get your stinkin hands outta me stock-ins or I'll piss all over the lotta yer!

Quick looks pale and nervous himself. His tunic is crumpled from holding her in the taxi. Elaine drifts by squinting with strain.

I don't know much about this stuff, Rose. I got the call and thought I'd better bring you. I thought you'd come.

The call from who?

Yer dad. Some bloke slipped a note in the mail box, I dunno, someone told him. I dunno.

Dad, you little mongrel, she murmurs. You gutless little runt.

350

Down the corridor the woman screams again. Aaargh!

You don't know what this is like, Quick!

He shrugs.

You've been sheltered from this sort of stuff, damn it!

He nods. Yeah, I'm finding that out, orright.

No one should make me do this again. I've told you all that stuff. They shouldn't make me.

Quick shook his head.

God, Quick, I'm married. I'm my own person.

She's yer mother.

I can't help that.

Neither can she. They said she wants you.

She can go to hell.

The voice is broken and hoarse now, pouring from that room. A man comes out sweating and closing a bag. The doctor. She'll settle now, he says leaving.

I think she's found Hell, someone says, by the sound of that.

Quick snatches up his cap. I've gotta go. Good luck. He turns on his boot heel and pushes his way through the doors.

Rose stands there with her hair about her like a stormcloud, all the steel gone out of her.

The Girl with the Brown Fatness of Hair

Dolly saw the girl swimming through the crowd. It was hard to see because she herself was lying on the bar with men leaning on her and their drinks on coasters balanced on her belly, between her breasts, along her thighs. They were squeezing her for it, those men, milking her tits for beer, foaming up their glasses, reaching inside her camisole, forcing her legs apart to get at things and dragging out coins, furniture, dead babies and old bottles. Between her knees and through the smoke and laughter she saw the girl with the brown fatness of hair. There was a great ticking watch on the girl's wrist, big as a saucer. Dolly heard it through the roaring mob and saw how it weighed the kid down. But

351

the girl waded on doggedly. She was strong, you could see, and she was coming, and the laughter was drying up and the hands were coming out as they all started dying around her.

A long time after everyone left, Rose stood by the bed. The old girl sagged back onto the pillows with her wild hair spread out upon them full of silver streaks, tobacco washes. She looked incredibly old and tired, more haglike than any pantomine witch. It was hard to believe that something like this could give birth to you. The whole house went quiet till it was just grinding on its stumps, like a ship at anchor.

You wanted to see me, said Rose dully after a long time.

Dolly closed her eyes.

Rose sat down.

I'm tired.

Well I'm tired, too, so get on with it.

Don't hate me.

Too late for that.

Why?

My whole life, Mother, that's why.

Dolly blinked. What did I do that was so bad?

Rose smiled bitterly. You've gotta be joking. You stole from me. My childhood, my innocence, my trust. You were always a hateful bitch. A drunken slut. You beat us and shamed us in public. I hate you for all the reasons you hate yourself, and I wanted to kill you the way you wanted to kill yourself. Everything, you stole from me. Even when I was a teenager you *competed* with me, your looks against mine. Shit, even my grief you steal from me. You can't imagine how I hate you.

You look sick, said Dolly.

I'm not sick. What is all this anyway? What's the summons? What've you been doing? Don't answer that, I don't wanna know.

I was sad.

What?

About Ted.

Oh dear. Here we go.

I loved him.

Your favourite.

People have em, Rose. You always loved Sam more than me.

He earned it.

People don't earn it.

They do with me. Listen, I'm going. This is making me want to vomit.

I wanted to talk to you.

I don't want any boozer's justifications and sympathy talk.

Come back tomorrow.

I've got my own life now.

Come back.

No.

Rose.

Why?

I want to talk, just to talk.

I'm busy.

Doing what?

I'm just busy.

Come tomorrow. Please. I'm beggin you to come back tomorrow.

Rose left. Lester drove her away. The house fell back against the night sky like a dying planet.

Go see her, love, said Lester.

Why?

I dunno. I can't stand the hate. It'll kill you. You're one of us now and I couldn't bear to lose you. Quick's hurtin. We all are. Go on with your life, love. It's all there is.

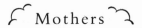 Mothers

In the morning, Rose went again but Dolly was asleep. She stayed in the house with Elaine and Oriel, narrowing her eyes at their noise and bustle, until Dolly woke.

She went in strangely robbed of her anger and unpre-
pared. She felt jittery and sad and feeble in all the ways she'd
planned against since her first ever period.

Dolly was sitting up in bed with pillows about her like
sandbags around a machine-gun nest.

Hello, Rose murmured.

Hello, said Dolly. A wan grin had fixed itself on her face
halfway between coming and going.

Better?

Feel like shit, but I reckon that's better.

Rose stood by the window where she could see the
peeling fence and the wall of weeds.

Look like you better sit down.

I'm alright.

You'll fall over. Siddown.

Rose pulled the chair over to the bedside.

Dolly raised her eyebrows. When you gettin pregnant
again?

I'm not thinking about it, Rose said, flushing. Besides
I haven't had a period for months.

You need to see a doctor.

That's a laugh.

Rose looked at her skirt, the way her knees made sharp
peaks beneath it. God, even the angles her body made were
mean looking now.

Anyway, why do you ask? she murmured, trying to
be calm.

I was plannin on bein a grandmother. This mornin.
That's when I decided. Be good for me, you know. Jesus, I'd
spoil em rotten, I would, givin em lollies and fizzy drinks.
Let em wreck the bloody place. Reckon I'd be the worst
bloody granma a kid could have –

Why not, Rose heard herself leap in, you were already
the worst mother.

Dolly didn't even stop.

They'd love me. I'd let em swear their heads off, give
em noisy toys, take em to the pictures an stuff em with fairy
floss. I wouldn't even make em wear clothes, I wouldn't

make em do anything as long . . . as long as they came to see me.

Rose saw the old woman's mouth sloping away toward weeping, and she realized that she had no teeth. She'd never noticed before. Rose had no idea what her mother would say next, no idea of what she might let out herself.

Outside it was a summer's day. That dry, wondrous heat of the west. Out there it would feel like the meeting of desert and sea, the heat behind, the dark coolness ahead. Rose thought about it. Yes, she could be down by the river now, with a baby, a brown sunny baby beside her on the sand. Water would lap like cat's milk and the air be heady with the scent of peppermint trees. There would be nothing to do but feel important and proud, to have the form against your body, to take a hand in your mouth and bite down those long, soft baby fingernails like some protective she animal, snuffle, smell, bask.

You're a grandmother already, aren't you? Rose said, finding her knees before her again. What about Ted's kids?

They're a thousand miles away. I don't know the girl. Don't know anything about em.

Well, one day, maybe.

Oh, yeah, they're gonna all get on the train an come an see Granma Dolly.

They've got money. Ted was a good jockey, they say. He rode winners.

Dolly laughed. Imagine bein around a man who rode winners.

They were quiet again a few long, awkward moments.

You reckon you'd have missed him more, if he was a sister?

What kind of question is that, Mum? I never had a sister.

Yeah, you wanted one, though, eh?

Rose looked at her mother whose white, puffy face was impossible to read just now. I suppose. I haven't thought about it much. I don't know if I ever really thought about it, but I guess it's true enough. I used to watch those Lamb girls and . . . think of the things they could tell each other. Used to watch that Hat, the eldest one, playing marbles with the boys, and I decided that the only way she could do it was because she had other sisters and it didn't matter somehow. She didn't have to play the part of the girl.

You turned out sort of prissy, didn't you.

I had to make myself something!

Don't worry about sisters, then. They always look better from a distance. I had seven. Sisters! Jesus, sisters. You're better off with brothers.

I just lost one, remember?

Well, he was lost to us a good while back.

God, you sound like a book.

I reckon you'd know. You turned out the bookworm. What did you ever get out of em, anyway?

Rose wrung her gloves and threw them onto the bed. Some idea of how other people lived their lives, Mum. A look at real people.

Ho, real people.

Like mothers. What mothers are supposed to be like.

Mothers! Sisters, mothers! You found out what a mother's like. You won't forget me in a hurry. Don't go moanin about sisters.

The heat went out of them quickly, surprising Rose, who had a thought that had never once come to her as a child.

What was your mother like, then? she all but whispered.

Dolly pulled the sheet up her body and slid down the pillows. Rose could have sworn the bed was shaking.

I had seven sisters. Jesus, I loved my father. My mother was always far away when I was around. There always did seem to be too many girls.

But what was she like? Your mother.

You should never trust a woman.

I thought it was men you hated.

Me? No, men are lovely. Gawd, I was mad about men all me life.

Yes, said Rose.

It's women I hate.

Daughters.

No, daughters are different, Dolly said with a grave,

356

measured tone. It's sisters I hate most. You should be grateful you never had any.

I don't get it, Mum.

My mother was my grandmother. My father was my grandfather.

What?

The second oldest sister, the one who made me feel like rubbish all my life, that one was my mother. There we were. There we were.

Rose felt things falling within her, a terrible shifting of weights.

My God. My God. Mum!

The old woman lay flat on the bed, bawling silently, her mouth wrought into the ugliest hole. She'd seen that ugliness before, the huge wordless grief of babies, in Quick's brother. There were no tears in the old girl's eyes; it was as though she'd been dried out forever in there. Rose Lamb got up out of her chair, put a knee up on the bed, hoisted herself, and felt the sobs beating up at her from the body beneath. The sound her mother made taking breath was like a window being torn from its hinges.

Oh, Mum. You never told me. You never ever said. Don't cry, Mum. Please.

Outside, it was a summer's day. The house twisted its joists, hugging inwards, sucking in air, and the two women wept together on the sagging bed.

Tonic

By the end of 1962 it looked as though the world might go on. The news in the papers got better, Quick got something of a pay rise, and Rose got a period. For so long there'd been things to fear. That someone might push a button, that Dolly would kill herself, that there would be no money at the end of the month, that their new house would never be finished, that Rose's body might beat her in the end. Before things brightened up a little, even Lester gave up saying: We had it harder in our day.

357

Rose was glad of those talks with her mother. She found soft parts still left in herself, soft parts in Dolly as well, and in a way she figured it saved her from herself. It was love really, finding some love left. It was like tonic.

Rose still went to see her mother every day or two and usually came back furious. The old girl sat out on her backstep feeding chunks of topside beef to magpies. She was often sober, always abusive, and after a time her cursing became almost soothing in its steadiness. Dolly bitched and whined about everything until Rose began to realize that half the time the old girl was bunging it on – she was play acting just to amuse herself. Sure, there was still heat in the old battleaxe, but not much of an edge. When Rose went round, Dolly made her a cup of tea. They'd feed the birds, the old woman would be abominable, feign deafness and raise a hedge of irritability between them, and Rose would go home.

Late in spring, Rose began to swim in the river at Peppermint Grove. She'd start out from the boatshed and swim right around the Mosman Spit. When no one was about she even tried a few bombies and tin soldiers off the jetty. She felt all the childish impulses of the Geraldton days, and she went home ravenous and kept her food down. With summer coming on, she woke in the mornings thinking of all the things she could do instead of listing the things she refused to do or was incapable of. Sometimes she felt all the blood rising in her skin, feeding her, overriding her will. She was alive despite herself. She got out the old books, spent entire mornings at the river in their worlds. In the evenings she planted little lovenotes to Quick around the flat: in his socks, pinned to his undies, between dusty packets of condoms. Poor Quick. How he'd waited for her all these months. It was that pigheaded Lamb patience, and you had to love him for it. She felt the shadow in her, this dark eating thing inside, like an anger, and sensed that it'd always be with her. But Quick would hold her up beyond reason, even when it went into stupidmindedness. It wasn't just the fact that she knew he could do it for her that made her love him. It was her certainty that he would.

As the weather warmed toward summer, Rose and Quick spent their spare time floating dreamily on the river in the Lamb boat. They talked like teenagers, catching up, making up time, finding words for how they felt. Marriage had been no dream. They'd worked their guts out, lived through sickness and worry and still their neat little suburban house wasn't ready for them. Rose thought about returning to work somewhere, but already she was staring at babies in the street again. Quick was promoted to riding the new BSA station motorcycle, an evil beast of a thing with enough compression to put you over the bars during a kickstart.

They came home from the river one day to find Lester Lamb waiting for them on the bonnet of an ancient Rugby, dressed in his threadbare suit and looking gorgeously pleased with himself. He showed them the car. It was a dusty, black old banger with tyres smoother than a baby's bum and rust beneath the paint like a spreading cold sore. He showed them every angle, every virtue, including the side-blinds he'd made himself from old X-rays which gave a curious effect of mortality to an afternoon drive: you saw the world through compound fractures, you saw the river in an old soldier's lungs, sky through the skulls of shellshocked corporals.

It's yours, he said, you need a car.

We need a car, said Quick.

But this is more than a car, said Rose, it's an experience.

By Christmas, Quick had that old scrumwagon Rugby up and running, Rose was pregnant again, and the house out in the suburbs was almost finished. Quick moonlighted in the day, driving trucks and hammering up cheap furniture in a warehouse while Rose took in ironing between river swims. Nights off they went dancing and made galahs of themselves at the Embassy and later drove out to Cottesloe Beach to make love under an upturned skiff.

We're getting somewhere, Rose thought. Our own house, a baby, money in the bank. She had dreams of furniture, neat rugs, lino tiles, a TV, the smell of Pine-O-Clean. A clean, orderly, separate place with fences and heavy curtains. Their own world.

By Christmas it looked a dead cert.

℩ He Does ℩

Red Lamb was a nurse and she liked to shock poor old Elaine.

Geez, I hate men's –

Red! Elaine winced, held up a hand.

Aw, Elaine, it's better to be disgusted than ignorant. Now did you know that –

Red, I don't need to know anything.

Crikey, what's this?

Into the kitchen came Lon all grazed and blackeyed and sweating, and by a stroke of bad timing he was followed in by his mother who caught one look at his face and shoved him cheeksfirst into the big freezerbox of the old Frigidaire.

Ice'll help, she said. What bully did this to you?

A man, blubbered Lon, a fullgrowed man. His voice sounded a longway off coming from the freezerbox.

What did he do? Now tell me, I'm yer mother.

Hit me. He hit me.

In public?

Only people.

Did you deserve some punishment? Oriel said, suddenly pensive. Red opened a bottle of mecurochrome the size of a stout keg and got together some swabs.

Lon?

There's a girl pregnant, said Lon from on ice.

No one could tell if Oriel fainted a moment or what, but she leant on that fridge door something shocking. You could hear Lon Lamb screaming three stops down the line.

Lucky it's only his head in there, Red said to the old man who'd come running; if it was me doin the business he'd be losin his play bits.

Lon was married inside a fortnight, and when the minister said: Do you Logan Fitzwilliam Bruce Lamb take this Pansy Mullet to be your lawfully wedded wife? Oriel murmured darkly: He does.

They took a room at Cloudstreet, Lon and Pansy, and filled it with rage and weeping.

Doomiest

Sam rolls awake in the night with his stump ringing with pain. It goes right through him, into his chest, down his side. Godalmighty, a heart attack, he thinks. But it goes on and on, emanating from pieces of him he no longer owns. No, he thinks, it's bloody doom. Big, big doomy doomier, doomiest. It hurt so much that tears roll back into his ears and the house seems to laugh at him. He wants to go to sleep and not wake up in the morning.

Flames

In her dream Oriel saw the bush and the city burning. People ran from their squawking homes to the riverbank with the flames gaining behind them, but they stopped, afraid, at the water and let the fire consume them on the grassy slope above the river.

The New House

Quick looks the business in his black helmet and leggings as he hammers the BSA out north to the new subdivisions. His Dougie MacArthur sunglasses flap against his cheeks. He leans, throttles into the turns, flies like an angel.

The new house stands in a street of similar new houses and Quick props the bike and goes in for a look. It's all there on its patch of rubblestrewn dirt. If he's honest, he'd like some weatherboard old joint to remind him of farm days, happy childhood days, or even of Cloudstreet, but he knows Rose wants it fresh, new, clean, apart. Yeah, soon there'd be kids in the street, and the sound of lawnmowers.

And then in the late afternoon gloom someone steps out from behind a wall and comes towards him. Quick knows him. Oh, he knows him. It's the blackfella wearing nothing but a beach towel and a pair of rubber thongs.

Go home, says the black man. This isn't your home. Go home to your home, mate.

Quick fronts him, emboldened by his uniform. This is a black man he's talking to.

But the man lays five fingers spread on Quick's chest. Go home. Quick turns. Already he's alone.

Christmas

At Cloudstreet on Christmas Eve the timbers rattled like bones in a box. Lester's marketfresh vegetables went brown in hours, and the milk curdled in the cans before the Lambs and Pickleses woke from vile, breathless dreams. A shitty smell came over the place and you'd swear there were more in the house than the headcount let on. Standing anywhere in Cloudstreet that day was like being in an overloaded ferry in a sou'wester. Oriel found herself needing the walls to keep her upright. The corridor was a lurching tunnel and the shop foetid. Sam woke and wished it was a work day so he could pack his gladstone and heave-ho. Dolly threw up her tea in the sink with spots in her eyes big as snarling faces. When you blinked, shadows ripped by. Out in the yard, the last of the shrivelled mulberries rained on Oriel's tent like a bloodstorm.

The pig sang all through Christmas with Fish sitting by beneath the fig tree listening and mashing his fists. What's he say, Fish? Can you pick it? Over and over, the same phrases. Carn, Fish, what's with the pork?

Sam went out in the afternoon to find that his cockatoo

was gone. Absconded bird. He went walking the streets calling Fair dinkum? Fair dinkum? All the old houses were coming down and salmon brick duplexes were going up in their place. The streets were full of jacked up FJs with foxtails and glasspacks. There seemed to be no children. When Sam came home birdless, Fish Lamb next door was bellowing and bawling and the piano was thundering.

On Christmas morning the house filled with foul and frantic shades and a howling set up in the surrounding streets. In the dawn the pig was nearly torn to pieces by a pack of dogs that jumped the fence while the lot of them slept on, resisting it as a dream.

Fish Lamb was strangely quiet. No hysterics. He lay on his bed and did not come out. Lester bandaged the pig, kissed its brow and prayed.

Summer Madness

And then the vile hot easterly blows them into summer proper, into a dry night-time madness that eddies under the eaves and shakes the rats out of every sleepout grapevine as a small man creeps through the back lanes between bin and gate and bloating fences itching with an inexplicable hatred. See him down there slinking along, snuffling and wheezing in your town, in your yards, your streets, and hating you, every whole one of you as you sleep moaning and turning beneath your sheet behind your flywire, past you as you sleep open on verandahs and on back lawns in the countrified manner you cling to. Oh, what hurt and malevolence glows in that shambling shape of a man. From beyond space and time I see him like a coal sputtering in the dark, rolling wherever the hot headachy desert wind blows him: West Perth, Dalkeith, Shenton Park, Subiaco, Mosman Park, coming by you, coming by you, coming for you. Against his chest he carries a rifle. For you all.

Bloody Mayhem

Quick wakes to the sound of a motor. It's high morning. A motorbike running under his window.

Lamb? Lamb!

Rose wakes next to him. Quick?

Sounds like Murphy from the station. Orright! Wait a second!

Get out here, mate! Get on this bike! We've got all shit goin up!

Quick got to the door in his undies. Gday, Murph.

Get fuckin dressed, mate.

What's up?

Bloody mayhem, that's what.

Well, says Rose, spose this is what you've been waiting for.

But when Quick is gone and Rose goes out for a paper, she finds it's worse than a bit of houseburning. The *West* is forecasting isolated thunder and broadcasting indiscriminate murder.

Heat of the Night

In the heat of the night with his barrel still reeking, the man with the hare lip and the cleft palate shifts through the dry night grass in someone's backyard and comes upon a sleeper behind insect wire. A sleeper: lips opening and closing in the great vacant journey of sleep, his breath coming and going like the sea. At the back of the house. In the big country town that wants so much to be a city, there's another sleeper and I can't stop this. I'm behind the mirror and in different spaces, I'm long gone and long here but there's nothing I can do to stop this. Every time it happens, on and on in memory, I flinch as that brow flinches with the cool barrel suddenly upon it. The sound goes on and on and matter flies like the constellations through the great gaps in the heavens, and I haven't stopped it again. Lester, Rose, Red – I can't stop it for you. When I'm Fish down there I just don't know, and now

364

that I'm what he became beyond it's all too late. I see it, I see it, all of history, and it sets me hard as spirit.

Right in Our Bloody Backyard

It's right in our bloody backyard, said the Sarge. Cottesloe, he shoots and wounds two in a car. Then he goes to a flat, puts a hole in a bloke's forehead. An hour later he shoots a bloke on his doorstep in Nedlands when he answers the door. Then he kills a kid sleeping on a back verandah in the next street. The CIB are shitting themselves. Your namesake, Lambsy, up at Central, he's like a cyclone.

What do we do? said Quick.

What we're told, said the Sarge.

It's madness, said Murphy.

Or evil, thought Quick.

Murder, Murder

Sam Pickles opened the *West* at lunchbreak, stinking of gold and silver and turpentine. DEADLOCK IN KILLER HUNT: STREETS STAY LIT. That's it alright. The shadow over the whole town. SHARK KILLS WOMAN IN TWO FEET OF WATER. Jesus. There's worse. RAIN DELAYS TEST PLAY.

The town is in a frenzy down there. This is what it means to be a city, they say, locking their doors and stifling behind their windows. On the streets at night no one moves. No one goes out. There's a murderer out there and no one knows what he wants, where he is, who he is, and why he kills. This is Perth, Western Australia, whose ambitions know no limit. And the streets are empty.

Quick crept the back lanes of Nedlands through the long, hot, wet nights. The CIB boys fingerprinted everybody in

365

the known world and the streetlights burned all night. Armed with his uniform, his handcuffs, torch and truncheon, Quick felt no fear, but he could smell it in the outhouses the length of every lane; it oozed from under the bolted doors, from every flue, vent and gully trap of the neighbourhoods he patrolled. He was alone out there with a gunman loose, and he wondered what evil really looked like, if its breath stank, if it could be stopped. The lanes were high with weeds and cast off junk. There was room, all the room in the world for a man to be abroad unseen. Quick didn't blame them all in there, tossing and rolling awake through the summer.

I'm scared, Quick, said Rose. I don't sleep all night. You can't leave me here on my own. I'm going mad. I can't even read. Even in the day, I'm frightened.

The new house is ready enough, I spose, he said, dubious.

I'd be alone there, Quick. I don't want to be alone. Have you seen that street? There'd be no one to talk to. I can't stand it while you're on nights, love. I've got the baby. There's some mad bastard out there and no one's caught him.

We'll think of something, love.

They're like rats in a fire down there. See, across the desert the train comes groaning with emergency supplies of locks and mesh. The fingerprint files of the CIB look bigger than the Doomsday Book. There's ulcers bursting, friendships and marriages lost. There's a murderer out there, a cold blooded maniac. Don't go out, they say. Ring three times, they say. Don't come calling, they say, it's too much for me, just don't come calling, just leave us alone, leave me be, leave us, leave us, oh God it's sweltering but don't go outside!

And someone else dies, regardless.

As Cloudstreet tosses and throttles, a queer point of lumi-
nescence in all that gloom, with its downpipes crashing in the
wind, its stonefruit falling dead from trees and the scarred
and hurting pig shrieking warning across the whines of
mosquito and the dead sobs in the walls, that man comes
wheezing. He steps lightly by stubbornly opened doors and
lifted windows, past the buckled shop shutters and the open
till within, down the swept side path into the heartland
where it smells of laundry and preserve bottling and wood-
work and vegetables and the hard labour of people, down
through it all with his heart a-dance, he comes wheezing. He
sees a tent billowing softly in the night light. He bites his lips
coming onward, bearing down, but out of the dark comes a
pink blur, a squealing snarling creature that uproots him and
sends him back in a tumble and he's running, grabbing for
the .22 before it can turn for another run, before he can find
out what it is.

And in the street, right under the light as he comes
running, is a man with black arms akimbo, just watching.
The gunman stops, draws a bead, and loses him in his sights.
Loses him from the street altogether. Someone's calling out a
foreign lingo. He bolts.

Rose shivers in her bed. We're alright, she says to the baby.
We're okay. Oh, Quick, come home!

After a night of endless lonely trudging, of holeing up in
ramshackle hollows and peering over back fences with thunder breaking the sky and the rain beating mud against his
shins, Quick clocked off the shift and went down to the river
to clear his head. In the dawn the sky was clearing and
summery steam rose off the jetty piles, and out of the steam
came the black man looking completely unsurprised.

Geez, said Quick, recognizing him fearfully. Haven't
you got a home to go to?

Not this side.

Quick looked across the river. Through the steam he

367

thought he saw moving figures, dark outlines on the far bank.

Are you real?

The black fella laughed. Are you?

Quick kicked the muddy grass before him.

You've got a home to go to, Quick. Go there.

Quick regarded the man. He was naked, naked enough to arrest.

Go there.

Orright, said PC Quick, already on his way. When he turned back, high on the hill, he saw more than one black man. He saw dozens of them beneath the trees, hundreds like a necklace at the throat of the city.

Home

Sam and Oriel and Lester met in the Lambs' kitchen at Cloudstreet before breakfast. It seemed to have occurred to them all at once.

Sam noticed that Oriel Lamb had the beginnings of a beard. Oriel Lamb still had a strange overwhelming parental power about her, and he imagined that crossing her would be like crossing luck itself. Sam felt himself shrinking in this engineroom of a kitchen whose walls throbbed with produce. From the window you could see the yard on the Lamb side, its terraces of flowers and vegies inside chickenwire, the stonefruit trees heavy, the redspattered tent sucking its cheeks in the morning wind.

This proposition's just more of an idea, said Sam.

Yes? Yes?

Let's get em back here.

Who?

Well, I worry about Rose.

That's my idea! said Lester.

Quick and Rose? said Oriel.

She's on her own too much, said Sam.

They've just built a new house, said Oriel.

She needs company, protection. She's havin a baby remember.

368

Gawd, it'd be good havin a nipper round the place again, said Lester.

We'll have one soon enough, said Oriel, thinking of Lon and Pansy.

They could have that big room at the top of the stairs.

Ugh, said Oriel.

Well? said Lester.

They'll never come, said Oriel. Rose's too proud.

Sam smiled.

And . . . and Quick too, she said trying uncharacteristically to be diplomatic, because any man could see the idea had taken root in her. No, no they're too proud. They'll never come home.

Quick and Rose arrived with the laden Rugby even before the Cloudstreet delegation set off.

Got a spare bunk? said Quick.

The families mobbed them on the verandah. It was a stampede, a door-flinging, board-bucking, fruit-dropping stampede down the corridors to reach them. Everyone grabbed hungrily at them, Rose with her big melon belly, Quick with his loose limbed nightshift body.

Just for a week or two, said Quick.

Yairs! Yairs!

It seems logical, said Quick through his teeth.

Aw, yairs.

I wasn't worried really, said Rose.

Aw, nooooo!

Fish came last down the stairs, thumping his way through the house. Aarr! Quick en Rose! Arrrr!

Quick felt safe here, he felt within his boundaries. Happy? he asked Rose amid the din. Happy, she said.

The Walls

But the library is horrible. And besides, Rose gets a late recurrence of morning sickness. She swears it's the windowless room. After long nights, Quick comes home to good old

Cloudstreet and crashes into bed with shop noise below him and old Dolly cursing gravity and time out the back somewhere, but it's not that which stops him sleeping. It's the old misery pictures on the wall. When he lies down and the door is closed, the room dark, quiet and airless, two strange miserables burst off the walls and at each other's throats. It's exhaustion he thinks, and lack of air. That steely old hag and the darkeyed girl going at it, mute and angry like the pictures on his wall in his childhood sleep. So he goes back on shift shitweary and useless.

The Light in the Tent

Nights were long out in the tent with no wood and glass to sleep behind. Oriel knew there was only fabric between her and death, fabric and strength of character. She took to leaving a lit candle by her bed. It stood in a saucer on the old family Bible, its flame curtseying before the draughts. Thundery showers peppered the tentfly and above it, the mulberry shook itself like a wet dog. Canvas. She knew how thin canvas was, but she refused to be afraid. True, she could move inside until the killer was caught, as Lester and Quick said, but that would be a surrender to things that hadn't even declared themselves and she knew that going inside would break her will.

Sometimes in clear patches of sleeplessness she stood at the flap and looked up at the old house and wondered why it still fought them so. Nineteen years, wasn't it long enough to belong? But it had got worse lately, this illfeeling coming from the place, unless she was imagining it and any fool could tell you she wasn't much for imagination.

All down the street and down every street men and women were sliding new bolts on their doors, locking windows, drawing curtains, dragging out dusty .22s and twelve gauges, opening bottles and whispering Hail Marys under the sheets while that candle burnt on the Bible in the tent behind Cloudstreet and that boxy little woman sat arms akimbo, waiting for something to show itself.

Only Streets Away

Only streets away a man with sinus trouble slips from yard to yard. Across a back verandah he creeps and a restless sleeping body catches his eye through a cool screen window. A sultry, sultry night. He slips a hand through the wire of the screen door, slides the bolt. The smell of lamb chops lingers still in the close air of the house. He's inside. He's decided something. This isn't madness. He's thought about it. He knows what rape and murder mean. He's just come to like them.

Fish Wakes

Fish wakes. Rose hears him sobbing. And then muttering, the crazy foreign talk from the wedding, on and on, until she hears Lester stirring.

He Knows What Rape and Murder Mean

Yes, it's a woman. Young. A short nightie rucked up in the heat. He steadies, drawing on all his skill. After all, he's the Nedlands Monster, no less. Finds the cord from the bedlight. It's so easy. And her breasts part as he slips it under her neck. She hardly makes a sound going off, throttling, writhing and choking and her legs spread in surrender so he goes to it on a spurt of triumph. He knows what rape and murder mean. He knows what he's doing. They're frightened of him. The whole city is quaking at the thought of him. This girl, even her dead body is afraid of what he's doing, repulsed at the look of triumph on his face, recoiling at the face itself.

Oriel Hears

Oriel hears the boy blabbering and wailing up there. All the houselights are on. She'd go in there herself and claim order, but Fish doesn't know her, doesn't see her, can't hear her and she isn't that much of a glutton for punishment.

Businesslike

With his seed in her the dead girl's gone all heavy. They're gonna come looking for him. The police, the screaming, hurting family, the whole defeated city. You have to be a winner. Even the short and ugly and deformed, they have to win sometimes. He's winning, beating them all. A little truckdriving bloke with no schooling, he's killing them in their beds and they're losing at last.

He drags the girl's strangled and defiled body out into the lane. Finds a hole in a neighbour's fence and stuffs her through, throws the nightie after her. Then back to the car, across the deadnight river to the missus and kids. Business-like, that's what he admires about himself.

Quiet

Oriel wakes from a doze and the candle is out. The house is quiet and there's light coming from the rim of the sky. Quick will be home soon from the shift. With news, she can feel it.

Loaded House

Lester steps out of Cloudstreet, crosses the road and looks back at it. There's something horrible about it lately. Something hateful, something loaded with darkness and misery. He doesn't know how much more of it he can stand.

Morning

Quick stands exhausted by the river. The old town isn't the same anymore, it'll never be the same. The sun is streaming out over the hills and onto the terracotta roofs of the suburbs where they'll all be waking up to the news. It's happening out there, he thinks, and we can't stop it, we can only clean up after him.

Quick moves along the bluffs above the river. He won't let himself think it, but he knows he's looking for that blackfella. He has to talk.

The City is Howling

The city is howling with outrage. They're talking of bringing in the army, bringing across the Sydney homicide squad, Scotland Yard. The whole city goes mad with fear and outrage.

Dolly and Rose

Out on the backstep Dolly feeds the birds their raw meat. They eye her sideways and snatch it from her to back off to a distance and hack away.

Garn, she says, you'd tear me bloody eyes out if I didn't come with a feed, wouldn't you?

A diesel rumbles past heading somewhere on the tracks. The birds flinch, baulk and Dolly laughs.

Well, you gutless wonders! You'd eat ya children!

She sees them now pecking at her bloated body out in the desert by the tracks that lead nowhere and bring nothing. Rose comes down smiling. Good old Rose, good old Rosie.

Bastard of a Place

Sam latches his gladstone bag, pops a morning peppermint in his mouth and steps down off the verandah where Lester is lifting the shop shutters.

Bastard of a place, he thinks vaguely, not knowing which place he really means.

373

Fish stands by and sees the shade ladies pressed flat against the wallpaper as Quick opens the wall up with a saw. Wood dust comes down and makes him sneeze. There's plaster like frost upon the floor.

Slip us the crowbar, will you, Fish.

This?

Yep.

There's sun coming!

Quick prizes boards away, knocks a cut beam aside, and a square of sunlight breaks into the room with a shudder and a riot of motes and spirits. Fish sees the shadows with their mouths wide in horror. He grips the saw, its handle still warm from his own brother Quick.

Well, look at that. You can see the backyard. Wave to Mum, Fish.

Fish looks gingerly out of the hole in the wall and sees some woman looking up from the flap of the tent.

Gawd, that's better. Some fresh air. You can feel the difference already. It was enough to make a bloke wanna puke in here before. You don't mind us using it, dyou, Fish? I mean I know it's always been kind of like your own den.

Fish is looking at the shadows creeping around the edge of the walls.

Well, it'll do till we get sorted out.

How's it coming along? Rose calls, hauling herself up the stairs. It's hard to recall so much light on the landing. It pours out of the old library instead of feebly trying to get in. She comes into the doorway and rests on the jamb looking flushed and loaded.

Well, that's an improvement. When's the window coming?

Dad's bringing it on the truck this arvo.

Just finish the job, I hate half-finished things.

Speakin of half-finished things, Fish's been askin about the baby. He wants to feel if it's true.

Fish looks at his great barge feet.

Cmon, Fish, says Rose. Hands on.

Fish shuffles over. He keeps his head down and puts his smooth, pale man's hands on her belly and smiles into his chest.

He's in there.

Well, that's what the doctor says. You could fool me.

The ladies won't like it.

Oh, I think they'll get used to being grannies, don't you?

You happy? asks Quick.

It could be worse, Rose says. We'll have a roof over our heads, even if it is the same old roof.

It's gonna look great. We'll bung our furniture in, splash on a bit of paint, and whacko-the-diddle-o.

It's the whacko-the-diddle-o that I'm worried about, says Rose.

Dolly finds herself at the Cloud Street Station in the long lull between Saturday evening trains. A smudge-eyed dog comes up to her and whines, slopes away. The solitary palm tree over the roof of the ticket office submits itself to the wind, and Dolly feels her false teeth slipping in sympathy. Right now, she can't remember ever having had her own teeth out in the first place. You wouldn't say she's drunk, that bulky, rumpled old woman on the bench there by the platform, though she's got a smell of brandy about her, a whiff of the old Chateau Tanunda. She just seems a little confused.

Now and then she gets up and goes out to the edge to look down on the rails.

They go somewhere, the bastards, she murmurs. I always wanted to go somewhere.

A diesel hoots down the line and a man and a boy buy tickets and wait out in the evening sun beside her. She watches them, observes the way the boy hooks his finger into the edge of his father's trouser pocket. Men. Don't they love each other. They should be enough for each other. We're not like that. I wouldn't let a daughter do that. I wouldn't. I just don't think I could.

375

The train comes into the station blowing fumes all over her. Two or three people step down, newspapers rolled in their hands.

Doll, what're you doin here?

Sam looks surprised but pleased to see her.

I'm sittin, that's all.

Hey, I won meself fifteen quid.

Who on?

That mad bastard, the Monster. I bet he'd strike within the month.

You sick bastard.

It's commonsense. Anyone who kills that many has to like it.

You should be put down.

I'll take you to the flicks, eh? There's Dean Martin and Sinatra at the Ambassador. Or *Hatari*, that sounds good.

I'm too old for the flicks.

Carn then, let's get home, I'm stranglin for a cuppa.

I'll give im lollies. I'll spoil im filthy if only he comes to see his old granma.

Carn, old girl, you're walkin with a winner.

No Man's Land

Rose settled down to read on the bed in their new room, their new home. There was an autumn chill in the air and the smells of paint and putty. She was damp still from her shower; she shivered a little, climbed in under the covers with her mound hoiking up the bedspread before her. Strange being in the house again, coming back from the bathroom down the hallway, wrapped and steaming, feeling like a houseguest or a new lodger, all selfconscious and prudish. Wireless sounds, cooking, a song coming from somewhere, the clunking of doors and a chorus of floorboards. There were two kitchens, two livingrooms, two families, and now they lived in the middle, in the old room they called No Man's Land.

It was a queer room, this. Even when she was alone in it

376

the place felt close, crowded. Certainly it was better than it had been. Hell, she could remember a time when she wouldn't even step inside the door. As a kid she'd hear music coming from here, Fish's weird piano fugues, and she'd come to the door to watch him, but it took a lot to get her to come inside. Fish didn't play in here at all now it was their room, though the piano was still there in the corner beside her dresser and the old sea trunk she stored her linen in. They'd even brought her old desk, the one the old man had bought her with winnings and never taken back to pay old debts. Quick had knocked up a few pine shelves for her John O'Haras, her Daphne du Mauriers and Irwin Shaws. No one touched that piano but sometimes Rose swore she could hear a note in the room. She listened hard at it when she set her mind to it in the middle of a sleepless bellyrolling night, and though she knew she heard a quiet unbroken sustained note in the air, she couldn't be sure it wasn't just the sound of silence ringing between the curtains and the sofa, in the new painted walls themselves.

Rose preferred the window open a little way and the curtains shucked back to ease her claustrophobia, even though she knew it meant having old Oriel monitoring them from her tent flap below. Quick seemed so damn happy to be back here, she could barely believe it. Being here relaxed him. He skylarked on the landing with his sisters, sat in the Pickles kitchen with Dolly like he'd been going in there all his life. She remembered the queer glow on him the morning he came off the shift with the idea to move back. He was glowing like a kid's night lamp. Deep in, when she let herself think it, she was glad to be back, even though it was this place. True, she felt a little guilty about it; it seemed like a surrender to her and she'd made up her mind a long time ago to neither surrender nor go back. She'd been trying to escape this place so long, and now here she was, married to a Lamb, having his baby and living back in the thick of it. The old man'd put it down to the Shifty Shadow, but it was their decision. So here she was. She couldn't say she was unhappy. Even this queer joint felt safer than a normal house, certainly it felt better than Mrs Manners' lonely bedsit. She didn't mind the noise that much; at least it was a sign of company and its protection. Oriel came up with pillowslips patched together from old pyjamas and made Rose do exercises that almost split her fanny to bits, but it didn't seem so bad somehow. Autumn came on and then winter and Rose grew big, so big she was disgusted with herself, but in the mirror her face was the face of a living woman, not a girl threatening the world with her death. She thought about Dolly, poor Dolly who was weak now, and confused, and needing love. Maybe she owed the old girl some of this happiness. She'd sit in the sun with her again today, hold her hand. She smiled at herself in the mirror and made herself laugh, and Fish came in. She let Fish lay his hands on her. He squawked with joy when the baby kicked and rolled under the skin of her drum.

The ladies won't like it, he laughed.

Quick came home grimfaced but he brightened at the sight of her.

I'm trying for a transfer to Traffic, he said.

Given up on fighting evil?

This bastard's got us beaten.

Will they let you move?

He shrugged.

Well, I never liked you prowling about all night knowing you might run into him. Now there's a baby to think of.

Yeah, he said, unconvinced of his own motives. Yeah.

Slipping

It's well after two and cold as charity in the cowering streets of Nedlands when Quick hears the BSA howling through the streets. It'd be Murphy come looking for him for sure. Something's up. A headlight swings into the street and Quick goes to meet it.

Get on, says Murphy.

What's up?

Christmas, what do you think? Hold on.

When they get there, only a street away, the CIB have a

378

car outside the house already and an ambulance is squealing down Broadway.

They go in and the body's still there on a sofa, a hole in her forehead.

Babysitter, says the dick with the notebook. The baby was still asleep when the parents got home.

We've gotta do something, says Quick. Bugger it, we've gotta do something!

Yeah, says the dick, start by makin us a cuppa, willya?

Day after day, Quick feels himself slipping. It's sadness coming on like the old days, the vast seamless hopeless weight of sadness looking for a place to rest. Willpower, he tells himself, willpower. But it's useless. Even on lonely night patrols that week he sees misery pictures dancing in the darkness. Indo-Chinese, shark victims, President Kennedy's dead baby, lynched negroes with newsprint faces. He's beyond willpower. He's getting hopeless like the Quick Lamb of old. They're losing. There's someone out there killing and doing evil and he's losing the fight with them, and day by day it gets him further into despair.

Does the Poo Hurt?

Fish finds Quick weeping in the outhouse.

Does the poo hurt, Quick?

But Quick says nothing.

Fish stands by the old pen where the rugged survivor of a pig rubs against a post. He goes up to the dunny door.

Quick?

It's orright, Fish.

Doan cry.

No.

The ladies like it.

Go back inside, mate. Leave me alone, orright?

Fish goes obediently.

379

Somethin's Up

Somethin's up, said Murphy. The CIB know somethin, they're settin somethin up. Even the papers know about it.

Hmm? said Quick by the urn looking at his own handcuffs.

The weapon. The papers are goin quiet. We've got him rattled, the sick bastard.

I just wish it'd stop rainin, said Quick.

You wouldn't notice yer own balls ringin vespers, said Murphy.

I could drive trucks, said Quick.

Jaysus, said Murphy.

Oh, see down there, Fish, see down there something happening at last. A tip, a copper's hunch, an old couple coming across a .22 under a bush above the river. And the net closing.

On Sunday, Murphy was on the shift fresh from midnight mass.

They got him, he said.

Who'd you get it from, said Quick, the priest?

Father of seven, said Murphy, can you imagine?

Sure, mate.

I know a journo.

And I know a load of bollocks.

The Sarge came in: You hear the news, Lamb? They got him, the Monster.

Who told you, Sarge? said Quick.

Murphy knows a journo.

That'd be bloody right, said Quick. He just wouldn't let himself believe it. No, they'd have this mad bastard hanging over their lives from here on in. He was here to stay.

Lamb? Lamb!

Sarge? What was that?

The phone was for you, you galah. You gone to sleep on us? Constable!

Sarge?

Get home.

Sorry, Sarge. It's just I'm . . . It won't happen again.

Go!

But Sarge!

Get him home, Murphy.

But *why*? Quick pleaded.

Because yer about to be a father.

It'll be in the morning papers, shouted Murphy riding through the streets on the single sidebanger.

My baby? said Quick.

The bloody murderer, you nong.

Oh, him.

Him

Him. Already they're bundling him into a paddywagon, disappointed at the size of him, the hopeless look of him ambushed and frightened and suddenly not winning. He's just a frustrated man with a hare lip who's gone back to his lifetime of losing, and the pathetic sight of him robs the detectives of the feeling they'd expected. The Nedlands Monster, the man who made the town a city, who had gallows written all over him. Him!

Wax Harry

All these months Rose has been rehearsing the whole business in her mind, the steady buildup of contractions, the developing stages, the orderly nature of nature, but what she finds when the contractions come is that this baby means business now and to hell with stages and order.

The house wakes inside a minute and Lester goes down-stairs like a falling cupboard to finish up naked and grazed on the corridor rug below. Pansy comes down scowling, with Lon behind. Fish wanders out with his slug tilting gamely from his pyjama bottoms.

Get to a phone, Lon. Lester calls once his specs are in place. Tell Quick to come!

Rose stands up for a few musclecranks and decides that she won't try the stairs alone. They are flurrying about down there like maggots in a Milo tin and she's having this squeezebox routine every minute or so. She sits down, puts a pillow in her mouth and she can hear a motorbike coming already – or is it her pulse backfiring?

Quick comes hammering upstairs. I've gotta get her to the hospital!

Get the truck started! says Lester.

I'm not going in that bloody truck! yells Rose, putting her head to the wall where a vicious white old woman looks down aghast at what's pinning her knees.

The Rugby'll never start in time!

I'll start the Harley! says Lon. She can go in the sidecar.

Oh. Gawd Aggie! Don't bother. I'm having it right here and now.

Lie down, Rose!

I can't.

Elaine gets her back on the bed.

Lester slips quietly off to get Oriel, but she's inside already with her gown sleeves rolled up and her specs on awry. Sam stumbles into the corridor.

Fire?

Baby.

Oh, gawd. Dolly's out to it.

Rose sees Oriel coming up the stairs two at a time with her mottley forearms swinging, her boots a-creak, and she's never been so grateful to see her. Already Rose is bearing down. She can't help but push.

Hot water, towels, boiled scissors and a laundry bucket! Oriel barks, and some purpose comes into the gathering.

Oohhhghm!

Rose feels herself lifted like a child. The library light comes on. There's the bed.

Take a rest, love, you'll tear your insides out. Fish, go to your room.

No.

Uughnnmmaah!

Let's get this nightie off. Good Lord who made us – there's the head.

Outside the Harley blurts up, sending out a volley of backfires.

No shoutin, no shoutin, the old woman says. We'll frighten the creature.

Quick comes in with patched towels as Rose draws herself up on her knees and strains with the sound of air through the neck of a balloon. There's gooseflesh big as acne on him. His mother's down there making a footstool of herself, her hairy bum showing shockingly in the gap in the back of her gown. Rose has fistfuls of fabric at Oriel's shoulder; she hoists with each burst of power.

Rose sees the stars and moon in the walls, the weft and weave of timbers behind the two strange spiritous women pressed away from her. It's like she's looking into the room on herself and Oriel because one is old and the other a girl, but the girl is black, bruise-coloured and the both of them are straining and it doesn't make any sense at all without oxygen in your head. Fish is at the piano, fisting it out all of a sudden and the women fade and for a moment Rose is frightened it means she's dying. They're fading, fading.

Here we come!

Ohmygawd, said Quick, about to howl.

The Harley revs impatiently.

Fish lets off a burst of wild singing. It sounds like a flock of galahs passing or a man strangled in a cement mixer.

Get the cord, Quick, take the cord.

Gawd, the baby's got his fingers crossed.

Ahhhh! goes the mob in the doorway.

You mean it's a boy?

Wait a sec, love, we don't –

He's all there, orright.

Don't worry, Sam calls shaky from the doorway mob. We all are, too.

Haah! goes Rose.

Lookathat.

Fish, cut it out!

The room goes quiet. The spirits on the wall are fading, fading, finally being forced on their way to oblivion, free of the house, freeing the house, leaving a warm, clean sweet space among the living, among the good and hopeful.

He's lookin at me, says Fish, shambling over. Oriel reaches out with one bloody hand to push Fish's dick back into his pyjamas.

Rose knows it's only her, it has to be only her, but the house is shaking.

Give him here, give him here.

Cover her up.

Oh to hell with it, Rose says, now you've all seen me bits.

They all circle around like a two-up school, peering down.

Thank God, says Lester, weeping fit to sweep away his specs. Thank God, thank God.

He's perfect, says Rose, and he's gonna have sisters.

Pass the bucket, Elaine.

You're not puttin im in the bucket? Sam protests.

She's got a placenta to come, you ignorant man, Oriel says with a grin.

She hasn't got her teeth in, thinks Lester grimly, she could've slipped her teeth in.

Wish Dolly could've seen it.

Shut up, Dad, and gimme a kiss.

After me, says Quick.

Don't get slushy, says Elaine.

Red shoulda been ere, she's the nurse.

Nah, she hates people's bits.

She'll be dark on us for doin it without her. She hates to miss out.

I don't reckon I can go through with it, says Pansy.

Shoulda thought that when you were goin through with

somethin else, Chub sneers.

Oriel glares and Chub backs off.

Make a pot, love, she says to Lester. And get the girl a drink.

He's hungry, says Rose.

He's lookin at me, says Fish. He knows me. He loves me.

We'll call him Harry, Quick announces.

Not on your life.

Lookit the little larrikin. He's a homebuilt Harry if I ever saw one.

Oop! Hold im Quick. I've got –

What? I can't do – I don't know.

Take him, you useless drongo, says Oriel.

Oooer, what's that? someone calls.

And to think we were blessed farmers, Oriel mutters, catching the placenta in the bucket and swabbing Rose a moment.

He's waxy, says Quick.

Wax Harry, Lester grins.

Put the kettle on, I said.

Put your teeth in.

What? Have I, oh I, my –

Wax Harry, says Fish.

Don't be ridiculous, Oriel says.

Is it alive? The ragged voice cuts the room silent. Dolly swings on her heels in the doorway, face yellow and streaky.

Yes, says Rose. It's a boy.

Well, Dolly says, squeezing out a silent belch. You can all just go out and leave her alone. I'm a grandmother. Good night.

The room sighs, the house breathes its first painless breath in half a century and outside the pig is going at it balls to the wall, giving it his all, like an angel in a pig's body, like a bacon choir, like the voice of God Himself pouring up through the fruit trees, rattling the tin fence, shaking the old smells from the walls and the worry from the paintwork, till it spills out on the street where they're already celebrating something else, something they've been waiting for in their beds all year.

385

Long, Hot, Peaceful Days

SUMMER came again to Cloudstreet. Quick got his transfer to Traffic. During the long, hot, peaceful days, Rose took Wax Harry down to the river and lay in the creamy sand with him the way she'd promised herself she would. Harold Samson Lamb fisted sand and dead jellyfish into his mouth. He was dark haired and black eyed, outrageously uncircumcized and stubborn. He grew browner, healthier, gamer. When Quick came home from a shift he couldn't wait to play with him so he took to waking him up at midnight, at six, whenever. Harry learnt to roll, to crawl. Jealous grandmothers sneaked him out to their own rooms to feast on him uninterrupted. The household spoiled him rotten.

The house was full of comings and goings. Repairs were planned, though nothing ever eventuated, and just the idea gave the place a fresh look. Out the front, the place looked like a dancehall parking lot. There was a Chev truck, the X-ray Rugby, an Oxford, an old Humber, a Harley and sidecar and Lon's new FJ Holden that would never be paid for.

Dolly had a few bingo friends come round occasionally nowadays. She often dragged them up to the library to see her grandson where they left fag ash all over the rug and cooed with the most breathtaking sincerity. To Rose they were a worthless mob of old croakers – bar leaners and bus stop bores – but that they so clearly adored her mother was enough for her to put up with these incursions. Sometimes Quick sat out on the stoop with Dolly to feed the magpies their topside chunks. He'd come to the conclusion that she was a bit of a character. Whenever Dolly was around the baby Rose got nervous. She was frightened of Dolly dropping him, full as she was at least half of the time, and she imagined him blinded by her jutting cigarette embers, clawed clumsily by her yellowing nails. Rose drilled herself in the discipline of refraining from panic, and as if to reward her, Harry was safe always.

Lon and Pansy had a baby girl in the hospital. The corridor at Cloudstreet was full of their squalling and the baby slept through everything. They called her Merrileen-Gaye. Pansy was pregnant again before anyone was willing to believe it. She and Oriel did not speak, and very loud they were about it.

Some afternoons Rose helped out down in the shop. Someone was building a modern supermarket across the rails, but the Lambs' place still won all trade, and no one believed it could be any different. Rose liked the smell of the shop, the crates of vegetables sloped back along one wall, the fatty cold meats, boiled sweets, the zinc odour of the bottle caps collecting in the bucket they'd send to the Blind School every Friday. She went down one afternoon looking for Harry and found herself serving in the afterschool lolly rush. A ha'ppenorth of umbugs, lady! Tuppence a pennysticks, missus! Please, please, a bag uv snakes! She fought with the lids of the great glass jars and felt the weight of kids pressing from the other side of the counter. Rose doled out generous serves and won hearts. Next day they asked for her. On the third day, left alone for an hour after the rush, she rearranged the jars in a more practical order and found them all firmly replaced next day. Elaine daydreamed all morning about her fiance who was stringing their engagement into its sixth year, and she found in Rose a willing ear, though she'd wait till Oriel was out of the shop before starting in on another story of real romance.

Lester came and went, as though distracted somehow. Rose sensed that he'd lost interest in the shop. He baked irregularly, made no icecream.

Within a week, Rose had feelings about the shop. If Harry was impossible and kept her from it, she regretted it. Oriel noticed.

They were wary of one another, Oriel and Rose. When Oriel came into the room she was all over it instantly, like a hot rash. She brought the place to attention just by entering it. Rose remembered the way she took command of a situation in a dozen crises – when Dolly was sick, when she herself was hurt, and she couldn't think why the very strength of that woman's actions felt so unforgivable. Her kindness was scalding, her protection acidic. Maybe it's just me, thought Rose, maybe I can't take it from her because my mother never gave it to me. What a proud bitch I am. But dammit, why does she always have to be right and the one who's strong and the one who makes it straight, the one people come to? Why do I still dislike her, because she's so totally trustworthy?

Geez, Rose, Elaine said offhandedly one afternoon in a quiet moment between the shelves, you remind me so

391

much of Mum when she was young. I can see why Quick married you.

He didn't, love, I married him, she said from some old reflex that took over in moments of terror.

Ha, ha! Just like Mum. You're a ringer, Rose!

Rose choked.

Oriel wasted nothing and she despised waste in others. There was no point walking from the shop to the kitchen for one task if it could incorporate five more and save walking. Nothing was thrown away, nothing written off to chance. When Oriel sent you to the butcher's she armed you with a diagram of the cut she wanted, the name, weight and a list of defects to watch for. There was one way of storing eggs, one way of sealing a preserve jar. There was a way of looking after your breasts, a better way of pinning a nappy and an inspired way to get the shit off them, and you couldn't take solace in the possibility that she might be wrong because she never was. You'd hold out stubbornly with your own inferior methods until you got sick of yourself and gave in with relief. When she found you doing it the right way she'd lay a hot, square hand on you and congratulate you as though you'd just thought up that ingenious method yourself.

Yer a wonder, she'd say, Rose yer the real thing.

And Rose never knew whether to leap for joy or puke.

Fortune

Sam Pickles was starting to slow down at work, all the blokes at the Mint knew it. He looked weaker these days and that cough of his took up as much of his time as working did. The men who worked on the hosco knew he wasn't worth his day's pay any more but they wouldn't see him laid off until the silly old bugger couldn't walk in through the gates of a morning. They were used to seeing him round; they liked to hear tips from him of a Friday afternoon about the weekend's punting. Stories had sprung up around him, that he'd lost his fingers in some covert commando exercise in the war. He'd been at the Mint so long the young bods figured there must be gold dust in his pores by now. All the stories of his legendary bad luck started to ring suspicious to the young crew.

Coming up for twenty years in the job, Sam still smuggled out duds, blanks and new releases, only nowadays they were for his grandson. No one checked him at the gate anymore, beyond the old question: Got any ingots in yer pockets, Sam? If he'd had any greed at all (some would have said any sense at all) he could have been making his pay ten times over.

Twenty years ago, Sam Pickles might have been invisible at the sorting table. Nowadays it was all: Gday, Sam, and What's the dirt, Sam? How's things today, Sam? They talked to him like he was management and they expected him to work about as little. The last few years he walked around all day with a smile on his face, and wondered why no one would believe he was that unlucky. He lost at the races every weekend, more or less without relief, and if he died tomorrow he wouldn't have enough money to bury himself, but the blokes swore he was onto something somehow, and their admiration was infectious. When he got home of an evening, Rose and Harry'd be in the kitchen often as not, and he'd sneak the boy a peppermint, bring down his two-up pennies and toss them off the paddle for him to get a giggle. Rose would fuss over his cough, pour him a cup of tea, and he was hardpressed to feel unlucky.

He seemed to be growing smaller.

A thought occurred to him. In a year or so he could sell this house, cop the profits and retire to some little place by the sea, maybe even back up in Geraldton, or Greenough – yes, Greenough where summers had been so good so long ago. He'd mention it to Dolly, he thought, but he never did. The two of them sat in the kitchen by the wood stove without real antagonism, in silence most evenings, with the sounds of the house around them. Harry might squeal upstairs at bedtime, kicking the wall in protest.

He's givin er a run for er money tonight, Dolly would say.

Yairs. Cheeky little bugger.

Needs is bum kicked.

Yairs. He's a one orright.

And that would be it. The kettle would growl. Water moaned in the pipes. The wireless came on.

Sam went to bed at nine with a *Daily News* and a glass of VO, thinking that he might just live to see his fortune. His hacking cough had become a comforting, familiar sound in the house, innocent as a boy's bronchitis.

News

The Nedlands Monster comes to trial but he's forced off the front page by the Kennedy assassination. Rose comes across the startling byline: *by Toby Raven, exclusive* and feels a smile on her face.

A letter comes from State Housing demanding that they move into their new house. She looks at it, gives it to Quick who sighs.

Soon, he says, when we're settled.

No hurry, she says.

1963 turned toward 1964. Cloudstreet sweetened up like a ship under full sail. The only shadows were the shadows of nature, the products of strong, direct light, and as the stonefruit came out again there was laughter, shopjokes at noon in the corridors, and kidsilliness all evening. The lines were strung with nappies that flapped like pennants above the tiny scratching chicks who escaped their mothers to forage in the grass. The place stank of happiness, but the world went on its way. The Nedlands Monster got the Hangman's promise. The city went wild with exaltation. There were hanging parties, theme nights, ugly jokes.

Whacko! said Quick, turning the pages of the paper. They gave him death. Thank God for that.

Good riddance, said Rose, giving Harry her breast.

Oriel and Lester looked horrified at one another. Lester put his finger to his lip, advising caution, but Oriel couldn't help herself.

Killin is men's business, she said, not God's. If you think it's somethin to celebrate leave God out of it.

Quick smiles in disbelief. What've you gone soft on the Monster all of a sudden?

He's only a man, said Lester.

What about an eye for an eye and a tooth for a tooth?

Barbarism! snarls Oriel. That's for primitive tribes.

Gawd, she's gone all modern on us. What about the Bible, Mum, that's your old inspiration isn't it? I've seen you out there with it, burnin the midnight candle. I know what you're doin out there where no one can see you.

Oriel flushed.

Oriel, come on outside, said Lester. The old girl had water on her cheeks. Rose gaped and even Wax Harry left off feeding to stare. Oriel held herself firm before them awhile, mustering up her message, but she seemed to collapse in the face right at the end, and went out running.

Gawd, said Quick. What was that all about?

Lester rubbed his hands together absently. Principles, Quick.

Quick winked at Rose whose face showed worry cracks all of a sudden. What's that? I thought she only cared about work. Mum's principles are work, work and work.

That's right.

Well?

Lester took off his glasses a moment: You don't understand what she works at, do you?

Obviously not, said Quick with a smirk.

Then Lester pulled a little book out of his shirt pocket the size of a harmonica. He found a page and read: *Master, which is the great commandment in the law? Jesus said unto him, Thou shalt love the Lord thy God with all thy heart, and with all thy soul, and with all thy mind. This is the first commandment. And the second is like unto it, Thou shalt love thy neighbour as thyself. On these two commandments hang all the law and the prophets.*

Quick snorted nervously. It's from another time. She doesn't even believe it.

She tries, said Lester, putting the book away. That's her work.

But she can't believe it, said Quick. Not since Fish. She *can't*.

But she tries, Quick, can't you see?

Now old Lester's lips began to quiver and he had to go outside to join Oriel.

Gawd, said Quick.

Fishing

Early Sunday morning, dressed for a fishing trip he never intended to make, Lester Lamb stands at the back of the cathedral and watches the micks go about their business. He can't make head or tail of what they're saying up front, and he doesn't quite know how to feel about the gorgeous vaulted ceilings of the place and the way it smells like a bank, but when it comes time for them all to file up the front and take the wine and the wafer he feels a sort of homesickness come upon him. Even the sight of them kneeling to the men in uniform doesn't poison it for him; it's the pleasantest kind of melancholy, and he knows there'll be other Sundays like this, secret, strange.

Afterwards he parks the Chev down by the river and plays his spitpacked old harmonica, wondering about himself.

The Past

On Rose's birthday, Quick slips into a florist's shop in uniform to buy flowers for Rose and Dolly and Oriel. Lucy Wentworth stares at him from behind the counter, huge in her pinny, lips painted up, teeth smudgy with the stuff, and she treats him like any girl will treat a traffic cop in leathers. Maybe it's the uniform, he thinks, uncertain whether or not

396

he should be grateful. He buys roses for his mother who won't approve of them and daffs for Dolly and Rose and watches Lucy wrap them in a trumpet of paper. She hands them over smiling. Quick gives her money, gets change and walks out. Riding home on the BSA, he feels the flowers pressed against his legs concealed beneath the wind tarp across his knees, and he can't help but be relieved she didn't recognize him. Maybe he owed her a favour because right now it felt like she'd done him one years back.

Waiting

In the tent at night, and sometimes on her knees on the duckboards, Oriel Lamb looks out at the house and wonders what it is that still holds her from it. It's full of light and sweetness now in a way it's never been before, but why can she still not go back? A whole life of waiting for answers that don't come. Wait, Oriel, keep strong Mum, keep the steel, you'll see. Oh, how I missed you all my life. You'll see it's best this way. Wait.

Floater

Quick likes it on Traffic. There's still some lair in him from younger days; the bikes and the speed still do things for him. He has the whole city as his beat either side of the river and all the way to the coast, and for the first time in months he relaxes a little. He knocks off drunks and speed merchants, faulty vehicles and sideswipers, and he turns up to prangs ahead of the ambulance, siren first, notebook later. It's cut and dried, rules and regs, safe as houses. Until the day he pulls in by the river for his cheese and pickle sandwiches late one afternoon and sees what two kids paddling an upturned car roof have already found. Facedown, a floater on the incoming tide.

Boots, leggings, leather and all, Quick slams into the water with the spray glugging up in his helmet. The river tastes sweet and rotten. A mullet bounces off his thigh and one of those kids is crying. When he gets to the facedown child, he hoists him over, ready to scream, ready to take this river apart, and he finds he's an hour late to save a life. Cold as welfare, a body light enough to lift one armed. With him over his shoulder and the other kids in tow, Quick wades out scowling before a crowd. On the bank he feels for a pulse, for any hope at all, but this boy is long gone. His skin is already doughy, his clouded eyes look up at the canopy of rising midges, his lips purse in a terrible, naked kiss which moves Quick to cover the face with his own hands. The sight sets off too many thoughts. In time, a siren comes keening, men come at the run, and Quick Lamb is forced to take his hands away and see it for what it is. That's Harry's face. That's his own boyhood face, that miserable washed out set of features there on the ambulance stretcher. That's the sight of the world ending, someone's son dead. Then it hits him. That's my brother. This is my life over again. This will always be happening.

You won't believe this, says the sergeant from the local station.

Probably not, says Quick, putting his wet boots back on, still jittery.

The kid's been missin since this mornin. He's the whatsisname's kid. The Nedlands Monster.

Quick sat there. It took a while to set on him. Him! Murderer, father of seven. The Nedlands Monster, the face of evil. That was his son he'd been holding and trying not to weep over in front of a crowd. He'd seen himself, Harry, Fish in that dead boy's face. Quick felt something break in him as he stared at his boots.

The poor bastard, he thought, the poor, poor bastard, sitting down there in Freo gaol waiting for the hangman, thinking there's no news worse than he's just heard, with *this* heading his way in only a few minutes time.

The mother's comin, said the sergeant. You better go.

Aw, gawd, why didn't you say before! Quick charged

398

the door, clipped the jamb and met her on the path. He wanted to tell her something, stop and give her something to go on, but he knew he didn't have it in him and the local sergeant would come down on him like a ton of bricks.

The murderer's wife. A man's wife. A man. With evil in him. And tears, and children and old twisted hopes. A man.

He blundered out to the BSA and nearly kicked it off its stand.

Quick rode to Cloudstreet feeling useless as a twelve year old, reckless across the Narrows Bridge, ready to drive into the river at any second. He caned the BSA up Mounts Bay Road, leaning into curves with only wind holding him free, past the Crawley baths where he'd swum as a kid where jellyfish piled up like church camp food and the rotting stink of blowfish blew past.

Put Yer Dukes Up, Woman!

That very morning, Lon Lamb has taken a sickie off work. A cold feeling drifts up through the house from the shop where Oriel is making up the day's deliveries, sorting them box by box, silent and ominous with it. She glances out now and then to see the dewstreaked paintwork of Lon's FJ Holden. Elaine bustles beside her mother, gnawing her lip. Baking smells sweep back from the kitchen as Lester slips around doing the lunchtime pasties and singing some old wartime song. Lon and Pansy's baby Merrileen-Gaye whimpers longwindedly on the landing outside her parents' door.

Aw, that kid, murmurs Elaine.

Not her fault, says Oriel, pushing a case of fruit and vegetables to one side.

Maybe I should go up and get her, says Elaine.

No. I'll do it.

Mum.

There won't be any problem.

Oriel takes the stairs one at a time. Rose has opened her door to see what's happening. Oriel waves her back. Merrileen-Gaye has a full nappy round her ankles and she looks broadeyed and uncertain at her grandmother, who strides past and throws open the door. Pansy and Lon are naked and conjoined somehow like a seesaw. They are plank and boulder, breast and bollock naked, and not altogether prepared for this.

We're doin deliveries this morning, Lon Lamb, same as every mornin, and if yer not goin to yer own work this mornin I'll thank you to be packin the Chev in ten minutes. Good mornin, Pansy. You're lookin advanced. Ten minutes.

Come ten minutes later, Lon Lamb is slinging crates up onto the flatbed and spitting out the foulest curses a Lamb could ever imagine. The sound of it, the sheer vicious unhappiness of it draws the household to its windows. Customers coming early stop to watch, as if they can sense the beginning of a shenanigan. By the time the truck is packed – higgledy piggledy, boxes all over – a small crowd has gathered. A shiver goes through it when Oriel Lamb steps out onto the verandah wiping her hands, squinting in the morning light. Old men take off their hats. Throats are cleared. Oriel ignores the lot of them.

We do things a certain way in this family, Lon. It's called the proper way. When we say we'll do something we stand by it. Pull it down and pack it properly.

It's fine as it is, Lon murmured.

You'll lose it the first corner you take.

I'm not takin it anywhere. I'm off work.

Pull it down.

Go to hell.

It's the word itself that sets her off. In a moment she's charged out there, torn the side off a pine crate and got him by the ear. The onlookers are too sobered to roar with surprise or delight. Now his wife is watching, and then his daughter.

Pull it down.

Go to hell, you rotten bitch.

Oriel bends him like a saw over her knee and gives him the pine across the arse; once, twice, and another full swing before Lon breaks away, a feisty wildeyed man of twenty-

400

two with his plumber's fists up now, prancing back before her, calling:

Carn, then put yer dukes up, woman! Put yer bloody dukes up!

And she does. She gives him a left – quick as a snake – coming up under his nose to shake the crowd from its silence and Lon Lamb from his moorings. He goes down swinging, with blood shooting, and does not get back up.

His feet are still planted, but his body has gone down between them completely untrellised.

Oriel wipes a pink smear from the back of her hand, and picks him up.

It's still my blood, too, you know. She looks round at the grinning faces, the elbows shoving, the hands across mouths.

These folk will help you repack it. That seems like a fair thing for a bit of entertainment, don't you think?

Ongh, says Lon.

We're cheap, but we've never been free.

The little woman stands there and faces them down while Lon teeters beside her. She doesn't go away. In the end the crowd feels shame and discomfort there in her yard, and the truck is packed in no time.

Turning

Quick clumped up the stairs and went into the library. Harry was asleep in his cot in the corner and Rose sat at the dresser with a candle. The mirror threw light all about as he closed the door, the candle guttering a moment. He sat on the big bed to pull off his leggings and boots. Rose wore one of his old sweaters and not much else besides. When she leant over the table he saw her cotton knickers white against her tan. She spun a butterknife on the dresser top.

See if it'll give me a holiday, he said.

You need one?

I need one. I need a holiday, Rose.

You brood too much.

Yes.

What? Why're you looking like that, Quick?

We all turn into the same thing, don't we? Memories, shadows, worries, dreams. We all join up somewhere in the end.

What are you talking about?

The gaols are full of blokes we'd swear are different to us. Only difference is, they did things you and me just thought about.

That's still a big difference, said Rose.

Maybe. A second's difference.

What's happened?

I pulled a drowned kid out of the river today. You wouldn't believe this, but it just happened to be *his* kid.

Whose?

The Monster.

Geez.

I've pulled a kid out of the river before, Rose. When I was eleven years old. My own brother. I know how it feels. I know how that poor bastard feels. And I got thinkin about my childhood, my life. I did a lot of feelin sorry for myself, those years. I used to see the saddest things, think about the saddest, saddest things. And those things put dents in me, you know. I could've turned out angry and cold like *him*. I can see how that evil little bugger might've just . . . turned, like a pot of milk.

So you've given away the old good and evil? asked Rose, amazed at all this rare talk from Quick.

No. No. I'll stay a cop. But it's not us and them anymore. It's us and us and us. It's always us. That's what they never tell you. Geez, Rose, I just want to do right. But there's no monsters, only people like us. Funny, but it hurts.

Quick shook and coughed up a great tearless sob.

You can't do the impossible, she said.

No, he murmured, unconvinced.

You do need a break. Let's go somewhere.

Quick Lamb wept. He cried like something had fallen on him from afar.

Quick. Quick.

Rose put the knife down and came to him on the bed. She pulled the sweater up and over her head and let her breasts settle hot on his chest. She wrapped her legs around him and lifted her breast, silvery with workmarks, and put it to his mouth. Her nipple like a hot coal on his tongue.

You need me, Quick Lamb, she said. That's why I have you. Just be happy. Be happy, Quick. It's us. You said it yourself.

Coming

Autumn comes and the long, cool twilights before winter hang over the rooftops of the city full of the sounds of roosting birds and quiet leaving. Down in the yard at Cloudstreet, down there in the halls and channels of time Fish and the pig exchange glances and dumbly feel the weather turning inward. The pig is battleworn, leathery beyond the threat of butchery and scarred like the trunk of an old tree. Fish handles him sweetly and without talk, just touches him on the moist plug of his snout and stands. What are you thinking, Fish? Do you feel that you're going, that you're close? Strange that you should be so hard to read these last stretching days. It should be rushing, like the whole planet is rushing down its narrow, fixed course. But I can't read your face. I stare back at you in the puddles on the chilly ground, I'm waiting in your long monastic breath, I travel back to these moments to wonder at what you're feeling and come away with nothing but the knowledge of how it will be in the end. You're coming to me, Fish, and all you might have been, all you could have hoped for is turning for you like the great river, gathering debris and nutrient and colour from every twist and trough of your story without you even knowing. The house is clear, the people are coming to things day by day and it's all that's left. No shadows, no ugly, no hurtings, no falling down angry. Your turn is coming.

Get a Haircut

Sarge, said Quick coming into the dry warmth of the office looking like a wilted celery, Sarge I –

Take a week off, Lamb, you look like shit.

Sarge, I –

Go now before I look at the roster and change me mind. And get a haircut.

Where will we go? said Quick that night in bed. We could go crabbin at Mandurah, or go for whiting at Parrys. There's fish up at –

No fishing, said Rose.

What?

No fishing. There will be no fishing.

But it's a holiday, love.

This time it'll be a holiday without fishing.

Quick lay there, suddenly without reference. Well, what would you like to do?

Rose turned into his chest and lay her hands flat on him. Let's just fill the car up and drive.

And drive?

And drive.

That's . . .

Not the Lamb way, I know. It's not practical, it's probably not even safe, but for once we can just go. We'll make it up as we go along. We'll just . . . *go*.

Sure you wouldn't rather go fishin?

Rose turned her nails into his flesh and he shook the bed with trying not to scream.

Lester on His Knees

Lester pulled the Harley over in the fresh, antiseptic street and lifted his goggles. He looked at the scrubbed bricks, the dinky letterbox, the planted lawns of Rose and Quick's new place. They'd been out here getting it ready. So, this was where they'd be. Lester looked up and down the silent street. He got off the bike, dropped his helmet in the sidecar, went down the side of the house and fell on his knees to pray. Somewhere, a long way away where there was still a native tree standing, a kookaburra laughed up a cyclone of derision which brought a flush to Lester Lamb's cheeks but did not keep him from his prayer.

⌒ Voting Day ⌒

Sam Pickles came back dejected and alone from the polling booth knowing his vote hadn't done the country a stick of good, and that those tightfisted boss lovers would be back for another term, sucking up to the Queen and passing the hat round to the workers again with smiles on their faces. When he turned into Cloudstreet the sun was on the rooftops and a man stood alone across the road from the big house. Sam shambled on up to him, lit a fag and held it out to the stranger.

Ta.

He was black as a bastard.

Got yer vote in?

The black man just smiled. He had a Ned Kelly beard and an old grey suit on with a pair of red leather shoes that must once have cost a fortune. The toes were cut out, and the man's toenails were horny as a rooster's.

Well, not that it's much use. It's a boss's country straight up.

The black man sniffed, still smiling. Only the bosses don't know theys the bosses, eh.

Sam blinked.

You live there, said the black man.

Yeah. I own it. Don't tell anyone, but in the new year I'm gonna sell it. Some rich bastard'll come along, bulldoze it and build a fuckin great block of flats on it. Salmon pink bricks, five storeys, ugly as sin. And I'll do orright.

Sam looked away from the house and found the black man looking at him. Jesus, thought Sam, paint him white

405

and he might be me old man. The black man's stare put a foul sweat on him. He damnnear asked for his smoke back.

You shouldn't break a place. Places are strong, important.

Bloody place is half fallin down orready. Can't hurt to give it a helpin hand.

Too many places busted.

Sam wandered half across the street, his hands in his pockets, his stump tingling a little. He turned back to the black man. I mean, lookit that joint, willya?

You better be the strongest man.

Sam looked at him. He felt blank. All he noticed was the way the black man's shadow came out on four sides of him like a footy player under lights at training.

How did you vote today, mate?

The black man dropped the smoke and toed it. He walked away shaking his head, his shadow reeling out all sides of him as he went.

Gift Horse

On Sunday morning, early, Dolly threw a chunk of beef into the long, wild grass. The maggies came swooping; you could hear the whooping of their wings as they came from out of the sun, wheeling round to land at her feet. Dolly's hands looked younger with the blood and juice of meat on them. They trembled, those hands, but the birds were used to it. Now and then one of the boldest would come and take meat off her palm and the force of the peck, the beak hitting her skin through the meat sent a thrill into her.

The last birds hopped through the bloody tangle of wild oats, checking the ground for remnants. Dolly's back ached, squatting the way she did, but she stayed there to watch the impassive heads of the magpies, trying to see a sign of disappointment or of satisfaction, or gratitude, and smiling when they left abruptly at the sound of a footfall.

Jesus, you'll be cookin rice puddin for em next, Sam said behind her.

So you got up, eh? Here I am, up before you.

Sam stood by her, weight on one leg, with his hands in his pockets. I've got a bloody hangover.

Well, that explains it. You're still a two pot screamer.

I was thinkin.

Never think n drink at the same time. Makes you miserable. What about?

Oh, Gawd, everythin. What we're gonna do about Chub, retirement. The house.

What about the house? Dolly's haunches hurt now, but she stayed where she was, with the breeze rattling up her thighs.

Well, it's the twenty years come summer. Joel said we could sell after twenty.

That was to protect us all from you.

Fair enough.

But what?

Sam scratches the inside of his calf with the heel of his shoe. I thought, well, twenty years is up. We could sell. They're goin mad in this town, buyin the old and buildin the new. We could make ourselves a pile.

And you believe in luck!

What?

Did you earn this place?

No. You know that. Joel gave it to me. Us.

You think it's good luck to sell what someone gave you as a present, a gift?

He sighed. Joel was the luckiest bastard on earth.

It didn't keep him alive this last twenty years.

Yeah, but it kept us alive.

Dolly spat on the ground and laughed bitterly. What's kept us alive is that friggin woman. A dead man and an ugly woman. Vanilla icecream, pasties and mullet.

It's a bloody horrible old house, Doll. We could do what Rose is doin – build a new place, out in a new suburb. This is old.

Oh, it's not so bloody horrible.

Jesus, you hate the place!

Dolly sniffed. I don't know about that. What was the

407

horse's name, the one Joel made all his money off?

Eurythmic. What a horse that was.

What is it they say about lookin a gift horse in the mouth?

My God, woman, you're the evillest bitch.

Dolly laughed: You dunno the half of it.

We must be fuckin mad.

Below Deck

The night before Rose and Quick's trip, Oriel put on a dinner in the big room where Lester slept. The bed was taken out and two tables were laid end to end, draped in a great white cloth that stank of mothballs and the *Reader's Digest*. It was getting stupid, Oriel decided, the way Rose and Quick wandered from kitchen to kitchen, not knowing who they were supposed to eat with, and besides, if they ate with the Pickleses it was a sure bet that poor Rose'd do all the cooking, and on the night before her first holiday in years, it wasn't right that the girl should cook. Anyway, it would save all kinds of embarrassment if a gesture was made, a compromise sealed, and they ate together. Oriel had a head-ache the moment she conceived the idea. But it had to be done. Someone had to take the initiative. Also, and she could barely admit it, the prospect of not having Harry and Rose and Quick in the house depressed her. After their holiday, now that their new house was finished, they'd be leaving Cloudstreet for good. It was weakness this silly dinner. It was hanging on to them, but Oriel considered she had the right to a bit of clinging.

When the big room was full of noise and laughter, Sam and Dolly came knocking. Red let them in. They looked overscrubbed and shaky. Fish was rolling soup bowls, Lester was giving the accordion a bit of a hiding, and Lon was telling a joke that no one could possibly approve of.

Come in, come in! said Oriel, brightly signalling them in and avoiding their eyes.

The stove roared, gusting hot air into the room beyond,

where the riotous mob was milling.

Welcome below deck! called Lester as they went through.

Geez, it's like the engine room, orright, said Sam to no one special.

Sit down, Mum and Dad, Rose said, trying not to bite her lip. Geez, you're all got up.

Dolly trod on Harry who had crawled under the table, and there was pandemonium. Dolly nearly fainted with guilt and embarrassment.

It's alright, said Rose. Relax, Mum.

Sam sat next to Fish who said: Who's got your fingers?

Lester insisted on singing 'The Wild Colonial Boy'. He sounded terrible, but everyone was grateful for the break, and while he was singing and squeezing, Oriel brought out the food with Elaine who passed hot plates that took the prints off a few fingertips. Out came roast lamb, cauliflower cheese, mint sauce, a tray of roast potatoes, parsnips, onions, pumpkins, cabbage, slabs of butter, hot white bread and Keen's mustard. There was a chicken stuffed with leeks, cold ham, beetroot, and a jug of lemonade the size of an artillery shell.

Everyone passed and grabbed. Plates disappeared beneath it all.

For what we are about to receive, Lester said, stopping them all dead with his mild voice, we are truly thankful.

Amen, said Sam.

Christ Almighty, look at the food, Dolly murmured. She's tryin to kill us.

They ate and passed and picked while Lester told them all stories that could only have been the weakest of lies, until there was steampud with jam, custard and cream. A pot of tea was hauled in, cups brought, chairs snicked back a little to allow legs to be crossed. Fish and Harry played under the table with Pansy's girl Merrileen.

I hear you're thinkin of sellin, Mr Pickles.

Quick put the teapot down: Mum!

Dolly rolled her eyes. Lester looked as though it was news to him.

I used to know this bloke, Lon began.

Shut up, boy, said Oriel.

Sam grinned, rubbed his nose with his hairy little stump of a hand. Call me Sam, whyn't ya?

With the sort of smile that put Lester in mind of the old Anzac Club days, her confident, gracious, fulldentured smile, Oriel took Sam's cup, held it out for Quick to pour tea into, handed it back and nodded.

Sam. It came to me that you were in the mood for leavin.

You were never a dawdler, Mrs Lamb.

Oriel.

Oriel. You're still a quick one.

The old girl raised her eyebrows, as if to say: Well, that goes entirely without saying.

Dolly lit a cigarette which caused a tremor of concern round the table.

I spose youse people'd be worried about your position, Sam said.

Well, they *are* paid up on rent till about Harry's twentieth birthday, you silly coot, muttered Dolly. We'd have to pay em to leave.

Well, Oriel said darkly, if we have to leave then there's nothin to be done. It's only a house.

I expect it'd be more wiser to buy your own by now, said Sam.

No. No, Oriel said, it does you good to be tenants. It reminds you of your own true position in the world.

Sam blinked.

A house should be a home, a privilege, not a possession. It's foolish to get attached.

Yairs. Yairs, Sam said. There's the practicals to be thought of.

Oriel put her elbows on the table and opened her stubby little workdark hands, leaning through them towards Sam Pickles whose understanding smile faltered somewhat.

But I have got used to it here, you know, she said. You might say I've come to love this awful old house. It was here for us when we had nothin. It never made it easy for us – and I tell youse, there's times I've thought the place has been

410

trying to itch us out – but I reckon we've made our mark on it now, like it's not the house it was. We're halfway to belongin here, and . . . I don't know where I'd go anymore. Out there, she flung a hand in no direction at all, they're bulldozin streets and old places, fillin in the river, like they don't wanna leave any traces behind. I reckon Harry'll never see the places we know. Can you imagine that? What am I gunna do – walk out into that? I'm sixty-three years old! This place has been good to me.

Everyone recrossed their legs, stirred their tea, felt a nudge from their neighbour, passed the fruitcake.

She's right, said Dolly. Yer right. Yer right. She muttered, unable to look Oriel in the eye. The bloody place has got to us.

Good on yer, Doll, said Quick.

Dolly scowled back a delighted grin and looked about, as though for a miracle in the form of a loose glass of gin.

It's twenty years soon, said Lester. He wheezed the accordion open. Twenty years.

Well, Sam said. That's it, then.

That's what?

We stay.

You weren't really gunna sell, Sam? said Lester, squeezing off an allergenic chord.

No. Some Abo told me it wasn't worth the money. Actually he said it was bad luck.

That was me! said Dolly, and I'm no Abo.

I dunno, I forget. It was election day. The bugger laughed when I asked him how he voted.

He didn't vote, said Rose, matter of fact.

What?

Blacks haven't got the vote, she said.

Sam put his cup on the saucer. Jesus, that's a bit rough, isn't it? They need a union.

Rose laughed.

Well, he was shitty for a reason, then. He basically said I was pissweak.

Remember which side of the corridor you're on! Oriel bellowed. The language!

Well, he was right, said Dolly.

Now, now, said Lester.

More tea? asked Elaine.

Yairs. A toast.

What to?

To us, said Lester. And this old place.

Ere, ere.

God bless er, an all who sink in er.

Gawd, he's gunna play the national anthem.

Lester! Give over.

Fish, get yer fingers out of it, let him play the song.

That's a royalist song. Play an Australian song.

They're all Irish.

The stove roared and hissed from in the kitchen, and heat swelled the house and pressed the families' shadows into the wallpaper. Oriel Lamb punished her multifabric hanky, thinking that it was something at least, a gain before a loss.

All down the street you could hear them singing, those mad buggers from Cloudstreet, sounding like a footy match.

Inland

Quick was up at dawn, folding some tarps, throwing a shovel and axe into the boot of the X-ray Rugby, carrying out a box of groceries, the billy and frypan, some blankets and toys with Fish at his elbow.

Quick? Quick?

Yes, mate. Hop out the way a sec.

Me, too, Quick.

Look out. Here, hold the door open. What?

I wanna go.

No, Fish.

I wanna.

I'm sorry, mate.

Please is the magic word.

You can't, mate. This is just for me and Rose and Harry.

And me!

Quick sidestepped him a little, but Fish pressed him against the cold, beaded fender of the car. He was big now, solid, going to fat, wetlipped and tonguesome, and Quick felt the power in the hands flattened against his chest. Oh, shit, he thought, I could do without this.

We'll see, orright?

Fish looked sideways, considering. I wanna.

We'll see. Just let me get packed.

Up in the old library, he woke Rose. She rolled his way in a spray of black hair, and he had a mind to slip straight in beside her without delay, but it didn't seem the moment.

Hi.

Everything alright?

Yeah, I'm packed and all. There's only breakfast to have. Bloody Fish wants to come, though. I'm tryin to figure out a way of tellin him. Thought maybe he'd listen to you.

Rose lay back with Harry stirring beside her. She let out a sour burst of morning breath and closed her eyes.

Get him packed, then.

What? This is our bloody holiday! We haven't taken a holiday in –

And neither's he, Quick. Get him packed before I change my mind.

I'll wait till you do.

If he wants to come, let him come.

Rose, we've orready got Harry to think of. Fish is a big retarded bloke and he'll cause us a lot of problems that we could do without on a holiday.

Rose grabbed him by the shirt. Listen to yourself. Big retarded bloke – it's Fish for Godsake.

Mum'll never let him go.

Oh, crap, You still afraid of your mother?

Why are *you* so keen?

Well, he's asked you, hasn't he? Probably begged you, I imagine. If I said no, we'd both drive out of here feeling like a pair of right bastards. They'd have to lock him in his room and you'd go dark on me for a week. I'd be sitting with Quick Lamb the Absent for a week. I want a good time. I've

413

brought *Anna Karenin* and I want to lie back somewhere feeding Harry with you reading it to us. Fish'll like that, too. He's always game for a story.

Gawd.

Go and tell them.

Quick slid onto her, tucked his head into her neck.

The things a man does when he's in love.

There's worse yet, Quick Lamb, I've got other demands.

From the forested hills, across the scarp and down into the green rolling midlands beyond, the old X-ray Rugby sputters and clatters its way east on the kind of late spring morning that promises hayfever, boiling radiators, carsickness and landscape fever. When they hit the wheatlands and they're all sung out from 'Roll Out the Barrel' to 'Rock Around the Clock', Rose slides across the seat to snuggle against Quick.

Well? Where to?

Quick shrugs. A fishin hole somewhere.

She cuffs him. Come on, let's decide.

It's an adventure, you don't decide these things.

Well, there's Harry and Fish to think of. We need a bit of a plan.

Now she says.

Quick watches the broad breadcoloured flatness spreading before him. He's thinking of what Sam said last night, a blackfella warning him off. It's like the stuff he learned as a kid. Wise men and angels. Fools and strangers. Principalities and powers. Works and wonders. He sees Fish watching him in the rearview mirror.

I always wanted to see Southern Cross.

Yeah? Rose sound dubious. Why?

Dunno. The name I guess. Because of the stars. I used to watch them out here when I was a shooter.

Is it far?

A few hours more.

Okay. Let's make a stop soon, though. Give the boys a stretch. Southern Cross, eh. That sounds like our adventure.

Lookit the water! The water! Fish yells. Lookthewater! His head shoves up over the seat and his arms spread up on the upholstery behind them. He points forward out through the windscreen at the heatripples pooling and writhing on the road in the distance. Ah! Hurry, Quick. The water.

They pass through bald, silent wheat towns: Cunderdin, Kellerberrin, Merredin, Bodallin, inland beyond rivers, beyond rain and pleasure, out to where they are homeless, where they have never belonged.

Southern Cross turns out to be just a wheat town. Squat. Plain. With a rarefied air of boredom, almost a tangible purity of boredom that blows in through the windows as they roll down the main street past diagonally parked utes and council bins. Harry and Fish are asleep on the back seat. Dust and pollen settle on the upholstery. Rose's eyes water and Quick can't help but smile.

Well. So much for that idea, Rose said through her hanky. On with the adventure.

You know, it's just how I thought it'd be.

How small our dreams are.

The main street finishes and they're back on the highway, still crawling.

Was that what you were expecting?

What did you want – Ayer's Rock?

I'm sorry.

It's just a wheat town. I used to live in one just like it. I went to a church there where they actually called me Brother Lamb, and at night I shot kangaroos. It was a nice life. Those kind of towns are like heaven, in a way.

Rose blew her nose. Why didn't you stop, then?

I only wanted to stop if I saw someone I knew.

Who're you gunna know out here, Quick? For Godsake.

I just took a chance. A Pickles sort of impulse.

And how did the knife turn, Lambsy?

415

Oh, I reckon it's still turnin.

I don't get you at all mate. I think I married a bloody lunatic.

Out on the plain Rose sees the great travelling shadows of clouds moving with them, overtaking them, marching east.

The Shifty Shadow, she says with a chuckle that isn't quite genuine.

They head north away from the highway on dirt roads until they come to a place called Bullfinch, which looks beyond the means or will of any bird at all.

The names of these places, says Rose. Wyalkatchem. Doodlakine. Burracoppin.

From the back, Harry begins to whinge and cry.

Harry's cryin.

Thanks Fish.

I need a poo.

Just wait a little bit, mate.

Quick.

Hang on, we're just lookin for a place to camp.

And generally being aimless and dithery, says Rose. Are we lost?

Fish begins to moan which sets Harry off at a higher pitch.

Por, what's that bloody—

I told you, Quick. But I told!

Oh, fuck a duck, he's shat himself.

Maybe we should have gone fishing after all.

Quick pulls over by a roadside ditch. The paddocks lie away on every side, waist high in wheat. The marbled sky hangs over them.

Now what?

Now you hop out and clean him up.

But Rose –

Don't look at me because I'm the woman.

I do Harry's nappies – fair go.

What a big boy. Now you can do your brother's.

Orright, orright. Come on, Fish. Stop blubberin. Hop out.

416

Late afternoon sun slants onto their backs in the roadside silence where only the tick of the cooling motor can be heard, the clink of a belt buckle. Quick kneels to take down Fish's trousers. He sees the white rolls of fat, the ramshackle patchwork of his undies, and it's not a body he recognizes.

Fish turns his head aside in shame as Quick slides the shorts off. Quick gags a moment before slinging them down into the ditch, glad his mother isn't here to see the wanton waste. He pours water over his hanky and begins to wipe shit away.

Bend over, he murmurs, the way he's murmured a thousand times to Harry.

The size of him, the stubbornness of shit in the black hair of him, the thought of how they've come to this threatens to break something in Quick's throat.

Rose leans out of the window and goes to hurry them up, but closes her mouth. The sill of the car door is warm beneath her arm. Against the back fender Fish's whole putty body is jerking; his buttocks shiver while Quick hugs his legs shaking with emotion as the wheat bends a moment to the breeze that has sprung out of the very earth itself.

Spaces

In the end they stopped looking for places because there were only spaces out here, and they found some mangy trees back off the road a way where they could make a fire, stretch some tarps from the car roof and fry sausages. The paddocks swallowed the pink pill of the sun. They went quickly grey and cool and then it was dark. The broad patch of uncleared mallee stood shadowy on one side, the luminous wall of wheat on the other. With its long quiet flames, the fire lit Rose and Harry and Fish and Quick while they ate. It warmed them when the sausages were finished, when the bread and butter were gone, the apple cores cast off. On blankets spread on the dry ground, the four of them lay wakeful and dreamy. Above them the black sky looked crisp

417

with its stars and configurations. Dots as worlds, and milky smears as worlds of worlds.

That's the Southern Cross there, said Rose. It looks better in the sky.

You feel like it's hanging over you like the top of a cathedral, Quick said with Fish's arms around him.

Water, said Fish. All the water.

Look, his face is shinin. The moon's on your face, Fish.

There is no moon, said Rose.

Fish rolled onto his back beaming and the sight of him stirred them deeply. Harry began to snore. Rose wrapped him in an old army blanket and got out a little bottle of brandy. Before long, Fish slept too, shining in the shelter of the tarp with Quick and Rose watching over him, sharing the Chateau Tanunda in little squinteyed swigs.

Remember the night in the boat with this stuff?

Quick nodded.

What do you make of this house business? All the oldies staying on.

I think they're right, he murmured. I reckon they belong to the place. Gawd, everyone knows that house. They know the shop, our families. It's like they've built something else from just being there. Like – he laughed at himself – like a house within a house.

Yes.

I just couldn't bear to think of em all leavin and those mongrel developers gettin their hands on it.

Tell you a secret, said Rose.

Orright.

You won't believe this.

Try me.

I can't bear to think of any of us leaving. We belong to it, Quick, and I want to stay.

What? What are you talkinabout? What about our place? After all this trouble. Our own place!

I don't know about our place, Quick. I like the crowds and the noise. And, well, I guess I like the idea, it's like getting another childhood, another go at things. Think of it: I'm in this old house with the boy next door and his baby, and I'm not miserable and starving or frightened. I'm right in the middle. It's like a village, I don't know. I have these feelings. I can never explain these feelings.

But you *hate* family stuff.

Rose laughed. But it's two families. It's a bloody tribe, a new tribe.

Don't you want to be independent?

Quick, I don't even know what it means anymore. If it means being alone, I don't want it. If I'm gunna be independent do you think I need a husband? And a kid? And a mother and father, and inlaws and friends and neighbours? When I want to be independent I retire. I go skinny and puke. You've seen me like that. I just begin to disappear. But I want to live, I want to be with people, Quick. I want to battle it out. I don't want our new house. I want the life I have. Don't be disappointed.

Quick took a suck on the brandy. Disappointed? Love, I'm putrid with . . . with happiness. I've been wantin to tell you for months.

He rolled a big dry mallee root onto the fire and a carnival of sparks went up reeling. Kangaroos thumped through the wheat invisible. The earth smelt golden.

Why *did* they call you Quick? I never knew.

Come on, I told you plenty of times.

In the night Quick woke with the moon white on his face, and Fish was awake beside him, kissing him on the cheek.

What's the matter, Fish? You cold?

The moon was all over his face, or it seemed to be until Quick saw that moony light was coming off Fish himself.

There was a long, steady rustling in the wheat, rhythmic as the sound of sleep. Quick thought of a herd of roos grazing, but it came closer and was too musical to ignore. He propped himself on an elbow and saw a line of figures moving between the trees. Fish sat up beside him and let out a gasp of delight. Quick shook Rose awake and saw the black widening of her eyes. They were children, naked children. Placid faced, mildly curious, silent but for their footfalls,

419

rising from the ground like a mineral spring, following the faint defile of the land to a gravity beyond them, faces and arms, eyes and legs travelling in eddies, some familiar somehow in the multitude that grew to a vast winding expanse, passing them with a lapping sound of feet. Rose sniffed, awake, but none of them spoke anymore, not even Wax Harry who watched curious as the tide of naked children swirled around them, dizzying, heady, making a vortex, an indrawing whirl deeper than exhaustion, until the stars were low enough to touch their eyes heavy, and the great adventure of sleep took them back. The children parted the wheat like the wind itself and took all night to pass.

Soon

Can you see, Fish, see me close as a whisper in the tidespace your longing has made? Pouring through a tiny crack we are, running to the sea which will not fill with us for we came from it and return to it, and this moment they have seen us too, your gift to them, the man, the woman, the baby, a gift bought with pain and shortening. Soon you'll be a man, Fish, though only for a moment, long enough to see, smell, touch, hear, taste the muted glory of wholeness and finish what was begun only a moment ago down there where the fire crackles by the bank and those skinny girls are singing, where the light is outswinging on the water and your brother laughing. The earth slips away, Fish, and soon, soon you'll be yourself, and we'll be us; you and me. Soon!

Stayin

Quick and Rose drove home wild as kids, roaring down the scarp into the city with a happy madness up their noses like lemonade bubbles. Harry and Fish roistered in the back with the fractured light upon their faces.

Quick pulled onto the front lawn at Cloudstreet as Elaine was opening the shop and the first dogs were gathering to beg out in front of the big old hemiplegic looking joint. The X-ray Rugby burst open with them all tumbling out wild as kindergarteners at lunchtime – Rose, Harry, Fish, Quick – taking Elaine so much by surprise that she dropped the shutter and damnnear brought down the wall with it. Windows opened, and the house grew heads. Roosters crowed up a panic, and dogs began to bark.

You're not due home, said Elaine who tried not to shout.

We're havin a picnic, said Quick. To celebrate.

What picnic? said Sam, hoisting his gladstone, fingering his work hat. Celebrate what?

Bush fever, said Lester, wiping flour from his arms.

What's this foolishness? roared Oriel, emerging from the shop. It's Wednesday morning, work to be done.

They're celebratin, said Sam.

All of us, said Quick.

We're staying, said Rose.

No, *we're* stayin, said Lester.

You're stayin? asked Oriel, lifting the shop shutter again. The heavy old tin flap quivered in her hands as she scrutinized Rose, the girl who took her son from within.

Long as it takes, said Rose.

To do what? As it takes to do what?

To get old and die. To count the angels on the head of a pin, I dunno. To get sick of it. A day, a week, a Test Match, a session of parliament, a decade, I don't know.

Oriel's fingers gave out and the shutter crashed to with a whang that sent a couple of weatherboards fluttering down from the top storey in sympathy.

Till the bloody walls come down, Oriel!

A dozen slack jaws wind up smiles as dust rises from the verandah.

Picnic, you reckon? says Lester.

Dolly goes inside for a hat.

Twenty years, said Quick.

What the hell, said Sam, throwing down his gladstone bag.

Don't stand there, youse bludgers! yelled Oriel. Pack the

Chev, lock the shop, grab a hamper. Let's go to the river. Let's do it right for once!

$\curvearrowleft$ Moon, Sun, Stars $\curvearrowright$

On the long grassy bank beneath the peppermint trees and the cavernous roots of the Moreton Bay figs, they lay blankets and white tablecloths which break up in the filtered sunlight and they sprawl in their workclothes and stockings, rollers in, buns half out. Out of the crates come hams, cold chickens, lettuce salad, hardboiled eggs and asparagus, potato salad and shredded carrot, chutney, bread, a jar of anchovies and a vat of pickled onions. Lemonade, Coke, ginger beer, squeezed juices and a hip flask of Chateau Tanunda. A collective groan goes up at the sight of the white linen napkins that Dolly hauls out.

A weddin present, she says. Could never think of a decent bloody reason to get them dirty.

The university clock chimes and a rowing team slides past with the sun in its eyes. A formation of pelicans rises bigbodied from the water, the sweet coppery water where jellyfish float and blowfish bloat and the slow wheeling schools of mullet divide and meet without decision.

And another crowd has gathered. I can see them in the shade of the trees, the river of faces from before, the dark and the light, the forgotten, the silent, the missing who watch Lester dance his silly longlegged jig while half choking on his roast chook. They hear his accordion burring like a deck of cards and see Sam feeling its wind in his face. Ah, to Sam it smells like fortune itself. The Lambs and the Pickleses begin to dance, Oriel and Dolly, Red and Elaine, and even Chub is up off his arse and dancing. Quick and Rose have Harry between them like a sail in the wind, now Lon is up with Pansy and the dance spreads, a mad, yokel twenty-year dance that sets the shadows moving in sight behind them where a black man leaves the trees like a bird and goes laughing into the sun with a great hot breeze that rolls the roof of the sky and tilts the leaves above them till the gathering is dizzy with

422

laughter, full and gargling with it. And someone else is going, his sweaty hands are flexing. He hears nothing but the water. The sound of it has been in his ears all his life and he's hungry for it.

Mind you, the world goes on regardless. In Fremantle Gaol they're cutting a man from the scaffold and taking the bag from his head still afraid, still hating him enough to deny him his final wish – to be buried beside his drowned son. Oh, yes, the world goes its way, don't worry.

But here, here by the river, the beautiful, the beautiful the river, the Lambs and the Pickleses are lighting up the morning like a dream. Students stop to watch. Council workers grin and nudge each other. It's a sight to behold. It warms the living and stirs the dead. And speeds the leaving.

Because there, down along the jetty, fat and barefoot, runs Fish Lamb with a great slack grin on his face shining with chickengrease and liberty. His shirt tail is out and so is his tongue. The boards rattle and ring with nails and years and spikes and barnacle chatter and dried bait leaps behind him. Below, the water flexes and falls silver brown gold black. Birdshadows fall across him. His trousers rattle with knucklebones, pretty stones and pennies to make running music, going music, blood music in his temples and ears till right out at the end he finds the steps and the landing, the diving board in its sheath of guano. And the water.

The water.

And the mirror it makes.

Ah, the water, the water, the water.

Beneath the trees, in the midst of the dance, someone stirs, comes running, comes shouting alarm.

A bird turns out of the sun.

Fish leans out and the water is beautiful. All that country below, the soft winy country with its shifts of colour, its dark, marvellous call. Ah, yes.

The man stops running before he even reaches the jetty. Quick makes himself stop and already he's crying.

Fish goes out sighing, slow, slow to the water that smacks him kisses when he hits. Down he slopes into the long spiral, drinking, drinking his way into the tumble past the dim panic of muscle and nerve into a queer and bursting fullness. And a hesitation, a pause for a few moments. I'm a man for that long, I feel my manhood, I recognize myself whole and human, know my story for just that long, long enough to see how we've come, how we've all battled in the same corridor that time makes for us, and I'm Fish Lamb for those seconds it takes to die, as long as it takes to drink the river, as long as it took to tell you all this, and then my walls are tipping and I burst into the moon, sun and stars of who I really am. Being Fish Lamb. Perfectly. Always. Everyplace. Me.

SUN poured careless into the quiet yard where vegetables teemed in the earth and fruit hung, where a scarfaced pig sang sweetly at the sky and a small congregation amassed in the light. Beneath the ancient mulberry tree whose blood stained the soil around her, a square little woman unpegged and folded a tent, taking it corner to corner, minding its brittle, rimed fabric, smacking the dust from it. Another woman stepped forward, tottering a little. She crossed the long gash in the ground where yesterday there'd been a fence, and she took a corner of the tent herself.

The little boxy woman and the big blowsy woman folded end to end till the tent was a parcel that they hefted to their shoulders across the greensmelling grass, and then they went inside the big old house whose door stood open, pressed back by the breeze they made in passing.